THE
TOMORROW
SEED

THE
TOMORROW
SEED

ANDREW BUTCHER

www.atombooks.co.uk

ATOM

First published in Great Britain in 2008 by Atom

Copyright © Andrew Butcher 2008

Excerpt from *Parasite Positive* copyright © 2005 by Scott Westerfeld

The moral right of the author has been asserted.

*All characters and events in this publication, other than those
clearly in the public domain, are fictitious and any resemblance
to real persons, living or dead, is purely coincidental.*

All rights reserved.
No part of this publication may be reproduced, stored in a retrieval system,
or transmitted, in any form or by any means, without the prior permission in writing
of the publisher, nor be otherwise circulated in any form of binding or cover other than
that in which it is published and without a similar condition including
this condition being imposed on the subsequent purchaser.

A CIP catalogue record for this book
is available from the British Library.

ISBN 978-1-904233-96-1

Typeset in Baskerville by M Rules
Printed and bound in Great Britain by
Clays Ltd, St Ives plc

Atom
An imprint of
Little, Brown Book Group
100 Victoria Embankment
London EC4Y 0DY

An Hachette Livre UK Company
www.hachettelivre.co.uk

www.atombooks.co.uk

ONE

It was a typical English village, picture-perfect in thatch and stone. A parade of pretty, lovingly tended gardens. The bright bloom of flowers like an Impressionist masterpiece fragrancing the air with summer. A welcoming shop. A congenial pub. The cottages old friends whispering silent gossip. The peaceful, weathered church presiding serenely over all. It was the kind of rural idyll that would clearly be a front-runner for Village of the Year.

Were it not for the corpses.

Some were in the street where they must have staggered at the last in hope of help that never came, lying now like litter, one middle-aged woman dressed for bed. Several slumped in cars, lifeless limbs unable to turn the ignition key, the road ahead invisible to sightless eyes. An old couple sat on their garden bench, their backs propped up against the wall, heads leaning close together and lips parted as if exchanging a final confidence, rotting in death with as little fuss as they'd gone about their business in life.

Most of the bodies, however, would be inside. Many villagers would have made it to the church, seeking comfort in its cool and meditative sanctuary; the stench precluded any need to check on that. More still would be hiding away in what had been their own homes. The six teenagers clambering out of the sparkling new 4×4 knew it would be so. Since leaving the Enclave a week ago, every village they'd passed through had been the same.

'Another day, another shit-hole,' grumbled Richie Coker.

'Don't worry,' said Travis. 'We won't be staying long. A quick restock and then we're out of here. Everyone armed?'

Everyone was. Travis and Antony with subjugators, the others with personal selections from the small armoury they'd amassed during their travels. Handguns for the three girls, a shotgun for Richie which he swung about with exaggerated menace.

'Yeah, and I reckon Freud'd have something to say about *that*,' remarked Mel.

'I don't know, Trav,' complained Jessica. 'Shouldn't we respect the homes of the dead? Taking weapons in – is it really necessary?'

'It's not the dead we need to watch out for, Jess,' said Antony.

'No.' Linden shuddered though the morning was warm. 'It's the living.'

The Scytharene. Or the feral gangs of youths like the few they'd already encountered, roaming the countryside directionlessly, driven mad by grief and horror. In a worse condition than those who'd been abducted into slavery by the alien invaders. Enemies and dangers on all sides. Linden gripped the handle of her pistol tightly.

'Ready?' said Travis. 'Then like the man in the movie says, let's go to work.'

At least there was one thing Richie was happy about. His clothes. The forced removal of his cherished hooded sweatshirt

2

and his favourite baseball cap aboard the *Furion* prior to processing had been calamitous enough, a major blow to his sense of self – 'a real bloody downer', as Richie had eloquently put it – but he'd been even less enamoured by the garments that had replaced them. The grey uniform of the slave while in the custody of the Scytharene. Similarly unprepossessing khaki combats once they'd escaped the aliens and joined the meagre handful of soldiers and scientists at the Enclave, all of whom had now gone the same way as the villagers. Over the past few days, though, the teenagers had been able to ransack stores and houses with impunity; everyone had found and now wore clothing in which they felt more comfortable. For Richie, the hoodie look was triumphantly restored. In fact, apart from the black hair beneath the cap having been allowed to grow a little, anyone seeing him now who'd also known him before the Sickness, recognising the heavy, naturally sullen features, might assume that Richie Coker was unchanged from the bully and all-round lout he'd been back then.

The anyone would have been wrong.

It was in the way he followed Linden Darroway around with his eyes, like they were trainee stalkers, like they were dark in colour because secrets could best be kept in darkness. Something was different about Richie Coker these days, though whether that something would improve him as a person or make him worse, perhaps time had yet to tell.

The Coker stare switched from Linden to Travis, the second of his two companions. 'So how does it feel, Naughton?'

'How does what feel, Richie?'

'This. Being a criminal. *Stealing*.'

Travis looked up from the cardboard box on the shop's

3

counter that he was busily filling with canned goods. 'We're not stealing. We're foraging for supplies.'

Richie chuckled mischievously. 'Which we're gonna pay for, yeah?'

Travis refused to rise to the other boy's jibe. 'If you put that gun down for a moment, Richie, you'll probably do a better job with your packing. And only liquids of a non-alcoholic variety this time, huh?'

'It's just that back at school and at Harrington and all, you were always such a stickler for the rules, weren't you, Naughton? Making a stand. Doing the right thing. And now you're up to your arse in stolen goods and you're not even thinking twice. What's happening, man? You turning into me or what?'

Travis grinned at the suggestion. Linden didn't. Linden suddenly hurled a can of beans across the shop that almost took Richie's head off. Her hazel eyes flashed with anger and her elfin face contorted, flaming almost to match her russet hair.

'How *dare* you say that, you ugly cretin? How *dare* you? Travis is nothing like you. What have you ever done for anyone but yourself? All you are is selfish. All you do is use people and hurt people. You're not fit to lick Travis's shoes.'

'Hey. Hey. Lin. Calm down.' Travis's brow furrowed as he placed his hands on the girl's shoulders. 'What's the matter with you?'

'*Him.*' Linden stabbed an accusing finger at Richie's heart. 'He's the matter with me.'

'I don't . . . must be PMT, Naughton,' said Richie innocently. 'Or else you're not treating her right. If you want a bit of advice, nudge, nudge, I know a few tricks to set a girl's pulse racing.'

4

'Get out!' Linden screamed. 'Travis, tell him. Tell him to get out. I can't even *look* at him.'

Puzzled, Travis nodded. 'Might be better if you waited in the car, Richie.'

'Sure be quieter. Try her on some of that vodka behind you, Naughton. Might chill her out a bit.'

'*Get* . . .' But before Linden could advance to '*out!*' Richie had got.

'Now maybe you'll tell me what's really the matter,' Travis encouraged with concern.

But, of course, she couldn't. Not exactly. Not entirely. Linden might not have felt able to look at Richie but she scarcely dared to engage Travis's gaze either. Those piercing, searching, irresistible blue eyes of his, they'd see through her for sure, identify her guilt and deduce its source.

'It's Richie,' she said. A lie with a grain of truth at its core was always more convincing than one with none.

'I kind of gathered that.'

'I can't stand him.' So why had she slept with him?

'Yep. Got that, too. And?'

'Isn't hating someone's guts enough to lose it once in a while?' Slept with him while Travis, her boyfriend, the boy she loved, the only boy she truly wanted to be with, was absent risking his life for each and every one of them, including Richie, out of sight for a few short hours. But to cheat on one boy with another only took minutes.

'Losing your temper's one thing, Lin,' Travis said, 'but you just took going ballistic to a whole new level. Like there's more to this than general hostility. I know Richie isn't going to be winning any awards for his humanitarianism, but he's no more of a thug now than he's ever been. I think, actually,

5

in some ways he's becoming almost civilised – he pulled Antony out of that Joshua, remember? Something's having a good influence on him.'

'Don't you believe it,' Linden muttered. Travis didn't know.

'What I'm saying is, you've never reacted to Richie like this before, and you've known him a while now.' He paused. 'Has something happened, Lin?'

'No.' Travis couldn't know, must never know. 'Of course not.' Never ever ever. For his sake as well as hers. 'Just . . .'

'Just?'

'Well, he was riling you, wasn't he? Provoking you. And he shouldn't. He hasn't the right.' She covered up her anxiety with a smile. 'Nobody speaks to my boyfriend like that.'

Travis took the cue and wrapped his arms around her, kissed her forehead. 'Well, I appreciate the sentiment, Linden, but the day I let *anything* that Richie Coker says affect me is the day I hand the keys to our little group over to Antony. I can handle Richie Coker.'

'I'd sooner you handled me,' Linden diverted, completing her deception by running her fingers through Travis's tangle of brown hair. 'If you know what I mean.'

'Sadly, I think we'd both better restrict ourselves to bottles and cans.' Travis glanced around at the half-empty boxes of supplies. 'We need to get on. And *you* need to try to get on with Richie, Lin. We're stronger when we're together. Will you?'

'Will I what?'

'Be nice to Richie. For me?'

'I'd do anything for you, Travis,' said Linden, and hated herself.

*

It wasn't the bodies that distressed Jessica most. She wouldn't go quite as far as to say that after you'd seen one victim of the Sickness, you'd seen them all, but the disease's trademark crimson circles scarring the flesh were pretty much identical on every corpse, and dead people in any case, she was finding, seemed somehow too remote from the living to be disturbing: unreal, inorganic, like statues carved by the most morbid sculptor in history. No, the deceased themselves were not the problem. It was what they left behind that upset her.

She should have teamed up with Travis, Linden and Richie at the village store. Plundering shelves of produce was neither as intrusive nor as emotional as picking through private houses that had once required an invitation even to enter. Nobody displayed the relics of their precious past where the public bought their vegetables.

Antony and Mel were upstairs. She could hear them rummaging. Jessica herself stood in the cottage's tiny parlour like a guest nervous of her reception. The curtains were drawn and she wanted them left that way. Greater light would reveal more starkly the owners of the cottage's belongings, and that could well bring tears. Not because of what the objects were in themselves – a cluster of matching tables, a Delft pottery milkmaid, a carriage clock – but because of what they signified. Lives had been lived here, and the furnishings, the ornaments had provided the backdrop for those lives, like a stage set for a play. But the actors were all gone now and the drama was ended. There could be little more lonely than an empty room.

The photographs were the worst. Strangers smiling though there was no one left to love them. Jessica's heart wrenched every time she saw the photographs, proudly arranged on mantelpieces and sideboards. This time she didn't look.

'Find anything good yet?' Mel barged into the parlour, made Jessica jump. 'What are you standing in the dark for? Let's shed some light on the subject.' Which she did, yanking back the curtains. She sniffed at the contents of the room like a unimpressed auctioneer. 'Nah, nothing of any value here. Bet there'll be an oil lamp or candles or something, though, in the kitchen. You all right, Jess?' Because the blonde girl was blinking her large green eyes and pressing her trembling lips together as if she wasn't.

'I'm fine. Something in my eye, that's all.' Probing it with a slender finger.

'You sure?'

'No.' The damn photographs. She hadn't been able to ignore them entirely in the flood of morning light. A grandmother, a little girl balancing on her knee and laughing at the precariousness of her position.

'Jessie.' Mel's voice was warm and tender. So were her arms as they enfolded Jessica.

It was akin to being embraced by night. Melanie Patrick's pre-Sickness wardrobe had been as black as the hair that cascaded over her thin shoulders. Post-Enclave, she'd reverted to type. Mel was the sartorial equivalent of Henry Ford and his Model T: she'd wear any colour you liked, so long as it was black. Baggy was also good, so the curves of her body couldn't be seen, so her sex could be obscured. But not her feelings. It took more than a few scraps of fabric to conceal what Mel felt for Jessica Lane.

Right now, Jessica didn't care about that. She was grateful for the comfort. 'It's stupid. I know. I'm stupid. It's just a

8

photo, people I never even. . . That old lady, Mel.' The grandmother. 'Do you think she lived here?' Mel's eyes strayed meaningfully to the ceiling. 'Oh, *God*.'

'She looks peaceful, though, Jess. Antony covered her up.'

'What about the little girl in the picture? What do you think happened to her?'

'I don't know.'

'Do you think she's still alive somewhere, wandering with one of those horrible gangs we saw? Or maybe she's in a cryo-tube aboard a slavecraft waiting to be transported to the Scytharene homeworld. Do you think she cries for her granny or her parents every night to come and save her?'

'I don't know, Jessie,' sighed Mel, 'and I'm not sure it does us any good to dwell on it. We can't help little girls like that. At least, not until someone's beaten the Scytharene.'

'So,' said Jessica bleakly, 'never, then.'

'What's this, a tea break?' Antony Clive breezed into the room looking as if he was about to depart on a bracing walk through the grounds of his own estate. A tweed cap wouldn't have gone amiss on his head of tight blond curls. His finely chiselled aristocratic features, however, darkened from a smile to a frown when they registered Jessica's expression. 'Jess?'

Grudgingly Mel stood aside. The boy hugged Jessica instead.

'I'm all right, Antony. I was saying to Mel . . . I got a little upset by the photos, that's all.'

'Maybe a bit of fresh air'll help,' suggested Mel. Bonus: she wouldn't have to watch Antony fondling Jessie like that.

'Good idea. Very good idea,' he agreed at once. And it must have been Antony's public-school, play-the-game upbringing, Mel reflected. An asset on the rugby field, no

9

doubt, but it had made the former Head Boy of the Harrington School absolutely bloody useless when it came to detecting hidden agendas. 'Mel and I can finish up in here, Jess. You pop outside.'

Jessica nodded. 'I think I will.'

And she did feel a little better in the open. Their car was parked about a hundred yards down the road, nearer to the shop. Richie was leaning up against the vehicle smoking. Jessica breathed in deeply. The cottage, all of the houses, they were more like graves these days. She closed her eyes, lifted her face to the sun, swept her long hair back and tried to forget for a moment where she was, tried to remember her life before the Sickness and the Scytharene.

The whine of a dog refused to let her.

Jessica opened her eyes to see it quivering on all four paws just inside the garden, the gate swung wide. The mongrel's fur was filthy and matted, its body so skinny every rib could be counted and each heartbeat bulged like a ball thrown against its chest from within. The animal seemed barely able to stand, but it found the strength to wag its tail feebly and its brown eyes appealed plaintively to the girl as they'd doubtless done to many humans before, begging food, craving affection.

Jessica felt an urge to supply both. The latter she could manage immediately. 'Hello, boy. Hello. What's your name? Are you a good boy?' She bent down, extended her open palm, inched closer towards her new little friend. She'd always wanted a dog, a collie like Lassie so they could have adventures together, or a beautiful Labrador she could have her picture taken with when she was famous. Dad had said no. Dad had said dogs were a tie. Dad had said dogs were more trouble than they were worth.

10

Perhaps Jessica could prove him wrong after all this time. 'Good boy. There's a *good* boy.' Closer to the whimpering, motionless canine, leaning forward, reaching out her hand to touch him, to stroke his muzzle. 'You don't need to be frightened. There's nothing to be—'

The dog went for her. One second it was whining forlornly, the next it was growling and predatory, its lips peeling back to expose sharp and snapping teeth. It lunged for Jessica's hand.

Which she snatched away with a squeal, recoiling in shock. The dog, undeterred, launched itself snarling at the girl. Jessica jerked sideways, avoiding the animal's leap. But though the dog landed awkwardly on the grass it twisted around like wire to confront her once more, eyes crazed, muscles bunched. Aiming for her throat this time. And Jessica back-pedalling frantically, fearfully. Stumbling.

She screamed again as she fell. How could she defend . . . The gun. Tucked into her jeans. If she could reach it. But the maddened dog was sensing easy prey. Its bark might almost have been of triumph.

A shot rang out across the garden with the stinging crack of a whip. Not from Jessica's weapon, though. From Mel's, her gun fired warningly into the air. She and Antony had heard Jessica's cries, were racing from the cottage.

The dog didn't care who they were. It knew only that they were enemies and more powerful than itself. It did what aggressors normally do when suddenly finding themselves outnumbered. It fled.

'You all right, Jess?' Antony kneeling beside her, raising her up. 'Did it bite you?'

'No. No. But it was *going* to. I mean, I think for *food*,

Antony. I think it would have tried to kill me if Mel hadn't . . .
God.' Her stomach heaved.

'What's going on? Who the hell's shooting?' Richie
appeared the other side of the garden hedge, flourishing his
shotgun as though keen to join in.

'Panic over, soldier. You can stand down,' Mel said. 'Man's
Best Friend turns out to be a bit of a bastard after all.'

'Come again?'

'We had Fido try to turn Jessie into a main course. Guess a
diet of nothing but meaty chunks out of a can and a few bis-
cuits must piss you off eventually.'

'A dog attacked Jessica?' Richie frowned.

'If only the examination system was still up and running,'
Mel said ruefully. 'You're a truly A-star student, Richie.'

'Drop dead, Morticia.'

'Do you think we can stop bickering?' Antony had helped
Jessica to her feet but she still seemed shaky on them. 'Let's
get Jessie to the car. It's okay, Jess. We've scared the thing
away. It won't be back.'

A distant barking drifting on the air.

Mel stiffened. 'Can we have that in writing, Antony?'

And multiplying. And approaching. And escalating in
volume.

'I reckon bloody Fido's gone to fetch his mates,' said
Richie. 'Maybe we should *all* get to the car.'

And not *barking*, either, not really. More of a baying, a
howling, insistent, inexorable. Chilling. Like a pack of hounds
on a hunt before they tear the fox to pieces.

'Oh, shit,' gulped Richie.

Bounding into the street from the other end of the village
to the car, dogs. Dozens of dogs. Every breed. Emaciated,

caked in dirt, some of them bloodied, all of them savage. Once, and not too long ago, either, they'd been domesticated, family pets, children's playmates, pensioners' companions. But the Sickness had deprived them of their owners and denied them their source of food. Starvation had done the rest. They'd reverted to the wild. They were wolves again. And the bloodlust was in them.

'Run!' bellowed Richie.

The teenagers did, sprinting for the car, but they weren't going to outpace the pack. The larger, stronger dogs in particular were gaining. An Alsatian with gristle where its ears had been. A Dobermann streaked with blood and slavering.

Mel fired her gun into the air again. This time the animals didn't even flinch.

'Not over their heads, Morticia, you tart,' Richie raged. '*At* them. *Shoot* the buggers.'

'I can't . . . I can't shoot a *dog*,' Mel moaned. Her finger was on the trigger but she hesitated.

The Dobermann didn't. Its black body and swiping claws were almost on her.

A white blast from Antony's subjugator froze the animal in its tracks and dropped it thudding to the road.

'Can't think of them as dogs, Mel,' he advised, firing again. 'They're wild beasts now.'

'Yeah, I can tell you've been on safari, O Great White Hunter,' Mel retorted. It was easy for Antony to mow the creatures down. The rest of them didn't have the luxury of his subjugator's stun function. When they opened fire, they were shooting to kill.

And she had no choice but to do that, to open fire. Blood sprayed from the Alsatian's chest. And as the animal yelped in pain and died there in the street where its owner might once have walked it, Mel felt like a murderer.

In the village store, Travis and Linden heard the gunfire. Drawing their weapons, they rushed outside.

Into a canine obstacle of their own.

Bare-fanged, ravening brutes numbering in double figures. Surging for them. Springing at them. Totally by instinct, Travis fired his subjugator, removed the threat of the lead dogs.

Linden was slower to react. When she'd lived with the Children of Nature, she'd been taught to love and care for *all* of Nature's creatures. Whether that instruction included those creatures seemingly intent on ripping her throat out was an issue she didn't really have time to debate just now. Sentimentality had already placed her at a disadvantage.

An Airedale clamped its jaws around the forearm she'd raised to deflect its flight. Just as well her sweatshirt had long sleeves. A Boxer and, absurdly, surreally, a poodle, snapped at her wildly kicking legs and feet.

'Travis!' Occupied with the elimination of their other assailants. She'd have to do the feminist thing and save herself. Just as well it was her right hand still free. Her gun hand. The Airedale was clinging on, its teeth biting through her sweatshirt, bruising her arm, about to puncture the skin. 'God,' she uttered. *Forgive me*, she felt.

Prodded the barrel of her gun into the dog's chest and blasted. Noticed the animal was still wearing a collar as its jaws widened in agony and its eyes glazed and her arm was her own again. Noticed the shiny silver disc still dangling from it. Read what it said.

Forgive me, she prayed again.

14

And maybe someone had. She didn't have to kill any more. Travis and his subjugator had been busy.

'Come on, let's get the car open and started up,' he urged, darting towards it and pulling her with him. The others were converging on the vehicle too but still embattled by the pack and further off. 'Hope Richie's left the key in the ignition.'

He had. And there was no building of tension like in the movies. The engine started first time, allowing both Travis and Linden to provide covering fire and help haul their friends into the car.

'Go, Naughton, go!' From Richie, sprawling unceremoniously across the back seat.

'Mel . . .' Travis said. The black-haired girl was still yards away.

'What's Morticia waiting for? A better offer? Get a bloody move on!'

'That's what's so inspiring about you, Coker,' said Antony acidly, piling in with Jessica. 'You're so concerned for the welfare of others.'

'Sorry I'm late.' Mel dived into the back too. 'Did you miss me?'

Linden and Antony slammed the doors shut. The dogs propelled themselves impotently, idiotically at the windows, their bodies thumping and slamming into the vehicle.

'Yeah, too late, you bastards.' Richie pressed his jeering face against the glass where, an inch away, a less than golden retriever howled its frustration. 'You want to take a bite out of us now, you need a can-opener. I hope you all die.'

'Shut up, Richie,' glowered Linden. 'This isn't the dogs' fault. They can't help what they're doing. The Scytharene have forced them into it. They're only trying to survive.'

'Us too,' reminded Travis as a bony greyhound somehow vaulted on to the bonnet and kind of butted the windscreen. Travis stamped his foot down on the accelerator. The greyhound slid off the car almost comically.

The crunching bumps as the 4×4's wheels ran over dogs too slow or too lunatic to get out of the way, however, were far from amusing.

Jessica peered through the rear window. Those animals that remained alive were compensating for the loss of their original prey. They were fighting each other for the right to devour their dead companions. Jessica turned away quickly.

'Everyone all right?' Travis said.

Mel broke into shrieks of hysterical laughter. 'All right, Trav? Sure. I've never been better. We've been chased out of a village full of corpses by a pack of homicidal hounds and who knows, just around the corner an army of albino aliens might be lurking to chuck us into slavery for the rest of our naturals. All right? How come you even have to ask?'

She was still rocking with bitter hilarity as the village vanished into the distance behind them.

Before the Sickness, Vernham Hill had been a notable beauty spot. Tourists had come to climb its steep, wooded slopes and to admire the breathtaking view from the summit. The crashed and blackened hulk of the Scytharene slavecraft *Furion* had put paid to that, gouging deep, dark channels in the earth and splintering once-towering trees into matchwood. The scars of the recent battle between the *Furion* and a force of Joshua Assault Vehicles, all of them destroyed, did little to restore tranquillity to the scene either. It would be a long time before sightseers returned to Vernham Hill.

Those who came here now had different priorities.

Scytharene warriors in their customary black armour, their helmets modelled after savage beasts or birds of prey, swarmed over the ship's remains like ants. Through vents and tears in the metal as well as more conventional hatches and portals, they ventured into the interior of the *Furion*'s broken crescent. When they emerged again, sometimes it was with something that in size and shape approximated to a body. On these occasions, they deposited their find on the ground where similar objects lay, zipped into bags and catalogued by comrades in red. Then they returned to the wreckage. This process was repeated very many times, with very many warriors participating. The rows of body bags stretched further than the eye might care to see. Even the pitiless, pupil-less crimson eyes of the Scytharene.

Which perhaps explained why two of their number stood at a distance from the majority's grim work, closer to the smaller ships that had brought them here and that now occupied the brow of the hill. On the other hand, perhaps it was the golden armour in which this pair were clad that distinguished them from their fellow Scytharene, in ways more profound than simple colour. They were a female in her twenties and a male more than twice her age who, unlike his companion, was draped in robes, also of gold. Neither wore a helmet, allowing direct comparison to be made between the facial features of the Scytharene sexes. Not that there appeared to be any real physiognomical differences. Both heads were entirely hairless, the skin utterly white, the white of bled meat, the white of fresh skulls, and in common too were the lumpish cartilage ears with the half-moon flap, the flat, ugly nose, the lipless mouth that unseamed itself when

17

preparing to speak like a wound splitting open, and those eyes, like jellied blood. Only at the bellineum was gender expressed. The jutting buttress of bone that bulged along the forehead above the male's eyes was as pale as the rest of him; the female's bellineum, however, in keeping with the traditions of her kind, had been painted in bright, seductive hues, decorated with symbols like hieroglyphics. Inscribed less permanently on each of the Scytharene's faces were the emotions of anger and loss, but whereas rage predominated in the male, with the female the gentler, sadder condition seemed to prevail.

A warrior approached the pair, punched his fist to his heart and bowed his head deferentially. 'Fleet Commander Gyrion,' he addressed the gold-robed male.

'Warrior-Prime Murion, report if you would.'

'We've already recovered a significant number of the crew's bodies as you can see, Fleet Commander,' said Murion, 'but I'm afraid the operation will take a considerable time to complete. Perhaps you might prefer to return to the Culler and I'll send word when—'

'I *prefer*, Prime,' corrected Gyrion, 'to remain where I am and not to have my movements dictated to me by my subordinates.'

'Yes, sir. My apologies, Fleet Commander, sir.'

'My son perished aboard the *Furion*, Warrior-Prime Murion. My son made the ultimate sacrifice for the Scytharene cause and proved himself worthy of his noble bloodline. My son is a hero of his race, and I will not leave this place until *he* does. Retrieve every one of our fallen brethren, Prime, and do so quickly.'

'Yes, sir, Fleet Commander Gyrion,' assured the warrior

subserviently. 'Then perhaps the Lady Dyona might be more comfortable . . .' Indicating the ships, seeking to redeem himself.

'Your solicitude is appreciated, Prime, but unnecessary,' said the female Scytharene. 'Lord Darion was my betrothed. My duty is also to remain here.'

'Of course, my lady. Forgive me.' Bowing his head once more, Warrior-Prime Murion beat as hasty a retreat as he dared. It was not sensible to risk the disapproval of even a single member of the elite Thousand Families, let alone two, and one of those Fleet Commander Gyrion.

Who stared after the soldier with contempt. 'There must be contamination in that one's bloodline, Dyona,' he observed coldly. 'An alien in the ancestry, as the saying goes. A poor example of our people, putting relaxation before revenge.'

'I'm sure that's not an error you'll make, my lord,' said Dyona, with a sardonic note that a more sensitive soul than Gyrion might have detected.

'Indeed not.' His eyes like lava. 'The Earthers will pay for the crime they have committed.'

Fighting for their lives against alien invaders whose intention was to enslave them, Dyona thought. Who were the real criminals here?

'This is a miserable, primitive planet,' Gyrion growled. 'I can hardly bear to tread its surface and its foul air is a corruption in my lungs. The impurities of alien environments revolt me. Thank Ayrion the slave harvest is well advanced. With our profits from the sale of these wretched savages I will build the finest mausoleum our people have ever seen in which to enshrine the body of my brave and beloved son, Darion.'

19

'I'm sure he'd appreciate that,' Dyona said. She was lying, of course, but her tears were true. They brewed scarlet in her eyes and coursed down her blank-paper cheeks like trickles of blood.

Their appearance embarrassed Gyrion. Blood was only acceptable when spouting from wounds inflicted in battle. 'You miss him, of course,' he said gruffly.

'I loved him.' And she still did. Not even death was mighty enough to change that.

'Then take pride in the manner of his passing,' his father said. 'Battling for what he believed in.'

'Oh, I do, my lord,' Dyona said fervently.

'The superiority of the Scytharene race.'

Hardly. Gyrion's ignorance almost made Dyona laugh. Darion had been killed alongside the crew of the *Furion*, indisputably, but he'd not been *fighting* alongside them. He'd opposed them. He'd despised them. He'd rejected every single tenet of his people's Master Race creed and allied himself with the Earthers. And at the last, during the final conflict, however it had actually transpired, whatever the details of Darion's death, Dyona was absolutely certain that her lover had been fighting *against* the Scytharene. Her heart exulted with that knowledge even through her grief.

'And at least the cursed traitor Shurion spoke of must have died with the rest.'

The traitor. Gyrion's own son.

'Indeed, my lord,' said Dyona. 'A most happy occurrence.'

And the traitor's body might have burned. Darion was gone. But his spirit and his inspiration would live on, Dyona vowed. *In her.*

*

'I'll miss my old Gameboy,' said Antony.

Richie swigged lager and leaned forward leeringly in his chair. 'You talking electronic leisure devices, Tony, or the kid in the next bed at that poncy bloody school of yours?'

'Oh, Richie,' complained Jessica, 'why do you always have to lower the tone?' She didn't glance Melwards.

'It's okay, Jess,' Antony said loftily. 'Richie can't help it. That's the problem with having more nostrils than brain cells. I mean computer games generally. I'll miss those. I know it's only a small thing—'

'Unlucky, Lane,' chuckled Richie, and had to duck to avoid the cushion flung like a Frisbee at his offending head.

They'd parked up for the night at an isolated and fortuitously corpse-free cottage. They'd shifted the chairs in the front room into a circle and by candlelight were sharing their thoughts on those items of pre-Sickness life they most regretted losing.

'Funny, I wouldn't have put you down as a fan of those shoot-'em-up games, Antony,' said Mel. 'Richie, yes – or would have been, if he could have worked out how to turn the computer on.'

'Bet I know how to turn you on, Morticia,' came the retort.

Mel snorted. 'What's in that can? Lager or libido? Get a grip, Coker – so to speak.'

'And actually, if anyone's interested,' Antony pointed out, 'I *didn't* play shoot-'em-ups or whatever you want to call them.'

'Not much need to now, anyway,' said Travis. 'These days we're shooting for real.'

'Yeah. Would have made a great game, though, wouldn't it?' Mel's voice became exaggeratedly dramatic: 'Will you survive "The Attack of the Scytharene"? Or, the Sickness was only the beginning. Now battle for freedom or become "Slaves of the Scytharene".' She shrugged. 'It's a shoo-in. If only the marketing people weren't all dead.'

'I preferred,' persisted Antony doggedly, 'more constructive games. Games where you built something rather than destroyed it, that tested you with something more positive than beating your best friend's body count. Were you familiar with *Pax Britannica*? You had to found a new British Empire in the twenty-first century. I used to spend hours playing that.'

'Me too,' Jessica laughed, clapping her hands with delight. 'Mum and Dad bought it for my fourteenth birthday. I loved that game.'

'Really?' Antony gazed at Jessica. He looked kind of dazzled. 'What a coincidence. How far did you get?'

'Oh, I never managed to civilise the *whole* world. The Middle East was always a bit of a problem. And Australia.'

'Well, I worked out a few short-cuts. . .'

'Lord save us,' groaned Mel. Something else Jessica and Antony had in common. *Damn.* 'Let me restore sanity to the proceedings and step in with some of the things I *won't* be sorry to leave behind. Politicians telling us to do one thing while doing the opposite themselves, like bog-standard comps for us, posh public schools like Antony's for their kids. Has-been rock stars flying round the world pontificating about how it's our moral duty to save the planet by – uh – *not* flying round the world. Talent contests for untalented wannabes where you phone in to vote but the results are fixed anyway. Any magazine with the word "celebrity" on the cover. Footballers earning more in a week than a whole football team's worth of nurses could in a year. Health and

22

safety regulations being used as an insidious form of social con—'

'Mel. Mel,' interrupted Travis. 'Thanks. We get the picture. Just a pity it's the wrong picture. What do you *miss*?'

'Well, we could do with a satnav system for the car,' Mel said moodily. 'Might help us find the next bloody Enclave a bit easier.'

'We'll be there tomorrow,' Travis promised, and with a pointed glance at Antony: 'Early.'

They hadn't been wandering aimlessly since the battle with the *Furion* and the fall of the first Enclave. The sheet of paper the late Dr Mowatt had given Jessica and Mel identifying the positions of other such military-scientific installations had become like a treasure map to the teenagers, offering a rich reward of hope. What if all, some or even just one of these other Enclaves turned out to be operational, occupied by living people, soldiers, scientists, *adults*? Perhaps there were experts in residence who already knew how to defeat the Scytharene, who even now were masterminding the perfect plan to expel the aliens from Earth, to send them scuttling and vanquished back into space. Or perhaps not. The group had located two of the Enclave sites so far. Both complexes had been hollow shells. What if, in time, Travis thought fearfully, hope became hollow as well? What would they do then?

He'd wanted to push on today, maybe even reach the next base before dark. Surely, the next Enclave would be the one. But Antony had proposed instead that they stop for the night in order to be fresh for the morning. The others had agreed with him, which perplexed and kind of annoyed Travis. He didn't understand. He never wanted to stop.

'What about me?' Richie was demanding. 'Don't you wanna know what *I* miss?'

'We already *know* what you miss, Big Guy,' Mel said. 'Pornography, amphetamines and kids with dinner money to extort. I'd rather ask Linden. Lin?'

Who, everybody realised, had been silent throughout the entire discussion. Five pairs of eyes turned quizzically to her.

'I don't . . . I'm not . . .' Linden looked away. 'I can't do this.'

She sprang to her feet and ran from the room.

'Lin? What's . . . I didn't mean to upset her.' Mel half rose from her seat. Travis saved her the trouble of the other half.

'It's all right. I'll go.'

'Chicks blubbing for no reason,' Richie grunted after them. 'That's something that'll *never* bloody change.'

Travis found her in the dining room, leaning her arms on the table and her head on her arms. She was crying quietly.

'You want to try my shoulder, Lin? Not quite so hard.'

She looked up and her face in the moonlight through the window was like silver. 'I'm sorry, Travis. I must have made myself look foolish.'

'Not to me you didn't. Not to the others, either.' He pulled up a chair beside her, twined a protective arm around her. 'What's wrong?'

Linden smiled wanly. 'I'm not sure it's worth me saying. It's stupid, really.'

'Foolish. Stupid. I'm beginning to see a pattern developing here. *Tell* me.' He stroked her cheek and dampened his fingertips with her tears. 'Trust me.'

'How many millions did the Sickness kill, Travis? Or is it

24

billions? And the Scytharene. So many people I haven't cried for, haven't mourned. And yet this morning I kill one dog, *one dog*, an animal, it wasn't even a human being, and I can't get it out of my head, and I'm sorry and ashamed . . .'

'Lin, you didn't have any choice . . .'

'I know. I know. Rationally, I know, but here, Travis' – pressing her hand against her heart – 'what I *feel* is different. The dog had a name-tag on its collar. I read its name as it died. Scamp. I killed Scamp. Some kid had loved that dog, Trav. I know it was a child, a little girl, a little boy. They'd loved him and they'd called him Scamp. In a different life they'd done it, a better, happier life, and I shot their beautiful dog dead.'

'Linden . . .'

'And I'm crying for him. That's the bizarre part, Travis. The human race virtually at the point of extinction and I'm grieving for a solitary dog, not all those people. There's got to be something wrong with me.'

'There's nothing wrong with you.' Travis cuddled her. 'Linden.' He adored saying her name. He'd never realised a word could be so stirring, so tantalising. 'Nobody can feel about millions the way it's possible to feel about one. A million deaths is a statistic. A single death – that's something else. That's an individual, and that's when loss can touch us, when we can begin to care. I mean genuinely. The way one person *can* care for another, get close to another.' And Travis could hardly have drawn closer to Linden right at this moment. Their bodies were locked together. 'The way one person can love another . . .'

'Do you love me, Travis?'

'Oh, yes.'

'I'm glad. I love you.'

'Linden . . .'

'Do you believe me? Do you believe I love you?'

'Lin . . .'

'Say you do. I want to hear you say it.' Anxiety behind the eyes.

'I believe you. I know you love me.'

'Then don't leave me tonight. Be with me. All night.' In urgent whispers. 'Sleep with me, Travis.'

And uncertainty in Travis's voice. Fear as well as longing. 'Lin, we said we'd—'

'We said we'd wait. I know. Until the time was right. But I think we've waited long enough, Travis, don't you? I can't – I need you loving me. Time's now.' She took his hand, squeezed, made to stand.

He checked her. 'Linden, it's just . . . You know I haven't . . . *been* with anyone before.'

'You told me that. Makes me a lucky girl to be your first, Travis Naughton.'

'It's just – I want this, tonight, to be special. You and me, Lin. I don't want to let you down.'

'I'm sure you'll measure *up*,' Linden grinned. She kissed him deeply, her tongue flickering hotly over his. 'Don't worry. Relax. Enjoy. Listen, I'm not exactly gossip column material myself.'

'Ash . . .'

'Ouch.' Masking a sudden fear with a short laugh. She hadn't wanted to hear *that* name tonight.

'Ash is the only boy you've ever – slept with?'

'Does it matter?'

'It matters,' said Travis, simply and sincerely. 'Maybe it shouldn't, but it does.'

26

So Linden lied. Richie she struck from her memory. Richie had never happened. 'Then yes. Ash is the only boy I've ever slept with – but he won't be for much longer. Will he?'

'No. Not for much longer.'

'Pleased to hear it. Shall we?'

And this time when she rose, Travis let Linden lead him to the stairs.

'What about the others?' he whispered, hearing their voices from the front room.

'I think it's better if we just keep it to you and me, for tonight at least,' giggled Linden. 'Let them find their own kind of fun.' She began creeping up the stairs. 'God, it's dark. I can hardly see.'

'That's good, isn't it?' Travis followed her into the blackness. 'Love is blind.'

Which was perhaps why neither of them noticed Richie Coker brooding in the shadows of the hall. Richie could see them, however. He'd been watching for a while. And he knew where they were going. And why.

His fists were clenched.

27

TWO

Travis remembered how his mates had talked about girls back at school: 'That Janine Collier, she fancies you . . . You're in there, mate, she's *gagging* for it . . . Cheryl Stone? You got more chance with *Sharon* Stone.' And gawped and ogled: 'Will you *look* at that bum. That's got to be one of the top ten bums in the world, that has . . . legs up to her armpits, yeah. Course, they've gotta be that long or they wouldn't reach the ground . . . Alison Grant? I *know*. She's so hot I could drink her bathwater.' And boasted: 'We *did* do it, I'm telling you. At Dale's party, in the spare bedroom, while everyone else was off their heads . . . While her mum was out shopping . . . She went to the loo and when she came back in she was starkers. I'm not kidding . . . In the back room of the youth club where they keep the old table-tennis tables . . . Babysitting for her next-door neighbours . . . All the way . . . Twice . . . Three times.' And largely fantasised.

Travis had joined in, of course. Leching over teenage girls was what you did when you were teenage boys, and from what Mel had told him –with a chaste touch of moral disapproval, as though she herself was immune to such predilections – the same was pretty much true in reverse for girls. But though he'd been happy enough to be lewd and vulgar with the rest of them if the conversation had taken a lewd and vulgar turn, generally he'd been quieter on the subject of sex and girls than most. Getting laid seemed to have been the central purpose of some of his mates' existences, their sole preoccupation, and while Travis had had no intention of leading the life of a monk, there'd been other, darker, more painful matters on his mind as well.

His policeman father, stabbed to death in the street. His widowed mother, sobbing herself to sleep at night. The evil that was out there in the world, prowling in the darkness like a beast and waiting to pounce. What to do about it. How to combat it, to make a stand against it. How to make his father proud.

Maybe it wasn't surprising that on occasion the joys of perving over Alison Grant's legs or Cheryl Stone's bottom had kind of passed him by.

It would happen one day for him, he'd known that. Somewhere, with someone he hoped he'd love.

But he hadn't expected to lose his virginity in a dead stranger's bed in a house he'd never so much as entered before and would never visit again. He hadn't expected his partner to be a girl who for most of her life had lived in communes and with eco-warriors out in the woods. He'd imagined Jessica might have been the one, if she hadn't seemed so afraid of anything that smacked of adulthood. Or Mel, if she hadn't been so wary of anything male.

But it was Linden. Linden was the one. Linden Darroway with her hair the colour of autumn leaves. And he was glad. Linden was the only good thing to have come out of the Sickness, meeting her, falling for her.

Slipping out of bed, Travis realised he couldn't do without her, not before last night and certainly not now. He studied

29

her with a kind of wonder as she lay curled up asleep. The covers had slid from her body. She was naked, vulnerable, perfect. But there was fear in his heart as well as exhilaration, because what if something ever went wrong between them? What if he ever lost Linden? If that happened, Travis doubted he'd have the strength to carry on.

But it wasn't *going* to happen. Ever.

'Are you staring at me, Travis?' Linden was grinning, her eyes open.

'I think admiring might be a better word.'

'Well don't. It's rude.' Linden giggled, stretched out. 'Can't you see I've got no clothes on?'

'Don't worry about it,' Travis responded. 'Neither have I.'

'Mm – so I notice. Maybe we should huddle together for warmth.'

'Much as I'd love to, Lin . . .' Travis sighed, glanced towards the window and the world that stretched beyond. 'We need to get moving. I want to reach the next Enclave as soon as possible.'

'Fine by me, Trav, but hey,' Linden recommended from the bed, 'I'd put some jeans on first, yeah?'

They didn't have to say anything. It wasn't hard for the others to work out that Travis and Linden had taken their relationship to the next level. Mel whistled and clapped as they ventured downstairs: 'Ladies and gentlemen, I give you the happy couple.' While Travis wasn't looking, Jessica hugged Linden: 'I'm so happy for you, Lin. Travis is the *best*.' While Linden wasn't looking, she hugged Travis: 'I'm so happy for you, Trav. Linden's lovely.' Between times, when *he* wasn't looking, she gazed, with a curious mixture of doubt and desire, of anticipation and

30

apprehension, at Antony. Who found a discreet moment to shake Travis by the hand, wish him a circumspect well done, and trust that they'd Been Careful.

Only Richie, if anything more sullen and morose than ever, made no reference whatsoever to Travis and Linden's nocturnal activities, however oblique. He merely pulled his hood up, his baseball cap down, and glowered in his seat as they set off for the Enclave.

It was Travis's turn at the wheel – except in the event of emergencies, they'd adopted a system of rotating drivers so that everyone over time could develop their confidence and skills on the road. Antony sat alongside Travis in the front and read the map.

'It might be wiser to keep to the minor roads,' he advised. 'Less chance of a close encounter with the Scytharene that way.'

'Yeah. And *more* chance of losing time,' Travis said. 'We could have been at this Enclave by now if someone hadn't wanted to stop earlier than necessary yesterday.'

'Well, if we hadn't,' Antony bridled with a sense of unfairness, 'someone *else* might not have started today with such a grin on his face.'

'Hey, the two with the view,' Mel called from behind, 'did you pick up a pair of handbags on the quiet at that last village or what? You're beginning to sound like a couple of old women.'

'Antony's only making a suggestion, Trav,' said Jessica.

'And Travis is only ignoring it,' said Linden.

'And we're gonna be in big trouble if we don't get off this bloody road *fast*!' Richie, breaking his self-imposed vow of silence. And for good reason.

31

Above the fields that spread out on either side of them, a Culler sliced across the sky. An alien slavecraft must be close by. Both types of ship had the same keynote design, the silver sickle of the Scytharene, but their dimensions were very different. The Cullers were launched from bays *inside* the significantly larger mother ships such as the *Furion*, and from within the Cullers themselves much smaller craft still could take to the air – as they did now. Panels in the undercarriage retracted. The battlepods billowed out like bubbles blown by a child. Battlepods, oval in shape, the lower half metal, the upper half transparent, each one able to accommodate a single Scytharene warrior, each one released with the express intention of harvesting human slaves for the cryo-tubes. The six teenagers had made their acquaintance before. Familiarity did not make them any the more welcome.

'Travis, those trees. Under those trees.' Which formed part of the nearest of a number of coverts that embroidered the roadside.

'I'm there.'

No disagreement now between Travis and Antony as to their course of action. The former sped for the shelter, braked sharply. Everyone jumped out of the car. The Culler was hovering some distance away with imperious aloofness but there was still the danger of being spotted by the circling battlepods. The car had to appear abandoned and the teenagers had to not appear at all. Luckily the grass in the adjacent field was long, like green wheat rippling in the breeze. Toting only their weapons, Travis's group threw themselves full length into it.

'Trav!' Mel hissed in dismay and pointed in the direction of the Culler.

So that was why the battlepods had been deployed. A small crowd of youngsters, some twenty or thirty of them, had been detected foolishly crossing open land, a nice little diversion for the Scytharene. At the first sight of the aliens the kids had obviously scattered, but it was going to do them no good.

'There's nowhere for them to run,' groaned Linden.

'Even if there was they'd never get there,' Travis said.

'I'm not watching this shit,' growled Richie.

From the swooping battlepods bolts of unerring energy flashed, cutting down the frantic children before most of them could even utter a cry.

'At least – at least they're not dead.' Jessica sought consolation as the last one fell.

'Maybe they'll soon be wishing they were,' Mel muttered grimly, recalling the cells of the *Furion* and the future life of a slave with which the virtual reality of processing had taunted her.

'We should have done something,' Linden said. 'We should have helped them – somehow.'

'We can't.' Antony winced at his own powerlessness.

'Maybe we can,' Travis contradicted.

The blond boy frowned. 'Against battlepods? Travis . . .'

'Not against the pods, no.' The blue eyes narrowed. 'Against the Scytharene themselves.'

Because the oval craft were coming in to land. The black-garbed Scytharene warriors were stepping out, laughing, congratulating each other. Prodding bodies with their boots. Some even removing their helmets, grinning through the bloody slits of their mouths.

Travis set his jaw. 'I get the feeling they think they own this planet already. I think we should put them right.' He raised his subjugator and aimed it at the gathering Scytharene.

'Naughton,' nodded Richie, 'I *like* the way you think.' Following suit with his shotgun. 'That guy from *The Last of the Mohicans* can eat his heart out.'

Antony grabbed the barrel of the shotgun and Travis's subjugator simultaneously. 'Have you lost your minds? What do you think you're doing?'

'Shooting alien bastards,' provided Richie.

'Yeah? Bringing alien . . .what you said down on top of us, that's what you're doing. Getting us caught is what you're doing if you open fire now.'

'Antony,' scowled Travis, 'you don't win wars by not engaging the enemy.'

'You don't win them by making futile and suicidal gestures, either,' Antony insisted. 'How many Scytharene do you think you and Richie can pick off – even all of us firing together – before the rest of them overwhelm us or signal the Culler? As if the Culler won't in any case think something's wrong and investigate as soon as it sees its people falling over for no apparent reason. And surely you're not suggesting we take on a Culler as well?'

'Okay. Okay.' Reluctantly Travis lowered his subjugator.

'Making a stand is good, Travis. But let's make it when we've at least got a fighting chance of staying on our feet.'

'I said,' Travis grimaced, *'okay.'*

'Shit,' commented Richie. 'I had one of those suckers right in my sights, too.'

'So what do we do, then?' Linden wanted to know.

'What Antony said,' Travis gritted. 'Absolutely nothing.' It irked him to give way to the Head Boy of the Harrington

School – he, Travis, was the group's leader, after all. But it frustrated him even more to know, deep down, that on this occasion at least Antony was right.

The battlepods' work completed, the Culler moved in. It hung high above the youngsters' bodies and from its under-carriage it shone a beam of dazzling white light that enveloped them all. As the light touched them, and despite their continued unconsciousness, the children stirred, lifted themselves from the ground as in a reverse-slow-motion replay of their fall. They were weightless now, as insubstantial as the air into which they rose, drawn inexorably towards and into the belly of the Culler. Like souls, Mel thought, ascend-ing to Heaven, and the notion inexplicably moved her. But in reality, of course, it was a Scytharene tractor beam in opera-tion.

Helplessly, despairingly, the teenagers looked on as the abductions continued.

But it wouldn't always be like this, Travis swore. It couldn't be. He wouldn't *let* it be. There had to be a way to defeat the aliens, and at the Enclave they would find it.

Darion's spirit would live on, she'd pledged, and she'd meant it. But who was she kidding? As the Scytharene said, the war-rior who lies to himself is no warrior at all.

Little by little, Dyona's strength was draining from her. Day by day, her life aboard the flagship *Ayrion III* descended deeper into nightmare. The horrors were all around her. The slave cells, packed to capacity with potential merchandise. The assessors, processing the captives around the clock, establishing which subjects were viable – likely to cope with the emotional and psychological stress of slavery on a planet

35

far from their own – and which were *un*viable. The disposal cells for the latter, screaming as they performed their fatal duty. And the vast cryo-tube storage chamber, filling with the former, hundreds of the long, transparent cylinders occupied, the bodies of the Earther slaves silent and sleeping.

Soon the Cullers would be required to transport this latest stock of cargo to one of the cryo-ships in orbit, thence to be conveyed to the distant galaxy and the sprawling markets of the Scytharene homeworld. Meanwhile, the Cullers would return to their mother ship bringing fresh supplies of untenanted cryo-tubes. The process would begin again, and it would continue, onwards and always, until the harvesting of further Earthers was deemed to be uneconomical. Only then would the Scytharene leave this plundered and depopulated world. And move on to the next. With Dyona no doubt still among them. It was a nightmare, and it consumed her every waking moment.

Most disturbingly and most disorientatingly of all, now that Darion was dead nobody else seemed to share her perspective. Her fellow Scytharene did not view slavery as a moral and cultural atrocity, as she did. Instead, they regarded the practice as natural and just, the strong exploiting the weak as was their birthright in a universe divided mercilessly but incontrovertibly into superior and inferior species, the conquerors and the conquered, the leaders and the led. Many Scytharene, particularly those with lower-caste bloodlines, were content simply to line their pockets with the profits of their trade and gave no thought to the philosophical implications of their conduct. Many more, however, especially among the elite, the Thousand Families of the Scytharene ruling class whose bloodlines could be traced back to the first founders of their kind, saw each enslavement as a crusade. In their minds, the Scytharene were the Master Race, and it was their duty and their honour to demonstrate at every stage their supremacy over the puny and primitive civilisations they inevitably came to dominate. This was done often with great ruthlessness and always with great relish. It was a mind-set that Dyona could not comprehend, that seemed to her brutal, twisted and insane. Yet in this matter she seemed to be in a minority of one. In most cultures she had encountered, a single individual whose beliefs were in such utter and dia-metrical opposition to the prevailing values of his society was himself likely to be deemed mad and locked away. In some, however, a lone voice crying in the wilderness was heard and revered as that of a seer, a prophet, the voice of the truth.

Which, Dyona wondered, was she?

Perhaps it might help her sanity if she was reassigned else-where. The *Ayrion III* was based outside the English city of Oxford, which, as an alienologist, had excited Dyona at first. Oxford was one of the most important centres of learning and intellectual achievement among the Earthers, not just on this tiny and otherwise rather inconsequential island but throughout their world. She'd eagerly anticipated the oppor-tunity to explore the Earther university here, to browse its libraries and study its buildings, its artefacts. It didn't matter that her official role was to produce scientific proof of the cultural, social and racial inferiority of the aliens. She herself would still have been able to learn about Earther civilisation, impartially, for learning's own sake, without judging. All knowledge was good knowledge, even when it was acquired on an alien globe. She and Darion had both believed that. It was what they had loved in each other.

37

But now Darion was gone. If only the same could be said of his father. Always a zealot for the Scytharene cause, since Darion's death Gyrion had become more fanatical than ever. He was planning on monitoring Dyona's researches in Oxford more closely and with greater rigour than she'd expected; she was to be allowed even less latitude than usual. Even the consolation of immersing herself in the mysteries of a gratifyingly non-Scytharene culture was, it seemed, to be denied her.

So was reassignment the answer? Sadly, she doubted it. Gyrion would be unlikely to grant permission, for a start, at least not without asking a lot of questions first, and the way she was feeling now, lonely, despairing, she might just let her mask of obedience and orthodoxy slip. That would *not* be good. It was probably more sensible to stay where she was and make the best of the situation. Gyrion wasn't intending physically to accompany her expedition into Oxford. That was something. The Spidroids had virtually cleared the dead Earthers with their possibly disease-spreading bodies from those areas of the city yet to be harvested, including the site of the university, which meant that she and her expedition could possibly set off as soon as tomorrow, certainly the day after.

Dyona was settled. Departure couldn't come quickly enough. Any time spent apart from Gyrion and the *Ayrion III* was time *well* spent. But first . . .

'My lady.' On cue, her loyal servant arriving to remind her.

'I know, Etrion.' Dyona glanced down at herself. Today was not a day for armour. Her flowing gold robes of mourning were edged with blue, the Scytharene colour of death.

38

'You are awaited, my lady, in the Chamber of the Ancestors.'

Darion's transcension ceremony was about to begin.

'Are you sure this is right, boys?' Mel gloomed from the back seat of the car. ''Cause it looks like a long way to send out for a pizza.'

'Top-secret military-scientific installations aren't as a rule situated in areas of high population density, Mel,' said Antony over his shoulder.

'Thank you, Professor Clive.'

Mel returned her attention to the scenery. It was not memorable. Travis was tearing along a rudimentary road that was slanting permanently downwards and had been cut between two steep rock faces. Dust flew up from beneath the wheels and hung in the air like white smoke. There was no sign of human life or activity.

'Trav, do you have to drive *quite* so fast?' Jessica wondered nervously.

Mel developed her critique of their immediate surroundings. 'Only, I mean, honestly. This is like some crummy old *Dr Who* set from the seventies where every alien planet looked like a gravel pit and every alien race consisted of three fat guys in latex and wigs who sounded like they'd been educated at Eton.'

'Wish that was the only kind of alien race we had to worry about,' remarked Linden.

'Wish this bloody car was like the Tardis and bigger on the inside than it is on the outside,' grumbled Richie. He shifted awkwardly in his seat. 'If you want to sit on my lap, Morticia, it's polite to ask first.'

'Stop moaning,' snapped Travis. 'We'll be stopping in a sec

and you can get out. They must be aware of us by now. They must have surveillance and monitoring systems in place, maybe more of those vigilanteyes.' He lifted his gaze to the sky as if hoping to see one of the flying globes floating there at that very moment. He was disappointed. 'They must have realised we're friendlies.'

The road, having reached its final destination, promptly ceased to exist. The rock walls parted and the teenagers found themselves entering the heart of an industrial-sized quarry. There were no other means of access.

'Oh, great,' Richie grunted. 'A big round dead end.' He yanked at the door handle as Travis slowed down. 'Well, at least . . .' And almost fell out as the other boy accelerated again. 'What the bloody hell . . .?'

'There. *There.* Can't you see it?' Travis jabbed the windscreen.

A rectangle of blackness in the rock face on the far side of the quarry, the outlines too precise to be natural.

'The door to the Enclave.' Travis beelined for it. 'They *have* seen us. They've opened it for us.' He was grinning. Everything was going to be all right.

Only he was wrong.

It was obvious from the moment the car pulled up and nobody emerged from the tunnel beyond the entrance to greet them, no soldiers with comforting automatic weapons, no scientists in lab coats with solutions to the Scytharene problem. The doorway gaped like a dead man's mouth, like Munch's *Scream*.

Like the darkness Travis saw when he closed his eyes and groaned.

*

Dyona didn't think it timely to point out to Fleet Commander Gyrion the similarities between a Scytharene transcension ceremony and the Earther custom of funerals. Indeed, every civilisation in the galaxy accepted the value of some kind of public ritual to commemorate the loss of a loved one. Which suggested to Dyona that the differences between intelligent species were as superficial as the pigmentation of skin compared to those monumental and universal experiences, birth, sex, death, that they had in common. Which suggested again that there was much the various races could learn from each other. But now was not the occasion to mention that, either.

The congregation maintained a respectful silence in the domed Chamber of the Ancestors while the priests droned their way through the ceremony. As was prescribed, in the very centre of the room the coffin had been placed on a high podium, around which the blue-robed priests circled in a clockwise direction, to symbolise the inescapable passage of time. Forming a wider and more static circle around the priests stood the mourners, and from the arches of the chamber and the friezes on its walls, at a greater distance from the recently departed in space as well as time, effigies and delineations of the venerated ancestors of the Scytharene people observed the rite also, as if to ensure that all was enacted in accordance with tradition.

It wasn't quite. The coffin ought really to contain the remains of the deceased, but there was no body here today. No identifiable trace of Darion had been found aboard the *Furion*. His casket was empty – and Murion had been reduced to the ranks. Secretly, the absence of a body delighted Dyona. Not because she harboured any impossible hope that her

41

beloved had somehow survived the ship's destruction after all, but because it allowed Darion to evade even involuntary participation in a ceremony he had in life despised.

The priests, needless to say, carried on as normal.

'. . . celebrate Lord Darion's liberation from the shackles of the flesh, his freedom from the bondage of time. As his soul rises now to join with the spirits of his ancestors and the totem of his bloodline, let us reflect with gratitude and pride on the deeds of a noble life . . .'

Dyona felt the grief welling up in her again. She heard herself sobbing. *Darion*. She remembered how she'd boasted to him that she'd joined the outlawed Dissident Movement, bragged how she intended to take positive action to disrupt the slave harvests and to protect the aliens, even if that meant inciting or actually engaging in acts of violence against her own people – she *disowned* her own people. She remembered thinking how exciting a little bit of covert terrorist activity would be. And she remembered how she'd mocked and berated Darion for his caution and his reluctance to make a stand in defence of the aliens. She'd believed that she was stronger, more committed than Darion, braver than her betrothed, but she'd been wrong. Immature. Frivolous. It was Darion who had found the courage of sacrifice, and she was nothing without him.

'. . . and as we say together the words we have been taught: Son of Ayrion, walk with Ayrion . . .'

By the gods, Dyona hoped not. Darion may have belonged to the bloodline of Ayrion, hero of the Scytharene, but he'd loathed his ancestor and all he stood for. She felt the same disgust towards her own bloodline of Lyrion.

Where were Travis Naughton, Antony Clive and Melanie

Patrick, the Earther youths they had aided before? Dyona would sooner walk with them than her own kind. She prayed they were safe.

'Darion, son of Ayrion, born of the noblest bloodline of them all, your time among us is over. Transcend now the limits of this life and ascend into the holy embrace of your ancestors.'

A blue light radiated from above to enfold the coffin, levitating it from the podium, bearing the casket to the domed ceiling of the chamber and a portal that opened to receive it. All denoting the deceased's acceptance into the next world, so it was said.

A hollow gesture, was Dyona's opinion, and for an empty box. If only it was Scytharene society itself that they'd come to bury.

And now that the central object of the ceremony had been removed, in her overwrought state it seemed to Dyona that the faces of the ancestors both sculpted and painted were turned towards her, glaring at her as if privy to her treacherous innermost thoughts.

She didn't care. The Scytharene of centuries past meant nothing to her. She no longer felt a sense of community with any of her race, living or dead. They were *alien* to her and she did not belong among them.

In a strange way, Dyona wished she was human.

'So we keep going. We keep moving.' Travis was illustrating his words by pacing the control centre in restless, relentless circles. The others were rather more stationary, slumped on chairs at computer consoles where technicians once had worked. 'If there's nothing for us here, we seek out the next Enclave.'

43

'Well there's nothing for us here, that's for sure,' said Mel emphatically.

As they'd feared from the first, this Enclave too was deserted, abandoned. A few putrefying corpses here and there provided the only indication that it had ever been inhabited by human beings. Though it was constructed on three levels like its counterparts the teenagers had already seen – military, scientific, and accommodation and recreation – there was little of value to be salvaged from any of them. Any equipment that had been at all portable was gone. They weren't even going to be able to expand their limited armoury, much to Richie's dismay. Power, at least, was still being generated, but the screens of the computers in the control centre were blank like the eyes of the blind.

'I realise finding the place like this is kind of disappointing,' Travis accepted.

'*Kind of,* says Naughton,' grunted Richie. 'It's like holding a party and nobody bloody turning up.'

'But we can't be demoralised. We mustn't give up.'

'Why not?'

The question came with the shock of an obscenity in a prayer, and all the more unexpectedly because of who had uttered it. Everyone's eyes turned to Antony Clive.

'Why *not?*' Travis repeated disbelievingly.

'I don't mean give up in the sense of surrendering ourselves to the Scytharene. Just – why don't we stop endlessly trailing around the country searching for something we might not ever find and we don't know for sure is even out there? Every time we drive there's a greater chance we'll be spotted by a Culler or a patrol of battlepods. Look what happened earlier. We were lucky to—'

44

'No,' said Travis flatly. 'We can't stop. I know moving about is dangerous, but the reward is worth the risk.'

'What reward's that then, Naughton?' said Richie.

'You know what.' Travis's blue eyes flashed with irritation. 'Contrary to the opinion of some, it means' – a frown in Antony's direction – 'sooner or later we *will* find the key to defeating the Scytharene.'

'Bloody sooner or later.' Richie shrugged. 'Later or *never*'s more like it.'

'Trav,' ventured Mel, 'I hear what you're saying, but we haven't really got anywhere so far, have we? And I mean, say one or more of the remaining Enclaves *is* operational and *can* fight back, they'll do that with or without us, won't they? I mean, what difference can we make anyway? The six of us.'

'It only takes one person to make a difference, Mel,' Travis said.

'Travis is right,' backed Linden.

Mel wasn't persuaded. 'In principle, maybe. In an ideal world. But this world is finished. Realistically, we haven't got a chance against the Scytharene.'

'So where do we go next, Melanie?' Hurt that Mel seemed to be opposing him. 'Or do we go nowhere? Do we just sit on our arses down here for the rest of our lives?'

'Actually, perhaps your time frame is a little extreme, Travis,' said Antony, 'but other than that . . .'

'*What?*'

'I think we *should* stay here. Keep ourselves hidden and safe. For a while, at least, until we have a clearer idea of how events are unfolding, whether there is any coherent adult resistance to the Scytharene.'

'Stay here, Antony?'

'Perhaps we might even be able to recruit others as we'd started doing at Harrington, organise, make rules, establish a proper community . . .'

'Here? What, holed up underground like rats?' Travis was contemptuous. 'We need to stand up to the Scytharene, not scurry away from them like bloody rodents.'

'Don't get angry, Trav,' Jessica said, a pained expression clouding her features. 'I think Antony's got a point. If we could just pause, rest for a while . . .'

'I'm with Tony too, Naughton,' said Richie.

'I don't give a toss who *you're* with. Lin?'

'Do you have to ask, Travis?' She smiled supportively.

'Mel?'

'Sorry, Trav. Not this time. Not without something more substantial to go on than faith.'

'Well – well that's great. That's just – great.' And maybe it was giddiness from those incessant circles he'd walked but the room seemed to be reeling. He *knew* he was sounding childish and petulant but he couldn't help it. Too much stress. 'You can say what you like. It makes no difference. I'm the leader of this group and all the while I am, policy is to stand against the Scytharene no matter what.'

'Then perhaps,' Antony advanced, 'we need a new leader.'

Travis jabbed an accusing finger at the blond boy. 'So that's it, is it, Antony? By "new leader" you mean of course you.'

And it kind of surprised Antony but yes, he *did* mean him. He hadn't originally intended to challenge Travis for the leadership of the group, only to raise an important issue he'd felt they should discuss, but *now* . . . 'Why not? I'm qualified.' When the staff had been succumbing to the Sickness, when the students had needed an authority figure to reassure them, Dr Stuart had chosen him.

'Yeah, that's right. Head Boy of the Harrington School.' And Travis knew he shouldn't take his frustration out on others – *his father would never have done it* – but he couldn't help that, either. 'And you did such a great job, the last time we saw the place it had been burned to the ground.'

'Travis, that's not fair!' cried Jessica.

'How dare you?' thundered Antony.

'Is it me,' chuckled Richie, 'or is Naughton kind of pissed off right now?' He glanced towards Linden.

'How *dare* you?' Antony was on his feet, confronting Travis face to face. 'Are you implying the destruction of Harrington is somehow down to me?'

'I'm just looking at your track record as a leader, that's all.'

'Well let's look at yours. Let's look at some of the people you see fit to trust, for example. Who then go on to betray us to the aliens and nearly get us all killed. Any names spring to mind?'

'Leave Simon out of this.'

'You should have left *Harrington* out of this.'

'Jeez, guys,' sighed Mel, 'can't we just leave the *testosterone* out of this?'

'Antony needs to back off.' Linden.

'Travis started it.' Jessica.

Both girls standing.

Richie leaning back in his chair with his legs stretched out and his hands behind his head. 'You chicks want to fight, don't mind me. But hey, Naughton, Tony, yell any louder, the Scytharene'll hear you and it won't matter a toss who's the bloody leader.'

47

'It's about your judgement, Travis,' Antony was pressing. 'Too often you make decisions based on what you *want* to believe, what you *want* to be true, whether it is or not.'

'Belief is what counts, Antony. Leadership is more than drawing up work rosters or allocating beds.'

'Uh, guys?' Mel, who had been distracted from the argument by the computer at her console.

'Leadership is about putting the group first, Travis. Seems to me sometimes you're more interested in your own agenda.'

'Fighting the Scytharene should be everyone's agenda, *Antony*. Unless your upper-class upbringing hasn't quite given you the bottle for it.'

'Ah, the tedious envy of the comprehensive-school student. I wondered when—'

'*Guys!*' Mel felt she ought to be heard this time. '*Look.*'

At the screen. Which was suddenly active, the words displayed clearly legible: *Is anyone receiving this message? Please respond. Is anyone receiving this message? Please respond.* Silence gripped the control centre.

'We are not alone,' said Mel.

Disputes were forgotten, for now at least. When Mel made way for Travis to sit at the computer, nobody protested, not even Antony. Everybody crowded around him as one as he prepared to open a dialogue with their mysterious contact.

'What if this is some kind of trap, though, Trav?' worried Jessica. 'Mum and Dad always warned me to be careful in internet chat-rooms.'

'Which this isn't, Jessie,' said Travis. 'Whoever's sending, he knows how to log on to a military network. And I don't think the Scytharene need to resort to tricks and deceptions

48

anyway. Not when they've got battlepods.' Travis glanced up pointedly. He was already regretting what he'd said in the heat of the moment about Harrington. 'Antony, what do you reckon?'

'I agree. Go ahead, Travis.'

He keyed in: *Your message has been received. Who are you?*

My name is Dr Crispin Allerton. Who are you?

'So he's human.' There was a wild hope in Linden's tone.

'*Says* he's human,' Mel countered.

'And with a name like Crispin,' commented Richie, 'only just.'

'But he's a doctor. A scientist like Dr Mowatt?' Jessica's voice too was rising with excitement. 'From another Enclave? Travis, you were right.' She squeezed his shoulders, was taken aback by the tension in them.

'Not yet I'm not. But I guess I'd better introduce myself . . .'

'Say you're an adult, Travis,' Antony advised. 'If he thinks he's only talking to teenagers, he might log off.'

'Definitely not an internet chat-room,' observed Mel.

Travis was nodding. 'Good idea.'

He typed: *My name is Captain Travis Naughton, British Army.*

The reply came back almost immediately: *Pleased to make your acquaintance, Captain Travis Naughton.*

Mutual, typed Travis.

Captain Naughton, how many men do you have in your command?

'Your *command*,' said Antony. 'He's optimistic, isn't he?'

'So am I,' grinned Travis.

Fifty.

Are you armed and mobile?

Yes. Why? Do you require assistance?

49

'Let's hope to God he doesn't, though,' Travis muttered.

Captain Naughton, my colleagues and I can help you more than you can help us.

What do you mean?

'I'd never have thought of that one, Trav,' Mel chuckled. For a second. She hadn't anticipated Dr Allerton's reply, either, and it didn't reduce only her to slack-jawed astonishment.

My colleagues and I have discovered the means to annihilate the alien invaders, once and for all.

THREE

Jessica blinked as though awaking from a long sleep. 'They know how to . . . It's like a dream come true.'

'A dream, yeah. So it can't *be* true.' But even Mel's cynicism had limits. 'Can it?'

'Let's find out.' Travis keyed in: *Tell us how.*

The response took a while to appear.

'If this Dr Allerton guy is lying,' Linden mused in the meantime, 'why? What can he hope to gain?'

'If he's not lying,' Antony was daring to believe, 'if there really is a way. . .'

'Alien ass is gonna get kicked,' said Richie with relish.

Captain Naughton, the text resumed, *our plan would take too long to explain communicating like this. Our power reserves are low and must be conserved.*

'Here we go,' snorted Mel. 'He's backing off already. That's the story of life, isn't it? Undying love declared one day, divorce papers served the next.'

All I have time to tell you now is that my colleagues and I belong to a government-sponsored scientific research programme called the Paragon Project.

'Paragon,' said Antony. 'It means somebody or something seen as a model of excellence.'

The Paragon Project has been studying the Sickness from the first,

Captain Naughton, and the aliens since their advent. We can defeat the invaders, but you will need to come to us to learn how.

'You sure Paragon doesn't mean sly git, Tony?' said Richie. 'There's the catch.'

'Yeah, well, let's allow him to think he's caught us for now,' said Travis.

He keyed in: *Where are you?*

The Paragon Project is based at Wells College, Oxford. Oxford is presently encircled by the aliens. Young people are being abducted. Then of course there is still the Sickness. It is too dangerous for us to leave the controlled environment of our laboratories.

'But not too dangerous for us to risk our lives going in.' Linden wasn't impressed.

'Travis told him we're soldiers, Lin,' Jessica reminded her. 'He's probably hoping for the SAS.'

Captain Naughton, you must find your way to us – fight your way through the alien lines, if need be. Save us from the aliens and we will save you.

'Bastard knows how to bargain,' Richie said with grudging admiration.

'So what do we tell him?' Mel said.

'At the moment, whatever we decide to do in the end, we'll follow in the great British political tradition,' said Travis. 'We'll tell him exactly what he wants to hear.'

Dr Allerton, he typed, *we are on our way.*

'Are we, though?' Jessica wanted to know as soon as the communication was ended and the computer screen returned to blankness.

'I guess the answer to that one depends on whether we believe this Dr Allerton or not,' said Linden. 'Do we?'

Antony considered. 'Well, there certainly is a Wells College in Oxford and it *is* renowned for scientific research and development. Named after H.G. Wells, the writer. I know how to get there as well.' With a surreptitiously superior glance at Travis. 'It's next to Merton College on Dead Man's Walk.'

'That's a hell of a promising address,' shuddered Mel.

Richie grunted. 'What, you got a GCSE in memorising maps, Tony?'

'No. I've been there. *Past* there, to be more accurate. My parents took me to Oxford a few times, to walk around the university. It was where I wanted to study for my degree – if I proved good enough to get in, of course.'

'Head Boy of Poncy Private School? Daddy a diplomat? I reckon you'd have been good enough to get in, Tony.' Richie winked.

'Actually, my parents wanted me to apply for Oxford too,' Jessica said, beaming at Antony.

'Why does that not surprise me?' said Mel. 'But what say we keep the discussion of our higher-education prospects for another time and kind of focus on the more pressing question, which is, what do we do *now*?'

'Of course, Mel,' Antony acquiesced. 'All I'm saying is that for an important scientific and research project to be based at Wells College is at least plausible.'

'That's helpful, Antony.' Travis rubbed his chin with his knuckles. 'What about Allerton's claim?'

'If only,' Antony shrugged. 'But I suppose the bottom line is, how can we tell for sure?'

'By going to Wells College,' Travis said. 'By doing what the mysterious Dr Allerton wants us to do. It's the only way.'

He gazed searchingly at his five companions. 'I know it'll be a risk, a big risk. We've not dared to enter any major town or city since before the Scytharene appeared. The aliens might not be the only threat. And I know most of you an hour ago would have been quite content to stay here where it's safe – safer, anyway – and not venture above ground for a while at all, and I guess I can see your point, though I don't happen to agree with it. But if we head for Wells and Dr Allerton, this Paragon Project, we won't just be trailing endlessly around the country, Antony, and we will have something more substantial to go on than faith, Mel. We *know* Dr Allerton exists. We'll have destination and purpose and hope. The greatest hope of all – that we can finally win our planet back. Yes, Allerton could be spinning us a line to get himself rescued, but he could also be telling the truth. And if he is, I know we're not the military but we've been inside a Scytharene ship, we've been in touch with Scytharene dissidents. Our knowledge still makes us useful. So I don't think we have a choice. We can't afford *not* to believe Allerton. We stay here the night, and then tomorrow I think we have to go.'

Linden: 'I agree.'

Jessica: 'All right, Travis. It makes sense.'

Mel: 'A clean sweep of the girls, Trav. Must be those baby blues of yours.'

Richie: 'Guess I'll run with the pack. You win, Naughton.'

'Antony?' prompted Travis. 'I'm sorry about what I said earlier.' He offered a conciliatory hand. 'I didn't mean any of it.'

'I know.' Gripping the hand firmly with his own. 'Neither did I.' *Except perhaps the part about me deserving to be leader.* 'And you're right, of course. If we don't go to Wells and meet this Dr Allerton, we might never forgive ourselves.'

'So,' said Mel, 'anyone for a group hug?'

There were enough rooms on the accommodation level for a dozen each and more, let alone one. The presence of both Jessica and Antony in the same room at the same time was not due to pressure of space. Neither was it entirely necessary for them both to be perched on the bed, given the number of available chairs ranged about, and the bed itself, being of conventional length, provided plenty of scope for two people to keep a polite distance from each other if they were so inclined.

It appeared that Jessica and Antony were *not* so inclined.

'I'm so glad you and Travis are friends again,' Jessica was saying, squeezing the boy's hands. 'I don't like you arguing. I don't think I could stand it if you fell out permanently.'

'We won't,' promised Antony. 'You think a lot of Travis, don't you, Jess?'

'I think a lot of you too,' Jessica said shyly, lowering her eyes.

Which Antony knew. Which elated him. Which, to have it confirmed by Jessica when they were alone together like this, kind of excited him. But he wasn't yet so confident of her loyalties as to ask her opinion regarding the group's leadership. Instead, 'Were you and Travis ever . . . involved, before the Sickness?'

'You mean were we boyfriend and girlfriend?'

'Yes.' Wanting to hear no.

'Kind of.'

Not brilliant, but it could have been worse.

'I mean, we went out a few times,' Jessica explained, 'but nothing happened.' What she couldn't really explain, though, was *why* nothing had happened. Or maybe she didn't trust Antony sufficiently yet to try. Her pampered, perfect childhood. Her fear of change. Her fear, when it came down to it, of boys, of the possibility of physical intimacies that boys brought with them and which would one day alter her life irreversibly and make her someone other than Daddy's Little Princess, would force her to leave the sanctuary of childhood behind her for ever. 'Travis and I sort of split up as a couple but there wasn't any bitterness. I love Travis – but like a brother. I know he'll always be there for me.'

'He's not the only one,' said Antony.

Jessica's face crimsoned. 'Antony . . .'

So at least Travis wasn't his potential rival in everything.

'Were you really going to Oxford?' Jessica asked suddenly.

'As I said, if my grades were good enough. My father went there.'

'Mine too.' Jessica marvelled. She had so much in common with Antony. They could have been made for each other. 'Do you think, if we'd both gone, I mean, if the Sickness had never happened and we were still living in the old world, the *right* world, do you think we'd still have met? At Oxford, I mean. At university. We might still have met.'

'I hope so. It's a nice thought. If we *had*,' Antony said, 'I know one thing, Jessica . . .'

'What?'

Reaching out and running his fingers through her long blonde hair. 'I'd *still* have been attracted to you. I'd still have wanted to kiss you.'

'How would you have kissed me?'

He showed her. Then he showed her again, and the taste of him lingered on her lips. And she felt close to him now, closer than she'd felt to any boy, even maybe Travis, and *comfortable* with him. His kisses thrilled rather than threatened. She wondered how much closer still she could or should draw to Antony. She thought of Travis and Linden: they were lovers now. Would she and Antony be like that? Did she dare take such a step? *Daddy's Little Princess*. But Daddy was dead. The world she'd grown up in was gone. Allowing Antony to – Doing It with Antony – that would be the last nail in her old life's coffin.

'Jessie,' breathed the boy.

'Antony, I think – I think we'd better get some sleep. Early start tomorrow, Travis said. I think you'd better . . .'

'Yeah.' Standing and understanding. 'That's fine. I'm going. See you in the morning, Jess.'

She wasn't quite ready to leave the past behind her. She couldn't. Its allure was still too strong. Perhaps one day she would be able to. Perhaps soon.

But not yet.

'God, Richie!' Linden cried out involuntarily as the boy in the baseball cap stepped suddenly into the corridor in front of her. 'What the hell do you think you're doing? Rehearsing for a mugging?'

'Sorry. Didn't mean to scare you.'

'Well you did. This place is creepy enough without you jumping out at people like that.' The silent labs. The empty corridors. The overriding sense of absence and loss.

'I wanted to talk to you.'

'Couldn't you have talked to me while we were all in the canteen eating?'

'I didn't think you'd want the others to hear what I've got to say, Linden.'

She closed her eyes and winced. She should have known. 'I don't think *I* want to hear what you've got to say, Richie.'

'It's about us.'

'Richie, there *is* no us, but if you're still confused on the issue let me run it by you one more time – one *last* time.' Linden's brow creased in pain at the recollection. 'I was weak – my fault. You took advantage – your fault. We're both to blame, though me more than you, if that makes you feel better. I was the one in a relationship. I betrayed Travis and I'm trying to live with that. But what we did was a physical act and nothing else, nothing more. Like exercise. Like going to the gym. It meant nothing, it was a one-off, and it was a terrible mistake. We need to forget it and move on. End of story. So talking of moving. . .' Linden gestured sideways with her hand. 'Night, Richie.'

Richie dutifully stepped out of her way – until she was passing him by. Then he grabbed her arm.

'Get your hand off me,' Linden snapped.

'I can't forget.'

'What?' There was a note in Richie's voice that Linden had never heard before, a kind of sincerity, a vulnerability, even a sadness. Whatever, it was very much at odds with the boy's hoodie fashions and heavy, sullen features.

'I don't want to forget.' Richie's sallow complexion was crimsoning with self-consciousness. Linden forgot he was still holding her arm. The yearning she could see in his eyes appalled her. 'Being with you, Linden, it was the best. It made me feel – you make me feel . . .'

'Oh, no. No no no. Richie, don't even go there.'

58

'I want you, Linden. I want you to be *my* girl.'

'Richie, you're mad. That's impossible. I've *told* you. I'm with Travis. I *love* Travis. Travis loves me. That's the way it is.' More sympathetically: 'I'm sorry, but you'll just have to—'

'Will Naughton still love you if he knows what we were up to behind his back?'

Finally Linden shook herself free of Richie's grasp. 'You said you wouldn't tell him. You promised.'

'People can't always keep their promises, Lin. People can let you down. You know that.'

'Don't do it, Richie. If you have any feelings for me at all, I mean genuine feelings, don't tell Travis.'

'I don't want to, but – you're on your way to him now, aren't you? We're not talking separate rooms either, are we? Or separate bloody beds. You and him. Thinking about you and him, together, it's bloody killing me.' His dark eyes flashing with anger and humiliation and longing.

'Then don't think about it,' recommended Linden, not perhaps too helpfully.

'I can't think of anything else.'

'Richie.' Linden shook her head in despair. 'Listen, you like Travis, don't you? You're always coming out with some smart-arse comments but it's obvious you admire him.' She interpreted the boy's silence as a grudging affirmative. 'Well if you tell him about us, you could destroy him. Do you want that, Richie? I don't think so. And you might succeed in splitting me and Travis up, but that won't bring me leaping into your arms instead – I'm *telling* you. So you could scar two people's lives, you could hurt me, hurt Travis, but you won't make yourself any happier if you do. And I'd hate you for it. *Hate* you, Richie. I mean it.'

'If I'm feeling bad, though, why shouldn't you? *And* Naughton? Why should I be the only one bloody suffering?'

'It's up to you, Richie,' Linden said. 'In the end, it's what the Children of Nature taught me: whatever we do affects other people, and we have it in our power in a million different ways to make them miserable or make them glad. We have to choose, every day of our lives, what kind of person we want to be, positive or negative, creative or destructive . . .'

'Load of bullshit,' Richie muttered.

'It's not bullshit. It's true. And right now, Richie, you have power over me and Travis. What you choose to do could alter the direction of our lives. Please' – her tone becoming pleading at the last – 'make the *right* choice.'

But as she turned and walked away without looking back, Linden dreaded what would happen if Richie did *not*.

The matter troubled her again later, afterwards, Travis lying alongside her and staring sombrely at the ceiling. 'I shouldn't have lost my temper with Antony like that before. It was unforgivable.'

'Don't be so self-critical, Trav,' she said. 'Or so absolute. Anything can be forgiven.'

'Some things can't.'

Linden looked at him suddenly. 'It was pressure, stress, that's all. It's gonna get too much for all of us from time to time. It's a miracle we're not all ga-ga by now anyway, considering the hell we've had to live through.'

'I'm only surviving because of you, Lin.'

'Travis Naughton, you sure know how to boost a girl's ego.'

'I mean it.' He turned his face to hers on the pillow. 'You're the only perfect thing left in the world.'

'Travis, I'm not perfect.' With a nervous laugh.

'You are.'

'I'm really not, Trav. I'm just a girl. Don't put me on a pedestal.' *Because how will you react when I fall off?*

'You are perfect,' said Travis.

Mel couldn't remember waking and dressing but she must have done because here she was out in the Enclave's corridors fully clothed.

She wondered why.

Maybe it was to investigate what had gone wrong with the power supply, because the lights had somehow failed and she was standing in more or less utter darkness. It was as if night itself had entered the complex. And she was reduced to a face and two hands and nothing else because the jet of her clothes had been woven into the greater blackness and the ink of her hair had flowed into it as well and the darkness was a grave into which she had fallen or a deep and icy lake in which she was doomed to drown.

Or maybe she'd left her bed and her room because she was lonely, to seek the company of the others. But where were the others? She drifted through the darkness as if she was floating on a river of oil and she called her friends' names but her words sank into the liquid pitch like silent stones. Travis and Linden, they'd be together. They wouldn't want her hanging around anyway. Jessica – Jessica had deserted her, was turning now towards Antony, leaving her behind and taking Mel's poor dreams of fulfilment with her.

She was alone. As, in truth, she'd always been alone. As she always would be alone, for ever and . . .

Someone was having a good time up ahead.

A blush of light on the dark, like a city seen from a plane at night. Laughter. Music. A door to step through.

Nobody had told Mel there was going to be a party in the Enclave tonight, but the organiser, whoever he was, had been busy inviting guests. There were plenty of guests. Mel knew some of them.

'Simon,' she said, and the bespectacled figure of Simon Satchwell grinned at her, raised a glass to her, looked happy to be here. Why not? Drinking and socialising surely had to beat lying cold and dead four feet under the ground – they'd wanted to dig the customary six so Simon's body couldn't possibly be disinterred for food by foxes or something, but they'd struggled to make it even to the lesser depth.

Mel moved on. 'Rev.' The biker she'd last seen broken and bleeding in the Scytharene slave compound. Rev who seemed to be harbouring no hard feelings towards the race that had killed him, given the apparent amicability of the conversation he was holding with Darion of the bloodline of Ayrion of the Thousand Families.

Mel was beginning to detect a pattern here among the guests.

And on the next table, Dr Mowatt, Dr Shiels, Mr Greening, Captain Taber, all of them grinning up at her, welcoming her, beckoning for her to join them.

As if she belonged with them.

They were standing now, the guests. And they were gliding hospitably towards her like creatures that had no need of muscles for motion. She'd been mistaken at first. She didn't know *some* of them. She knew *all* of them. *Had* known all of them. When they'd been alive. And they were surrounding her, converging on her, reaching out to her, and on the air their voices were carried like distant sighs: 'Stay with us. Stay with us.'

And Mel was backing away, finding her voice at last. 'No. I don't want to stay. No.'

She didn't get far.

Hands like fetters clamping around her shoulders. Mel screaming, twisting round to confront her captor. Screaming again.

'Melanie,' smiled her dead father, 'but I *insist* . . .'

'You okay, Mel?' Travis asked her the next morning as they packed the few items they thought necessary into the 4x4 prior to departure. His voice was edged with concern.

'Why? Don't I look okay?' Hers was defensive.

'Actually, not really.'

'Next place we stop I'll book a facial.'

'You know it's not that. You haven't said two words to anyone today. Something bothering you?'

Mel shrugged her bony shoulders swathed in black. 'Didn't have a very good night, that's all, Trav. What you might call bad dreams, if you'd also call the Great Flood a spot of rain.'

'I've heard bad dreams can be a symptom of stress.'

'Linden been sharing the homespun wisdom of the Children of Nature with you again, has she, Trav?' Mel chuckled bleakly. 'I bet she knows some great natural remedies for the common cold as well.'

'Mel,' Travis said affectionately, immune to her sarcasm, 'what's wrong?'

Mel sighed. Travis's gaze was on her and she couldn't defy it. 'Belonging,' she said.

'Say again?'

'I don't know where I belong any more, Trav. Or with who. I don't know what I'm doing or where I'm going. I don't know what I'm *for.*'

'That's just the effect of what's happening – first the Sickness, then the Scytharene. The world we knew's been torn away from us, the lives we led there, everything that gave us – I don't know – *foundation.* Stability. Adjusting to the new realities isn't going to be easy.'

'You seem to be managing, Trav. Linden seems to be helping you,' Mel added archly.

'She is,' Travis admitted freely. 'Everybody needs somebody, Mel. You can't cope on your own.'

'Some of us don't have a choice.'

'Come on, what are you talking about?' Travis protested. 'You're not on your own. You've got us. And to answer what you said before, you belong here. You belong with us. Your friends.'

Mel felt stupid tears stinging her eyes. 'For now, maybe. But what if you and Linden get all coupley, Trav, you know, all wrapped up in a world of your own kind of thing?'

'Mel, even if there was such a word as coupley and even if Linden and I were it, that wouldn't make a difference to you and me. Friends are for ever.'

'Promise?' Mel said cautiously.

'Do you trust me?'

'I trust you.'

'I promise. Now come here.' They hugged. 'Feel better now, Melanie Patrick?'

'Better,' she said.

Mel wasn't the only member of the group to appear uncharacteristically withdrawn this morning. Linden was keeping an anxious eye on a reticent, moody Richie Coker. He obviously hadn't told Travis about the two of them yet and maybe – *please God* – he wasn't planning on doing so at all. But the grooves scoring the one-time bully's forehead indicated a state of deep thoughtfulness not normally included among Richie's repertoire of expressions. He was clearly considering his next move. Linden was equally clearly not yet safe.

It should actually have been Richie's stint at the wheel today, but Jessica had suggested that maybe Antony should drive, by virtue of his superior knowledge of their destination, and Richie did not object. As the journey commenced, Antony's spirits were as high as it was possible for them to be, given the prevailing circumstances. He'd been accepted by everyone, even Travis, as the group's expert on all things Oxford. He'd therefore assumed a leadership role, at least for now, which was what he wanted. And Jessica was sitting alongside him with the road atlas – in case his memory or the signage failed him.

Jessica. He did what he shouldn't and glanced at her constantly instead of keeping his eyes on the road. He couldn't help it. Jessica was way more gorgeous than the road. She'd wondered last night about whether they might have met at Oxford, the important thing was that they could both have been there in the first place. The trajectories of their former lives were amazingly similar. Even before the Sickness, both he and Jessica had been moving in the same direction and from virtually identical starting-points. Their backgrounds, their attitudes, their expectations, all pretty much interchangeable. It was destiny for them to meet, a destiny that went beyond the physical and emotional attractions that drew them closer every day. In Antony's mind, he and Jessica could become more than just another couple. They could be the representatives of a whole way of life. They could be the pre-servers of their parents' values.

They decided to ditch the car before they'd even gained the outskirts of Oxford. For one thing, vehicles either empty or occupied only by corpses had begun to obstruct the road and make passage difficult. For another, and more disturbingly, Scytharene activity was becoming visible both in the sky and on land.

Cullers soared intermittently overhead like hungry birds of prey; the group had to be close to a slavecraft like the *Furion*. The ships' vigilance had obviously been rewarded many times already. Travis, Antony and Mel recognised the tall sentry posts and blue force-field fences of Scytharene slave compounds spanning large areas of land, high-tech versions of the prisoner-of-war camps familiar from old movies. The three teenagers had briefly sampled the hospitality of one such institution. Thanks to the intervention of Darion they'd escaped, but those they'd had to leave behind were now no doubt being held under more restrictive conditions still, con-fined to the one-man cells that were the cryo-tubes.

'I hope they've got enough beds for us in the nearest one of those slave camp shit-holes.' Richie had evidently decided to abandon thought and return to the comfort zone of his usual foul-mouthed self. ''Cause that's for sure where we're gonna end up if we keep heading in *this* direction.' Stabbing a pugnacious finger forward. 'We're never gonna get where we're going, all these alien bastards around. It's bloody madness.'

'Thanks for that typically intelligent analysis, Richie,' said Travis. 'You want to turn back, feel free. The rest of us are going on.'

'Bloody madness,' Richie repeated in case there was somebody who hadn't heard him the first time, but he didn't turn back.

Travelling on foot rather than driving reduced the risk of being spotted. Travelling on foot by *night* reduced it further. They physically only left the car behind them when it grew dark.

'We should take our packs with us,' said Antony.

Travis disagreed. 'Weapons only. Packs'll slow us down and if the worst comes to the worst we might need to run.'

'You're filling my heart with gladness, Naughton.' Richie.

'Food and water they're bound to have at Wells.'

'Water for sure, Trav,' joked Mel lamely. *'Wells?'*

Antony conceded the point to Travis with an unconvinced kind of shrug. 'I'm taking these, though,' he said, retrieving from his rucksack a pair of army binoculars. He'd found them at a previous Enclave and had assured everyone that sooner or later they'd prove their worth. He slung them around his neck. 'Shall we go? We don't want to keep the good Dr Allerton waiting.'

They remained on the road, picking their way past the traffic's idle rabble. When necessary, they ducked down beside this car or that truck to shield themselves from the probing, prowling searchlights of the Cullers still in the air. Mel reflected on her dream, how terrifying the darkness had seemed then, and smiled ruefully. Right now, darkness was their friend and *light* their enemy. The betraying beams of the Cullers. The beacon flames of—

'What the hell are *they*?' Mel murmured. She crouched behind a car with the others and stared in stupefaction.

The open land most adjacent to the city the Scytharene were putting to a different use than the incarceration of slaves. In what looked suspiciously, horrifyingly like examples of a series of such sites, perhaps a ring of them encircling all of Oxford, fires raged in huge pits. Even at the teenagers' distance from the scene, which they were more than pleased was considerable, they could see that each pit had to be dozens of metres across. The blaze from them blistered the black night red, flames rising, falling, then rising again as if new fuel was continually fanning the inferno.

But what fuel? And to what end did the bonfires burn?

Shapes and figures seemed to be shifting around the fire pits and there appeared to be numbers of sizeable blockish objects suspended in the sky, but it was impossible to distinguish anything precisely with the naked eye.

'*Told* you,' grinned Antony, boosting his sight with his binoculars. His grin lasted only as long as it took him to focus. He'd almost sooner have been blind. 'Oh my God.'

'What is it, Antony?' Jessica entreated. When she touched him, he was shaking. 'What can you see?'

'Cremations.' Antony spoke in an icy whisper. 'Bodies. I can't . . . Hundreds of bodies. *Burning*.'

Antony beheld the terrible scene thrust cruelly before him by the binoculars. High above the pits themselves, hovering just out of reach of the flames, a succession of craft lined up in orderly fashion. They were of grey metal and rectangular, large containers of some kind – Antony was reminded of skips. He could make out glowing propulsion units in all four corners of the containers' undercarriage, though the things

68

were patently remote-controlled: their sides were completely blank, offering no viewing point for a pilot. They carried cargo, however, and the undercarriage of each in turn slid open and emptied it into the fire. Emptied *them* into the fire. Human bodies. Human beings who'd once laughed and loved and *lived* before the Sickness had deprived them of all that and made of them material fit for kindling. They spilled from the containers' dark interiors, clothed or naked as they'd been for their final breath, and they dropped inelegantly into the grasping flames. Antony thought of the damned plunged into the eternal fires of Hell. He thought of the chimneys of the Auschwitz crematoria belching smoke in great abundance and blackening more than the sky. Most of all, he thought of 1665, the Great Plague, the vast communal graves in which the countless dead had been heaved from groaning wagons, swiftly and unceremoniously, to prevent the further spread of disease. The Scytharene were undertaking the same operation here.

They were cleansing the city of dangerous corpses. They were disposing of the dead.

But they weren't doing it alone. In fact, perhaps they didn't have the stomach for it at all, or maybe supervising the mass burning of bodies was deemed to be a duty beneath the dignity of a Scytharene, because there were very few warriors in attendance. Instead, the work seemed to have devolved to artificial life, giant mechanical spiders, silver robots as tall as a man, their sleek bodies glittering in the satanic glare of the pyres, their eight pylon legs extending from steel abdomens and finding footholds in the soil. The spiders scurried around the pit distractedly. Some took possession of those container vessels that had discharged their human contents and landed, ready presumably for a further foray into the deceased city, ready to be replenished. Others rose up before the flames on hind legs and swayed as if in worship, or as if they were warming their metal shells by the heat of the incineration.

Ashen-faced, Antony passed the trembling binoculars to Travis. Moments later, Travis handed them to Mel. Everyone took their turn and saw. Once Antony had received his binoculars back, Travis stood. Everyone followed suit. They moved off again towards Oxford and Wells College, perhaps even more urgently than before.

Nobody said a word.

For once, Travis was content to let Antony lead them. His mind was tortured by the memory of the fire pits; his dreams, he knew, would be haunted by the falling bodies igniting in the flames – his nights might soon become as tormented as Mel's seemed to be. And with the horror came doubt. How *could* they hope to defeat an enemy capable of such atrocities? An enemy powerful enough to topple civilisations and reduce great cities to wastelands?

He looked around him. Gutted, blackened buildings, some still smouldering. Streets strewn with shattered glass and rubble and the debris of lost and ruined lives. An endless crush of vehicles, burned out, upended, on their backs like dead metal tortoises. But no bodies, not in this part of town anyway. The Scytharene had seen to that. And no sound – any likely slaves from here had been harvested. Only darkness to shroud the desolate city.

Travis flirted with despair. Who would not? He and his friends were weak and helpless children with delusions of grandeur. They should repudiate the folly of resistance and submit to the inevitable. The struggle, the stand; in the darkness he was forced to acknowledge that they were wearing him down. How much longer could he stay strong?

And then Linden was gazing at him, searching for comfort with wide, anxious eyes. And he smiled and kissed her forehead reassuringly. He shrugged the blackness from him. Linden was the answer to that question. So were Jessica and Mel, Antony, even Richie. How much longer could he stay strong?

For as long as it took.

The complexion of the city was changing now as Antony guided them into the heart of the university district. The façades of the buildings on either side of the teenagers paled in colour, not simply an effect of the moonlight but the result of an architectural transformation. The centuries seemed to slip away as the conventional structures seen in any major city centre were superseded by the noble elegance of the Oxford colleges. Somehow, the damage inflicted elsewhere had made no impact here. Still proud, still haughty, serene despite the disaster that had befallen their students and dons, the colleges rose above the teenagers in all their Gothic splendour. Travis's sense of hope soared with the spires and the pinnacles of the university, his courage bolstered by the buttressed walls that had withstood everything that time had thrown at them.

'These places, they look a bit old, don't they?' sniffed Richie. 'All the rich kids who came to this bloody university, you'd think they'd have the money to pull 'em down and put up something modern.'

Travis laughed out loud. He couldn't help it and it felt good. He could have hugged Richie Coker.

'Pull them down? You're looking at St John's College, Richie,' Antony said indignantly. 'This frontage dates from 1437.'

'What I said, Tony. Old.'

'The colleges,' Linden observed, 'they look like decaying wedding cakes.'

'And that beautiful example of neoclassical architecture over there,' continued Antony, 'see the columns, Richie, the pillars? Neoclassical. That's the Ashmolean, one of the finest museums in the country.'

'I've never been inside a bloody museum in my life, Tony,' declared Richie as though it was a point of honour.

'I'm sure they're grateful,' huffed Antony.

'Yeah,' said Mel. 'As much as I'm enjoying the tour, guys, do you think we can move on? I'd feel better inside, you know? Out of sight. I mean, am I paranoid or do the rest of you get the feeling of being watched?'

'You're paranoid, Morticia,' diagnosed Richie.

'It's all right. It's all right.' Antony hurried them on. 'We're almost there.' They emerged from one narrow thoroughfare on to another, slightly wider road. 'This is Broad Street. We take a left, follow along—'

'Antony!' Jessica clutched his arm.

They were not the only tourists in town tonight. Swarming forward from the right skittered a host of the Scytharene's robot spiders. For the first time the teenagers could see their eyes, cold and calculating computer screens. Container vessels like giant coffins floated in the air above them.

'*Now* tell me I'm paranoid, Coker,' snapped Mel.

'Save your breath, both of you.' Travis grabbed Linden's hand. 'Run!'

They fled along Broad Street. The robots pursued them. However, 'They're not going any faster, Trav,' Linden reported.

'Hey, Lin,' called Mel, 'are you complaining?'

Maybe the spiders didn't need to increase their pace. Antony raced with Jessica down a right turn, the others hard on their heels. On a collision course towards them from the opposite direction, more of the robots. The teenagers' options were diminishing rapidly.

'Have you never been in a library either, Richie?' Antony said. 'No? Well the Bodleian's a good one to start with. Come on.' He darted into a palatial building to their right, his companions behind him. Only the faintest of light filtered through leaded and stained-glass windows. 'Split up. Hide. Hope to God they can't track us down.'

'At least we'll be able to read a good book while we're waiting to find out,' quipped Mel. And split up? Oh yeah. Antony vanishing into the dark with Jessica in tow one way. Trav and Linden making tracks another. Splitting up as in leaving her behind. What had Trav said earlier? But maybe she shouldn't blame them. She certainly wasn't hanging around for Richie.

The spiders were at the door.

Mel retreated fleetly but judiciously deeper into the building: injuring herself in a collision with some practically invisible piece of furniture would not enhance her chances of survival. She ghosted through dim galleries, beneath vaulted ceilings. The place was more like a church than a library and it seemed to go on for ever.

At last she found herself in a long room where the shelves, loaded with weighty tomes, reached to the ceiling. What had to be reading desks loomed around her, their deeper darkness like stains on the night. This was better, she thought. There'd be somewhere to conceal herself in—

She tripped over something soft and yielding on the floor, fell to her knees on top of it. A body. She was sprawled over a dead man, her face brought so close to his that even in the dark she could make out his grey beard, his glasses, and the scars of the Sickness disfiguring his face. His eyes were open as if he'd like to carry on reading. Maybe he'd come here to die because he'd loved books more than anything. Ironic, really. Mel had come here to stay alive.

If the Scytharene's robots would let her.

There were two of them in the doorway. It wasn't so much the black bulk of their shape that announced their arrival, or the steel click of their legs on the flagstoned floor. A searchlight beamed from each of their brows, knives to slice open the darkness and discover what hid inside.

Mel stifled a moan, rolled off the corpse, didn't dare risk standing, scrambled away backwards on her heels and hands, not unlike an ungainly insect herself. But the spiders were preternaturally alert to both movement and sound. The searchlights swept in her direction. One picked out the dead man and lingered. The other found Mel.

Dazzled, she froze. She was unable even to produce her gun, little good that would do against a metal-encased machine in any event. If she screamed, would that bring Travis or somebody rushing to help her? If it did, wouldn't they only get themselves caught too? Mel remained silent and motionless.

The spider advanced upon her. The spider stood over her. It regarded her with something like curiosity or uncertainty, data flickering in its computer eyes.

74

Its partner approached the man's body and seemed much clearer about its task. Its head inclined as if nodding approvingly. A small aperture opened in the lower portion of the head, perhaps mimicking a mouth.

Thick and sticky webbing spat from it.

The late reader was enmeshed, the webbing like a net. The spider began to drag the body towards the door. From there, it didn't challenge Mel to guess, to one of the container vessels. Finally, to the fire pits.

The prospect of that grisly fate was too much for her – as her own potential captor seemed to reach a decision and activated the aperture in its head. Mel screamed, threw up her arm in token self-protection, scrabbled back further still, expecting to be ensnared at any second.

She wasn't. No webbing spewed out to entangle her. The aperture closed.

It *closed*.

The spider was suddenly totally indifferent towards her, turning its back as if she was no longer worthy of its attention. It was the kind of slight to which Mel would once have taken indignant and vocal exception. Now, however, she whooped with glee. She jumped to her feet, punched the air, burst into almost hysterical laughter (it seemed to be becoming a habit). The spider continued on its way without so much as a pause.

Because it had no interest in her. None of the robots had. Why should they? Their job was to gather the dead for cremation. That was all they were programmed to do, and on a fairly primitive level at that: sound and movement. As soon as she'd indulged in both and proven conclusively to the machine that she was alive, it ignored her. She and the others had never needed to panic and run in the first place: the spiders were scouring the colleges to collect corpses, not harvest slaves.

But she ran now, back the way she'd come, and she yelled at the top of her voice: 'Trav! Jessie! Can anybody hear me? You're not gonna believe this!'

It was disconcerting to see the spiders, gleaming in the moonlight, crawling over the venerable university buildings. Mel's deductions, however, did appear to be true. The robots were going about their business with the mindless diligence of the automaton and seemed quite content to let the teenagers go about theirs. In actual fact, the former's numbers seemed to be gradually reducing as their function became redundant: not a great deal of cargo for the container vessels here.

By the time Antony stopped and announced that the grand façade in front of them belonged to Wells College, the spiders had disappeared altogether. No sign of death at Wells, evidently. Precious little sign of life, either.

'Are you sure this is the right college, Antony?' enquired Jessica gently as they explored the dark – and entirely uninhabited – interior. 'It looks just as deserted as the others. I mean, at night and everything, maybe, well . . .'

'Tony's taken a wrong turn,' grunted Richie.

'I haven't actually, Richie,' Antony said scornfully. More tenderly to Jessica: 'This is right. We're here.'

'But is Dr Allerton?' Mel said.

'He has to be,' Travis stated flatly.

No diners in the long college halls. No worshippers in the chilly college chapel. No students strolling the corridors or the quad.

'Allerton!' Travis suddenly cried, and Linden detected a note of desperation in his voice. 'Dr Allerton!'

She added her shout to his. 'Dr Allerton! Anyone!'

The others joined in too, like a tuneless choir. They bellowed the name into the darkness as if expecting it to reply. Eventually, it kind of did.

'Trav, look.' Linden's sharp eyes spotted him first.

A boy with shaggy brown hair, about fourteen or fifteen as far as she could tell in the dingy light, emerging cautiously from behind a pillar and bobbing his head and torso up and down like a nervous animal. Richie swung his shotgun round and the boy flinched back.

'Richie, you neanderthal.' Linden swatted the gun aside. 'It's all right,' she coaxed, approaching the boy as she might a timid animal. 'We're not going to hurt you. My name's Linden. What's yours?'

The boy answered only with a beckoning gesture before darting away.

Linden looked to the others. 'Do we follow him?'

Mel seemed to think so. 'We could starve waiting for the mysterious Dr Allerton to turn up.'

Travis nodded. 'Follow him.'

Along the wide corridor, down a flight of worn stone steps.

'Terrific,' Richie muttered. 'The kid's gonna show us the basement.'

Into subterranean darkness. Not even moonlight penetrated here. Within moments, their guide had become invisible.

'Perhaps we should go back.' Antony realised his hand had dropped instinctively to his subjugator. 'What if this is some kind of trap?'

'We're armed,' came Travis's voice from a shadow nearby. 'But you could be right. This is going no—'

A sudden glow of light silenced him. It came from possibly thirty yards ahead of them, where what the teenagers could now see was a broad but low corridor ended in a sheer stone wall. The light radiated from *between* the stones of the wall, as if luminosity had been applied there instead of mortar.

The shaggy-haired boy was doing his bobbing thing directly in front of the wall, grinning at Travis's group as if he'd outwitted them somehow. He looked like he'd benefit from a wash and a general tidy-up. His clothes, shirt, jumper and jeans, appeared to have been recently trampled on. Soap seemed to have been boycotting his skin since before the Sickness.

But he spoke as though participating in an elocution lesson. 'You are aware of Dr Allerton? Do I take it you would like to meet with Dr Allerton?'

'That's right,' Travis said eagerly. 'Do you know where he is?'

'Oh yes,' said the boy, and promptly stepped through the wall.

'Tell me I didn't see that,' gasped Richie.

The tousled head poked back again, like the decapitated and mounted trophy of a hunter. 'If you want to meet Dr Allerton you have to follow me. It's quite safe. A hologram. Science can allow you to walk through walls, you know.'

'It's what's on the other side of the wall I worry about,' Linden muttered.

Travis seemed to have no such qualms, though he did draw his subjugator. 'You want to know what's on the other side of this one, Lin?' he said, striding forward. '*Answers.*'

He was swallowed by the stones but the only sensation was a slight cooling of his skin. The ambient temperature had dropped: air-conditioning at work. The reverse of the hologram had not been designed to masquerade as old stones. It imitated instead the metal limits of a lab. The rest of Travis's new surroundings showed why. Computers, scientific equipment in generous amounts, solid doors in solid walls no doubt leading to more of the same. But it wasn't the high-tech facilities that attracted his attention primarily, nor that of his five companions as they also emerged from the hologram.

It was the lab's other occupants.

Shaggy-Hair had joined two more teenagers, both a little older than Travis's group, seventeen or eighteen. One was male, one female, the boy fair, his hair clipped short in military style, the girl brunette and rather unflatteringly pigtailed. The boy's attire was impeccable but bland, every garment white, even his shoes, perfect creases in spotless trousers; his companion wore clothes that her mother might have dressed her in before she hit puberty: a knee-length blue-striped dress, pleated, puff-sleeved, and white socks, and sandals.

The girl patted the younger boy on the head as if he was a pet dog who'd successfully performed a trick. She and the fair boy studied the six newcomers dispassionately.

'Yes?' said the boy at last.

'We're . . . uh' – Travis fought confusion – 'we're looking for Dr Allerton.'

'Then congratulations. You've found him.' The boy's thin lips twitched a cursory smile. '*I* am Dr Allerton.'

FOUR

'But you can't be Allerton. It's not – Dr Allerton's a grown . . .' Travis was about to say *man* before he realised: the truth was that up to this point, Dr Crispin Allerton had only been words typed on a screen. Travis and the others had *assumed* that their contact was an adult.

He struggled for the disappointment in his features not to darken into despair.

'I assure you, I am who I say I am,' said the fair boy. 'Perhaps if you put your guns away, we might be able to proceed in a more civilised manner and introduce ourselves properly. Thank you. Interesting firearms, those.' Indicating Travis and Antony's subjugators.

'They belonged to the aliens,' Antony said.

'Really? Mm.' The fair boy sounded almost impressed. 'But introductions. Dr Crispin Allerton. Ruth Bell.'

'Hello,' said the girl.

'And this is Geoffrey Thomas.'

'We've already met,' Shaggy-Hair chuckled.

'Now perhaps you'd like to tell us who *you* are, and how it is you come to know of me.'

'I'm Travis Naughton.' His name sounding fraudulent on his tongue.

'*Captain* Travis Naughton?' The fair boy's turn to feel cheated.

'Well, yes and no. Travis Naughton, yes.'

'Captain in the British Army commanding fifty men, clearly no,' Crispin Allerton deduced. 'It seems you have been somewhat economical with the truth, Naughton.'

Ruth Bell perked up as if she'd just been asked out on a date. 'Recent research suggests that the propensity of some individuals to resort to falsehoods as a matter of course is the result of an electro-chemical disorder in the synapses of the frontal lobe of the brain.'

'Nothing that a little surgery won't cure,' said Geoffrey Thomas, fluttering his filthy fingertips.

'You freaks calling Naughton a liar?' Richie stepped in combatively. Linden had been right yesterday about him admiring Travis. It actually went further than that. If Richie Coker could be reborn, it would be as Travis Naughton, and not just because Travis was sleeping with Linden. He also happened to be everything that Richie's woeful life-choices had precluded *him* from being, and the former bully was not prepared to stand by and let him be criticised. 'You disrespect Naughton, pal, you're asking for trouble.'

'Mm.' Allerton inspected him with interest. 'And who is this aggressive specimen?'

'Richie Coker, that's who' – living up to the adjective applied – 'and don't you forget it.'

'Why would Crispin want to forget your name if he's just requested it?' said Ruth Bell curiously.

'All right, Richie,' said Travis. 'Thanks for the support.' The atmosphere calmed again, he introduced the others to their three new acquaintances. 'And yes, Crispin, I lied about my title when we were in communication before – thought we might get taken more seriously if you believed we were

81

adults – and I'm sorry about that.' Travis added pointedly: 'But I obviously wasn't the only one.'

'Mm, but yes you were, Naughton,' said Crispin. 'I really am *Dr* Allerton. I hold a PhD in genetics awarded by Oxford University.'

'But how can you?' Jessica asked. 'You're only – seventeen?'

'Eighteen, though I completed my doctorate at sixteen,' said Crispin modestly. 'How? Put simply, I'm a genius.'

'Genius my arse,' muttered Richie.

'We're all three of us geniuses,' supplemented Ruth Bell.

'Prodigies,' nodded Geoffrey Thomas.

'Paragons.' Antony raised his eyebrows. 'So you were telling the truth about this Paragon Project, too.'

'Of course,' Crispin said. 'Though we are the last of its number.'

'So what was it, the Paragon Project?' said Mel. 'Kind of like extra science lessons for gifted kids?'

'Rather more than that, Patrick,' sniffed Crispin.

'*Mel.*'

'As you wish. The Paragon Project was initiated by certain agencies within government first to identify and locate young people of extraordinary talent in the fields of science and mathematics, then to bring them together as a single elite group in an environment conducive to discovery and achievement, a place where its inhabitants could live and work beyond the reach of what might be termed "typical teenage distractions".'

Linden translated. 'So they locked you away down here, stopped you from seeing other kids of your own age and forced you to slave away in a lab twenty-four hours a day. Genius sounds like a short straw, if you ask me.'

The Paragons laughed. It was the kind of laughter heard in school canteens when some hapless student trips and spills the contents of their lunch tray all over the floor. Unsympathetic. Ridiculing.

'Did you see a lock on the door as you entered, Darroway?' challenged Crispin. 'Did you see a door at all? Even before the Sickness we were at liberty to leave the programme at any time if we so desired. We did *not* so desire.'

'Nobody here ever forced us to do anything, Linden,' said Ruth Bell. 'It was the advancement of knowledge that drove us on, the thrill of what we might accomplish . . .'

'But didn't you want to live a – normal life?' Jessica sounded appalled by the Paragons' experience.

'What is a normal life?' Crispin Allerton countered. 'That of a comfortable middle-class family residing in a leafy Surrey suburb? Or that of an impoverished child in Asia or Africa, compelled to work from the age of six or younger simply to survive? Normality is a concept devoid of true meaning – these days more than ever before.'

'But what about home? And parents?' Jessica persisted. 'Didn't you ever want to go back to them?'

'We were *chosen* to come here,' said Geoffrey Thomas proudly. 'Out of the many, we were the few. They knew our value here and we were respected, not like at home. There were no rules controlling our behaviour at Paragon, no adults ordering us about. We were our own authority, Jessica. We could do whatever we liked. And what we didn't like, we didn't do.'

'I guess you never liked to wash, Geoffrey,' commented Mel.

Travis's tone was more serious. 'I'm assuming the work you

were doing was all kind of hush-hush, though, Crispin, yeah? Underground labs. Holographic walls. Exploitation of minors, however big your brains are.'

'The existence of the Paragon Project was not public knowledge, Naughton, you are correct,' conceded Crispin. 'Your point being?'

'Secret government-sponsored scientific research projects. In all the movies I've seen, they tend to be bad news. Treating life like an experiment. Crossing lines. Dr Allerton, meet Dr Frankenstein. If you were allowed to *behave* however you liked, I doubt there were very many limits placed on your work, either.'

'None,' declared Crispin Allerton triumphally. 'Convention is a cage, Naughton. Morality is a prison. Genius must be permitted to transcend both. Genius is a bird that should be free to soar beyond boundary and restriction and alight wherever it wishes. The only rule that governed our research was that there *are* no rules.' The Paragon smiled with perfect teeth. 'You look as though you disapprove, Naughton.'

'Can't say I'm jumping up and down with joy,' Travis admitted. 'One group thinking it's above the rules usually means trouble for another group. You might dismiss morality, Crispin, but I think right and wrong are kind of important.'

'What a disappointingly small mind you have, Travis,' commiserated Ruth Bell.

'Now, Ruth.' Crispin raised a finger admonishingly. 'Naughton and his friends are our guests. But Naughton, you should be grateful to us. We Paragons were trained to become sheer mind, and it is only *because* of that fact that you and the remaining children of Earth will be saved.'

'What?' It couldn't be, could it? 'Are you saying you *do* know how to defeat the Scytharene?'

'I never implied to you anything else,' said Crispin Allerton, assimilating Travis's last word thoughtfully. 'The Scytharene. Mm. The aliens. Oh, we can defeat the aliens.'

'Then what are we waiting for? We can help you.' Travis started forward so eagerly it seemed he intended to embrace the Paragon. 'Standing around jawing, we're wasting time.'

Crispin checked him with a cautioning palm. 'Too hasty, Naughton. You're getting ahead of yourself. We were willing to divulge our plan to *Captain* Naughton of the British Army, chiefly because it would have required his men and his resources to implement it successfully. The nature of your true identity has rather changed the situation.'

'No.' Travis refused to accept Allerton's contention. 'Nothing's changed. And the only situation that matters is the one going on above our heads, the Scytharene enslaving kids like us. If we can do something to put an end to that, we need to do it now, soldiers or no soldiers.'

'He's passionate, isn't he, Crispin?' remarked Ruth Bell.

'But reason, Ruth, not passion, brings progress to the laboratory,' said Crispin. And to Travis: 'Naughton, it's late. We can offer you accommodation. I think it wise if my fellow Paragons and I discuss our best course of action alone and that we then all reconvene in the morning.'

'That's not good enough,' Travis protested.

'Trav, it looks like it'll have to be.' Linden squeezed his hand. 'We can't do anything tonight anyway. Be realistic.'

'Mm. I would listen to Darroway, Naughton,' advised Crispin Allerton. 'It is never sensible to antagonise a potential benefactor. And one more thing for you to consider whenever you begin to feel a rush of moral indignation. For one who claims to value right and wrong, which of us has so far been more honest in our dealings together? Interesting, mm?'

Travis's group was escorted to a conference room that had been converted into makeshift sleeping quarters, sheets and mattresses hauled down from the college's hall of residence and piled in a heap on the floor.

Richie for one didn't seem too happy with the arrangements – or with anything else connected to Wells College and the Paragons. 'Those smart-arses are creeping me out,' he shuddered, wrinkling his nose. 'You see the way they look at you? Like they're visitors at the zoo or something and you're in the cages. 'Specially that freaky Geoffrey kid. He's definitely a few Bunsen burners short of a chemistry set, if you ask me.'

'They are a little odd, Richie, I'll grant you that,' said Antony. 'It's the effect of the cloistered life they've led.'

'I don't give a toss what kind of life they've led,' remarked Richie, 'even if I knew what the hell cloistered meant. But I reckon we'd be better off out of it.'

'What do you mean, Richie?' asked Mel.

'Isn't it obvious, Morticia? There's the door. We go through it. We find that bloody holographic wall again and we go through that, too. We put major distance between us and the freaksome threesome. They're bad news. They're not like us.'

'Ordinarily, anyone not being like you, Richie, I'd say was *good* news,' Mel said, 'but this time I'll make an exception. I agree with you.' Turning to a brooding Travis: 'I think

Richie's right, Trav. There's something sus about anyone who believes they're perfect – and that Crispin Allerton, sorry, *Dr* Allerton, he struts around like he's God's gift to creation. I don't trust him.'

'I think you're both exaggerating,' mused Antony. 'Assuming we believe what they've told us, and we've no reason so far not to, they *are* prodigies, and all geniuses tend to be a little eccentric.'

'Do they tend to be serial killers as well, Tony?' grunted Richie. ''Cause I reckon that creepy bloody Geoffrey Thomas has got a successful career as a mass murderer ahead of him.'

'Don't be ridiculous.' Antony dismissed Richie's comment with a wave of his hand. 'They've studied at Oxford. That must count for something. And they know how to beat the Scytharene.'

'*Claim* they know,' Mel pointed out.

'Well, what if they *do* have all the answers? Surely we can't just leave? What do you think, Jessie?'

'I've heard of Ruth Bell before,' the blonde girl said. 'Seen her. I remember my parents watching a programme years ago, a documentary about this little girl – the same sort of age I was then, ten or eleven – and this girl was one of the youngest people ever to go to university, she was a mathematical genius or something, exceptional. It was Ruth Bell. I'm sure of it.'

'That's a pretty handy memory you've got there, Jess,' said Mel.

'I remember it because the programme was all about her leaving home to go to university, and Dad said to me would I like to go to university too one day and – well, it's embarrassing now but I burst into floods of tears because I thought he meant soon, tomorrow, that minute, like the little girl on the telly, and I didn't want to leave home, leave Mum and Dad, not ever.' Jessica smiled weakly. 'I'm afraid I wasn't the boldest or bravest of children.'

Mel said, 'Don't worry about it' and Antony, 'Neither was I' simultaneously, both reaching out to touch Jessica's hand. Antony got there first. With a frown, Mel had to divert her own hand to her sweep of black hair. She scratched her head vigorously.

'It was Ruth Bell, though.' Jessica was emphatic. 'Same plaits and everything. I remember – she looked so sad and lost. Her parents kind of abandoning her at this huge old building like an orphanage. I felt sorry for her. I think I still do.'

'Me too,' contributed Linden. 'This so-called Paragon Project, it's nothing more than rationalised child abuse. It's unnatural – focusing on the mind, the brain, to the exclusion of everything else. What did Crispin say? They were trained to become "sheer mind"? That's bound to damage you emotionally in the end, isn't it? Lead to the repression of feelings that ought to be expressed. If emotions can't find their natural outlet, they'll twist inside you, become like poison. Human beings, we're not just brains. We're bodies, too, and if we want to stay healthy we have to use our bodies, celebrate being physical . . .'

'Please, Lin,' laughed Mel, 'stop there. Before you get us all excited.'

Linden coloured slightly. 'Yeah, well. And the *other* thing that bothers me, a group that lives together in isolation from the rest of the world – not good. Particularly not if they're all believers in some cause greater than themselves. I've had personal experience of that with the Children of Nature and a few others. It creates a kind of siege mentality, an us versus them syndrome. It cuts you off from other people, limits your ability to socialise and sympathise beyond the group.'

'You seem to have managed it successfully, Linden,' said Antony.

'Why thank you, kind sir.'

'Perhaps the Paragons will as well.'

'Let's hope so,' Travis broke in, 'because whatever we might think of them personally – and I understand where you're all coming from, I don't disagree with any of you on this one – we simply can't afford to take off yet. Sorry, Richie, Mel. We have to step back, take a long, hard look at the Big Picture, the one with the Scytharene in it crushing all before them. If there is even the slightest chance of stopping that, we have to be around to take it. And if that means tolerating the Paragons' weirdness for a while, that's what we're going to have to do. Like it or not, we'll be seeing Dr Allerton and his friends again in the morning.'

Dyona had arranged for her alienological expedition to the University of Oxford to depart the *Ayrion III* at dawn. Shortly after dawn, therefore, she was pounding on the door to Fleet Commander Gyrion's private quarters, demanding entrance with a disbelieving outrage she could scarcely contain.

Gyrion was breakfasting at his table. He did not rise to greet his irate guest nor was he surprised by her arrival or her manner. He had been expecting both.

'Is it true, my lord?' Ignoring the social niceties of greeting. 'Has permission for my expedition been withdrawn?'

'I'm afraid it has, Dyona,' Gyrion confirmed calmly.

'By you?'

'As commander, I am responsible for all orders issued aboard this ship, my dear, you know that. I understand your disappointment, but come, won't you join me?' Indicating the spread of food and drink in front of him.

'No thank you, my lord. And is the reason I have been given for this sudden prohibition also true?'

'That would depend, I imagine, on the reason you have been given.'

'The city of Oxford is to be razed to the ground?'

'That is so,' stated Gyrion.

If it was possible, given Scytharene pigmentation, Dyona would have blanched then. 'On your order.'

'Indeed.'

'But you mustn't. You can't.'

'Further slave harvests here are becoming uneconomical, Dyona. The Earther settlement has fulfilled its purpose. We no longer require it.'

'That may be the case, my lord, but it is not usually policy wantonly to destroy whole cities after harvesting – certainly not before the work of the alienologists has been carried out.'

'In this instance,' said Gyrion, finally standing and sauntering to the floor-to-ceiling window, 'I am making an exception.' He stared out towards the distant dreaming spires of the university. 'I anticipated such a heartfelt reaction from you, Dyona. I know how committed you are to your work and I have always admired you for it. Naturally, I do not need to justify my decisions to anyone, but as you hold the privileged position of having been my son's betrothed, and as we both belong to the Thousand Families, this once I will explain. The settlement called Oxford was a significant centre for what laughably passed as culture among the aliens – you know that better than I, Dyona. It will be obliterated not simply as a further proof of the utter defeat of the human race but as a fitting tribute to my fallen son.' Gyrion turned to face Dyona and his eyes were red like the fires that would soon engulf the city. 'The annihilation of Oxford and its primitive places of learning will provide awesome testimony to the Scytharene superiority in which Darion so ardently believed.'

Dyona felt a sickness in her stomach. At that moment, she loathed and despised Fleet Commander Gyrion more violently than she'd hated anyone ever before, more virulently than she'd believed it was possible to hate. His brute arrogance. His cold cruelty. He was the evil essence of his kind personified.

And he had to be opposed.

'*No*,' issued dangerously, foolishly from her mouth.

'No?' Gyrion's bellineum knuckled like a fist.

'I mean, not yet.' Betraying her true loyalties would benefit neither the Earthers nor herself. 'We must . . . as you yourself were perceptive enough to note, my lord, Oxford was of great cultural importance to the Earthers. The wealth of knowledge stored within the buildings of its university, the centuries of learning protected and preserved there, surely it cannot be right to eradicate all that before we have a chance to study—'

'False knowledge,' decreed Gyrion. 'Sham learning. There will be other sites for you to examine, Dyona.'

'But none as rich as this, my lord,' pleaded Dyona recklessly. 'Please, delay this destruction for a short time. A week.

A day. Let me at least lead one expedition to the city's heart before you still it for ever. Darion would not have agreed with this.'

She'd gone too far. She sensed it immediately. She should have left her lover's name out of it.

'My son would have approved of my action a thousand times,' boomed Gyrion. 'My son was a patriot and a true alienologist, one who knew well that the purpose of his art was to expose the poor inferiority of alien civilisations compared to our own. If I didn't know you better, Dyona, if Darion had not chosen you to be his bride, I might almost suspect you of valuing this alien culture for its own sake, as if it contained elements of genuine worth. It does not.'

'Of course not, my lord.' Abject retreat for Dyona. The only way to save herself. 'A savage, degenerate culture. Pitiful. I thought it would be my own small tribute to Darion if I could prove it so scientifically. But you are absolutely right, of course. An unnecessary endeavour. Who cannot already see that we Scytharene are the masters and they, the aliens, the slaves? I bow to your greater strength and wisdom.' Flattery, the last resort of the desperate. 'Lay waste to what you will.'

Gyrion appeared mollified. 'It seems I owe you an apology, my dear. My criticisms were quite without foundation. Forgive me. I should have recognised the truth of the matter at once. You are still mourning for Darion.'

Not only for Darion now, Dyona thought bleakly. For Oxford, too, and any unfortunate Earthers left inside the city.

Not all the conference rooms in the Paragons' laboratory complex had been given over to accommodation. Some retained their original function. In one such, around a central table, two parties of teenagers gathered. Travis's group by necessity wore the same clothes as yesterday, but the three Paragons seemed almost disturbingly unchanged, like they were action figures rather than real human beings.

'We were occupied very much with genetics and genetic theory before the Sickness struck,' Crispin Allerton explained nonchalantly. 'Playing with the findings of the human genome project, toying with amusing little tweaks to the DNA of pigs and sheep – as you might expect from someone with my academic background.' The boy's prevailing fairness of complexion and hair, seen close up a second time, seemed less a colour than an *absence* of colour, as if the vitality had been washed out of him. 'Geoffrey here's field is biology and bio-engineering . . .'

'I like to take things apart and find out how they work,' added the youngest Paragon, whose hair had clearly not been in the same vicinity as a comb overnight. 'Living things.'

'And then do you put them back together again?' Linden asked with a degree of revulsion.

'Sometimes. Sometimes I change them about a bit.' Geoffrey Thomas giggled.

'Ruth's specialism is mathematics,' said Crispin. 'Mathematics underpins all our work.'

'Numbers are everything,' extolled Ruth.

Mel grunted. 'Bet you were a whiz at the lottery.'

'Mm.' Crispin continued. 'When the Sickness came, however, in common with every other government-funded science project, all research programmes were suspended until a cure for the virus could be found. I'm afraid we have yet to find one.'

'Guess you're not such a genius after all, Crispie,' smirked Richie.

A comment Crispin loftily ignored. 'Our failure has not resulted from lack of effort. We have made some progress. We were given access to the bodies of many of those unfortunates who had perished from the disease, to analyse, to examine. . .'

'To dissect,' enthused Geoffrey Thomas. 'If we felt it was necessary, of course.'

Travis imagined with distaste that Geoffrey probably found dissection essential, and actually, rather a lot of fun too. He focused on the older boy. 'Let me tell you what you found. The Sickness virus attaches itself to the telomeres that protect the chromosomes of human cells, but only those telomeres that have deteriorated with age beyond a certain point, which is why adults were infected but not anyone under twenty or so. We get to build up a natural immunity so the Sickness can't ever harm us.'

Richie applauded. 'Forget *Captain* Naughton. Way to go, *Dr* Naughton.'

'Mm. Very impressive. And entirely accurate.' Travis saw that Crispin Allerton was trying hard not to seem taken aback by this unexpected knowledge, but his eyes betrayed not only surprise but a certain amount of annoyance, too. 'I take it you learned this from the same source that supplied you with the name of our invaders and occupiers. The Scytharene, didn't you call them?'

'That's right,' Travis said. 'And it's the Scytharene who are responsible for the Sickness.'

'I deduced that much the instant the spaceships appeared,' put in Ruth Bell. 'Statistically, the likelihood of a global pandemic and a species' first contact with an alien race occurring at the same time by chance is highly improbable. The two events were clearly related.'

'Who told you how the virus works, Naughton?' Crispin enquired coolly.

Travis pursed his lips and raised his eyebrows. 'Could be privileged information, Crispin. I'm not sure I should divulge it just yet. Tell you what, though, you finish telling us *your* story, and while you're doing that I'll consider whether I feel able to tell you ours.'

The Paragon's lips twitched that figment of a smile that seemed to be the best he could manage. He wasn't enjoying losing even a tiny measure of control of the conversation. 'We have little more to relate,' he said. 'The adults supervising the project died, including presumably the one or two who left at the last – they claimed to fetch help – and whom we have never seen again. One by one our fellow Paragons also fled, though foolishly. They would have been safer staying at Wells with us. Several talked about going home to learn the fate of their families.'

'A nonsensical exercise,' tutted Ruth Bell disapprovingly. 'Statistically, the chances of their parents not being either dead already or infected and about to die were infinitesimally small, negligible. What was the point of returning to them?'

'Perhaps,' Jessica felt impelled to respond, vaguely offended by Ruth Bell's words, 'they wanted to comfort their parents, to be with them at the end.'

'Why?' said Ruth Bell blankly.

'In time we were alone,' Crispin pursued. 'Our computer system here is networked with other covert, government-sanctioned initiatives such as the Enclaves, so we tried to contact them in the hope that adult authority still existed somewhere. Instead, we found you.' He didn't sound overenthusiastic.

'And we found you,' echoed Travis, 'and that's good for all of us.' He became brisk and businesslike. 'Okay, no more games. My group clearly can't match yours in terms of intellect, and if you really do have a way of overcoming the Scytharene, you're just about the most important human beings on the planet. We need you. But you need us too, Crispin. You're not the only ones who can bring something to the table. We know things you don't. How did we learn about the virus? Had it explained by a Scytharene himself, Lord Darion of the bloodline of Ayrion. We know a lot about the aliens and their society. We were prisoners aboard one of their ships, went through slave processing, escaped, were part of an attack – *with* adults – that brought a slavecraft down. We've fought the Scytharene and survived.'

'Did *you* fight them?'

It took Antony a moment to realise that Ruth Bell was addressing him. 'Uh, yes, I did. We all did.'

'You must be very brave,' observed Ruth. But the *you* seemed reserved for Antony alone.

'The point is,' Travis was pressing, 'we can contribute. Our first-hand experience of the Scytharene can only be an asset. Maybe there'll even be something in what we know that'll ensure your plan works – if you ever see your way to sharing it with us in the first place.'

'Mm. Very well,' agreed Crispin, though without consulting either of his fellow Paragons. 'Perhaps your people will be of use, Naughton. In any case, the key to defeating the Scytharene is really quite simple. I'm surprised you haven't already thought of it. We turn the aliens' own virus against them.'

There was a moment's awkward, uncertain silence before Travis burst out incredulously: 'That's it? Your master plan? Turn the aliens' own— The Scytharene are *immune* to the Sickness. It doesn't affect them. Don't you realise that?'

'Of course we realise that,' said Crispin Allerton supercil-iously.

'Then how can you hope to—'

'Travis,' said Antony, 'let him speak.'

'*Thank* you, Antony. You're so respectful.' And Ruth Bell smiled.

Jessica suddenly did not. She was beginning to wish that Ruth Bell had remained a figure confined to the television screen, glimpsed once, harmlessly, many years ago.

'The aliens and infection,' Crispin lectured. 'Let us first assume that Scytharene medical science is sufficiently advanced to provide vaccinations against indigenous Earth diseases. At the same time, the Scytharene's physiology, their physical make-up, precludes them from contracting the Sickness. But what if we could *modify* their cellular structure, their DNA, so that they *are* susceptible to it? A fitting form of retaliation, mm?'

'They stuck it to us so we stick it to them. Like it.' Richie was beginning to think Crispin Allerton might not be such a dick after all.

'Pleasingly ironic,' commented Antony, as if critiquing a poem.

'So long as it works.' Jessica remained concerned. 'So long as anything works.'

Travis concurred. 'Theory good. Practice – how?'

'The Sickness only attacks human cells,' said Geoffrey Thomas. 'Animal species are unaffected.'

'Dogs sure are,' frowned Mel, remembering the other day.

'So the greatest weapon we have is already inside us. The carrier of our genetic information. The building blocks of life. Human DNA itself.'

Linden half expected the wild-haired boy to rub his hands together and cackle. 'I'm not following,' she said.

'We create a new virus, Darroway,' expanded Crispin with teacherly exasperation. 'Bioengineered under laboratory conditions. Airborne like the Sickness. A virus which will introduce into the systems of all the Scytharene who breathe it human DNA – harmless to us, of course. A virus that will graft that human genetic code to Scytharene cells and by combining the two sets of DNA, human and alien, fundamentally alter the genetic make-up of the host body. In effect, the Scytharene will become less alien and more human.'

'We kind of infect them with humanity,' Mel said.

'And the part that's human will make them vulnerable to the Sickness virus still in the atmosphere. They'll contract it just like the adults did.' Travis saw the beauty of the plan.

Linden saw the ugliness. 'They'll die from it just like the adults did. How much more death can the world take?' Instinctively, she moved closer to Travis.

'It'll have psychological effects too, won't it?' Antony speculated. 'Even on any Scytharene who aren't infected. A corruption of their gene pool. A blow to their mad obsession with racial purity. What'll they suffer when they realise they can fall prey to the Sickness just like the inferior Earthers?' His brow darkened. 'Can't say I'll be feeling sorry for them.'

'It's called gene transfer technology,' concluded Crispin.

'I don't care what it's called. Will it work?' Travis demanded.

'Naughton, don't you trust us?'

'With Crispin's genius for genetics and Geoffrey's bioengineering expertise,' Ruth said, 'of course it'll work.'

'So why haven't you developed this virus already?' Mel, suspiciously.

The Paragons exchanged glances.

'This is why we needed the military,' said Geoffrey. 'There is certain equipment we require that is not available here at the Project.'

'We hoped armed soldiers with transport would be able to procure it for us,' appended Ruth.

'So now,' Crispin addressed Travis's group generally, '*you'll* have to.'

'Now *we'll* have to? What are we all of a sudden, the bloody hired help? You can kiss my—'

'Richie,' Travis intervened. 'I don't think that'll be necessary. But I *do* think you need to talk to us a little more like we're equals, Crispin. Because we are.'

'Mm.' Crispin did not appear unduly convinced.

'Yeah, you can't just start ordering us about,' protested Mel. She'd never taken kindly to the impositions of male authority figures.

Crispin seemed genuinely bewildered. 'But every group needs a leader.'

'We've got a leader,' Linden said. 'Crispin, meet Travis.'

'Mm. With respect, I'm sure Naughton has done a competent job for you thus far, but now that you're throwing in your lot with us, it's obvious that *I* should take over as leader.'

'Obvious you're an arsehole,' muttered Richie, who'd returned to his original estimation of Crispin Allerton's personal qualities.

Ruth and Geoffrey, on the other hand, were both nodding their heads in approval.

'Obvious why?' Mel again, much to Crispin's umbrage. 'If I've permission to speak, Dr Allerton, sir.'

'Of course, Patrick.' Rising above the sarcasm. 'It's *obvious* because even among my fellow Paragons, all modesty aside, it has to be acknowledged that mine is the most brilliant mind of all.'

'I don't see the connection,' Linden said stubbornly.

'Then perhaps you need some work done on your eyes.' Geoffrey's own glinted as if he'd be in the market to carry it out for her, possibly with a scalpel.

'The best must always lead,' declared Crispin with the certainty of infallible truth.

'Well that's open for debate,' Travis himself finally responded. 'Define best, for a start. What's certainly true is that a successful leader has to be able to inspire confidence in those around him – or her. A good test for that is a vote. I assume you're familiar with the concept of democracy down here?'

'A statistically suspect form of social control,' Ruth Bell said sorrowfully. 'It pretends to be about majorities and choice when in fact only a decreasing minority of people vote, and for increasingly similar political parties.'

'It's still the fairest kind of government there is.' Antony leaping to the defence of the system he'd been brought up to revere.

'If you say so, Antony,' beamed Ruth Bell.

'So let's vote for leader,' Travis proposed. 'Me or you, Crispin.'

'But there are more of your followers than there are of mine,' Crispin pointed out mildly.

'If you're so sure you're the best candidate, that won't matter.'

'Mm.' Crispin Allerton's pale eyes narrowed. He was only too aware he'd been backed into a corner by this upstart Naughton with the disconcerting gaze – younger than him, patently his inferior in terms of intelligence, probably still struggling with GCSEs or whatever the examinations were called these days in moronic subjects ending in 'Studies'. There ought to be no question which of them should lead. Leadership was Crispin Allerton's right. Naughton's companions, despite their intellectual limitations and tribal loyalties, would surely be able to see that. If Crispin believed in anything at all, it was himself. Therefore, 'Very well,' he consented. 'We'll vote. Who wants me to be leader?'

His own hand went up, of course. Ruth's. Geoffrey's shot up with the obedience of a dog given an instruction by its master.

He felt the humiliation coming even before: 'And who wants Naughton?'

The girls, the black-haired one with too much to say for herself and the redhead slightly quicker with their hands than the blonde. Girls were *not* reliable – even Ruth's only fault was her gender. The thug, of course, arm outstretched like a gorilla reaching for a banana. Naughton himself. Clive too, to make it unanimous within Naughton's group, but markedly slower than the others, the endorsement granted almost reluctantly, as if he secretly favoured another candidate for the position. The wretched Patrick girl whooped with delight

101

at the election's result – he wouldn't forget that – but despite the outcome, Crispin was not entirely downhearted. Between Naughton and Clive, he sensed an undercurrent of friction. Division could always be exploited.

Crispin Allerton would assume his rightful position yet.

'So?' Travis challenged.

'You win,' the Paragon conceded. *For now.*

'Yay, Trav!' cried Mel. Linden embraced him.

'That's not fair. It isn't fair.' Geoffrey Thomas did not take their defeat gracefully. 'We were outnumbered.'

'Ruth said it,' Linden reminded him. 'Numbers are everything.'

Crispin waited for the immediate reaction to die down before he spoke again. His tone was as superior as ever. 'This election does not alter the fact that equipment and materials still need to be acquired and brought here before we can begin work on the virus. You, Naughton, and your friends will still need to find and fetch them for us.'

'Well if we need the extra technology, add a please and I doubt any of us are going to complain – but shouldn't you come too? If we're looking for specialised equipment, how can those of us who aren't scientists be sure we're identifying the right stuff?'

Why not vote on it? Crispin thought bitterly.

'*We* can't leave Wells,' Geoffrey snorted, as if Travis was insane to think otherwise.

'The Project is our home,' Ruth added plaintively. 'You understand, don't you, Antony?'

'Well, actually . . .'

'This is where we belong,' Crispin insisted. 'This is where we're safe.'

The conference room seemed to tremble, just a little. The faintest of rumblings sounded, like the distant echoes of an avalanche.

Linden lifted her eyes automatically to the ceiling. 'What's that?'

If she'd been aboard the *Ayrion III*, she'd have known. The demolition of Oxford had begun.

FIVE

Travis and Antony volunteered to find out what was happening outside while the rest of the group remained below ground. They didn't need to go far. The essentials were all too chillingly obvious from the college's main entrance.

The slavecraft hung in the morning sky, monumental in size and scale even though it presently hovered above the far side of the university, beyond spires that bristled and jabbed upwards like defensive ranks of spears. The bright blade of the ship's sweeping crescent appeared more like a gigantic, ruthless scythe than ever. The smaller Cullers fanned out on either side of it. Energy bolts flashed from each and every vessel; they struck the city in a storm of lightning, relentless, remorseless. The naked buildings found no defence. They were pulverised.

The armada advanced ponderously but purposefully, with the inevitability of death.

'My God. My *God*.' Antony stared in horror, could hardly speak.

'They're levelling the place. The whole city.' Travis, though equally appalled, retained the power of decision. 'We have to leave. Now.'

He turned to race back down to the Paragon Project and inform the others of that imperative. Antony grabbed his arm.

'Run away? But Travis, we can't just – can't we do something?'

'Get real, Antony. In a few hours this city's going to be nothing but dust and ashes.'

'But they mustn't – it's not just a city, Travis. This is Oxford. Oxford means something.'

Antony's gaze was transfixed by the approaching destruction, brick and mortar and stone thrown up into the air in a solid wave. Architectural masterpieces lovingly, reverently erected over centuries, shattered in seconds. Shrines to the ingenuity and creativity of the human mind violated, smashed by the brute force of ignorance, like a gentle, beautiful face pounded into a bloody pulp by a fist. The frontage of St John's had been breached by now, Antony knew, the neoclassical splendour of the Ashmolean reduced to rubble, its wonderful, irreplaceable exhibits crushed or burning.

'I was going to study here. They're taking my future away from me. They're taking everything away.' Despair was etched across the blond boy's features.

Travis had seen Antony like this before, when the Harrington School had fallen victim to the Scytharene. He felt a surge of sympathy for his friend, recent disagreements forgotten in the agony of the moment, in their shared adversity. 'I know. I'm sorry. But Antony, we have to move. If we stay here, we'll die here.'

'You're right.' Antony squeezed his eyes shut, nodded his head once, emphatically. 'You're *right.*'

By now the very foundations of the city seemed to be shaking. Behind the holographic wall, the other teenagers were nervously awaiting Travis and Antony's return. Even now, they formed two distinct groups, the three Paragons and the

105

boys' four original companions. Everyone, however, seemed relieved when their scouts reappeared safely.

The feeling didn't last.

'We've got to get out of here. Right now.' Travis's tone brooked no dissent. 'The Scytharene are destroying the city. We need to grab our guns and go.'

'Now you're talking, Naughton.' Richie darted off to fetch their weapons.

'I'd better make sure he doesn't accidentally shoot himself,' said Mel, following after him.

'Trav.' Linden comforted her boyfriend with a hug.

Jessica joined Antony and did the same. 'Are you all right?'

'I will be when we're on our way.' His tone sharpened. 'Are you three just going to stand there?'

The Paragons had not moved at all, though Ruth and Geoffrey did seem to be looking to Crispin for a lead.

'We told you, we can't leave,' he said. 'You'll have to bring help.'

'There's no help to bring.' Travis gaped in amazement. 'What's the *matter* with you people?'

'A vehicle at least,' Crispin compromised. 'You could find a car, couldn't you? We can't be expected to run. We're not accustomed to physical activity.'

'Well you'd better bloody well *get* accustomed to it!' Travis cried. 'Because if you think I'm leaving you behind when you're our best hope of beating those bastards, you've got another think of your very exceptional brains coming. I'll drag you out at gunpoint if I have to.'

'Please.' Antony hadn't intended to adopt Travis's earlier words, but he couldn't think of a better phrase of his own. 'If you stay here, you'll die here.'

'Crispin?' Ruth Bell bit her lip anxiously.

Richie and Mel charged back into the room with the group's firearms. 'Tooled up and ready to rock,' grinned Richie, who always felt more confident with a shotgun in his hands.

Mel distributed weapons. 'So what are we waiting for?'

'Crispin's still not convinced,' said Jessica.

'Then Crispin's an idiot,' said Mel scornfully.

The Paragon might have objected to such an assessment had the lights not chosen that precise moment to extinguish themselves. Temporarily. A few seconds of total blackness and then power was restored. Perhaps the next time, however, the failure would be permanent. Perhaps Wells wasn't so safe after all.

'Very well,' Crispin decided. 'We'll come.'

'That,' said Travis, 'is all I wanted to hear.'

They reached the street outside the college before the Scytharene did. It was fortunate that the aliens were as thorough and methodical when laying waste to a city as they were in every other aspect of their operation. The swathe of devastation was closer than it had been only minutes before, the ground now quaking and the cacophony of exploding buildings deafening, but it would still take the energy bolts several minutes more before Wells came within range.

By then, the teenagers would be long gone.

'At least we know which way,' said Linden with a bleak smile.

'My binoculars,' Antony suddenly remembered. 'I've left them behind.'

'Don't even *think* about going back for them,' Jessica warned.

Richie waved his shotgun at the ships. 'You don't need binoculars to see *those* bloody things, Tony. Use your bloody eyes.'

'Oh, I intend to.'

And Antony gazed one last time upon the extinction of Oxford. The Bodleian, its precious volumes cindered. The Sheldonian Theatre where the university's degree-giving ceremonies had taken place, atomised like the hopes and dreams of the graduates. So much of value expunged from existence. Antony suffered with the city, but in a strange way he was also beyond despair now. His heart was hardening with hatred, gaining strength from anger. He knew why the Scytharene were doing this – it was an attempt to eradicate an entire intellectual and cultural heritage, an attempt to break the spirit of any human resistance fighters still at liberty. It wouldn't work. It hadn't worked. Antony felt the courage of defiance energising every fibre of his being.

'Antony, let's go!' Travis calling. The others scurrying off already.

'*Antony.*' Jessica waiting for him, looking concerned. She didn't need to be.

'It's okay,' he said. 'I'm coming.'

They would escape the ravaged city. They would find a safe place and concoct the Paragons' lethal virus. They would retaliate.

They would win.

Dyona sat alone in her private quarters, hunched over a table and staring desolately at the dagger she'd placed on it. The knife was a Coriolanian redemption blade, the opulent gleam of its richly bejewelled handle distracting the viewer only briefly from the deadlier glitter of its six-inch serrated cutting edge.

Through Dyona's researches on the now-enslaved world of Coriolan she'd learned that every member of that planet's ruling class was presented with a redemption blade when they reached maturity. The gift was not simply ceremonial in nature, though neither was the knife intended to be employed against Coriolan's enemies, who apparently had been numerous. No, the owner of a Coriolanian redemption blade was only ever expected to use the dagger on a single victim – himself – and only under certain circumstances, of course. If he failed in his duty. If he disappointed his family. If he was defeated in battle or racked with despair. If any of these conditions prevailed, it was seen as legitimate by the Coriolanians for the sufferer to plunge the blade into his chest up to the hilt or to saw away with it at his wrists until the steel was washed red with blood. Suicide as a form of compensation for one's faults or failures. The ancient Romans on Earth itself had often taken their own lives as a noble way out if the fates or the Senate had conspired against them, Dyona knew.

She was wondering whether to follow their example.

An U'lau lament was playing in her rooms, more loudly than normal to drown out the sounds of Oxford's destruction. She couldn't bear to hear the fierce, discordant music of the energy blasts; she couldn't bear to see the ruin they wreaked. Dyona had dimmed the windows of her quarters almost to darkness. In the shadowy light, the artefacts she'd preserved from a dozen conquered civilisations and that now adorned the walls and display cabinets appeared like ghosts, phantoms of a lost and unattainable past. What relics of

Earth would she have been able to add – if she'd planned on living longer?

Dyona's fingers stroked the haft of the dagger. Once, she'd entertained the ridiculous notion that she could rebel against her people and inspire a revolution, free the slaves. How much like truth woeful self-delusion had seemed while Darion had lived. But her lover lived no more and neither, Dyona felt wearily, did her courage or her strength to resist. She couldn't pretend any longer, couldn't continue her soul-destroying masquerade as a good, dutiful Scytharene.

She picked up the knife.

The blood of her species ran in her veins. Perhaps she could expiate the guilt that tormented her and find her own redemption if she let it out, let it flow freely, if she drained her body of its Scytharene inheritance. It would be easy to do. The dagger digging into her flesh, a single moment of pain and penetration – then peace.

She laid the flat of the blade on the forearm she'd bared in advance. It was cold, like death. But no colder than her present life. To pierce the skin, a little additional pressure. Surely she could achieve that. Surely she could—

'My lady!' The U'lau lament was silenced as Etrion switched off the sound system manually. Dyona hadn't even heard her servant come in. He stood regarding her with horror.

She crimsoned in the dark, put down the dagger with a suspect's swiftness. 'How dare you intrude upon me without permission, Etrion. I told you I wished to be left alone.'

'Alone to do what, my lady?'

'Whatever I do is none of your concern. Remember your place.'

110

'Oh, I know my place, Lady Dyona. My bloodline has served yours faithfully and with pride for generations. My place is here, and *everything* you do is my concern. May I speak frankly, my lady?'

'You have already been presumptuous enough for me to have your tongue cut from your mouth if I so wish. You had better speak while you still can.'

Etrion stepped forward. His voice was that of a friend rather than a servant. 'What you were contemplating before I entered, my lady, it's not the answer.'

Dyona gave a nervous laugh. 'And exactly what, Etrion, do you imagine I was—'

'To take your own life, my lady, it's wrong.'

'I was not . . . let me tell you, Etrion, in Coriolanian culture—'

'Suicide is for the weak, my lady,' the servant said clinically. 'Suicide is for cowards. You are neither of those things.'

'Am I not?' Dyona lowered her gaze. 'You have too high an opinion of me, Etrion.'

'No. What I have is an excellent memory, for I can remember what you appear to have forgotten. The dream of revolution you shared with Lord Darion. How you risked your life to save the young Earthers at Clarebrook House. Conviction and determination still reside within you, my lady. Look for them again. Find them. And then direct that dagger not against yourself but against the authors of your misery.'

'I want to believe you, Etrion. I *want* to,' Dyona agonised. 'But monsters like Gyrion, there are too many of them. I can't stop them. I can't change anything.'

'You can try, my lady,' urged Etrion, 'as Lord Darion tried.

To fight for one's beliefs even at the cost of one's own life, that is the *true* route to redemption, not' – gesturing dismissively towards the dagger – 'not this. My lady, Lord Darion would not have wanted this.'

Dyona closed her eyes and sighed. 'Etrion, you are wiser than your bloodline should permit.'

For the first time, the servant allowed a slow smile to sneak across his features. 'Wisdom is a matter of brain, not blood, my lady.'

Dyona smiled too, though warily. 'True, Etrion. And I owe you a debt of thanks for your intervention. Are you gifted with prescience as well as wisdom to appear in my quarters at such a timely moment?'

'I'm afraid not, my lady,' admitted Etrion. 'I was simply wondering if you required any refreshments?'

'I think I do,' said Dyona. At last she stood. 'I seem to have regained my appetite.'

Two cars drew to a halt in a country lane. Neither saw fit to pull in to the verge, as if both assumed there to be little danger of collision with oncoming traffic. If there was any threat at all it was likelier to come from the rear, where a dark pall of smoke lingered above the distant horizon and whatever remained of Oxford like a bruise on the sky.

Travis, Antony, Linden and Jessica emerged from the leading vehicle, Mel, Richie and the three Paragons from its shadow.

Mel had been driving the second car and seemed unhappy to have her fun curtailed. 'What have we stopped for? You run out of gas, Trav? *Men* drivers, huh?'

'Nothing like that,' said Travis. 'It's just we've probably put

Oxford far enough behind us now to think beyond where we're driving *from* and start considering where we're driving *to.*'

Geoffrey Thomas bobbed his torso up and down as was his habit, glanced from side to side like a hunted animal. His voice was a little-boy whine. 'I don't care where we go as long as we get there soon. I don't like this.'

'What?' quizzed Mel. 'You mean my driving or the great outdoors?'

Linden saw that Ruth Bell looked pale and queasy and that even Crispin appeared ill at ease. It occurred to her: 'They did let you out of your precious Paragon Project from time to time, didn't they? I mean, you haven't spent the last however many years cooped up underground, have you?'

'We could come and go as we pleased, Darroway,' snapped Crispin, offended. 'We weren't prisoners. We simply chose to stay where we were more in control of our environment, where we could concentrate exclusively on our work.'

'Statistically,' put in Ruth Bell, 'do you know how unpredictable life is when you begin to factor in all the possible variables of people and places?'

'No, but life's *supposed* to be unpredictable,' argued Linden. 'That's its beauty. Not knowing what's going to happen is what keeps life fresh, new, exciting.'

'Dangerous,' shuddered Ruth.

'That too, sometimes,' Linden conceded, 'even before the Sickness and the Scytharene. But that's the reality we all have to face. You can't live life under controlled conditions, shut away in some lab or something.'

'Speak for yourself,' said Geoffrey. 'I'll wait in the car.'

'As for labs,' Crispin added, 'I wouldn't be too critical,

Darroway. Unless we find one soon, and a well-equipped one at that, we might not be living at all.'

'Fair point,' acknowledged Travis, 'which kind of sorts out the *where to* problem, doesn't it? Jessie, where's the next Enclave on your list?'

Richie groaned. 'Here we go again.'

Antony filled the Paragons in on the group's recent disappointing experiences with Enclaves. 'You know about them in any case, didn't you say? You tried to contact them?'

'We did,' said Crispin. 'The only response was yours.'

'So they could all be deserted.' Travis refused to give up on the Enclaves. 'But one of them could *still* contain all the materials and all the resources we need.'

'They haven't so far, though, have they, Trav?' Jessica said cautiously. 'They've all been pretty much stripped bare.'

'I know one that'll be fully equipped,' said Crispin.

Jessica peered closely at the paper she'd produced from her pocket. 'Which one?'

'It won't be on your list. It won't be on any list. Enclave Zero doesn't have a code reference like the others.'

Mel laughed sardonically. 'Enclave Zero? You sure your PhD wasn't in creative writing, Crispin?'

The Paragon ignored her. 'I was amusing myself one day by hacking into the security services' top-secret files and happened to learn of its existence. *And* its location.'

Mel's laugh became a moan. 'Why do I get the feeling this news is not going to be good?'

'Enclave Zero lies directly beneath Whitehall and the Houses of Parliament.'

If Richie's face had fallen any further, it would have had to be scraped off the road. 'The Houses of Parliament in London?'

'As opposed to the Houses of Parliament in Chipping Sodbury, Richie?' Linden taunted.

'It's a bunker-style complex begun during the Second World War and enlarged and extended over the years since. Its function is to shelter the members of the government and other key figures in the civil service in the event of a surprise attack on London.'

'Yeah, yeah,' grumbled Richie. 'So when the shit starts flying and the bombs start falling our wonderful bloody politicians save their own arses first as usual.'

'If any Enclave remains in possession of the resources we require,' concluded Crispin, 'it'll be Enclave Zero.'

'Yeah, and zero's our chances of getting there in one piece, if you ask me,' said Mel. 'Even if you *don't* ask me.'

Linden tended to agree. 'Oxford was difficult enough, but *London. . .*'

'It would certainly be a challenge.' But one that Antony seemed to be prepared to tackle.

'Those spider robot things might have cleared away the bodies,' said Jessica. 'We shouldn't have to worry about disease.'

Travis fixed Crispin Allerton in his piercing blue gaze. 'You know *exactly* where this Enclave Zero is, Crispin? And you can get us in?'

'Of course. The entry codes were in the files. I memorised them.'

'Lucky for us, huh?' said Mel sceptically.

'Mm. I memorise everything. And forget nothing,' added Crispin, turning pale and humourless eyes to Mel.

'So what does everyone think?' canvassed Travis. 'It's going to be hazardous getting there, but this Enclave Zero might just contain everything Crispin and Ruth need to develop their gene transfer virus.'

'It's the Harrington motto,' said Antony. *Avoid the Easy Way.*'

Richie applauded ironically. 'Oh yeah, top-bloody-hole. That'll look just great on our tombstones, Tony. Here lie all of us: "They Avoided the Easy Way".'

'I wish we could avoid you, Richie,' Linden muttered before turning away in disgust.

Moments later, two sets of car doors slammed. Two engines started up. With a full complement of nine teenagers between them, the vehicles resumed their journey.

To London.

They stopped for the night at 'Hey, a lonely, isolated farm,' gasped Mel ironically. 'Guess it makes a change from a lonely, isolated cottage.' On the plus side, the cars could be shunted inside a barn, hidden from the eyes of any prowling Culler. On the minus, the farmer, his wife, and an elderly relative of indeterminate sex, given that individual's advanced state of putrefaction, were still in residence. The boys – excluding a fastidious Crispin but *in*cluding a fascinated Geoffrey – had to lug the bodies down to the cellar wrapped in blankets. Even though after this operation accommodation became available in all the farmhouse's bedrooms, it wasn't perhaps surprising that people preferred to stretch out downstairs.

Mel left the building entirely and wandered out to the farm gate as the sun began to set. Ensuring the others didn't spot her, Jessica followed. She wanted to talk to her best friend alone.

'Sneaking out too?' Mel grinned when she saw her. 'Trav'll be doing a head count and panicking.'

'I don't think he'll even notice we're missing,' Jessica grinned in return. 'Problems with the sleeping arrangements for our Paragon friends. They each want a room to themselves and I think Crispin's demanding sterilised sheets or something.'

'Crispin is, to coin a phrase,' said Mel, 'an arsehole.'

'He speaks highly of you too.'

The two girls leaned side by side on the rusting gate and gazed across rolling hills towards the sinking sun. They shared the sweetness of the evening's stillness and silence together.

'You know what my favourite movie scene of all time is?' Mel said at length.

'Don't tell me. It involves (a) zombies, (b) decapitations, (c) Satan and his demons, or (d) all of the above.'

'You've got me all wrong, Ms Lane,' protested Mel, feigning hurt. '*None* of the above. It's that scene in *Chitty Chitty Bang Bang* after Dick Van Dyke's sung "Hushabye Mountain" to his kids in the windmill.'

Jessica laughed. 'You're joking. Mel, I didn't know you'd even *seen Chitty Chitty Bang Bang*.'

'I kept it quiet. Didn't want to spoil my image. Now we're never going to see another film again in our entire lives, I think I can afford to reveal the shocking truth. You know the part I mean? Dick Van Dyke's all kind of gloomy and depressed because he hasn't got the money to buy that wrecked old car for his kids – can't fulfil their dreams, that's what it means. And he's kind of solitary and lonely and he's out gazing across the fields and it's sunset and the windmill's turning and it's all kind of beautiful and sad at the same time. Remember that part?'

'Of course. Watching *Chitty Chitty Bang Bang* every Christmas in our house was as much a tradition as opening our presents.'

'Yeah. Well, just as Dick Van Dyke's about to give up, just as it looks like there's no chance for him to save his kids' dreams, he sees the travelling fair coming, the wagons and the people all strung out in silhouette along the horizon. And he can hear the sound of fairground music drifting on the air. And that gives him inspiration, doesn't it? It's like the fair's coming to his rescue and he's not gloomy and depressed any more. He's got hope again. I love that scene. It always used to make me want to cry.' Mel scanned the barren horizon fruitlessly. She spoke softly. 'What I wouldn't give to hear that fairground music now.'

'I preferred "Me Ol' Bamboo" myself.'

'Jessie.' Mel smiled affectionately. 'Well, so much for fresh air. You want to head back?'

'In a sec. I want to ask you something first, Mel.' Cautiously, Jessica's expression uncomfortable. 'Advice?'

'Ooh, *advice*.'

'It's about Antony.'

Mel winced. Why did it have to be about Antony?

'And that Ruth Bell. I'm – I think she's got her eye on him.'

'No worries, Jess,' Mel said briskly. 'As the song says, Antony's only got eyes for you.'

'Well, I hope so, I *think* so, but it's made me wonder, if I want to keep him . . .' Jessica coloured. 'He isn't putting any pressure on me or anything, and I do really like him, it's not casual, and what with Travis and Linden, well, you know, I'm wondering whether I ought to – well, *sleep* with Antony.'

'Oh, Jessie, Jessie.' Mel threw up her hands and shook her head. 'Maybe you should talk about this with Linden. I'm not sure I'm the right person to give advice on who you should or shouldn't commence sexual relations with.'

'Why not?'

'Why *not*?' Sometimes Jessica's essential innocence became almost criminal naivety. 'Because unless you've repressed the memory entirely, and I wouldn't blame you if you have, not so long ago I was sadly guilty of trying to coax you into commencing sexual relations with me.'

'I haven't forgotten,' said Jessica, and tenderly, without the shock and revulsion that had characterised her initial response to the revelation of Mel's feelings. 'But I thought we'd sorted that out, got beyond it. I thought we were friends again like before.'

'Friends again, yes,' Mel said. 'Like before, no. It's impossible for us to be like before, Jess. Sorry.'

'So am I.' Jessica's eyes clouded with tears. In some ways, she wished she felt differently, wished she could have responded to Mel's admission of love as her friend had longed for her to respond, then she'd be making Mel happy instead of miserable, but she couldn't do it. How complicated sex made relationships (but also, in Travis and Linden's case at least, it seemed, how wonderful). 'Mel, can I ask? Do you still have . . . feelings for me?'

'You know the questions, don't you, Jess?' Mel sighed. 'If I say yes, you'll probably run screaming back to the house.'

'I won't. That's ridiculous.'

'But if I say no, I'm lying.'

'So you do . . .'

'I want to be with you, Jessie, of course I do. I've tried *not*

119

to want that. I've tried to get rid of my feelings, kind of expel them like naughty schoolchildren, block them out of my mind, deny them, convince myself they're bad and wrong and I should just sort myself out and start thinking and behaving like a nice, normal girl who wants to get married to a nice, normal boy and settle down and have kids and lead a conventional, socially acceptable, heterosexual sort of life. I've tried all that. None of it's worked. If I cut out my heart it wouldn't change anything. What I feel for you is in my soul, Jess, I love you in my soul and I'm afraid I always will.' She gave a short, sorrowing laugh. 'But don't worry. I'm containing myself. I'm not going to suddenly leap on you in the middle of the night when you least expect it. Self-control. I'm good at that. I know we won't ever be together, Jessie. I've just got to learn to live with it.'

'I'm so sorry,' Jessie said. 'I'm hurting you and I can't help it. Mel . . .' She reached out her hand.

Which Mel didn't dare take. From which she flinched reluctantly away. 'No. Jessie. Don't touch me right now, not after I've just come over all emotional. I can't . . . even my self-control has limits.'

'You'll get through this, Mel,' Jessica said hopefully. 'You won't always be thinking about me. You'll find someone else and then there won't be room for me any more.'

'Yeah, maybe I could get Ruth interested, do us both a favour and leave you with a clear run at Antony.'

'I'm serious, Mel. There'll be someone for you.'

'I'm serious too, Jessie. There won't.' Mel smiled wryly. 'But what the heck? I've been on my own my entire life so far. It's not that I'm not used to it. Someone has to be the outsider, don't they?' She glanced up at the sky. The sun had gone and darkness was taking its place. 'Come on, let's get to the house while we can still see it. Oh, and advice, Jess? Whatever I said would be useless even if I felt able to give any. Bottom line is, you have to make up your *own* mind about Antony.'

While Jessica and Mel were discussing matters potentially romantic at the farm gate, the subject of the blonde girl's indecision was swigging Coke from a can in the farmhouse kitchen. His parents had always disapproved of carbonated soft drinks but Antony had carried on guzzling regardless, a habit that pretty much qualified as his only modest rebellion against parental authority. He only wished his mum and dad were around now to scold him and warn apocalyptically of his teeth rotting in his head if he didn't switch to sugar-free cordials or bottled water. He'd never believed that bit about the teeth, of course, though he was unlikely ever to be in a position to verify or disprove it now. The stockpile of fizzy drinks was finite and shrinking: in time it would run out. No more Coke really would mark the end of the world as they'd known it. Since the Sickness, therefore, he'd savoured every can as a connoisseur would sample a fine rare wine, relishing the flavours that in years to come would never be tasted again.

But he was still too polite to hog their whole store for himself. 'Fancy a can?' he offered as Ruth appeared hesitatingly in the kitchen doorway.

'Oh, Antony. Really?' She surged forward.

'Uh, sure.' You would have thought he'd asked her to marry him.

And actually, considering there'd been complaints from all

three Paragons about having to share rooms for the night, Ruth seemed suddenly to have abandoned the doctrine of personal space. If she was to stand any closer to Antony she'd be wearing his clothes – which might be an improvement over her own.

'Well, here we are then,' Antony said, virtually pinned against the sink and reminded by the candlelight rather unsettlingly of cosy and intimate dinners for two. 'Cheers.' They clinked cans. Ruth giggled, peered into his eyes like an optician. 'Um, you haven't seen Jessica around, have you?'

'Oh, it's my turn to talk to you now. I've been wanting to talk to you properly all day.'

'Have you? Well, that's very, very . . . um, very . . .'

'Mel told me in the car that you went to the Harrington School.'

'That's right.' In fact, he wished he was there now.

'I've heard of it. It had a very good reputation. You must be quite bright for a normal person.'

Antony wasn't sure whether he should feel complimented or insulted by that. 'I was Head Boy,' he said, as evidence of an achievement beyond criticism.

'Really? Oh, that must have been exciting, everybody looking up to you,' admired Ruth, looking up at him.

'Um, what about *your* schooling, Ruth?' Antony said. 'Did the people who ran the Paragon Project oversee every aspect of your education?'

'Oh, the Project was our lives, Antony,' smiled Ruth nostalgically. 'I told you at Wells, it was our home.'

'Yes, but not your real home, though, was it?' Ruth looked blank. 'I mean, not where you grew up and . . . what about your parents?'

'What about them?' said Ruth, with a lack of emotion so total that Antony was both startled and disturbed.

'Well, don't you miss them? I mean, when you found out what the Sickness was doing, didn't you contact them, or they contact you? Didn't you want to be with them? I wish I could have been with mine – at the end.'

Ruth inclined her head to one side as if she didn't quite understand the language Antony was speaking. 'No,' she said.

And Antony could tell she meant it. He was feeling tears pricking his own eyes, as they still did every time he thought of his poor, lost parents, but there was not a trace of moisture in Ruth Bell's. Her grey eyes sparkled, as soulless as glass. 'Aren't you even grieving?'

'For my parents? No.' The idea seemed faintly preposterous to Ruth Bell. 'Why? Should I? Sexual reproduction is a biological necessity; our desire to participate in it is programmed into our genes. Giving birth to and rearing young are routine functions in life in order to perpetuate the species. There's nothing special or worthy of praise in parenthood, Antony. My parents, by bringing me into the world, were merely fulfilling their physical obligations to the human race.'

Antony was stupefied. 'There's more to it than that, Ruth. Human beings – we're not just robots controlled by our genes. We don't breed like . . . well, we're not animals.'

'*Reasoning* animals, Antony,' said Ruth, by way of mollification.

'But what about love?' Looking for a way to slip out between the girl and the sink. 'I'm sure your parents didn't have you because they were keen to do their bit for the survival of the human race. They had you because they loved

123

each other and wanted a family. Didn't they love you? Didn't you love them?'

'I suppose I was grateful to them,' Ruth allowed. 'For my life. But they did their duty and their time is over. It is the nature of things for each new generation to supplant the previous one, and we have greater motivation than ever to do that after the Sickness and the Scytharene. We are all that's left.'

God help us, Antony thought.

'Which is why I wanted to talk to you, Antony.' Was Ruth casting her eyes down bashfully? Was she simpering? 'You may not be a match for Crispin or Geoffrey intellectually, but physically I find you rather impressive. *Attractive*.'

'Well, I'm obviously flattered, Ruth' – Antony played for time – 'I'm really, really . . .' Finally managing to sidestep her, turn so his back was to the door and hers to the sink. 'The thing is, though, I'm with Jessica. She's my girlfriend. We're a couple. I'm not interested in anyone el——'

'But she won't make such a suitable partner for you as I will, Antony,' said Ruth with absolute certainty. 'Physically there is no real difference between us, and I have a far more able mind.'

'Relationships aren't about listing assets, Ruth. They're not about reason. They're about emotions, feelings. I *love* Jessica.'

'That word again,' Ruth registered, shaking her head pityingly. 'Love is a mathematically unsound concept, Antony. It can't be measured or calculated, therefore its value is severely limited. Think of it as a distraction for the sentimental and the immature. We must conduct our lives with more intelligence than to let our choices be influenced by an unsatisfactory impulse like love.'

'Well, as you've already pointed out,' said Antony, 'I'm *not* a match for you Paragons in terms of intelligence. So perhaps we're not as well suited as you might think.'

'Oh, no. We are. You're just taking a while to accept it.'

'Needs reversing, Ruth. I don't want to sound harsh, but I think *you're* taking a while to accept that I've got a girl already and her name's Jessica.'

'Should my ears be burning?' Jessica popped her head into the kitchen. She seemed to be seeing Antony with Ruth – which was worrying – but from their respective reactions to her entrance, her boyfriend breaking into a smile and the Paragon into a frown, what she was *really* seeing was Ruth with Antony. Which was a different proposition altogether – but actually, even *more* worrying.

'Jessie, where've you been?' Antony enfolded her in his arms, she sensed in relief as much as anything.

'Only outside. With Mel. Did you miss me? Looks like you've found some other company to compensate.'

'Ruth and I were talking.'

'About me? What were you saying?'

'Only good things,' said Antony.

And Jessica believed him, of course. She felt secure in his arms. She trusted Antony. But she glanced at Ruth Bell, and though the Paragon girl was smiling now too, Jessica realised she didn't trust her in the slightest.

Next morning Antony was up early and taking it upon himself to load the group's meagre supplies into the cars. Partly he was doing this to ensure that everything was in readiness for a prompt departure after breakfast. Partly, however, it was to avoid Ruth Bell.

125

He'd told nobody about the true topic of their conversation last night. If their exchange could simply have been dismissed as the weirdest attempted chat-up in history, he might have been tempted to confide it to Travis or even Richie (though *never* Jessica), but ultimately he'd decided that if some of Ruth's stranger ideas became common knowledge, particularly her attitude towards parents, they might well foster bad feeling within the group as a whole. Richie and Mel were already suspicious and distrustful of the Paragons. It wouldn't do to risk making matters worse, not when the teen geniuses' help was vital in the war against the Scytharene. Besides, eccentricity had never been a criminal offence, and that was all the three prodigies were. Eccentrics. A little odd. Too much time spent in secret labs and not enough in the real world. They just didn't know how to behave around normal people. They'd learn – and *soon*, in Ruth Bell's case, Antony hoped.

Someone cleared their throat behind him. *Please, don't let it be her.*

'Shouldn't Naughton be out here checking on the cars?' said Crispin, as punctiliously dressed as ever. 'Morning, Clive.'

'Morning.' It was the first time Antony had been positively *glad* to see Crispin. 'And why do you say that? I don't mind doing it.'

'I'm sure you don't.' The fair boy strolled forward. 'I simply would have thought that taking care of our transport was such an important task that a leader would want to attend to it personally, and Naughton is our leader, isn't he?' Crispin allowed his gaze to stray pensively back towards the farmhouse. 'Though I imagine he's still dallying with the lovely Linden somewhere, mm? I suppose one can't blame him for putting desire before duty once in a while, especially when there are those willing to cover for him.'

There was a slyness about the Paragon's tone that irritated Antony. 'Travis has never let us down yet,' he snapped, though, to be fair, maybe Crispin had some kind of point. Maybe Travis should be around and organising.

'Ruth tells me you were Head Boy of the Harrington School.'

'That's right.' And Antony hoped that was *all* she'd told him.

'I might have guessed. I could see you were used to authority and responsibility from the first. I'm sure you made an excellent Head Boy, Clive.'

'Thank you, Crispin.' Antony liked to think so. After all, he'd rallied the students after the Sickness, hadn't he? He'd kept the community flourishing – at least until Travis and his friends had turned up. *That* was when things had started to go wrong, first Rev and his biker gang attacking because Harrington was sheltering Travis, then . . . But no. None of that was Travis's fault. Rev had been a thug back then and might have picked a fight in any case, and the real catastrophe had been the arrival of the Scytharene, which nobody could have predicted or done anything about.

'Actually,' Crispin was confessing, stepping conspiratorially close to Antony, 'even before I learned you'd been Head Boy, I was mildly surprised you weren't leading the group. Rationally, given your background and experience, you seem to me the ideal choice, mm?'

'Travis is our leader,' stated Antony, pleased with Crispin's praise nonetheless.

'Oh, I know. I know that. Naughton is our leader. I meant no disrespect. I'm sure we're all mightily happy with the situation. Mm.' Crispin's pale eyes narrowed. 'I'll leave you to get on. I haven't had my breakfast yet. Perhaps our leader's managed to stir himself by now as well, what do you think?' They both laughed.

And Antony thought, as Crispin Allerton sauntered back to the farmhouse, that the oldest of the Paragons was actually quite a good guy after all.

Of course, he might have reached a different conclusion had he been present inside the farmhouse some minutes earlier when Crispin and Travis, from the parlour window, had seen him crossing towards the barn and the cars.

'I'd better go help him load up,' Travis said. 'Make sure the cars start and everything.'

'Mm, no need,' Crispin discouraged. 'I'm sure Clive can manage. Besides, while it's just the two of us, Naughton, I'd like to say, no hard feelings.' He specified: 'The election.'

'Well, I'm glad, Crispin. And it's mutual,' Travis said magnanimously. 'At least now when we get to Enclave Zero you'll be able to concentrate exclusively on the gene transfer virus while I do the tedious stuff like organising the foraging for food.'

'Exactly. Exactly.' Crispin was all charity and generosity of spirit. 'The best man won. *I* think so, anyway. Mm, it's just a shame that certain other— No.' Doing the right thing and stopping himself in mid-sentence.

'Certain other— No? What do you mean?'

'Mm, nothing, nothing.'

'I don't believe you ever mean nothing, Crispin.'

The Paragon turned away. 'I don't want to sow discord in the group, Naughton, not now we're beginning to get along so well.' He turned back. 'On the other hand, perhaps you *do* have a right to know.'

'To know what?'

'The things that Clive has been saying about you. Behind your back.'

Travis scoffed. 'I don't believe Antony would say anything about me behind my back. We're friends. Friends don't do things like that.' Though the two of them *had* been arguing a fair bit lately. Travis had thought they'd got over that before they'd set off for Wells College, but maybe some of their disagreements still rankled with Antony. And he *had* directly challenged Travis for group leadership at the last Enclave. But even so, snideness wasn't the Harrington style. 'You've got it wrong, Crispin.'

'Mm, I thought as much. I was sure I must have misheard, or taken Clive's remarks out of context. He wouldn't really be claiming he ought to be leader, would he?'

'Is that what he was saying?' It was what Antony had said before.

'Because "Travis is losing it", I think it was. Mm. But it can't have been, can it? You're friends, aren't you? And friends are honest with each other. I'm sure I misheard.'

But Crispin could tell from the other boy's frown that Travis *wasn't* sure, not absolutely, and doubts, once planted, tended to grow thick and fast. The Paragon's day was starting well.

It improved further still when Travis and Antony opted to travel in different cars for the next leg. No reason was given and nobody else seemed to think anything of it, but Crispin settled back in his seat, congratulated himself on his mischief so far, and prepared to enjoy the journey.

*

129

'What the hell is this?'

Richie, at the wheel of the first car, with Travis, Linden and Geoffrey Thomas his passengers, squinted through the windscreen. A grey and sullen drizzle had been falling virtually since they'd set off, so visibility could have been better, but what was travelling along the road towards them could not be mistaken. Vehicles, numbering in double figures, a motley convoy of cars and vans and trucks.

'You reckon trouble, Trav?' Linden leaned forward from the back seat to Travis in the front.

'Might we have to shoot somebody?' Geoffrey asked with glee.

Linden felt she might like to shoot *him*. She'd had to endure the vaguely sleazy experience of boys undressing her with their eyes before, but when Geoffrey Thomas stared at her, which this morning, given their unfortunate proximity, had been often, it was more like he was *dissecting* her.

'Slow down nice and easy, then stop, Richie,' said Travis. He'd been able to make out the driver and front passenger in the convoy's lead vehicle, a battered Land Rover. 'They're kids like us.'

'*Rev* was a kid like us,' Richie pointed out, remembering their former ambush. 'You want to take a chance *again*?'

Travis grinned. 'You've got to learn to trust more, Richie. People don't always let you down.'

The boy in the baseball cap said nothing but did as instructed, braking gently. Travis opened his door and climbed out.

'Are we taking our guns with us, Travis?' asked Geoffrey hopefully.

'No, we're not. We only want to talk.'

'Let's hope the guys who outnumber us six to one feel the same,' grumbled Richie.

The car driven by Antony pulled up behind them and disgorged the rest of the group. Following Travis's lead, they also left their weapons in the vehicle. Fifty yards or so ahead, the convoy too was easing to a collective halt.

Mel darted to Travis's side. 'Who do you think these guys are, Trav? Where do you think they're heading?'

'I don't know, Mel. But I intend to ask them.'

Members of the convoy were emerging from their vehicles. They were as diverse a band as their transportation, ranging in age from eight or nine to eighteen or nineteen, boys, girls, a mixture of ethnic origins. Not one of them carried a gun. A good sign, Travis thought.

'Well, as we forgot to pack the flag of truce . . .' He raised his hand slightly and stepped forward. 'Wait here.' Addressing the convoy in general: 'Morning. Not the best day for a drive.'

'Not much choice.' The driver of the Land Rover, an Asian boy of Travis's own age, advanced to meet him. 'Name's Sadiq.'

'Travis.'

Halfway between the two groups, Travis paused and offered his hand. Sadiq took it. With mutual grins and nods, any tension that might have existed evaporated. Both parties joined their leaders, mingled and chatted. Only the Paragons held themselves aloof.

'You're going the wrong way, Travis,' said Sadiq. 'Aliens behind us.'

'Behind us, too.'

'The bastards get everywhere, don't they?' Sadiq winked.

'Well, they haven't caught us yet, and if I have anything to do with it, they won't.'

'You've got a fair number of people with you,' Travis said admiringly.

'Yeah, and we could always do with more. Safety in numbers.' *Numbers are everything*, Travis recalled Ruth Bell professing. 'You're welcome to join up with us.'

'Actually, you might want to join up with us. We're heading for London to—'

'London? *London?*' Sadiq threw back his head and roared with incredulous laughter. 'Man, you really *are* going the wrong way. London is one place you want to steer *well* clear of, and I don't just mean 'cause of the congestion charge.'

'Have you come from there?'

'I lived there. Peckham. Left while I could during the Sickness. Roads are pretty much blocked and impassable now, but I've heard things, what it's like.' Sadiq grew troubled, fearful. 'The aliens are at work in London now. The city's ringed with pits of fire, huge – cremating the bodies of the dead. I've heard the smoke hangs in the air like night, and the *smell* . . .'

'Yeah. It's like that in Oxford, too.'

'Well the aliens have divided London up into sections, sec-*tors* might be more like it, and they're overrunning them one at a time, sweeping 'em for prisoners, slaves, whatever the hell it is they want us for.'

'Slaves,' Travis said. 'So I've heard.'

'Yeah, well, every park and green space in town is a prison camp now, and there's no shortage I hear of kids to put in 'em, so unless you want to wind up in one too, Travis, I suggest you turn your cars around, and whether you come with us or not, drive in the most opposite direction to London you can go.'

'I'm afraid we can't do that,' Travis said grimly. 'We have – business in London.'

'Then change your line of work. I'm not pissing about, Travis. You go anywhere near the city and you'll end up either in a cage or in the ground.'

'You didn't tell Sadiq about Enclave Zero, Trav,' observed Jessica as they watched the convoy driving off into the distance and the rain. 'Why not?'

'No point. They weren't going to come with us even if I had,' said Travis. 'Sadiq's reaction as soon as I mentioned London . . . he'd never have turned round.'

'You never gave him the chance,' Antony objected. 'We should have discussed among ourselves what we were prepared to reveal about our intentions *before* . . .'

'There wasn't any time for that, Antony,' Travis cut in irritably. 'And anyway, did you see how young some of those kids were? What right did we have to jeopardise their safety by dragging them into London?'

'We would have gained nothing from allowing that pack of imbeciles to accompany us,' declared Crispin Allerton loftily. 'Didn't you hear? They're wandering aimlessly. Like cattle. They have no idea where they're going. They'd only have slowed us down. Now shall we drive on or do we intend to stand around in the rain all day?'

'Got a point. We're getting pissed on here,' said Richie.

'Let's go, Trav,' urged Jessica, who'd always hated her hair being wet and still did, even when such trivialities should really no longer have mattered.

'Wait a minute, though.' Linden. 'If everything Sadiq said is true, how are we even going to get into central London? Roads sound like a no-no. Prison camps. Scytharene. We're supposed to tiptoe past all that on foot?'

'We won't be on foot, Linden,' Antony announced, a superior grin spreading across his face.

'You planning on hijacking a Culler or something, Tony?' Richie twirled his finger at his temple to indicate his assessment of the blond boy's sanity.

'No, no. It'll be plainer sailing than that.' Antony couldn't resist a faintly triumphant glance at Travis. 'We go by boat.'

SIX

Perhaps she should do it here, Dyona thought, on the bridge of the *Ayrion III,* while the mighty flagship was soaring through alien skies as it was now, while its commander stood draped in the regalia of his office, tall, proud and arrogant beside her.

Perhaps this was where she should kill Gyrion.

She'd selected the murder weapon already, though, of course, political assassination was not really murder – justifiable homicide at worst, and at best, the way Dyona interpreted the death to come, a righteous blow for freedom. It was appropriate that she'd chosen the Coriolanian redemption blade to strike that blow, fitting that Gyrion should perish by an instrument representative of a civilisation he had enslaved.

The stabbing would be bloody, she realised that. If Gyrion was to be dispatched in public he'd be wearing his armour, so she'd have to attack the neck and the throat rather than the body. But then, perhaps the bloodier the better. How much blood was already on Gyrion's hands? He ought to shed copious amounts of his own in recompense.

And as well, if she committed the assassination in full view of the bridge crew, she herself would not escape the scene alive. The dagger would scarcely have found its mark, she imagined, before the Blackhearts, the most militant Scytharene warriors, who made up Gyrion's personal bodyguard, would cut her down with their subjugators, *not* set to stun.

But the propaganda value of her future deed outweighed all other considerations. A Fleet Commander slaughtered on the bridge of his own flagship, the place where he should feel more powerful, more invulnerable than anywhere else, such an unprecedented event would surely serve to inspire dissident Scytharene throughout the Empire and pierce the heart of her people's complacency. Her own death as a consequence would be a welcome bonus. She would leave life a martyr, a figurehead, a symbol of resistance. She would die, like Darion, with purpose.

There would be no more pain.

She must have smiled at that, because she was suddenly aware of Gyrion studying her almost kindly, almost caringly. Almost like a father. 'You seem a little more restored today, Dyona,' he said. 'A little more like your old self.'

'I think,' Dyona replied, visualising the blade sinking into Gyrion's fleshy neck, the blood spouting from his ugly mouth, 'I am, my lord.'

'The eradication of Oxford has obviously had a therapeutic effect on you, my dear.'

'It has certainly stiffened my resolve, my lord, to conduct myself as a true Scytharene should.'

Fleet Commander Gyrion was both relieved and delighted to hear it. 'Perhaps our change of scene will refresh you further.'

If Dyona had had lips, she would have pursed them. 'Yes, I imagine vistas of wasteland where a city used to stand become rather wearisome after a while.'

'Not so, my dear. Invigorating,' claimed Gyrion. 'For a warrior at least, destruction has its own beauty, the right kind of death its own captivating charm.'

'Indeed, my lord.'

'In any case, even if the wretched settlement of Oxford still survived intact, we would have to leave. It is only right that the Fleet Commander responsible for this area of operations – myself,' he added with excruciatingly false modesty, 'should be present to supervise the final stages of the slave harvest at such a location as – what is it called again, Dyona?'

'London, my lord,' she supplied.

Gyrion grunted. 'These Earther names, so undistinguished. Barely language at all. But yes, London. This island's capital and one of the great settlements of Earth, I understand – relatively speaking, naturally. It will be a notable moment in the enslavement when all of London is ours.'

A moment you will not live to see, Dyona vowed. But she lowered her eyes. She had to be careful not to give herself away as she'd almost done before.

She needn't have worried, however. Gyrion was no longer interested in her but was gazing with eyes half closed into the future. 'The completion of the slave harvest of London is a milestone I intend to mark,' he said, as much to himself as to Dyona. 'The *Ayrion III* will host a celebratory summit meeting for myself and my fellow Fleet Commanders, in the conquered heart of the capital, to commemorate all we have so far achieved and to determine all we have yet to accomplish before we can begin to think of returning home with our spoils and abandoning this mudball for ever.'

You'll never leave this planet alive, Gyrion, Dyona longed to say, and if the Coriolanian redemption blade had been in her possession at that moment, she doubted she could have resisted the violent desire to wield it against him there and then. As well she was weaponless. Gyrion's self-congratulatory scheme for a summit had given her a new idea.

To kill one Fleet Commander would be dramatic enough. To kill *all* of them, at the same time, in the same place, not only might that terminally damage and bring to a premature end the enslavement of Earth, but the shockwaves of such a mass assassination would rock the Scytharene homeworld itself, perhaps crack the very foundations of her people's twisted and repellent society.

The Coriolanian redemption blade would remain in the display cabinet.

Gyrion had rediscovered his interest in her. 'Dyona, what do you think of the idea?'

'I think it's perfect, my lord,' said Dyona.

The teenagers found a marina ideal for their purpose on a genteel stretch of the Thames to the west of London. Moored along what had been a private area of the jetty they could see launches and small motorboats, one or two larger cabin cruisers, even a barge, while water craft evidently for public recreation, when the public had existed, included a pleasure cruiser and a line of rowing boats huddled under tarpaulin and feeling sorry for themselves. Vandals had been at work. Several of the boats had been damaged, with others untied and left to drift rudderlessly on the current. Even so, there remained a sufficient number of craft in good shape to give Antony a choice as to which they should commandeer. As the only member of the group with experience of sailing – his father had owned a twenty-foot motor launch – Antony had assumed an authority, for now, at least, which was unchallengeable even by Travis.

He'd led everyone to Wells College; now he was leading them to Enclave Zero. Travis had only led them around in circles. Antony was revelling in his moment.

'The pleasure cruiser's obviously too big. The rowing boats are obviously too small.' He grinned at his wit as he paced up and down the jetty. 'Other than that, anything that's seaworthy is a possibility. Let's board a few, make sure they're in good order and some little miscreant hasn't been poking holes in the hull.'

'Make sure there aren't any kids still aboard below decks or something.' Mel had glimpsed younger children darting between the shops and cafés that fringed the marina. They seemed to be afraid of the newcomers, hiding from them rather than approaching either in friendliness or hostility. Probably just as well. Now was not the time for introductions.

The Paragons, needless to say, deigned not to involve themselves in the boat selection process. They stood on the jetty and peered warily at both the river and the vessels bobbing upon it.

'I wonder what it's like,' Geoffrey Thomas said, 'drowning. Holding your breath and holding your breath until your lungs are on fire and your eyes bulging and you know it's not going to save you, you know you can't hold your breath for ever, and your mouth opens and—'

'Be quiet, Geoffrey,' said Crispin.

'Do we *have* to go by boat, Antony?' Ruth Bell asked forlornly. 'I don't think I like water. Couldn't we stay in the car and drive?'

'I'm afraid not, Ruth,' said Antony, and because it was him, Ruth simply nodded and thereafter accepted her lot.

Richie was only too glad to get out of the car, though not because he preferred boats as a means of transport. His only encounter with water craft before now had been on a boating lake at Whitley Bay when he was seven, and that had lasted less than five minutes because he'd insisted on ramming *his* pedalo into those of his fellow mariners. No, Richie could simply no longer abide being in such an enclosed space with both Linden and Naughton. It was, to coin a phrase, *doing his head in*. Linden so near, and him wanting her so badly, so overwhelmingly that he could hardly focus on anything else, like he was sick or something, and if he could only reach out and take her . . . But then Naughton alongside him, like a counterweight, trusting him, having faith in him, and Richie also craving Naughton's respect, his approval, his friendship, but how could he hope to gain any of those when he was secretly lusting after the other boy's girl, when clandestinely he'd *slept* with the other boy's girl? Guilt and desire contended in Richie Coker's brain, loyalty and longing. There could be no reconciliation between the two; it was a conflict in which one impulse had to triumph over the other. As the party split up to explore the boats, Richie finally felt that a winner had been declared.

He cornered Linden below decks on one of the larger motor launches.

The redhead's face was expressing disgust, though not, at present, with Richie. 'Someone's been here before us,' she coughed. Whoever it was had wrecked the cabin and left behind a reeking, revolting calling card – over much of the floor. 'I guess this is what happens when the chemical toilet fills up. We can't use this. Let's go.'

'Not yet.' Richie barred her exit.

Linden's hazel eyes flashed with anger. 'Richie, if this is about you and me again, I've already *told* you . . .'

'Yeah, you have.' At least he could get straight to the point. 'So now I'm telling you. I know what I want and I get what I want.'

'Oh, *please*. Richie, I'm already on the brink of throwing up with the stench in here. Don't give me any *more* shit.'

'This isn't shit. It's my final offer.'

'Your final . . .? God, just let me past.' Richie put out his hands to prevent her and Linden flinched back. 'Touch me, Richie, and I'll scream and I'll cripple you, though maybe not in that order.'

'Don't waste all that energy now, Lin. Keep some of it for bedtime.'

'You what?'

'Yes. I've decided. I don't care about Naughton or what he thinks. I care about you.'

'This is not caring, Richie.'

'Whatever. You're gonna sleep with me, Linden, whenever I fancy it, whether you like it or not – or else . . . or else I'll tell Naughton everything and put the bloody kibosh on your precious bloody relationship. If I can't have you, I'll make damn sure he won't *want* you.'

'Blackmail, Richie?'

'Call it what you like. I call it—'

Linden slapped him so hard around the face that she physically staggered him. 'So you're exactly what Mel and poor Simon used to say you were. A total bastard. And to think, not so long ago I was starting to believe there was more to you than meets the eye. Got that wrong, didn't I? There's *less*. And I'm gonna call your bluff. *Tell* Travis about us – if you've really got the bottle to. I'll deny it. Who do you reckon he's going to believe? And that'll be the end of you in this group, Richie, and right now I'd say that'd be good riddance. Now get out of my way.' She shoved the unresisting boy to one side. You're a turd, Coker.' Linden gestured with contempt to the cabin behind her. 'Why don't you do us all a favour and stay down here? You'll feel right at home.'

Only after she'd left him did Richie press his hand to the cheek she'd struck. His fingers were trembling with fury and self-loathing. He could have raked his own flesh with them.

Not that Linden herself was feeling a great deal better. She'd kind of betrayed Travis again in the way she'd countered Richie's plodding blackmail attempt. If it actually came to it, *denying* their one-night stand would still be lying to her boyfriend when, if she genuinely believed that Travis loved her, she ought to be able to tell him the truth because he *ought* to be able to forgive her. And if she wasn't sure of that, how certain could she be that their relationship *was* the real thing?

She'd called Richie's bluff, yes. She only hoped he wouldn't call hers.

'Linden! Lin!' And Travis was calling her from further along the jetty. 'We've found our boat.'

'Coming.' She ran towards him, smiling as though nothing was wrong.

Antony had selected a cabin cruiser to take them downriver. It was a forty-footer called *Kingfisher*, its hull painted appropriately in the brilliant turquoise of kingfisher blue; the upper bodywork that enclosed the forward cabin was white. A short flight of steps to the left of the wheel and control panels led down into the accommodation areas below decks, though the cockpit itself, the open seating area towards the aft of the craft, was spacious enough for all nine teenagers to congregate at the same time.

'It looks,' said Antony proudly, 'like it's in perfect condition.'

'Yeah, well, that's all jolly spiffing, Tony,' said Richie, who'd been last to join the rest of the group aboard, 'but assuming it doesn't come with the keys in the ignition, how do we get the bloody thing started?'

'Oh dear, Clive hasn't thought this through,' Crispin whispered in Travis's ear. 'And he imagines he's better leadership material than you.'

'Well, there are plenty of tools in this cupboard if we need them,' Antony said, opening the receptacle in question. 'Surely we can hot-wire a motorboat in the same way as a motor car? Your area of expertise, I think, Richie?'

Richie magnanimously declared he'd See What He Could Do.

While he did, the others dragged aboard the tarpaulin that had been sheeting the rowing boats. It was Travis's idea, the exercise seeming pointless to his companions until he explained why there was every point to it. Nobody protested after that.

The cabin cruiser's engine chugged into life. Everyone cheered and applauded – except Linden, whose fists were clenched and whose mouth was set in stony silence. 'Har, har, me hearties,' Richie gurned piratically from the wheel. 'Am I the new Captain Jack Sparrow or what?'

'I think that's a what, Richie,' said Antony. '*Thank* you.' Taking charge of the wheel himself. 'Shall we cast off? We don't want it to be too dark before we reach Westminster Bridge.'

'Who's Captain Jack Sparrow?' Ruth Bell asked blankly.

'You really *do* need to get out more,' said Mel.

Freed from its moorings, and with Antony steering, if not expertly, at least competently, the *Kingfisher* eased out into the central channel of the Thames. As it did, 'Look!' yelled Mel. A number of ragged urchins emerged from various buildings and trudged down to the jetty to watch their departure. With a pre-Sickness instinct, Mel and Jessica waved. The observers did not reciprocate. Their faces wore the remote, desolate expressions of the recently bereaved, as if they never expected to see either the *Kingfisher* or its self-appointed crew back again.

Everyone crowded to the side apart from Antony and Crispin Allerton, who joined him. 'You've done well, Clive,' the Paragon commended. 'Without you, we'd have stood no chance of reaching Enclave Zero. Naughton couldn't have managed it.' Confidentially: 'I suppose it's no wonder he's not happy with you.'

'Not . . . what do you mean?' Antony frowned.

'Oh, nothing.' Crispin shrugged innocently. 'At least, I imagine it's nothing. I just heard him muttering something about you stealing his thunder, and "Who does Antony Clive think he is? I'm the leader here."' Hurt and angry, Antony glared towards Travis, whose back was presently to him – *like he's shunning me*, Antony thought. 'He clearly doesn't appreciate what you've done, Clive, but take heart. The rest of us do.'

And as luck would have it, at exactly that moment Travis turned. His and Antony's eyes met but neither boy could hold the other's gaze. They both glanced away, brows furrowed. Neither noticed Crispin Allerton's slow, insidious smile.

At the cabin cruiser's safety rail, Jessica closed her eyes. 'You know,' she said dreamily, 'if we didn't know any better, if we could forget the Sickness and the Scytharene just for a moment, this could simply be a normal, ordinary pleasure cruise on the Thames on a beautiful summer afternoon. We could be back in the old world. All we have to do is shut our eyes and not open them, not look.'

'Jessie,' said Mel, whose eyes were always open, 'you're my best friend and I love you, but you are *seriously* deluded.'

Not even Jessica could sustain the pretence for long. The Thames had changed. Perhaps it had never been the cleanest stretch of water in the country, even outside of London, but it had never been littered and polluted quite like this before. The wreckage of other boats came first, shattered and over-turned hulls looming in the *Kingfisher*'s path like rocks which Antony had to be vigilant to avoid. And then cars, submerged in the shallows but visible nonetheless, like dead metallic fish.

'They must have been driven deliberately into the river,' Mel said sombrely. 'Why would somebody do that? Some kind of warped suicide attempt? You think there might be bodies still in the cars?'

'Do you think we'll be able to see them?' Geoffrey Thomas craned his neck over the side.

As they passed under bridges, they realised that Mel's guess was right. The ghostly hulks of vehicles quivered in the depths below, out here in the middle of the river where they'd plunged from above. Looking up, the teenagers could see the breaches battered in the bridges' parapets, too many of them to have been made accidentally. The cars had plummeted to their watery graves like lemmings.

And there was other debris in the river, the abandoned

trappings of lives brought by violence and disease to a premature end: papers, books, items of clothing, personal belongings, all gradually drifting downriver to the sea as if the minutiae of a defeated civilisation was being flushed away.

As the obstacles increased in number and variety, Jessica and Mel took on the role of lookouts at port and starboard respectively, warning the skipper of any floating dangers off either bow. Jessica, however, had to ask Linden to replace her when the bodies began to appear. Adults, children, the former unwilling to wait for the Sickness to finish them off, the latter unable to face the prospect of survival in the post-Sickness world, fully clothed corpses bobbing, some on their backs, most on their fronts – mercifully. Only Geoffrey seemed capable of meeting the vacant yet somehow recriminating stare in their eyes. The *Kingfisher* nosed its way politely through the crowd.

'Antony,' appealed Jessica, looking queasy, 'this isn't such a good idea. Can we turn round? I want to go back. I really want to go back.'

Antony removed one hand from the wheel to hug her to his side. She was shivering. His eyes flickered to Travis who was watching them. 'We can't go back, Jess. We've come too far now. We can only go forward.'

Towards skies black with smoke. Sadiq had not exaggerated. They could see the dense and dismal plumes long before they reached the outer boroughs of the capital, and smell them too, choking and acrid and worse, the stench sickening with the tang of roasted meat.

The fire pits began in Bushy Park, Hampton Court Park, Richmond Park, but though they were still belching out flames and the smothering, suffocating smoke, though the teenagers could feel the raw, scorching heat of them on their flesh, the infernos' task seemed to have been completed. There were no mass cremations in progress at any of the pits, no corpses or container vessels, no steel spiders, no immediate Scytharene presence at all. The fires were simply burning themselves out. The slave compounds were empty as well, left like bitter memorials to the crimes that once had been committed there.

'They've moved on,' Linden said. 'Burned all the bodies. Enslaved all the kids. No need to stay here any more. They've just moved on.'

'Bastards,' gritted Richie. At least he and Linden could still agree on *that*.

'Means we haven't got to move to the next stage of the plan yet.' Travis gazed ahead to darker waters. 'Maybe we'll get away with it.'

Closer they sailed to the heart of the city. Teddington Lock in ruins. Kew Bridge. No way for Antony to avoid the flotsam in the river now; they had to hope the *Kingfisher*'s hull was sturdy as it bumped and cannoned its way on. Chiswick Bridge. Hammersmith Bridge. Roads clogged with silent, rusting traffic.

Though they'd left the Scytharene fire-pits behind, as the city grew around them they could still glimpse blazes on both sides of the Thames. Arson or accidental, it hardly mattered. There was no fire service left to extinguish them.

Putney Bridge. Antony, absurdly, was reminded of the Boat Race. It had been one of his more far-fetched ambitions to be part of a victorious Oxford crew in the Boat Race. Wouldn't happen now, even if he could row.

Even if he could stay alive.

'Ahead of us. Look. Look up!' When Jessica wound her arms around him this time, he was trembling too.

Cullers hovered in the sky above central London, some of them with their tractor beams operating, white spears into city streets. Battlepods flitted through the air like glistening insects. There was nothing random in the positioning of the Scytharene craft, that much quickly became obvious. They were working in two distinct groupings, one on either side of the river, their movements organised, systematic, unstoppable.

'This is it,' breathed Travis. 'The front line of the harvesting.' His eyes blue steel, he addressed the group as one. 'Get ready. Antony'll keep us going as long as he can, but we might need to kill the engine any time from now. You know what you've got to do.'

At Battersea Bridge, the Scytharene had been busy. Boats had been strung together beneath it to form a barricade manned by black-clad warriors. Further passage downriver and to Westminster was impossible.

'Guess we're walking to Parliament from here,' Linden smiled weakly, squeezing Travis's hand.

'Everything's going to be fine,' her boyfriend promised.

Antony switched off the engine.

Warrior-Recruit Varion wanted action. His father, who'd seen service at several enslavements including Orsk and Mamamatou, had made it clear to him before his departure for Earth that if he didn't come home having performed some brave and glorious deed to the honour of his bloodline, he shouldn't trouble himself with coming home at all. It was a challenge the young Varion was only too keen to take up.

He was brave, he knew that, braver than any miserably primitive alien, anyway. He longed for glory. He dreamed of returning to his family a Blackheart. *That* would delight his father and impress his ancestors.

But so far, Varion had found little opportunity to distinguish himself. The virus had done its job almost too well. The adult Earthers had been wiped out so efficiently there was nobody left to fight, nobody against whom he could demonstrate his courage and prove his skills in battle. The enslavement would be over soon and Varion would have gone through it unnoticed by his superior officers. It was all so frustrating. He wanted *action*.

He doubted he'd find any on his present assignment. He, Pyrion and Atrion had been posted to the river blockade, to ensure that no potential slaves evaded the harvest via the Thames.

'This is no good,' he was complaining tetchily to his comrades. 'We shouldn't be wasting our time here.' They were patrolling down by the water line on the north bank of the river, checking for refugees in the few boats that hadn't sunk and that remained secured to the landing stages. Varion plainly expected to find nobody. Unlike his companions, he wasn't even troubling to wear his helmet but was carrying it and slapping it restlessly against his thigh. 'We need to be where the *Ayrion III* is going to be, where Fleet Commander Gyrion can notice us.'

Pyrion noticed a large boat drifting towards the bank. It was blue and white, the hull splattered with muck, and it looked likely to collide with one of the landing stages. He suggested they tie it up there, board it and perform an inspection. Atrion agreed.

Varion did not. 'What for? It's empty. You can see it's empty. A derelict. We'd be better occupied thinking of how we can bring ourselves to the attention of Fleet Commander Gyrion.' He grumbled on while the others hauled the boat alongside and secured it to the landing stage. 'We should ask for a transfer to the Regent's Park slave camps, for a start. Nyrion told me that's where they're going to station the *Ayrion III*.'

Pyrion and Atrion were climbing aboard the boat, subjugators drawn. They asked Varion if he was coming too or whether he intended to spend the entire day moaning.

'No, you can carry out your pointless little inspection yourselves. Why bother? We're not going to make our names . . . oh, very well. Why not, I suppose?' Sighing defeatedly and donning his helmet, Varion joined his companions on board. 'But I'm telling you – see? Nothing. A heap of some kind of canvas on the deck and that's all.'

Pyrion suggested they explore below decks. Atrion agreed.

Varion did not. 'What for? I'll tell you what'll be below decks.' As his companions turned towards the cabin steps. 'The same as up here. Nothing. The best you'll find is a dead and rotting Earth— *Urgh* . . .'

The Earther who'd shot him in the chest, a fatal subjugator bolt stabbing through the tarpaulin, was very much alive. Varion's last thought was of his father. If he couldn't come home in glory . . .

Warrior-Recruit Varion wasn't going home at all.

Travis tore the tarpaulin away, fired again. Linden followed suit. Richie's shotgun blasted, the force of the shell's impact propelling Pyrion backwards.

The Scytharene had been terminally slow to react. But there

150

was still a chance for Atrion to eliminate one of the three teenagers who'd hidden beneath the tarpaulin – until a sub-jugator bolt from Antony, bursting from the cabin with Jessica and Mel behind him, sent the warrior pitching to the deck to lie alongside his already fallen comrades.

'Bloody hell, it worked. We're still alive.'

'You sound surprised, Richie,' Travis smiled grimly. 'Don't you trust me?'

'Who's for subjugators?' Mel was wresting one from Varion's lifeless grasp.

'Not us,' Crispin declined, the Paragons emerging from the cabin last of all. 'We abhor physical violence.'

'Unless someone else is saving your arses with it, right, Crispie?' Richie snorted. 'You chicks can have 'em. I'm happy with what I've got.' Patting the barrel of his shotgun.

'Give your spare weapons to Crispin, Geoffrey and Ruth,' Antony directed the girls. 'We should all be armed whether we like it or not.'

'We'd better learn to like it,' Mel said meaningfully.

Because the Scytharene who'd boarded the *Kingfisher* had not been the only patrol. Hostile shouts from the right, towards Battersea Bridge. Half a dozen Scytharene opening fire from the street that ran along the embankment above the teenagers. Deadly blasts flashing close.

Ruth and Geoffrey squealed.

'We're sitting ducks down here. Come on.' Travis glanced about. 'The steps.' Concrete steps which led up from the water line to the embankment. He was leaping to the landing stage and racing for them immediately, maintaining a cover-ing fire as the others followed. The Scytharene saw the teenagers' destination, began their own charge towards it.

151

Travis bounded up the steps, and whether he tripped near the top of the flight or whether he threw himself to the ground deliberately in the event didn't matter. The recklessly advancing Scytharene had only his head, shoulders and arms to aim at; Travis had the aliens' entire bodies in *his* sights.

He exploited that fact. Six became five.

Antony dropped heavily to the steps alongside him, Jessica and then Mel to the blond boy's right. The report of a shotgun announced Richie's arrival to Travis's left. The pavement in front of them sparked like flint when the Scytharene's subjugator blasts fell short, other bolts seared the air above the teenagers' heads, but the aliens had yet to find a lethal range.

Unlike Jessica. They were already reduced to three when she opened fire. Seconds later, the battle was over. Antony stared at her, awestruck.

'What?' Jessica said defensively. 'So I got in some practice at the Enclave.'

'You're amazing,' Antony declared.

Ruth Bell, perhaps unsurprisingly, seemed to think otherwise.

'Okay.' Travis scrambled to his feet. 'We've done the heads-down bit, now it's the heads-up. Streets. Now. And keep together. *Now.*'

They had to use the city to their advantage, he knew. The clash of combat had alerted still more Scytharene to the group's presence, inflicting fresh pursuers on them, but these were a handicapping distance away and the teenagers were sprinting with breakneck speed. They could outstrip the aliens, *had* to outstrip them, lose themselves in the maze of car-cluttered streets, the labyrinth that was London where those giving chase could be shaken off, hide in the vacant shops and office blocks with their multiple entrances, multiple floors, lie low, wait for the Scytharene to give up their search, and then continue on to Enclave Zero concealed by night.

Good stuff in principle, Travis knew, as he hared down the middle of a road, one hand clutching Linden's and the other his subjugator, firing to the rear to deter the aliens. Everyone was keeping up, even the wheezing Paragons. And everyone was staying together. They could do this. They bloody well *could* outpace the Scytharene warriors.

A whoosh through the air above and behind them announced a new source of danger.

Yeah, good stuff in *principle*, but in reality the rules were always changing. Inwardly, Travis groaned.

They'd never outrun a battlepod.

SEVEN

Suddenly the city itself seemed to be siding with the Scytharene. Ahead of the hurtling teenagers a concertina crush of vehicles blocked their path, formed a solid barricade across almost the entire width of the street. In length it stretched as far as Travis could see, the aftermath of countless desperate but doomed attempts to flee a diseased London. The vehicles' drivers had failed – by now they must all have died – and their legacy could well have been to condemn those still seeking escape to the same fate.

The energy bolt that flared from the battlepod and tore up the tarmac of the road was yellow, not white. The aliens were taking no prisoners.

Give us a chance, Travis pleaded in silent dismay. *That's all we ask for. A fighting chance.*

'Travis, what now?' Linden yanking at his arm.

He felt the despair welling up in him again, the hopelessness, the surrender. Like grief. A wall of cars in front of them, death in a blinding flash of light behind. What could they do? What would his father have done?

He wouldn't have given up, that was for sure.

Travis recollected himself, remembered his responsibilities. Okay, so rules changed. So could tactics.

'Scatter!' he yelled. Forget about staying together for now.

That would only make things easier for the pilot of the battlepod. 'Give him something to think about!' *Confuse* the alien, hopefully. Cut down on the casualty rate. Some of them might make it. Linden, for one.

He wanted to keep her with him but that wouldn't do. He pushed her away. 'Run, Lin.'

'Travis, where . . .?'

Was he going? To give the battlepod some target practice.

Travis vaulted on to the boot of a car, on to its roof, turned and fired a futile but defiant subjugator bolt at the swooping battlepod. 'You want me, you bastard? Then come and get me.'

The battlepod tried. Its opening blast as it swept low above Travis's head struck a car several vehicles away from the boy, shook it loose from those it had crashed into, blew it several feet into the air. The resultant shockwave knocked Travis to his knees. He slid forward on to his car's bonnet. The battlepod was a pendulum in the sky between the high walls of office blocks – about to swing back again. When it did, Travis could not afford to be where he was now.

'Need a hand?' Antony was extending one.

'What are you . . .? You should have got away, Antony.'

'My thoughts entirely.' The blond boy's balance on the bonnet was far from perfect, but he wasn't going to be out-performed by Travis Naughton.

Travis's legs were shaky now, too. No time to ask about the others as he managed to stand, though he thought he could make out through the smoke of the battlepod's blast Linden and maybe Mel or Jessie running parallel to him and Antony along the narrow gap between vehicles and buildings. He hoped everyone else was doing the same.

A second explosion of cars all but buffeted the two boys into the street.

'Scenic route,' Travis gritted. He bounded from one car to the next, clambered over their roofs, Antony following his lead.

Behind them again now, the battlepod renewed fire. A wave of heat scorched the boys' backs and the metal surface beneath them shuddered and rocked. No chance to stand and shoot. Neither Travis nor Antony even dared to turn round or focus on anything other than their next hectic and treacherous step. A foot through one of the shattered, gaping windscreens and it was all over. A twisted or broken ankle from slipping on the sloping roofs and bonnets and it was all over.

They'd succeeded in drawing the battlepod down on the two of them alone, but if the pilot found his range in the close confines of the street, then . . .

Somebody had intended to leave the city *very* far behind them. Their petrol tank must have been filled to the brim. When the energy bolt hit it, the fuel ignited. An incendiary bomb could hardly have wreaked greater havoc.

Travis cried out as flames erupted searingly behind him, as a deadly chain reaction was set off and other vehicles combusted, turning the street into a furnace, as he was thrown helplessly forward, flailing, no possibility of keeping on his feet any longer. Bruises and blood as he slammed on to a car roof, but nothing broken, he could feel that. And he'd have been ashamed of his cries if it hadn't been for Antony screaming in concert, thudding alongside him.

Travis squirmed on to his back, thrust his subjugator into the air, gripped it with both hands. Through plumes of black smoke he distinguished a darker shape yet, and spherical. The battlepod. He'd keep shooting at it as long as there was breath in his body. But the Scytharene craft as it streaked above his head was itself ablaze, engulfed by the inferno its own weapons systems had unleashed. Travis would have laughed if his pummelled diaphragm had let him.

The battlepod spiralled crazily, out of control. It plummeted into the cram of vehicles and the explosion must have been the fiercest and most devastating yet. None of its predecessors had plunged Travis into unconsciousness.

But not death. He was alive. His hacking cough, his bleeding mouth and nose, the pain in his limbs told him that. Linden's arms around him, her warmth and softness against him, the wetness of her tears and her lips as she kissed him told him that. And he hadn't been out of it for long. The street was still burning. He and Linden were huddling in a doorway. Antony was with them, also stirring back towards consciousness. Someone else was tending to Antony.

Ruth Bell.

'You're all right. You're all right, Trav,' Linden soothed. 'We dragged you off the cars.'

'The others,' Travis said, squeezing her arm tightly. 'Mel. Jessie. Richie. Where are the others?'

'We don't know, Trav.' Linden's eyes flickered to the blazing street. 'We've lost them.'

The silence that succeeded Dyona's words was long and sombre, like that observed at the end of a transcension ceremony. Etrion seemed reluctant to break it without direct instruction. He appeared content to remain hunched forward pensively on the chair in his mistress's quarters where she had invited him to sit. Dyona herself stood equally motionless by the window. Outside, in Regent's Park, Scytharene warriors went about the business of slavery as briskly as ever. In this room, however, it was as if life had been drained away entirely.

'Well, Etrion?' Dyona finally prompted.

'Well, my lady.'

'It is a simple plan, is it not?'

The servant was forced to concede that his lady's scheme was, indeed, clear and uncomplicated. 'You bide your time until all twenty-four of our Fleet Commanders are gathered here aboard the *Ayrion III* for Fleet Commander Gyrion's celebratory summit,' he rehearsed. 'You then conceal an explosive device . . .'

'I plant a bomb, Etrion,' Dyona simplified, her eyes gleaming.

'Forgive me, my lady. You plant a bomb in the chamber where the Fleet Commanders will be.' He paused, asked mildly: 'Do you know how to make such a bomb, my lady? I was not aware that the manufacture of explosives was a subject traditionally included within the education of female members of the Thousand Families.'

'I know how, Etrion,' Dyona said stonily. 'Darion showed me.'

The servant nodded. 'You plant the bomb. You detonate it from a safe distance. You slaughter twenty-four of your own people in one fell swoop.'

'Assassinate, Etrion. And don't you think that this twenty-four at least *deserve* to die?' Dyona's mood darkened. She paced the room restlessly, huntedly, like a scarath in a cage. 'How many alien lives have been lost because of Gyrion and his kind? How many innocents murdered or enslaved? And yet, if I do nothing, in a few days' time these very monsters will congregate ten decks below us in the Chamber of the Triumph and rejoice at the destruction they have wrought, the planets they have ravaged. They will revel in the fall of Earth as if they were heroes. It's sick, Etrion, it's immoral and I will not tolerate it. Gyrion and his Fleet Commander accomplices are criminals, guilty of crimes against the peoples of the universe on an almost incalculable scale. They deserve to be punished. If justice is to be served, they must die.'

'Perhaps, my lady,' shrugged Etrion.

'*Perhaps?*'

'What our fellow Scytharene deserve or do not deserve I cannot be certain, my lady. All I know is that in life an individual must choose his beliefs, his values, must decide upon his loyalties of his own free will and remain true to his personal morality until his dying day. If and when one comes into contact with another whose beliefs challenge or even contradict one's own, there is always likely to be conflict. More often than not, there will be violence. This is the way the world works. In the end, one set of values, one moral code will emerge victorious and be accepted as the absolute truth, everywhere and by everybody.'

'I'm not sure I understand what it is you're saying, Etrion,' Dyona frowned.

The servant smiled gently. 'Just that I am a humble and ignorant being, my lady. Only time will tell if slavery is right or wrong: I cannot. But I know where my loyalties lie. With *you*, my lady Dyona. Always.'

'So you'll help me, Etrion?' Dyona grew urgent. 'Because

I need you if this is going to work. I can't do it without you. You'll be able to collect materials for the bomb from parts of the ship where my appearance as a member of the Thousand Families would attract unwanted attention, if not suspicion.'

Dyona was aware that she was engaging with Etrion far more freely than should have been the case between mistress and servant. She didn't care. Equality had to exist *within* races as well as between them. Dyona knelt before Etrion and clasped his hands. 'Will you do it? Will you help me?'

And there was sadness too now in Etrion's smile. 'I would give my life for you, my lady.'

Eventually, Mel stopped running. Not because she felt any safer – to drop gasping to her knees even on the unsympathetically concrete pavement was by now a physical necessity. Besides, Jessica was collapsing too, and even if her legs were capable of further immediate movement, she'd never leave Jessie behind. The same wasn't true of Crispin Allerton, whom Mel would happily have deserted at the *Kingfisher*, if not back at Wells College, Oxford. But for some reason the Paragon had latched on to her from the point at which the battlepod had attacked, and somehow he'd managed to keep up. He lowered himself delicately to the ground as if his foremost concern was dirty marks on his trousers.

'Mel,' Jessica was panting, 'what happened to . . . Antony? Trav? Where's Linden?'

Mel didn't know. She'd lost sight of the others at the first explosion. The streets that had been a dizzying blur as she'd pelted aimlessly through them had now steadied themselves and become reassuringly static again, but grim in the encroaching darkness of imminent night, and desolate, like cities evacuated in times of war. There was no sign of human life.

On the plus side, there wasn't a trace of alien life, either.

'They got away too, didn't they?' Jessica pursued anxiously. 'Everyone else.'

'Of course they did.' Mel sounded more certain than she felt for her friend's sake.

'Only, Antony and Travis, the last I saw of them, on the roofs of those cars . . .'

'They're fine, Jess.' And any excuse to wind her arm around Jessica. 'They're close by somewhere and they're fine. I promise.'

Crispin snorted sceptically.

'You got something to say, Doc?' Mel snapped.

'No, no. Not really. Mm, I was merely wondering how you can promise something that is clearly beyond your power to guarantee. It seems to me a faintly ludicrous thing to say. As you asked.'

Mel glanced at the Paragon. 'Yeah, well, you and ludicrous things to say must go way back, Crispin, you know what I mean? The others are fine. In fact, I wouldn't be surprised if any minute now . . .'

But when the steps were heard to their left, belonging to two dark figures picking their way through a jumble of cars, Mel's first reaction was to threaten with her subjugator and steel herself for violence.

'Careful, Morticia, someone might think you're not too pleased to see us.' The taller figure raised his hands. One of them held a shotgun.

'Richie.' Mel almost smiled. Until she saw who was with him. She didn't particularly wish Geoffrey Thomas any

161

harm, but she'd sooner have been greeted by Travis, Antony or Linden.

The new arrivals, however, had seen nothing of either the two boys or Ruth Bell.

'Soon as our noble leader said scatter, I bloody well scattered,' Richie said. 'Naughton wants to prance about like a prat where that bloody pod could see him, good luck to him. You won't get any grandstanding like that from Richie Coker, let me tell you.'

'By grandstanding, you mean risking his life to give the rest of us a better chance of surviving,' Mel said. 'No, I'm sure we won't get that from you, Big Guy.'

'An inclination to grand gestures of self-sacrifice is often symptomatic of deep-rooted psychological problems,' intoned Geoffrey Thomas, who was kind of squatting on the pavement. 'An attempt to compensate for an earlier traumatic event which the subject was unable to prevent, for example.'

'Hey, Geoffrey,' hailed Mel. 'You heard the phrase "Silence is Golden"?'

'Yes, but . . .'

'Then do us all a favour. Go for gold for a bit.'

'Let's not bicker,' Jessica intervened. 'We ought to be searching for our friends.' For Antony. If she couldn't find him, if she never saw him again . . . she didn't want to go there. It struck her that she'd begun to envisage only a future with Antony in it, the two of them together.

'Jessie's right.' Mel lined up alongside her. 'The sooner we start, the sooner we find them.'

'But it's gonna be dark sooner than *that*.' Richie was more reluctant. 'I know night's your favourite time, Morticia, but . . .'

'Just get your arse in gear, Richie.'

'They can't be too far away,' said Jessica. 'If we try to retrace our steps . . .'

'What if the Scytharene are still searching for us?' Geoffrey said fearfully.

'Mm. Indeed.' Crispin glanced to the deserted office block behind them. 'Perhaps it would be wise to discuss our options *inside*?'

'Options?' Mel said suspiciously. 'What do you mean, *options*? This isn't a choice. It's a duty. We have to find the others.'

'Actually we don't,' Crispin opposed. 'There's nothing compulsory about it. Expending valuable time and energy scouring the streets for those who may very well in any case, to put it euphemistically, no longer be with us . . .'

'They're alive, Crispin,' declared Jessica with feeling.

'. . . is not a useful occupation. It would make more sense for us to push on to Enclave Zero in accordance with our original plan. Enclave Zero should be our first priority.'

'You can shove Enclave Zero where the sun don't shine,' Mel retorted. 'I'm sure you'll have room. *My* priority is my missing friends – maybe they're hurt and need our help – but then I don't expect you to understand about loyalty and friends, Dr Allerton. As far as I'm concerned, you can come with us or you can go to hell. Let's get out of here, Jess.'

'Just a moment, Patrick.' Crispin stopped her. 'We're a group, are we not? We need to stay together.'

'So come with us, Crispin, Geoffrey,' Jessica exhorted. 'Don't you want to find Ruth?' Not that she was sure *she* did.

'A *democratic* group.' Slyly.

'What are you getting at, Crispin?' Mel said.

163

'We voted for leader. In his absence, why don't we vote on our course of action?'

Richie listened to Allerton droning on. He wasn't sure that old Crispie hadn't been *watching* him before he suggested the vote idea, kind of weighing him up. He didn't know why. Maybe the Paragon was a bit of a woofter on the quiet. He didn't care why – as Morticia and the Little Princess said they'd go with the majority decision like good little democrats. He knew which way *he* was going to vote.

'We search for the others.' Morticia.

'We locate Enclave Zero.' Crispie.

'We have to look for our friends. They'll be looking for us.' Jessica.

'Enclave Zero.' That freaky bloody Geoffrey, like Allerton's pet.

Linden. All she'd had to do was dump Naughton and take up with him, Richie, instead. That was all. Then Richie reckoned he'd have put himself out for her all right, looked after her, protected her, the kind of things that seemed to come easy to the likes of Naughton but that he'd never thought before were for the likes of him, things he'd used to laugh at, take the piss out of. She could have dumped Naughton. What was the big deal? Where he came from, chicks cheated on their boyfriends all the time.

'Richie. *Hello?*' Moriticia, sticking her face in his and waving like he was some retard.

'What?'

'Say you're with us and let's get moving.'

Hippie Chick. Not Linden. Just Hippy Chick. And Hippy Chick *could* have chosen him. Only she hadn't. She'd chosen Naughton. So to hell with her. And to hell with Naughton, too.

'I'm not with you, Morticia,' growled Richie Coker.

Mel's turn with the '*What?*' And Jessica, disbelievingly: 'Richie?' Almost hurt. Almost like she'd been relying on him.

But it was too late now. He pulled the peak of his baseball cap down so they couldn't see his eyes. 'I'm looking out for *me* now. Number one. Richie Coker. Traipsing round these bloody streets is gonna get us killed. So I'm not with you, Morticia. I'm with Crispin.'

Who perhaps tried but certainly failed to stifle a smug little giggle. 'Ah, democracy. You know, Patrick, I think I'm beginning to warm to it after all.'

'Richie,' Jessica accused him, 'how *could* you?'

'Get lost,' Richie scowled sullenly.

'Jess, we don't have to abide by the vote. It's not compulsory.' If Mel stared at Crispin Allerton's superior, self-satisfied face a moment longer she wouldn't be able to resist the tempting urge to give it a good smack. She turned to the blonde girl. 'We can still go and look for the others. You and me.'

'No. We voted.' Jessica shook her head helplessly. 'We have to obey the rules. That's what Antony would say.'

'Well, then.' Crispin Allerton rubbed his hands together in a businesslike manner. 'If we're ready, I suggest we make a' – his optimism suddenly deflating – 'start . . .'

This time the figures emerging from the shadows were not familiar, and there were very many more of them than of the small group they quickly surrounded, and they were human at least, youths from a range of ethnic backgrounds, but all of them were armed, and every weapon was trained on the five teenagers who drew instinctively closer together and raised their hands in surrender.

'Looks like we're all in the minority now,' Mel muttered.

*

They considered yelling out the others' names as the gloom of evening deepened but decided against. It probably wasn't sensible to risk attracting the attention of anyone who *didn't* answer to Jessica or Mel, or Richie or Crispin or Geoffrey for that matter, especially when such unknown elements might also prove hostile. But they weren't giving up on their friends, Travis made that clear. He expected to find all of them alive and well.

'Shouldn't we stay and search the streets around here, then?' Antony said. 'This is where they're likeliest to be, surely.'

The quartet themselves had fled the area where the battlepod had been destroyed and the cars still burned as expeditiously as possible. Progress in any direction since then, however, had been slow, hampered by the injuries sustained by both boys from the explosions. Travis was favouring his right leg, leaning on Linden from time to time for support, while Ruth was fussing around a hobbling Antony whether he wanted her to or not. Their wounds were superficial, even so, nothing that relaxation and a few good nights' sleep wouldn't cure. Unfortunately, since the Sickness, both relaxation and good nights' sleeps had been in short supply.

'We need to put distance between us and the Scytharene, Antony,' said Travis.

'What Scytharene?' the blond boy protested. 'I don't see any Scytharene.'

'If you did,' Linden said, 'it'd already be too late.'

Travis nodded. 'We need to keep moving. The others will be.'

'What if they're hurt or something and they *can't* move?'

Travis ignored Antony's question, though the same possibility had already occurred to him. All he could really do was to decide honestly on what he thought was the right course of action, stick to it, and hope for the best. 'We can't afford to wander around in circles. That won't do anyone any good. We all knew where we were going before we got separated. I think it's a fair assumption that sooner or later that's where everyone'll head. Parliament. That's where we'll all meet up again so that's where we go.'

'You'd better be right,' said Antony, with a sullenness of which Richie Coker would have been proud.

He was worried about Jessica. He was worried about *everyone* who was missing, of course, and if any of them were dead he'd mourn them and try to move on, but if something had happened to *Jessica* . . . he didn't think he'd be able to recover from that. He glanced across at Travis and couldn't help but feel resentment. Travis with Linden beside him, Linden with her arm around him. Travis's girl was safe while Jessica – God, he hoped she was too. If she was with Mel, that would be good. Mel wouldn't let any harm come to her. In her own fashion, Mel loved Jessie as much as he did. But it would be infinitely preferable to have Jessica here, as Linden was here with Travis. And Antony felt a bitterness coursing through him like poison. How was it that everything always went *Travis's* way?

'Ruth,' the group's leader was saying, 'do you know how to access Enclave Zero?'

'Not without Crispin.' She hoped Antony wouldn't be disappointed in her. 'I know there are entrances to the complex in Ten Downing Street and the Houses of Parliament themselves, Crispin told us approximately where those two are – there are other ways in and out as well, apparently – but the doors will be camouflaged, concealed, and even if we found

167

them we'd need the entry codes that were stored in the files Crispin hacked into. He memorised them.'

'So we really need Crispin.' Travis frowned.

'Dr Allerton seems to be getting into the habit of making himself indispensable,' Linden observed, and in a quieter undertone, 'sadly.'

'Don't worry, Lin,' said Travis. 'We'll find a way inside the Enclave somehow, even if we *don't* find Crispin.' He squeezed the handle of his subjugator. 'Even if we have to blast our way . . .'

'Hey. Hey!' Antony was suddenly breaking away from Ruth and into a run. 'Jess . . .' But neither of the two figures who'd darted from one of the shops just ahead of them was Jessica. They were shorter, they were younger, and in a splash of moonlight it could be seen both to Antony's dejection and embarrassment that they were also male and black. It wasn't just the pain in his legs that brought him to a halt.

His companions caught up with him as the two kids vanished into distance and darkness.

'Do you think there might be an optician's around here somewhere?' he joked bleakly. 'I think I need to get my eyes tested.'

'Antony.' Linden touched his hand understandingly.

And he brightened. 'Perhaps we should chase after them anyway, whoever they are. They're obviously locals. Perhaps they've seen Jessica and the others. They can tell us where they are.'

'I don't think so,' Travis said.

'You don't think so what?' With more than a note of paranoia. *Travis, everything always going his way.*

'I think it might be safer if we just carried on.'

'But if there's a chance? Don't you want to – don't you want to find the others, Travis?'

'Antony.' Stung. 'Of course I do. You know I do. But look. Look.' Indicating the empty street. 'If there was a chance, it's gone. So should we be.'

'No.'

'Pardon me?'

'You heard. Or are your ears as useless as my eyes? Or is selective deafness another one of those leadership skills you seem to have mastered so well?'

'Antony, what are you talking about?'

'If we're not going after those kids, I say we rest for a bit, get some food and drink inside us. *You* look.' Antony jabbed a finger at the establishment from which the two boys had swiftly exited. Back when such designations had mattered, it had been a mini-mart. Now its windows were smashed and its door seemed to have vacated the premises entirely. 'There might still be some supplies in there.'

'We don't have time to stop, Antony.'

'Why not? Because you say so, Travis?'

'What . . .? We need to press on.'

'Because you say so. Because you know best.'

'Is this a sulk, Antony? Is that what this is?'

'The rest of us aren't imbeciles, you know. I was Head Boy of the Harrington School. I deserve to be listened to.'

'Is that why you've been slagging me off behind my back?'

'I have *not*—'

'Reckon I've risen above my station, do you? Well let me tell *you*—'

'*Stop it!*' Linden joined the two boys in sudden disregard for the notion of making their way through the night-bound streets *quietly*. 'Stop it, both of you. Just . . . bloody hell!'

'Lin?' Travis read fear as well as anger in Linden's features. He moved to embrace her but she swatted his arm away.

'No, Trav. Not until – you should listen to yourselves, both of you. What the hell's going on? What's gone wrong?'

'I can assure you, Linden—' Antony began, but of what he never got round to saying.

'This arguing, this constant sniping at each other, where's it coming from? Why? You're at each other's throats like – I was going to say bickering children, but it's worse than that. It's like all of a sudden you're rivals or enemies, and you're not. You're allies. You're a team. Have you forgotten that? You're friends. And friends don't . . . You mustn't turn against each other. Antony. Trav.' Her voice wavered. 'The rest of us need you. Both of you.'

'Okay, Lin. Okay. I'm sorry.' This time, Travis's hug was not rejected.

'*We're* sorry.' Antony regarded the other boy soberly. Leaders didn't reduce those who relied on them to tears. He suddenly felt ashamed. 'Travis . . .'

'Antony!' Ruth, almost forgotten, crying out and pressing her hands to her temples. Ruth, looking dizzy, looking faint.

Antony caught her before she could fall.

'I'm all right, I'm all right.' Travis and Linden helped lower her to the ground but Ruth's arms entwined around only one of her three attendants. 'I'll be all right now,' she said with an expression of fortitude.

'Are you sure? Are you in pain?' Antony's medical knowledge was limited. He was genuinely concerned for Ruth, but kind of hoped there wasn't any loosening of clothing on the horizon.

170

'I'm just . . . I just feel weak,' the girl self-diagnosed. 'I think . . . something to eat and I'll be fine.'

Antony consulted Travis. 'The mini-mart?'

The mini-mart. Which, miraculously, was still reasonably well stocked. Chocolate bars and cans of fizzy drinks were pressed into service to boost the sugar content of Ruth Bell's blood. The others didn't feel that they could let her eat alone and plundered the shelves themselves. And Ruth had been right. All she'd needed was some sustenance. She'd barely taken a bite or a swig before she appeared remarkably refreshed, virtually back to normal. Maybe part of her recovery was due to the careful attentions of Antony.

Travis munched chocolate and eyed Ruth thoughtfully.

'Okay,' he said when cans and wrappers were emptied. 'Pit stop over. Time to go.'

'You're going nowhere, man.'

A male voice threatening from the doorway. Shadows coming alive and surging inside. Travis, Antony and Linden reached for their subjugators. The steel glint of light on the barrels of automatic weapons already prepared to shoot. 'I wouldn't do that if I were you.'

Travis opted to keep his hands outstretched and visible instead. 'We don't want any trouble.'

'Too bad, man. Trouble is what you got.'

'In deep shit, man, deep and drowning shit.'

The voices multiplying as their owners poured into the store.

'You shouldn't be here.'

'You shouldn't have come here.'

'Now you're gonna wish you hadn't.'

'This is Phantom turf, man.'

The four teenagers were overwhelmed, their guns snatched from them, restraining hands grabbing them. Ruth squealed, Antony shouted, Linden swore and Travis simply gritted his teeth. The two black kids had come back – if that was them hopping nervously from one foot to the other in the light through the hole where a window had been. They looked very young now. Those they'd brought with them were older. The gang dragged Travis's group out into the street and every one of them was of Afro-Caribbean descent. Seemed the newcomers would have trouble fitting in in more ways than one.

But Travis had to try. 'Listen, you don't have to do this. We're sorry. We didn't know this was your territory. We didn't mean any dis—'.

'Respect, man.' As Travis was shoved sprawling on the pavement, his companions, too. 'You got to learn respect.' As the gang encircled them, like a noose at a lynching.

'Trav.' Linden clutched his hand. Hers was cold.

'Antony,' whined Ruth.

'This can't be happening. This *can't* . . .' But Antony knew it was.

'Trespassers on Phantom turf, man. . .'

'. . . will not be prosecuted.'

'Don't.' Travis. '*Don't.*'

'They will be shot.'

A dozen weapons took aim.

The five prisoners were hustled through streets not too far away. Mel derived a degree of comfort from the fact that no actual violence had been inflicted on them so far, but she didn't want to tempt fate by making a break for it or anything.

She did as she was told and kept her mouth shut. She also kept close to Jessica.

Most of their captors acted as though they'd been delinquents long before the Sickness. On first-name terms with young offenders' institutes throughout London, she had no doubt. She was surprised they hadn't welcomed Richie as one of their own instead of prodding him along with the rest of them. She was surprised Richie hadn't *volunteered* to join them. So it wasn't much of a shock to find that the gang was holing itself up in an old-style gymnasium. No computer-monitored strength machines, saunas or adverts for Pilates classes here: punching bags, scuffed medicine balls, crumbling walls, oil lamps and a full-size boxing ring at centre stage, roped up and ready for a bout. Just the kind of place tough, unruly kids would be sent to channel their natural aggression into more disciplined and socially acceptable directions. The gang didn't only consist of young men, however. There were a number of girls, sitting or lying listlessly on the floor among outbreaks of bedding and mounds of food, the occasional gas stove.

It was a boy, though, who approached them. He was white, or rather, closer to red, like he'd been boiled in the not too distant past, seventeen or eighteen years old, shaven-headed and piggy-eyed. The T-shirt he wore bore a fading picture of the boxer Mike Tyson, the former world heavyweight champion's name and the barely legible slogan 'K-ng of th- Rin-'. Tyson was obviously a hero of the wearer's given that he had evidently sought to emulate the boxer's physique. He'd done pretty well, too – he was an imposing physical specimen to start with, bigger and bulkier even than Richie – but some of the muscle seemed to be debating whether or not its future

173

really lay in fat. The gang leader (Mel assumed) had probably been a regular at the gym in the old days, though if he'd been in training to be a fighter his trainer – had he somehow survived the Sickness – ought to be sued. One cauliflower ear, one broken nose and several missing teeth. Mel remembered the old gag: 'You should see the *other* guy.' She wasn't sure whether she should be afraid of this muscle-bound bruiser or amused by him.

She was even less certain when he lifted his fists to defend his face, dipped his shoulders, and bobbed and weaved in front of them. 'So,' he said, 'what have we got here?'

One of the gang told him. Apparently, what he had here were five strangers who'd crossed into the Kings' territory without permission.

'The King's?' Mel was emboldened to query. 'She's probably dead by now anyway, but don't you mean the Queen's?'

'No queens in *this* gym, love,' Shaven-Head snorted. He regarded Crispin dubiously. 'Not till now, anyways. The *Kings*. Kings of the Ring. That's us. We make the rules around here. We say what's what. And I'm Cooper. I'm the king of the Kings.'

'Care in the community, more like,' Richie muttered.

'Okay. If we're doing names . . .' Mel performed the introductions. She was thinking that this Cooper guy seemed reasonable enough. Maybe they weren't in such big trouble after all.

Then Crispin piped up. 'It's intolerable that you've forced us to this disgusting slum. It's no doubt infested with rats. I demand that we be released immediately to go on our way.'

Cooper and his fellow Kings of the Ring hooted with hilarity. 'Will you listen to this guy?' In a high-pitched squeak

174

which almost brought a smile to Mel's lips: 'I *demand*. It's intol-erawhatever.' Cooper's voice dropped a couple of octaves as he ducked his torso and jabbed his meaty fists to within inches of Crispin's startled face. The Paragon staggered back-wards. The barrel of a gun bored into his spine. Geoffrey was whimpering, his own upper body bobbing up and down as was its habit. Mel no longer felt any inclination to smile. 'This guy,' Cooper was chortling at Crispin's expense. 'Bet he's never stepped one prissy foot inside the ring. Bet he's never sparred a single round. Jeez, bet he bleeds real easy, real bright. Hope they pick you, Pretty Boy. Yeah, Pretty Boy Allerton versus King Cooper.' Bizarrely, Cooper switched to commentator-speak. 'It was the mismatch of the century down at Kenton's gym tonight when Pretty Boy Allerton faced the undefeated champion of the Kings of the Ring, King Cooper himself. And the crowd went *wild*.'

'Sorry. Sorry.' Mel interrupted the boxer's monologue. 'I apologise for Crispin. He's not really comfortable around people who haven't won the Nobel Prize. We generally ignore him.'

'Patrick,' bridled Crispin, 'how dare—' A glare from Mel silenced him.

'But he's kind of got a point. If we trespassed where we shouldn't have, we didn't mean to. If you let us go we'll just go. I mean, we could be out of here in, like, seconds. Sooner. Right now. We don't want to cause you any problems.'

'You're not causing *us* problems, love,' grinned Cooper. 'Picking you up makes a change from having to duck and dive round those bloody alien bastards. Haven't landed 'em a knockout blow yet, but when Coop gets a chance there'll be no stopping him. When Coop sees an opening, *blam*.' His

175

knuckles grazed Mel's chin but she didn't jerk away. She didn't even flinch.

'Are you finished?' she said.

'What did you mean,' Jessica wondered, 'you hope they pick Crispin? Who's they? And to do what?'

'*They* is *you*, Jessica Lane,' said Cooper. 'You have to pick one of your little group to be your champion.'

'What for?' Richie said with dread.

'To fight me. To take me on. In the ring. Seconds out, round one, all that shit. Oh yes, and Coop is the King of the Ring, undefeated. The contenders go down. See, we can't just let you leave. That's not the way things are done around here.'

Mel felt her heart sinking. 'So how exactly *are* things done around here, Cooper?'

'You step on to our turf, even by accident, we take that as a challenge to the Kings of the Ring, and Cooper, he never shirks a challenge.' In fact, he seemed to be growing increasingly enthusiastic about the prospect. 'One of you is gonna have to pull the gloves on and fight old Coop for the sake of the rest.'

'What if all of us refuse?' Mel said.

Cooper winked. 'Then all of you die. We gotta make sure no-one messes us around, see. We gotta show we mean business. But don't get too depressed. If your champion wins and Coop goes down, undefeated no more, then all of you live. Course, that's never happened before, but you get two fighters in the ring and anything's possible . . .'

'Ah, Cooper?' Jessica this time. 'What if our champion loses?'

'Same as if you don't fight at all,' Cooper said. 'You're

176

dead. Them's the rules.' With a final combination of blows which, if the air had been flesh and blood, would surely have laid it flat out, the burly Cooper danced away on his toes. 'He floats like a butterfly. He stings like a bee. Get the ring ready, boys,' he called. 'We've got us a *contest*.'

EIGHT

Travis burst into laughter. It wasn't the reaction he'd expected to give, on his knees as he was and staring up at the business end of a machine gun, but somehow it seemed appropriate. His amusement, bitter, ironic, reverberated between the shells of empty buildings in the dark.

'What's so funny, huh?' the holder of the machine gun demanded.

'*You* are,' Travis accused with his finger. 'Your stupidity is.' His blue eyes blazed without humour. 'Are you really going to murder us in cold blood, just mow us down? Is that really what you think's the best idea with the world in ruins all around us? Is it? And why? Because you reckon you own these streets or something? Because you reckon you're the main men on your pitiful, piss-pathetic scrap of "turf"? Because we're "disrespecting" you by crossing into your territory while trying to stay alive? Great set of priorities. Maybe you should put up a sign warning strangers to keep out – what do you think?'

'I think you'd better keep your smart mouth shut,' counselled the youth with the machine gun. He was Travis's age or perhaps a year older, well built, short-haired and with a scowl that seemed like a permanent condition. The rest of the gang appeared to be looking to him for direction. 'Shut up and stay *down*.'

But Travis was rising to his feet defiantly. 'Or is the problem the fact that we're white? Hmm? Is this a little racism you've got going on here to compensate for injustices in the old world? Well, you heard the one about two wrongs not making a right?'

'I *said*—' threatened the teenager with the scowl.

'Because let me tell you, seeing as you're obviously too bloody *dense* to have worked this out for yourselves, the only white skins you might want to resent now belong to the Scytharene. The aliens. You might have seen them. They travel in spaceships and they're kind of keen on slavery. Now *that's* something you should know about. You want a closer look? It won't take you too far out of your way. The aliens are maybe a mile from here in all directions – and they're moving in. They could be here tomorrow and they might just want to dispute who these streets belong to, and the whole damn city besides. You gonna tell *them* they need to learn respect?'

'It won't matter to you what we tell the aliens, man. You'll be past caring.' The youth with the scowl prodded Travis's chest with the machine gun.

Travis knocked the weapon away. 'And you're clearly past listening. Don't you get it? Kids shouldn't be pointing guns at other kids. Kids aren't the enemy. The aliens are. Kids – every single human being left alive – should be coming together to fight them. We should be standing side by side to defeat them and save what's left of our world. That's what we should be doing, "man", you and us together. But hey, if the truth's too much for you to handle, then do the Scytharene dirty work for them. Go ahead. Shoot me. I can't get away.' This time Travis seized the barrel of the gun and held it to his chest. 'Go on, if you really want to. Kill me. I *dare* you.'

'Travis, no!' Cries from Linden, Antony and Ruth as they too now scrambled to stand. The gang grabbed them as they did, kept them from joining Travis. Linden struggled but to no avail.

'You know, my friend,' the scowler was considering, 'I am sorely tempted.'

He and Travis were close, the length of the barrel apart. Their gazes were locked on to each other like gunsights, Travis's blue, the other's brown, both piercing, both intense and strong in self-belief, and in the battle of wills between them neither blinked or flinched or looked away.

'I am *seriously* tempted.'

'Then do it or back off.'

'The Phantoms *never* back off.'

'There's always a first time, Dwayne.' The teenager to the scowler's right laid his hand on the machine gun and eased it downwards.

'What the hell are you doing, Danny?' Scowler protested, though without true anger in his voice.

'I'm saving you from making a mistake and I'm saving *this* guy's life. I think he's got a point.' The boy called Danny was a year or two younger than his fellow Phantom, longer-haired and milder-featured, perhaps as likely to smile as to scowl. Other than that, the two teenagers looked very similar.

They didn't, however, appear to share the same ideas. 'Yeah, Danny, you *think*,' complained Scowler. 'That's all you do. I'm the one who makes the decisions round here. I'm the one who acts.'

'You're the one who assumes everyone's an enemy, Dwayne,' the younger teenager pointed out, 'whether they are or not. A *word*.'

His features still wearing the expression that came naturally, Dwayne nonetheless signalled to the rest of the Phantoms to let Travis's companions go. He turned aside to converse with Danny.

'Oh, Trav!' Linden flung her arms around him. 'What did you think you were doing? I really thought he was going to shoot you.'

'Got a death wish on the quiet, Travis?' Antony said with a weak smile.

'Pointed out a few home truths, that's all.' With Linden wrapped round him, Travis extended his hand to Antony who took it, but briefly and without the warmth that had once characterised their relationship. 'Didn't you know? The truth always wins out in the end.'

'Well it was touch and go there for a while,' Antony said.

'I'm glad we're safe,' Ruth Bell whispered in his ear. 'I'm glad *you're* safe, Antony. Don't take risks. Let Travis do that.'

'Shut up, Ruth,' frowned Antony.

'Shouldn't we get out of here?' Linden breathed to Travis. The Phantoms' attention just now seemed focused more on Dwayne and Danny than on the four of them. 'We could make a run for it.'

'I don't think we'd get too far. We have to convince these guys we're on the same side.'

They'd soon know whether they had. Dwayne was approaching them again, Danny at his right shoulder. Travis hoped that the scowl did not necessarily signify bad news.

'You're coming with us,' Dwayne glowered.

Progress. 'That's good,' Travis said, 'but—'

'But one step out of line and bang, you hear me?' Mock-firing the machine-gun.

So progress, yes. But not much.

'No.'

'No?'

'You got cloth ears, Morticia? *No.*'

'But Richie, you have to. You're the only one of us with a chance.'

'A *chance*, Jessica, ain't bloody good enough.' Richie crossed his arms defensively, turned away from Jessica. Her bewildered but kind of recriminating expression was reminding him uncomfortably of the kitten from next door after he'd kicked it on those mornings when he could be bothered to go to school. 'Find some other sucker to end up with his neck broken in that bloody boxing ring.'

'Sadly, Richie,' sighed Mel, 'we don't have an unlimited number of "suckers", as you so deftly put it, to choose from.' She glanced around the lamp-lit room where they were incarcerated, the room that had once functioned as an office for the gym and whose door was presently locked and guarded, its single small, high window barred. 'I count five.'

'Good for you, Morticia. But I ain't the *one.*'

Mel closed her eyes and wished they could stay that way. She'd never realised before the Sickness and the Scytharene that fatigue could come to resemble a physical pain, an ache tormenting her every fibre that had to be endured and managed. If only she could rest. If only she could sleep and be at peace. If only the nightmare she was living wasn't real. But it was. And insane though it was, one of them had to volunteer to face Cooper, pretty much immediately. They'd

182

been given a half-hour deadline to decide and the clock was ticking.

'I thought we'd been through this once already, Richie,' Mel said, 'but if a recap is gonna help . . . It can't be me or Jessie – neither of us are physically powerful enough to match Cooper. Same for Geoffrey, and he's too young besides.'

'If it was a quiz I'd be able to compete,' the younger Paragon said.

'Terrific. So what about Crispie here? He's older than any of us.'

'You surely can't expect *me* to engage in fisticuffs with a shambling brute like Cooper as if I was a common thug.' Crispin shuddered with horror. 'The very thought makes my gorge rise.'

'Yeah, thanks for that.' Mel shook her head dismally. 'We have to rely on you, Crispin, the Kings may as well save time and shoot us in the head right now. Which is what they're gonna be doing anyway unless you find some guts from somewhere, Richie.'

'Travis would have volunteered,' commented Jessica pointedly.

And didn't Richie just know it. *Naughton.* Oh yes, Naughton would have had his hand in the air bleating 'me, me, me' without even having to be asked. Naughton would take it as an honour to be beaten to a pulp by Cooper for the greater good. And no doubt Naughton would be proud of Richie, admiring of him at long last if he put himself on the line for the others, made that sacrifice, was selfless, even – *especially* – if he got the shit kicked out of him for it. But Richie had turned his back on Travis Naughton and all he stood for, hadn't he?

'I'm not your precious Travis,' he loured.

'Don't we know it,' Mel responded. 'You're Richie Coker, a selfish, cowardly shit. You always have been and you always will be.'

'Shut your face, Morticia,' Richie growled half-heartedly. What did she know?

'No, I won't, and you'll be glad that I won't, Richie, when you hear what I've got to say. *I'll* fight Cooper.'

'What? *You?*' Richie was startled.

Jessica was shocked. 'Mel, no. You can't.'

'Someone's got to. We're dead for sure otherwise.' And she couldn't let anything happen to Jessica. That imperative would keep her alive, help her find some way to outwit and outfight the boxer. 'I've seen *Million Dollar Baby* and those *Karate Kid* films, picked up a few moves. Wax on, wax off. I can take Cooper.'

'You *can't.*' Jessica appealed not to Mel but to Richie. 'Richie, *tell* her.'

'You are being even dumber than usual, Morticia.'

'As if *you* care,' derided Mel.

Her contempt hurt Richie, but not as much as the truth. 'Shit,' he muttered. Because he *did* care. It seemed he was only capable of realising it now, at the moment of crisis. He *cared* what happened to Mor— Mel Patrick. He cared what happened to pretty Jessica Lane. Not because he fancied them. Not because he wanted to get inside their knickers. But because they were his friends. Because they were important to him. Because they mattered more than he did. 'Listen' – he tried to drive his feelings away, to step back from the dangerous place they were leading him – 'these bloody Kings of the Ring, they're not serious, are they? They're not actually

184

gonna kill us whether someone fights bloody Cooper or not, are they?'

'Oh, I think they are,' piped up Geoffrey Thomas brightly.

'Who asked you, freak-features?' Richie snapped.

As the key turned in the lock. They heard it. As the door swung open. They saw it. *And* the group of armed Kings who entered, grinning, anticipating splendid entertainment – of one kind or another.

Shit, swore Richie deep inside himself. *Shitshitshit*.

'Who is it, then?' came the question.

Mel opened her mouth to speak. 'M—'

A hand on her shoulder, surprisingly gentle, silenced her. 'Sorry, Morticia, Cooper'll snap you in two like a twig.' Somebody else stepped forward. 'It's me. I'm the one,' said Richie Coker.

The Phantoms had made their home in a building whose open-plan offices would never again resound with the gossip of working life, the complaints about missed promotions, the exorbitant cost of living in the city and the ordeal of commuting, the praise and flattery of superiors to their faces and the carping and criticising behind their backs. It was an incongruous residency for the gang in some ways: very few of its members would have been likely to find themselves in this or a similar environment under the system that had prevailed in the old world – unless they were mopping the floors, of course. Which was why politicians had always secretly been happy for gang culture to exist: it helped keep the poor in their place.

Almost every square inch of available space was occupied by a kid or a group of kids and their scant belongings:

blankets, sleeping bags, lamps, cans of food and bottles of drink, here a book or a magazine and there, sometimes, among the younger children, a forlorn cuddly toy. Danny and Dwayne conducted Travis as leader of the newcomers to a private room where they could talk. The others were being held under guard on the main office floor, and though Danny was no longer armed, Dwayne hadn't let go of his machine-gun for a second.

'My brother isn't very trusting,' said Danny.

'My brother's *too* damned trusting,' said Dwayne.

Dwayne and Danny Randolph. Dwayne seemed pretty much the Phantoms' undisputed leader; his younger brother's role seemed more complex. Like Jiminy Cricket to Pinocchio, Travis thought. If he could reach Danny, he could reach Dwayne.

'Sit down,' Danny Randolph gestured to him, turning up the light of an oil lamp on the desk.

'But don't make yourself too comfortable,' Dwayne cautioned.

Travis grunted. 'With your gun still looking eager to provide me with some extra ventilation, that's hardly going to be likely, is it?'

'We're sorry about the hostility earlier, Travis,' Danny said, settling into a chair on the opposite side of the desk.

'No we ain't.' Dwayne preferred to stand, just behind Travis. 'We ain't sorry 'bout nothing. We don't take chances. Not with anyone who ain't one of us.'

'How do you define "one of us", Dwayne?' Travis challenged. 'A survivor? Someone who wants to live? Someone who wants to fight the Scytharene, maybe? Or do you just mean someone who happens to be black?'

'Skin matters, man. Don't give me that shit that it don't. Only the world's winners and wealthy ever say that, 'cause money matters more than skin, and I don't reckon most of 'em believe it anyway, but it makes 'em sound good. Where we come from, the colour of your skin is the first thing people see, and for most of 'em it's the only thing. Where we come from, skin is destiny, man. There ain't no getting away from that.'

'Where you come from, Dwayne,' Travis said, 'no longer exists. Where I come from no longer exists either. The Sickness changed the world. We've got to change with it.'

'People don't change,' Dwayne retorted. 'They only say they do. Let me tell you something, Travis, something me and my brother don't tell many people. Our dad got beaten up by racist skinhead thugs when we were small. He was minding his own business, walking down the street where he lived in broad daylight in this wonderful multicultural country of ours – you know the one, where things can only get better – and these four bastards jump out at him and they kick the shit out of him. Yeah, and they're calling our dad nigger and black bastard and that, our *dad*, and when they get bored they just leave him there lying on the ground in a pool of blood and they run away laughing. *Laughing*. Never caught, of course. Maybe they joined the police force when they got older.'

'No,' said Travis with feeling. 'That's not true.' There'd been good men in the police force he'd known. His father. Uncle Phil. Men who'd made a stand for what was right regardless of the consequences. Men who'd put their lives on the line for the greater good. Men who, in some cases, had lost them.

187

Dwayne might have seen something of that in Travis's eyes as the white boy turned to face him, because all of a sudden there seemed to be uncertainty in his. 'Yeah, well, maybe they didn't do that, but it don't matter 'cause the point I'm making is, you reckon bastards like *that'll* change? So the Sickness will have killed 'em and I hope they suffered, but anyone who was a racist bastard before, you reckon they're not still racist bastards *now*? You reckon black kids don't still have to stand up for each other, don't still have to be prepared to fight for their rights? Our dad, his body recovered from that beating, eventually, but his mind never did. He was never the same. He was beaten *inside*, you know? And you never get over that. When he died I was ten years old. At eleven I was out on the streets with the Phantoms. At twelve I was tooled up and we were out there every night, looking after our own, making the streets our own, doing what the law didn't do and protecting our own kind – and anyone on our turf who shouldn't be there, we'd teach 'em respect, in *pain*. Might be aliens now – Scytharene, did you call 'em? – but nothing really changes. Sickness and Scytharene or not, the world is still full of bastards.'

'With one or two exceptions, Dwayne,' Danny revised.

'One or two, maybe.' His brother made the concession grudgingly.

'Some people you can trust. Some people you can rely on, black or white. I believe that. Why we're talking, Travis, is so we can decide whether you're one of them or not. Dwayne thinks you and your friends might be spies from the Cutters or the Hardcore.'

'The who?' Travis shrugged. 'Never heard of them. Sound like bad punk rock bands or something.'

'They're neighbouring gangs,' Danny said. 'Rival gangs.'

'Don't tell me you don't know that,' Dwayne snorted. 'Everybody round here knows that.'

'We're not from round here,' said Travis.

'So what are you *doing* here, then?'

'Looking for a way to strike back at the Scytharene.' Though Travis was not yet prepared to divulge details. To Danny Randolph on his own he might have done, but he couldn't yet be sure of Dwayne.

The suspicion seemed mutual. 'Strike back? Yeah, right. So what part of town *are* you from?'

'Actually, we're from out of town.' Travis explained how his group had arrived in London and been separated. Both Danny and Dwayne appeared impressed by the body count Travis's people had accumulated, but the Phantoms had encountered no wanderers fitting the others' descriptions.

'Maybe another gang's got them,' Danny said. 'Since the Sickness and the death of the adults, London's fragmented, been kind of smashed into little pieces. It's not one city any more but a patchwork of territories staked out by gangs like ours, all at odds with each other, fighting, feuding, constantly in conflict. Not good, really, with the aliens advancing street by street, all the time forcing the gangs back and into closer contact with one another.'

Travis leaned forward on his chair. 'Maybe you should think about getting closer still. Combining. Uniting to confront the Scytharene.'

'I've sometimes wondered if we could,' Danny said dreamily, distantly. 'I've hoped. If it was possible—'

'It ain't possible,' broke in Dwayne hastily. 'It's bullshit, man. But you even suggesting the gangs join forces proves you ain't lying about comin' from out of town, Travis. Only someone who don't understand London would say that with a straight face. See, London works just like the old world. Nothing changes.'

'I think what Dwayne is trying to say,' Danny took over, 'is that this wasn't much of a *united* kingdom even before the Sickness, was it? The country lost its shared sense of purpose a long time ago. Politicians too afraid or too embarrassed or too cynical to propose a common British identity simply gave up on the idea and left us with nothing more than a competing mishmash of so-called "communities". The Muslim community. The gay community. The generally hard-done-by community. None of them interested in the country as a whole, just in pushing their own, self-serving little agendas. And it's the same now with the gangs. We've all segregated ourselves from each other. All-black gangs like ours – I admit it. We're no better than anyone else. All-white gangs like the Cutters. Muslim gangs hiding out in mosques. Christian gangs holed up in churches. The Sisters, feminists only. Gangs of kids from this street. Gangs of kids from that street. We live in a divided, irreconcilable society and there's no point in pretending otherwise.'

'Which is why you can't afford to care about anyone but your own kind,' said Dwayne.

'But if everyone thinks like that, Dwayne,' Travis protested, 'nothing *will* ever change. Somebody's got to make the first move, take the first step, whatever. Take a chance. Reach out to the other groups, *try* to unite them.'

'Who's gonna be bloody stupid enough to do that?' Not Dwayne Randolph, evidently. 'Reach out to some of those bastards and you'll get your hand chopped off.'

'It might not be easy, Dwayne,' said Travis. 'It might not be safe. But it'd be *right*. And to be more pragmatic about it, with the Scytharene breathing down your necks, the only chance any of your London gangs have got of avoiding a slave camp is to unite and fight as one.'

'Yeah, yeah. Thank you, bloody Winston Churchill.' Dwayne shifted his weight uncomfortably. 'But you might have more to worry about than the damned aliens, man.'

'Trigger finger getting itchy again?' Travis said.

'There's a gang Danny didn't tell you about. The Scavvies. Scavengers who live underground, in the tube stations, in the tunnels. Guess they started going down there 'cause they thought it was safe in the dark. Now they only come up at night – for food.'

Danny winced. 'And they seem to have developed some unpleasant eating habits. Not too many stray animals in this part of town, and quite a few unexplained human disappearances as well.'

'Wherever you go,' warned Dwayne, 'steer clear of the tube.'

'Wherever we go?' Travis seized on the Phantom's words eagerly. 'Does that mean you're letting us leave?'

'*I* certainly don't see you as spies or a threat,' said Danny. 'Dwayne?'

His brother shrugged noncommittally.

'And giving us advice, too, Dwayne,' Travis pursued. 'Doesn't that qualify as helping those who aren't your own kind?' Danny laughed. 'Maybe some things change after all. Maybe some people do.'

Dwayne Randolph scowled. 'Don't push your luck. You

might as well stay here the night now. Tomorrow, I don't care what the hell you do.'

But Travis didn't believe him.

He was in deep shit now. Richie groaned inwardly as two members of the Kings of the Ring bundled him unceremoniously towards the raised and rope-framed structure that had given them the second half of their name. Up to his eyeballs in the brown stuff. He glanced down at himself, the boots one size too small, the shorts one size too baggy, the fraying tan boxing gloves that were kind of like mufflers on his hands, his bare chest that at least looked stronger and more powerful than its owner currently felt. He wished he could have kept his baseball cap on. But he'd only got himself to blame for this. Putting himself on the line for others? What the bloody hell had he been thinking of? He should have just let Morticia get on with it and while Cooper was giving her a hiding sneaked out the back. He'd have played it like that in the old days.

Too late now.

The gang hooted and roared with sadistic anticipation when they saw him, every one of them from eighteen to eight years old crowded round the ring, pressing forward and straining their necks to be sure of a good view once the massacre started. They didn't expect it to last long. Limbering up, gloved and in shorts as well, Cooper was waiting for him.

Richie turned to one of his escorts. 'Listen, we couldn't just put the fight back a bit, could we? I kind of need the men's room.' There might be a window he could squeeze through.

'It's bad luck for a fighter to take his gloves off once he's

192

put 'em on until after the bout,' said the King. 'You can go if you like, but we'd have to help you out – and put you back in again.'

'You know what? I think I'll wait.'

The mob parted to let him through. Fists and fingers jabbed at him, partly in rage, partly in ridicule. He was jostled as he passed, back and shoulders slapped. Faces thrust close to his then jerked away again like punches thrown at an opponent, and on some of them was hate, and on others a kind of jest, on all of them an appetite for violence and on none of them an iota of support for Richie Coker. Where were Morticia and Jessica? Didn't they have the nerve to watch him, the faith that he could win? Maybe *they* were off doing a runner somewhere. He couldn't blame them if they were.

Richie remembered seeing a picture at school of French guys with frilly shirts and wigs on being cheered to the guillotine: they hadn't looked too happy about it. He knew how they felt.

And why did they call the bloody thing a ring anyway? It was square.

'Up you go, fodder,' grinned his two guards, shoving.

'And the challenger steps into the ring.' Richie could hear Cooper supplying his own commentary as he danced from one side of the ring to the other. Didn't the ugly fat bastard ever shut up? 'But Cooper's prepared. Cooper's focused. The undefeated champion of the Kings of the Ring is ready to do a job of work tonight and the contender is going down.'

Which probably wasn't the ideal moment for Richie, emerging through the ropes, to begin to ask 'What happens n—?' What happened n— was that Cooper charged forward and clubbed him around the side of the head with one gloved and considerable fist. Richie didn't hear birds singing as he crashed to the canvas, just a burst of enthusiastic approval from the crowd and the belated jangle of the ringside bell to announce the commencement of hostilities. Through dazed eyes he saw Cooper strut away with his hands held triumphantly high: 'And the champion strikes first. A devastating right poleaxes the contender and leaves him in no doubt that Cooper is not an opponent to be taken lightly.'

'Goddamn . . .' Richie felt the bruise swelling on his cheek.

'Get up. Richie, get up.'

'*Richie.*'

Morticia. And Jessie. And those two freaky Paragons as well, Crispie not looking too healthy. They *were* here. Practically pinned to the side of the ring. The chicks looking worried. He couldn't have that.

''Sokay. I'm just lulling him into a false sense of security.' With a wince of pain, clambering to his feet again.

'Richie, be careful.' Morticia screaming above the tumult of the horde. 'No rounds. No referee. No rules. That's what they said.'

'And the contender's up once more, but Cooper's moving in . . .'

No surprise attacks, either. Not now, anyway. Not with Cooper broadcasting his every move in advance. At least this time Richie got his gloves up to protect his face. Cooper switched his assault to the other boy's body, pummelling his ribs, driving the air from Richie's lungs in agonising explosions. 'The champion goes to work with a lethal combination. And the crowd goes wild.'

Richie swung; Cooper swayed. Richie missed but the

momentum of his punch lurched him forward. Cooper slammed both fists down in a piledriver blow on the back of Richie's head. The canvas slapped him in the face for good measure as the two of them renewed their acquaintance. Richie was sure the ring had been stationary when he climbed inside. How come it was whirling in giddying circles now? Maybe *that* was why it was called a ring. He thought of the little kids he used to terrorise when he was small himself, them cowering on the roundabout in the playground, clinging on for dear life as he pushed it faster and faster, and them crying out feebly, 'Richie, please, make it stop! Make it stop!'

He'd make it stop now. The bastard Cooper wouldn't get the better of Richie Coker.

He squeezed his eyes shut, pushed himself up from the floor. The world reeled sickeningly but the pain was that of a dislocated joint being slotted back in place: once it was over, everything was returned to normal.

His legs were unsteady but he could stand on them. His sight was blurred but he could see. And through the ocean dashing itself against the rocks somewhere in his inner ear, 'And the challenger thinks he can still take the fight to Cooper but it's clear what the champion thinks about that. In three words, what an arsehole.'

The blows rained in again but Richie resisted valiantly – *valiantly*: now there was a Naughton word – soaking up the punishment, defending himself as best he could, lashing out at the reddish shape looming in front of his damaged vision, the lump that was Cooper, even making contact. He felt some of his punches striking home. And why not? Richie Coker wasn't a slouch in a brawl. He could fight, retaliate. He had all the right muscles in all the right—

Cooper's boot thudded between his legs with blistering agony. *That* was below the belt. Richie's hands dropped instinctively to the injured area. *No rules.* Exposing his nose and jaw to Cooper's hammering gloves. A bright spray of red from lip and nostrils splashed the canvas like Jackson Pollock in his prime as for the umpteenth time Richie went down.

Cooper wasn't letting up this time. 'The champion goes in for the kill. Cooper gives Coker the *boot*.' In his stomach, again and again. The Kings of the Ring howling like animals. Blood smearing from Richie's face over the floor of the ring. Richie himself curling into a ball, a coward's retreat to the womb. No thought of retaliation now. No resistance. It was all over. He was beaten. He was beaten and he didn't care. He just had to escape, to get away from Cooper's crunching kicks to his belly, his back, his head. (He probably didn't need *all* those teeth, anyway.) He had to get out. 'And Cooper has the contender on the run. And the crowd goes wild.'

Not on the run. On the crawl. Richie heaved himself by his elbows across the ring, had this vague notion that if he could make it to the ropes, slither underneath them like the snake some had always said he was, the beating would stop. If only the beating would—

He flailed forward, grabbed the bottom rope with one gloved hand.

Mel was the other side of it, and Jessie. They were gazing at him imploringly. They were beseeching him, pleading with him, urging him on: 'Richie, get up.' (Easy for *them* to say.) 'Richie, don't *give* up. Please. You can't. You mustn't. Stand. Fight back. Please.'

196

It was like they were depending on him.

'And it can't end yet. The crowd want more. Cooper wants to *give* them more.' Seizing Richie's legs and pulling. Richie struggling to hold on to the rope.

More than that. Struggling to hold on to the belief in the two girls' eyes. They needed him. They were willing him on. They were on his side, maybe for the first time ever. They were looking to him as they looked, when things were bad, to Naughton.

And Richie felt a great surge of emotion inside him that he couldn't quite identify. It might have been pride. It might have been courage or determination. It might even have been heroism. He didn't know. He'd never experienced it before. But two things he *did* know. First, it wasn't submission. Second, it felt good.

Cooper yanked him from the ropes, dragged him into the middle of the ring by his boots, and the mob cheered because they thought Cooper had managed it through strength, but Richie was smiling because he'd let go of the rope by choice. He was smiling at Mel and Jessica to let them know he wasn't giving in. Naughton would never have given in.

'Should Cooper stamp on the challenger's face?' Working his followers into a frenzy. 'Let him hear you. *Should Cooper stamp on the challenger's face?*'

The general consensus seemed to be that yes, Cooper should, and quickly, and often.

Richie breathed deeply, let his battered body relax just for a second, gather its strength. What was happening was what he'd wanted for a long time. Here and now, he could match Travis, be equal to Travis, and not in a sleazy, shameful way, seducing his girlfriend. In a good way. By fighting for his friends. The expressions on Mel and Jessica's faces told him that. But better still, here and now he could *exceed* Travis. Naughton had a weakness. Naughton could only ever fight fair. Travis would never beat Cooper. *No rules.* But Richie Coker could. Richie Coker could fight dirty with the best of them – and the worst.

And he bloody well would.

'And Cooper lifts his foot to bring it smashing down on the contender's—'

Richie swept his opponent's other leg from under him. Cooper, startled by both the swiftness of the apparently defeated challenger's counterattack and the irresistible force of gravity on his own not insignificant bulk, dropped like dead weight. The ring shook with the impact of Cooper on canvas.

'And the crowd went *wild,* you bastard.' Richie scrambled to his feet, noting that the boxer had fallen heavily, awkwardly, his right arm twisted painfully under him. The crowd had in fact pretty much as one gasped in horror at what they'd witnessed, and there was a moment of shocked immobility around the ring, as if the scene had suddenly been freeze-framed for posterity. Cooper had *gone down.*

But he was getting *up* again. Richie had to press home his brief advantage. He darted to one of the corner posts where a kid nominally acting as timekeeper was standing with the bell in his hand and, in common with the rest of the Kings right now, his mouth hanging open slackly. It wasn't his mouth Richie was interested in. He'd snatched the bell from the kid's grasp before the boy could protest. It was an old-fashioned bell, metal with a wooden handle, the kind teachers had once used to ring for the end of playtime.

It could double up as a club just as easily.

Richie whirled, and with a massive swipe of his arm cracked the bell against Cooper's temple. 'Time to ring the changes, fat boy.' Struck him on the other temple on the return arc. 'Ding bloody dong.' Cooper staggered groggily, blood seeping from his gashed forehead into his eyes. For the first time, his defence faltered.

Richie nutted him. Crude but always effective. Blood burst from Cooper's nose. It was probably used to it, it had been broken before. 'And *this* is for earlier.' Boot to groin in one simple, satisfying movement.

'Cooper comes under . . . attack . . . but he's still . . . champion . . .' Reeling drunkenly, swinging blindly.

'Yeah, well, you got yourself a bit of a public, I can see that.' Richie clutched at the off-balance Cooper's arm and tugged hard. 'Why don't you go meet them?' His muscles straining, he propelled the heavier boy towards the ropes, *through* the ropes.

If the gang members crammed closest to the ring had stayed where they were, Cooper might have enjoyed a softer landing. They didn't, so he didn't. He kind of bounced on the timber floor. Blood kind of bubbled from his lips. He looked very red indeed now.

'And the gloves are well and truly off.' Richie casting his aside, leaping from the ring to thump on to Cooper's back. Not one of the Kings attempted to stop him or to interfere with the now inevitable course of the contest in any way. They had their own sense of honour, it seemed.

'No referee, I'll do the count myself.' Richie rolled Cooper over as his punches punctuated his words. 'One-a, two-a, three-a.' As silence descended on the Kings of the Ring, their champion undefeated no longer. 'Four-a, five-a.' Unconscious, though, probably yes.

'Richie, stop, you'll kill him.' Jessica.

'There's a thought. Six-a, seven-a.'

'No, keep hitting him. Hit him hard. Look at the blood. We could probably clone him from that.' That freaky bloody Geoffrey.

'*Richie.*'

'Eight-a.'

Morticia. 'You've proved your point. Stop now.'

'Nine-a. You reckon? One more. And *ten*.' A final thud on the red meat of Cooper's face. 'You're out, you bastard. Out for the count. And the winner is' – labouring to his feet, punching both fists to the ceiling despite the pain of his own injuries, throwing his head back – 'Rocky, sorry, *Richie Coker*.'

And, kind of unexpectedly, the crowd went wild.

'Travis, can I have a word?'

It was after midnight. Most of the Phantoms, apart from those on guard duty, had settled down to sleep. Travis and Linden were making themselves as comfortable as possible too, stretching out between a desk and a partition wall. They'd thought Antony had already bedded down.

'Can't it wait until morning?' Travis said with an uncustomary lack of sympathy.

'I'd sooner it didn't.' Antony glanced sheepishly at Linden. 'A private word?'

'Okay, if you must.' Travis stood reluctantly. 'But make it quick, Antony, yeah?'

They picked their way over recumbent bodies to the windows overlooking the street. Beyond, London lay in darkness. There was little to see but, arms crossed, both boys still preferred to stare outside than to look at each other.

'You know, my mother, Travis, when she was still alive, she used to say that you should never let the sun go down on a quarrel. Well, we're too late for the sun, but in the spirit of what she meant, I want to apologise.'

'Just generally or for something in particular?'

'For the tension there's been between us lately. For the infantile arguments we've been having. It's all my fault and I'm sorry.'

Travis glanced sideways at Antony with interest and renewing affection. It was difficult to stay mad with him for long, however valid the reason. 'Why do you say that?'

'Because it's true. This is hard for me to admit' – indeed, it had taken Antony the hours since their seizure by the Phantoms to muster the courage to broach the subject with Travis – 'but I fear I was beginning to resent you, to be jealous of you. You were leader. You'd become leader by common consent, almost by right, and yet before you arrived on the scene, at Harrington, *I* was in charge. It was me who appointed you Deputy Head Boy, remember that?' Antony smiled wistfully. 'It seems so long ago now. Anyway, part of me still wanted to take over again and that's what's been creating the friction between us – from my side, at any rate. At the Enclave before we found out about the Paragon Project. Even more idiotically, at the mini-mart.'

'You said part of you wan*ted* to take over again, Antony,' Travis pointed out. 'Past tense. Has something changed?'

Antony sighed. 'Not so much changed as been clarified. The way you stood up to this Dwayne Randolph, Travis, the whole gang. Impressive stuff.' He turned to his companion

201

too now and it was admiring envy in his eyes rather than bitter jealousy. 'I couldn't have done that, acted like that. I *didn't*. But you did, with your defiance, your courage, your strength of purpose . . .'

'Steady, Antony,' Travis laughed. 'I'm with Linden.'

'No. It just made me see, made me realise that a true leader needs to possess qualities I don't have. Self-belief. Vision. The ability to inspire. The only genuine ability I have is to organise.'

'Don't knock it. Communities need organisers,' Travis pointed out warmly. He let his arms drop to his sides.

'They do. That's true. But first and foremost they need inspirational, clear-sighted leadership. And among us, Travis, you're the only one who can provide that.' Antony clasped his hands behind his back. 'I can't compete with you and I no longer intend to. It was foolish of me to try, wrong for the group. I'm sorry.'

'Well, if you need to apologise, Antony,' Travis said ruefully, 'so do I. We should never have allowed something so important to become like a competition in the first place.'

'No disagreement there. Though I think I might have accepted reality a little sooner if Crispin hadn't kept encouraging me to believe that I deserved to be leader more than you.'

'What?' The blue gaze sharpened suspiciously.

'But it wasn't good form to denigrate my contribution to the group even so, Travis.'

'And again: what? You actually heard me, did you, Antony, slagging you off?'

Antony frowned. 'Well, no. Not *actually*. But Crispin told me. . .'

'You want to hear what Crispin told *me*?' Travis shook his head in disbelief. 'That *you* were going around criticising *me* behind my back.'

'But I wasn't – I wouldn't. So that's why you said what you did at the mini-mart.' Antony regarded Travis earnestly. 'But it's not true.'

'Neither's the idea that I spend all my time putting you down. You're my friend, Antony.'

'But that means . . .' Aghast at the truth.

'Exactly. That's what it means. The inestimable Dr Allerton has been playing us off against each other, dividing no doubt in the hope of conquering. Leadership candidate number three.'

'The frightening thing is,' Antony said, 'he almost succeeded.'

'But he didn't.'

'We've been fools, playing into his hands.'

'Not any more. Here's *my* hand.' Offering it. 'I think you overestimate me, Antony, but to use your terms anyway, any community that's going to survive needs inspiration *and* organisation, working together.'

'Then that's what we'll provide.' Antony gripped Travis's hand firmly. 'Let's not fall out any more, Travis. Over anything.'

'We won't,' Travis vowed. 'And when we finally meet up with Crispin Allerton again, let's make damn sure he knows it.'

Antony felt better having cleared the air with Travis. He lay back on a mattress on the floor with his shoes off and a blanket over him and entertained what was becoming an increasingly absurd notion since the Sickness, that he might actually be able to grab some sleep. If only he could be sure that Jessica was not in danger somewhere. If only she was *here*, ideally, beside him, with her arms around him, but he'd have happily settled for the certainty of her safety. As for the rest, if he did manage to sleep, perhaps he'd dream of her.

Antony never got as far as dreaming.

His eyes were closed, though, when the body slipped under the blanket and snuggled against his. The warm body, the naked body, bare skin touching his clothed form. His eyes popped open again pretty quickly. The body with the female curves.

'Hi,' simpered Ruth Bell.

'Bl . . . bl . . .' If his parents hadn't taught him never to swear, and never *ever* in the presence of girls, Antony would certainly have done so at that precise moment. Instead, in his sudden panic *not* to be in such intimate contact with Ruth Bell in her present state of undress, he jerked violently away, slid off the mattress entirely, and banged his head against the floor for good measure.

It probably wasn't the reaction Ruth had been hoping for.

'What the . . . what do you think you're doing?' Antony blinked as if half in hope that this was after all a dream – or a nightmare – which could be banished without embarrassment by waking.

'Ssh,' Ruth whispered. 'Antony. We don't want everybody looking, do we?'

Everybody? Antony didn't want to look himself. Luckily, the few lamps that remained lit cast only the faintest of glows over the two of them, while the still and huddled shapes scattered across the floor suggested that the rest of the company was in any case more concerned with slumber than shenanigans.

'Come back under the blanket,' Ruth coaxed. 'I thought we could be together tonight.'

'I thought I told you I wasn't interested,' Antony gulped.

'You *said* you were in a relationship with Jessica,' Ruth corrected. 'Well, you're not any more.'

'What do you mean, I'm not any more?' Antony's tone hardened as he began to recover from his initial shock.

'Jessica's dead. Or if she isn't, she's lost like the others. We'll never find them.'

'We will find them.'

'We won't, Antony. Be realistic. You'll never see Jessica again. Statistically, the chances of us—'

'I don't *care* about statistics.' Anger forcing his voice towards dangerous volumes. 'We will find Jessica and we'll find her alive. I don't want you even thinking otherwise.'

Ruth regarded him with bemusement. 'I'm only telling you what's likeliest to have happened. I'm trying to help you, Antony. You shouldn't waste time dwelling on those who are gone. Turn to those who are here. *I'm* here.' Antony could certainly see that as Ruth drew back the blanket; top to toe she was here. 'Surely my body is perfectly acceptable.'

And Antony knew he ought to look away. He *wanted* to look away. But it was difficult, impossible . . .

Ruth giggled, wiggled her hips. 'You see? Don't be embarrassed by your excitement, Antony. It's perfectly natural.'

Antony shook his head. 'Cover yourself up,' he mumbled awkwardly.

Ruth didn't. 'We don't have a choice in these matters,

Antony. Only sentimentalists and fools think we do. Desire is in our genes.'

'I said—'

'And on the subject of jeans, I wonder what else is in yours . . .'

Antony seized Ruth's hand as it reached for him. His parents had taught him never to be violent to a girl either, but he could apologise to their memories later for breaking that injunction. He squeezed Ruth's fingers so hard the knuckles ground together. 'I *said* cover yourself up.' Hissing through gritted teeth.

'Ah, Antony, you're hurting me.'

'I'm *warning* you, Ruth.' Though he did let go of her hand, largely so he could employ both of his to pin her down in the blanket, wrapping it tightly over the contours of her body, making of it a net. 'If you try something like this again, you'll be in real trouble. That's a promise on my honour as Head Boy of the Harrington School. I don't want you. And after this and what you said about Jessica, I don't even like you. You keep your distance from me from now on, Ruth, do you understand? I'll be keeping my distance from you.'

As if to prove his point, Antony promptly jumped to his feet and stalked away across the office floor. Ruth watched him go and there were tears in her eyes. Not of sadness, though. Of rage. She'd offered herself to Antony Clive and he'd refused her. She wasn't used to being refused. A Paragon was never refused anything. Paragons could do whatever they liked and *have* whatever they liked because they were, well, Paragons. Exceptional. Antony Clive was not only stupid and sentimental to reject her advances, but he had no *right* to do that. He ought to pay for it, be punished for it. His behaviour was unreasonable, unacceptable, unforgivable. *Rejection* was unforgivable.

But it was interesting, even so.

Ruth Bell had lived an emotionless kind of life at the Project. Now, however, she sensed mysterious new feelings inside her. That burning pain, for example, could that be jealousy? She'd certainly never experienced it before. She found it stimulating in a masochistic sort of way. And that bitterness, that darkness that seemed to be rising in her, perhaps that was hatred. Vengefulness. Almost definitely it was.

Naked and alone, Ruth Bell savoured the mysterious, compelling emotions growing within, wallowed and luxuriated in the passions they were beginning to generate. When they fully came to birth, she wondered where they'd lead her.

'How do I look?' asked Richie nervously.

'Well, put it this way,' said Mel, unable to suppress a grin completely, 'it's just as well you weren't exactly Orlando Bloom in the first place. But never mind, it's what you are inside that counts.' She patted his bare chest above the heart.

'Thanks a lot, Morticia. I *don't* think.'

'Your cuts and bruises'll soon heal, Richie,' Jessica chipped in encouragingly, 'and Mel's right. If it wasn't for you, we probably wouldn't be here.'

Here was the former office at the Kenton Gym that had served as their cell before last night's fight. With the addition of some rudimentary bedding, it had resumed that role until now, the grey light of dawn peering in at the window but perhaps understandably seeming reluctant to enter.

Crispin, with Geoffrey bobbing by his side like Igor to his Frankenstein, looked on critically as the two girls dabbed at

207

Richie's wounds with liniment. 'I'm sure we all appreciate your pugilistic endeavours, Coker,' he observed, as though speaking on behalf of everyone but himself, 'but they do appear to have been in vain, do they not?'

'What are you on about, Crispin?' sighed Mel exasperatedly. 'As if we really care.' She screwed the cap back on the bottle of ointment she was holding. The Kings of the Ring had been unexpectedly generous in supplying them with treatments for Richie's battered body. 'There you go, Big Guy, you can put your sweatshirt back on now.'

'Thought you chicks might prefer me with it off.' Richie flexed his biceps ostentatiously.

'I'm taken, I'm afraid, Richie,' Jessica reminded him.

'And I'm trying to get through the day without throwing up,' Mel said. 'So sweatshirt. On.' Richie obeyed, wincing as he stretched his aching limbs. 'And to cap it all.' She handed him his treasured baseball cap.

'Thanks.' Richie perched it tenderly on the top of his head. The chicks might be geeing him along, but he knew he must look a state. Black eye, burst lip, bruised cheek and purpled torso. He *felt* like he was in a state, his body one huge ache. But at least he wasn't suffering like he'd been six hours ago. He was strong. Like Jessie said, he'd get better. There was something driving him now which yesterday and all the days before that there hadn't been, something that would help him overcome his pain, something more powerful than any of the oils the chicks had slapped over him since the fight. He reckoned Naughton would call it self-belief. Richie called it pride.

If only bloody Crispie would stop whingeing. 'You're not listening to me, are you?'

208

'Actually, no.' Morticia really couldn't stand the git, could she? Richie would have laughed if it didn't hurt so much.

'Then you should be. Our lives are still in danger. In case your memory functions have become so addled by loud music and cheap alcohol that you're mentally incapable of remembering, the arrangement with this horde of thugs was that if our challenger defeated their champion, as Coker did indeed put that imbecilic Cooper lout in his place, then we were to go free. We are still under lock and key.'

'Yeah, I know,' Mel said acidly. 'And believe me, I'm enjoying your company just as much as you are mine. But actually, if your memory's got room for more than genetic theory and the history of condescension, Crispin, you'll recall that Cooper only said we'd *live* if we won, and if you had a heart you'd find it's still beating.'

Jessica frowned. 'To be fair to Crispin, Mel, I assumed Cooper meant they'd let us go too.'

There was movement outside the door as someone unlocked it.

'Maybe we'll get a chance to ask him,' Richie said, and in a lower tone: 'So long as he's not after a bloody rematch.'

Flanked by a brace of Kings of the Ring, Cooper limped into the room. He was as much the worse for wear as Richie, if not more so, though oddly he also seemed a lot happier. His smile was like a broken glockenspiel. He was wearing his Tyson T-shirt again and over one shoulder he'd slung an oversized leather belt ornately embellished with silver. One hand held the belt – the other he extended to Richie. 'And the morning after the fight, the fallen champion offers his congratulations to the triumphant challenger.'

'Come again?' said Richie, wondering whether Cooper

wasn't about to switch from boxing to wrestling and throw him if he took his hand. He was aware of Crispin and Geoffrey sidling behind him.

'Shake,' said Cooper. 'Never let it be said that Cooper can't show dignity in defeat. No tricks. Dignity in defeat's all part of the noble art of boxing. You did good, Richie Coker.'

'Yeah. Yeah. Okay.' Richie clasped his former opponent's hand. No tricks – so far. Richie's eyes strayed to the open door. 'Did I do good enough for me and my friends to walk out of here?'

'Oh, no,' tutted Cooper.

'No?' Tensing, Richie snatched his hand away.

'No. You don't want to do that. This is yours too. By right.' Cooper hauled the belt off his shoulder and showed it to Richie. 'Lonsdale belt. In the old world they used to be awarded to boxers who won titles. With the Kings of the Ring, this one still is.'

Jessica couldn't care less about the significance of a Lonsdale belt. 'Cooper, you implied we could leave if Richie won,' she said with a sense of grievance.

'You can, yeah, if you really want to, but maybe you *won't* want to.'

'Why might we not want to put this macho boxing bull-shit behind us as quickly as humanly possible?' wondered Mel.

Cooper was behind *Richie*, buckling the heavy belt around the victor's waist. ''Cause there's one thing you weren't told before the fight 'cause old Coop didn't think he'd get beat. But he did, and now he's just one of the gang again and the Kings of the Ring have found themselves a new champion.'

'And?' prompted Richie.

'You won the fight, Rich. You won the belt. Not only do you get to live, you get to lead. You're the top man around here now. Gang's yours. Cooper bows his head to the new King of the Ring.'

NINE

Before he drifted off to sleep, Travis decided that in the morning he'd let Dwayne and Danny in on the full story behind his group's presence in London, Enclave Zero, the gene transfer virus, everything. Maybe the Phantoms would help them. Maybe they'd found some explosives or something among the materials the army had left behind, dynamite or grenades powerful enough to blast their way into the Enclave if they found a door before they found Crispin. Travis reckoned the brothers could be enrolled in their cause at that level even if working with the other gangs still proved a step too far. Even there, though, he sensed that in time they could be persuaded. Danny was practically a convert already, and Dwayne needed only a push. Travis had taken heart from their earlier discussion. He felt confident that he could provide that final incentive himself, given the chance.

He didn't get the chance.

Dwayne was leaning over him, shaking him roughly. 'Naughton, get your pale arse in gear.'

'What's happened?' Travis sat bolt upright immediately. He was growing used to waking and acting in the same moment. A lie-in was a luxury lost for ever.

'Trav, what's going on?' Linden stirring alongside him.

A grey dawn, leprous light sufficient to read both resolution and fear in Dwayne Randolph's features. A sense of the building vibrating as though afraid itself of what was to come. An awareness of distant engines.

'Scytharene,' Travis said grimly.

'Street patrol says they're on the move and coming this way. Soldiers and ships. Time for you and yours to get the hell out.' Dwayne thrust subjugators into Travis and Linden's hands, tossed her more conventional firearm to Ruth groping from under a blanket nearby. She was clothed, which didn't surprise Travis in the slightest. Apart from their shoes, so were he and Linden.

'Where's Antony?'

'Danny's fetching him.'

Had fetched him. Travis saw the two of them hastening across the office floor, approaching. He also saw confusion and desperation among the Phantoms as their older members barked orders, boys and girls together grabbing guns and rushing to the stairs. The smaller children stayed where they were, huddled together. Some of them started to cry.

'You all right?' Travis checked with Antony, whose subjugator had also been returned to him. The blond boy nodded tersely. 'Then lead us to the front line, Dwayne.'

'No way.' Dwayne's refusal was unexpectedly final. 'You need to get wherever it is you're going while you still can. This is our turf. It's our fight.'

'It'll be your funeral too,' Travis warned. 'You need all the help you can find.'

'Don't bloody tell me what *we* need, man,' glared Dwayne.

'What my brother is trying to say,' Danny arbitrated, 'is that you'll probably help us more by being free to do what you really came to London for. We're not stupid. Nobody

213

with half a brain would come here without a damn good reason. You're not searching for family or friends but we know you're searching for something. I have a feeling it's important for all of us that you find it.'

'You're right, Danny,' Travis said simply. 'It is.'

'Then why are you still here?' snapped Dwayne. 'We can keep the aliens off your tail.'

Briefly, Travis was torn. Part of him wanted to stand and fight. There was always honour in that, even when the cause was hopeless, maybe *especially* when it was hopeless. But another part of him knew that the Phantoms would fall, and that if he and his companions fell with them, there'd be no gene transfer virus and no ultimate triumph of the human race.

So he had no choice in the matter, either. Travis gripped Dwayne Randolph's hand warmly. 'Good luck.'

Sometimes, though, luck couldn't save you. The four teenagers seemed barely to have embarked on their eastwards course towards the Houses of Parliament before the Culler that dominated the sky behind them was deploying the blinding light of its tractor beam. The Phantoms' resistance must already have been ended. The Randolph brothers' territory now belonged to the Scytharene.

'Come on. Quicker,' Travis urged at a run. 'They could be here soon.'

'Trav, what if they keep advancing?' The streets around her seemed like a trap to Linden, with no way out. 'What if they reach Parliament before us? What if this is their final assault on London?'

'Then we'll have to adjust our strategy,' Travis said, 'but right now we'll stick with Plan A. *Run.*'

'I can't. I can't,' bleated an ostentatiously exhausted Ruth.

'Antony' – who was keeping his distance – 'help her.'

Gritting his teeth and unable to decline, Antony took Ruth's hand. He hissed at her: 'There's nothing wrong with you, is there?'

'Not now,' she returned slyly. She and Antony were soon matching Travis and Linden pace for pace.

The Scytharene outstripped all four of them.

Twin battlepods streaked above the street, flying from the east. The teenagers flung themselves down among the corpses of cars while the 'pods passed above them.

'Do you think they spotted us?' Ruth said fearfully.

'If they had, they'd have shot us.' Linden struggled to sound reassuring. 'Wouldn't they?'

'Maybe they're leaving that to their mates,' Travis said.

In the wake of the 'pods, black-armoured warriors on foot, fanning out across the street and proceeding inexorably towards them, dozens of Scytharene, peeling off in groups to enter the buildings, prying even into the vehicles' metal shells.

'Searching for slaves,' Linden whispered.

'Let's reduce their likely find by four.' Travis signalled Antony and Ruth to slink back the way they'd come.

Ruth Bell, however, evidently believed that retreats should be undertaken speedily whatever the circumstances. Without waiting for Antony or the others, she made a wild break for it.

And was seen. A Scytharene shouted. Ruth screamed. Travis swore. Linden and Antony opened fire. And sometimes, maybe luck *could* save you. In the blistering barrage of subjugator blasts from the aliens, it could only have been sheer good fortune that not one of the four teenagers was hit.

Travis didn't intend to hang around to put the theory to further test. 'Let's go!'

Nobody asked where but everybody raced after him. Energy bolts sizzled where they struck vehicles, sparked from pavement and road: it was as if the group was being pursued by angry fireworks. Straight ahead as an option for escape ceased to be viable. More Scytharene, possibly alerted by their comrades to the rear, and the battlepods back again to render futile any direction taken by foot.

Except maybe one.

Desperate times called for desperate measures. Travis clearly remembered what Dwayne Randolph had told him last night about the Scavvies and where they dwelled. But the gaping entrance just yards away to Pimlico underground station was looking undeniably tempting. Darkness and the unknown awaited within. But when what was *known* included the fact that the force of Scytharene closing in on you couldn't fail to shoot you down any second now, the *un*known did have its attractions.

'Tube station,' Travis yelled. 'Now.'

They leapt down the steps into the station's concourse. At least they'd put the battlepods out of the chase but they didn't dare pause because the Scytharene warriors were no doubt still hot on their heels.

Someone had been here recently. Yes, there was darkness, a subterranean darkness of burials and caves, but a row of lamps had been placed on the tiled floor, oil lamps that were still alight and whose guttering yellow flames illuminated the station's payment points and enquiries window, the iron railings and ticket barriers that fenced off the floor space leading to the escalators. Someone had removed a section of the railings. The lamps marked out a path from the outside to the escalators – or from the depths to the surface, the disturbing thought occurred to Travis. *Scavvies*.

'What are those doing here?' Antony was frowning, indicating the lamps.

'Saving our arses.' Travis snatched one up. 'Come on. Take one. One each.'

Obeying, only now did Linden venture anxiously: 'Trav, where are we going?'

'You know where, Lin. We'll lose them in the tunnels.'

'Travis, I can't go down there.' Underlit by the lamp, her face was a mask of terror. 'It'll be pitch black, like entering a grave. I can't do it, Trav.'

'Lin, I know how you feel. I feel that way too. But we have to go down.' The first clatter of boots on steps. 'Or we lose.'

When Linden nodded despite the horror shining in her eyes, Travis loved her more than ever.

'Smash the other lamps,' he said, kicking out at those nearest to him, shattering the glass and extinguishing the light. 'Let's find out whether those red eyes can see in the dark.'

'Antony,' Ruth pleaded as with every lamp blinded blackness pressed ever nearer to them, overwhelming. 'Let me stay close to you. Please.' There was no cunning or hidden agenda in her voice now. Her eyes were wide and staring.

Antony nodded. For once the need was mutual.

The trail of lamps ended at the escalators. Nothing but darkness yawned below; it was like they were standing on the edge of a mineshaft. The foursome might not have found the courage to descend clutching their pitiful glimmers of light, even Travis might have baulked at such an ordeal, but the harsh stridor of Scytharene voices behind them drove them on.

Each teenager uttering a silent prayer, they plunged into the pit.

Travis's mum had always called them moving stairs, but the escalators weren't in motion now, nor ever would be again. The steps were solid and real underfoot, however, and that was good enough when the black void around and above them seemed endless and impalpable. It could have been the universe before creation. It could have been the nothingness of death. Travis breathed harder to remind himself that he was still alive. The flicker of their lamps was the promise of hope.

They reached the bottom of the shaft. Ruth for one sobbed with relief.

'Can't we stay here?' Linden said. 'Just stay where we are – wait for the aliens to lose interest and go. They won't follow us down here. We'll be all right if we just—'

An immeasurable height above them, it seemed, bolder beams of brightness stabbed into the body of the dark, multiplied and slowly descended.

'They've got – they must have lights in their helmets or something,' Antony reasoned.

'Yeah. Well we've got a head start.' Travis backed away from the escalators, which was just as well.

Flashes of subjugator blasts scorched through the black like meteors at midnight, struck the stairs and the walls of the shaft, ads displayed there for shows that had staged their final performance. The Scytharene were firing blind but they obviously still meant business.

The teenagers fled into the nearest tunnel. Its roundness

revealed by the lamps made it appear almost organic, but there was nothing natural about their predicament. To Linden, the darkness was like a dreadful flood that had submerged and would drown her. 'Trav, if we ever get out of here, remind me never to take up pot-holing.' She tried to laugh.

Ruth Bell screamed. 'There's something on me! *There's something on me!*' Dropping her lamp.

In the second it hit the floor they saw the rats, coiling around Ruth's feet like furry lengths of rope. Then the lamp shattered and darkness smothered the vermin again. But they were still there. Linden now felt claws scurrying over her feet, the loathsome rodent bodies rubbing against her ankles, squirming between her legs. She couldn't help but cry out as well. She wanted to hear Travis calm the situation with a regulation 'don't panic' speech but he was too busy kicking at invisible rats himself and the words that spat revoltedly from his lips tended to contain only four letters.

'A light! I can see another light!' Antony blurred past her. Linden looked where he was going and he was right. And more. . . Human shapes crossing the tunnel up ahead, glimpsed so fleetingly they might have been figments of an overwrought imagination, or ghosts. 'People. Travis, there are other people down here . . .'

'Don't go after them, Antony,' Travis warned. 'They're not people we want to meet. Damn *rats*.'

But the creatures seemed to have dispersed, Linden registered. Or were they only inches away from them, lurking in the darkness, regrouping, waiting?

'Why don't we want to meet these people, Travis?' Antony said.

'They must be the Scavvies. Dwayne Randolph told me about them. They've made the underground their home. Apparently, they've also developed one or two unpleasant little habits.'

'Like what, Trav?' Linden gulped.

'Let's just say it'd be wise to keep out of their way.'

'And theirs.' Raised Scytharene voices drifted through the tunnel. 'Ruth.' Antony called her to him protectively. To everyone: 'These Scavvies scampered off to the left. I suggest as soon as we can we turn right.'

'You're better than satnav, Antony,' Travis nodded.

They moved forward urgently. The tunnel came to a T-junction, the point at which the Scavvies had crossed it. An information board affixed to the wall indicated the north-bound Victoria Line platform to the left, southbound to the right. South, back towards the Thames. Sooner that than the Scavvies, though, and the Scytharene voices seemed to be gaining.

The teenagers ran, yellow light spilling and splashing crazily around them as the lamps swung and jumped in their hands. Steps leading to lower reaches yet. The tunnel opening out on to the southbound platform itself. No train in or expected, needless to say. But that didn't stop people waiting.

In Richie's absence, Travis mouthed his usual line for him: 'Oh, shit.'

Scavvies. They were squatting on the platform in groups around lanterns and lamps, torches and even one or two fires fuelled by burning books and magazines. There were both boys and girls, mostly teenagers, it seemed, though some kids younger than that, and all of them ragged, wild, almost savage, scarcely human. White faces, lolling mouths, blank eyes, like inmates at a lunatic asylum. Their larder was heaped up against the wall: dead cats, dead dogs, dead rats, the blood and bones of the eaten among the meat of future meals. Other, rarer dishes too, larger joints. For the first time, Travis was grateful for the absence of electricity – the obscuring darkness meant he could spend the rest of his life convincing himself he'd been mistaken in what he thought he saw.

The Scavvies saw the four intruders clearly enough. High-pitched, mindless giggles burst from those closest to them. A little girl with very red lips clapped her very red hands. Some of the boys barked and howled. Some crouched on all fours and bared their teeth at the newcomers and growled.

'Bloody hell.' Antony felt sanity slipping from him. He held on to it as tightly as he did his subjugator.

'This is madness,' Linden cried. '*Madness.*'

One of the Scavvies somehow owned a machine gun. He opened fire on Travis's group. The rattle of bullets in the enclosed space was deafening. The Scavvie's aim was rudimentary at best. He wounded the wall, didn't scratch the living. A single blast from Antony's subjugator ensured that would remain the case.

But the tube-dwellers were on their feet now, roused. Their community was under attack. They had enemies to kill. They were hungry.

They fell on the four teenagers in a frenzy of snapping teeth and raking fingers.

Like the dogs, Linden thought in horror. *They've become animals down here in the dark. They're beasts.* And in a way she was glad she could distance them from her like that. It made shooting children that little bit easier.

Their subjugators were set to stun in any case, white bolts paralysing the Scavvies the instant they struck, dropping them to the platform. But there were so many of them. A boy seized Linden's left arm and she had to let go of her lamp, wasn't going to be able to bring her gun hand around before . . . Ruth retrieved the lamp and smashed it down on the Scavvie's head. Ruth was the only one of them not firing, apart from that single moment of violence cowering behind Antony. The boys had also dispensed with their lamps in order to grip their subjugators with both hands and sustain a relentless defensive action. But their backs were against the wall, literally, Linden crushed against an empty chocolate vending machine. The nightmare faces that thrust towards her, that contorted and turned ghost-white for that single moment of energy-bolt impact, one of them she'd fail to stop in the end. She imagined teeth sinking into her neck as sharp as a vampire's.

Travis sensed her faltering faith. 'Keep fighting, Lin,' he urged. 'Keep firing.'

Because suddenly they weren't alone. A fusillade of subjugator bolts erupted from the tunnel to their left. A drove of Scavvies dispatched in one. But the Scytharene scarcely qualified as allies.

Warriors blasted their way on to the platform, ruthless, unstoppable. Their helmets were indeed equipped with lights, drilling into the dark from the middle of their foreheads. The helmets crafted to mimic the predators of another world; their wearers confronted by a new breed of beast on this. *Caught between two kinds of aliens*, Linden thought.

'Lin. *Lin.*' Travis was grabbing her hand, pulling her along the platform towards the tube tunnel itself. The Scavvies' attention had been diverted by the greater threat of the Scytharene. Clearing a path with their subjugators, the teenagers battled towards their only possible escape route.

They jumped on to the tracks. Linden landed on a rat, felt its spine snap beneath her heel.

'Wait.' Antony dashed back to the platform, snatched up the only lantern within reach. 'We're going to need this.'

They paused to look back at the station. There were adult screams in the chaos of combat now. Maybe the first Scavvies Antony had sighted had come back, were ambushing the Scytharene from the rear. Maybe the black-armoured warriors weren't going to have it all their own way after all. Travis found it hard to care. Let their foes eliminate each other. 'Let's get out of here,' he said.

One feeble light now between the four of them. They crowded close together, linked arms and didn't let go. Ruth held the lantern while the others kept their subjugators at the ready. But there was no sign of pursuit from Pimlico station by either Scavvie or Scytharene, and as the tunnel wound towards the Thames, the sights – quickly – and then even the sounds of conflict were left behind. The teenagers were cocooned once more in near total blackness.

'Tread carefully,' Travis advised unnecessarily. Nobody wanted to sprain or break an ankle by tripping over the rails.

'How far do we think to the next station?' Linden asked.

'Every step takes us closer, Lin,' said Travis, which was a more inspiring way of admitting he didn't know.

'At least we finally seem to have shaken off the Scytharene,' Antony said. 'Let's count our blessings.'

'I'm good with numbers,' Ruth reminded them. 'One, no Scytharene. Two?'

'Ruth' – Antony almost laughed despite everything – 'I didn't mean *count* . . .' The tunnel suddenly shook and rumbled. 'What's that?'

And shook again, more violently this time, like an avalanche building. The teenagers felt themselves swaying.

'Can't be a train coming, can it?' Even knowing the idea was ridiculous, Travis still glanced in both directions.

'That's no train.' Antony raised his eyes to the impenetrable blackness above. 'But something's happening. Up there.'

A third shudder, the ground vibrating, the whole tunnel physically rocking. A kind of booming sound far away. Nearer to home, a cracking of concrete.

'What the hell?' Travis gazed upwards too. Everyone did.

'What if,' Linden guessed, 'what if the Scytharene have called in an air strike, Trav? A Culler or a slavecraft. Like we saw at Oxford.'

'An air strike against what?' More cracking, like ice breaking on a frozen lake where it was deadly to skate, like a fissure widening in parched desert soil before an earthquake. Travis's lips were dry. If they could see the roof, would it be splitting open?

'Against the Scavvies. Against the station.' A calamitous thought occurred to Linden. 'Trav, we're not under the Thames here, are we?'

Antony supplied the answer with a shout of horror. 'Water. It's pouring down!'

In icy, oily gushes. Linden was suddenly drenched. Ruth was suddenly screaming. Whatever the cause, the dam of the tunnel had burst, and without its protection they were in effect stranded at the bottom of a mighty river.

A while ago Linden had imagined that darkness was drowning her. Now, as mortar too began to fall from the fractured ceiling, it seemed the waters of the Thames had plans to do it for real.

Why couldn't they see it? Dyona marvelled. Why couldn't her fellow Scytharene see the treason in her eyes?

Inside herself, her appetite for assassination had grown so overwhelming that she could scarcely believe it wasn't also communicating itself physically, facially, publicly. Betraying her before the moment came. But the ship's officers with whom she exchanged cordialities on the bridge, the crewmen who passed her in the corridors, none of them seemed to notice anything untoward. None of them seemed to have the slightest idea that she despised them all.

Of course, it helped that the lower orders of her people were not permitted to stare directly *into* the eyes of a member of the Thousand Families.

But Gyrion could. And Gyrion suspected nothing. So, the Fleet Commander was a fool after all. He *ought* to be put out of his misery and he would be. Dyona could pretty much predict the exact time of his richly deserved death.

It would be three evenings from now. Following this morning's advance through the areas of London known as Pimlico and Holborn north of the Thames and Lambeth to the south, Gyrion had ordered his forces to halt. Westminster and St James's, the centre of the British Earthers' political life, including the palace where their late monarch had resided, he was reserving for three days' time, to coincide with the arrival of the other Fleet Commanders aboard the *Ayrion III*. The final assault on those symbolic districts would mark the completion of the enslavement of the United Kingdom, a fallen kingdom now. At that point, celebrations could justly commence. A little later, they would be disrupted – *fatally*. Dyona pictured Gyrion with a drink in his hand and a smug smile on his face as the bomb went off and the explosion tore through the Chamber of the Triumph. She visualised him with a scream on his lips as his white flesh charred black.

She saw herself rejoicing. And safe and unsuspected. This was how it would happen. The obliviousness of those around her to Dyona's intentions was boosting her courage, her certainty of success. As she announced herself to the door of her private quarters, that barrier obediently sliding open to admit her, she felt powerful, serene, in control.

Etrion was sitting waiting for her.

'Ah, Etrion. I recruit you to my conspiracy and immediately you take advantage. Servants should stand in the presence of a member of the Thousand Families.' Dyona smiled. 'But if you won't tell, I won't. I assume you're here because you've procured those materials I need for our special party surprise. Where are they?'

The servant wasn't saying.

'Etrion?' Dyona's smile was replaced by puzzlement. 'Are you all right?'

Not prepared to discuss his health, either.

Cold fear clenched Dyona's heart. 'Old friend . . .'

She could see he was dead before she touched his shoulder and he slumped sideways on the chair.

'Physical contact with a servant,' Gyrion observed, stepping from one of the inner rooms. 'Another charge to add to your list of crimes, Dyona.' He held a subjugator. He pointed it at Dyona. 'And well you might look shocked. I'm afraid your little game is over.'

They weren't picking their way forward so cautiously now. They couldn't afford to. Black torrents of water were sluicing through the tunnel's ruptured roof. Chunks of concrete rained down upon them too. Linden was bleeding from her forehead where cascading rubble had dashed against it. They floundered on, feet splashing through the rapidly rising flood – soon they would be wading.

Ruth had cried that they should go back, turn back, but Travis had yelled that there was no way of knowing which direction provided the shortest route to safety and that going back would only deliver them directly to the Scytharene. So they'd persisted with forwards, and Ruth had stumbled and fallen and the lantern had broken, its thin glow submerged in a liquid black as oil. Antony had hauled her up again but they'd all had to fend off the showering debris with their arms, desperate to protect themselves from injury. They'd lost their hold on one another.

Now they couldn't see each other, they couldn't feel each other. It seemed that they were alone in a lightless cavern, blundering blindly, and the water was at their knees.

'Shout your names out!' Travis's voice. Linden heard it ahead of her and hastened towards it. 'Shout your own names. Travis! Travis!'

So they could find each other again, keep together even without touch, be sure that all four of them were well. 'Linden!' she bellowed. 'Linden!' Not feeling stupid or self-conscious in the slightest. Survival kind of superseded embarrassment.

'Ruth!'

'Antony!'

Crying out their names like rallying calls.

'Travis! Tra—!'

'Actually, Naughton,' came a metallic voice out of nowhere, 'I heard you the first time.'

'*Crispin?*'

Linden felt her head spinning. Crispin? How was that . . .? Maybe she was hallucinating or something. Maybe that was it. That sudden, shining door set into the wall up ahead, the tunnel peeling back from it like skin, that couldn't be real, could it? Illuminating the bedraggled, exhausted forms of Antony and Ruth. And *Travis*. She groped forward to embrace him. But probably none of this was real. The metal door rising and the bright steel corridor beyond. A Near-Death Experience, that was what she was undergoing. She'd read about them. Those on the brink of dying passing through dazzling tunnels to the afterlife. Maybe *she* was dying. It would make more sense than this. But she'd fought so hard to—

'If you want to live, I suggest you step through the doorway,' advised the disembodied voice of Crispin Allerton.

'Linden, come on.' Travis hugged her reassuringly. She felt his body through their sodden clothes. Travis was still real so their rescue was, too – if utterly inexplicable.

They dragged themselves to the doorway, into the corridor on the other side, leaned gasping and spluttering against smooth walls humming with power as the door lowered into place and sealed off the flooding tunnel. The water that had spilled in with them drained away. They were cold and they were soaked but they were *alive*.

The intercom crackled once again. 'Welcome to Enclave Zero,' said Crispin.

'Did you kill him, Gyrion?' Dyona felt herself shaking with the intensity of her hatred and her rage.

'I didn't. Of course not.' Gyrion scoffed at the suggestion. 'No decent member of the Thousand Families would lower himself to killing a servant. One of my loyal Blackhearts ended Etrion's worthless life. After torture, needless to say.'

'You . . . tortured him?'

'Oh, considerably. He gave us little choice. He simply refused to confirm what in any case I knew to be true.'

'What was that?'

'That you are a traitor to your race, my dear,' Gyrion said conversationally. 'That you have been plotting against us.'

Dyona wasn't wearing her subjugator. Aboard the *Ayrion III*, why should she? And the Coriolanian redemption blade was out of reach, in a display cabinet the far side of the Fleet Commander. Effectively, she was at Gyrion's mercy. 'I . . .'

'Don't attempt to insult my intelligence with denials, my dear. I have harboured my suspicions since your intemperate outburst over the razing of Oxford. A little too much passion in the settlement's defence, I thought, suggestive of an impure mind, a mind tainted with affection for mere aliens, an un-Scytharene mind. I've had you watched since then, you and your servant. When Etrion began appropriating materials useful for the manufacture of a bomb, I thought it was time to act.' Gyrion gestured to the corpse with his weapon. 'Unfortunately, even when his treacherous tongue had finally been loosened, he could not tell me everything I wished to know.'

229

Etrion, Dyona mourned. He'd said he'd give his life for her and he had. One more grievance to address. One more reason for revenge. 'You imagine I'm likely to be more forthcoming, you murdering pig?'

'A foul mouth is the mark of a foul mind, Dyona, do you not remember your etiquette instruction?' Gyrion twitched a brief smile. Then his expression hardened into open hostility. The subjugator quivered in his grasp. Dyona realised that the Fleet Commander too was beginning to struggle to contain a molten inner rage. 'The *Furion*, Dyona. Are you culpable for its loss? Were you in collusion with the filthy traitor we know was on board? Are you responsible for the death of my son?'

Ah. So that was it. Darion. 'What if I refuse to speak, Gyrion?' Dyona taunted.

'You *must* speak. You *will*. I'll make you.' A madness gleamed in Gyrion's blood-red eyes. 'I'll tear the words of your confession from your throat myself.'

'Oh, there won't be any need for that,' Dyona said. 'I'll talk. I want to talk. It's time you heard the truth, Gyrion.' Particularly as she had nothing to lose now, and a father ought to know what kind of person his son really was. 'But I warn you, you'll wish you hadn't.'

'You betrayed Darion, didn't you? You turned against your own betrothed.'

'It wasn't like that, Gyrion.'

'It was. How can it have been otherwise? You hid your criminal nature from my trusting, noble son and deceived him into believing you a fit recipient for his love.'

'No, I never deceived Darion. But he deceived you, Gyrion.'

'What do you mean? How dare you . . .'

Had he guessed already? Dyona wondered. Gyrion's reaction was more defensive than surprised. Was that the real reason for his wrath? She said: 'I did conspire with the revolutionary aboard the *Furion*. Both of us belonged to the Dissident Movement. But there was no need for me to conceal my political beliefs from Darion. He shared them, Gyrion. Your son himself was your "filthy traitor".'

And Gyrion groaned. 'No.'

'Darion died helping the Earthers, fighting for the end of slavery.'

'No, he did not. You're lying.'

'Darion died loathing you, Gyrion, as I loathe you. He died despising you and everything you stand for.'

'Lies. Fabrications.'

'And I loved him for it.'

'Be *silent*. You don't know the meaning of love, Dyona,' Gyrion said, and for a moment there was a grief in his voice that in anybody else's would have won Dyona's sympathy. 'My son was pure. The blood of Ayrion flowed in his veins and he cannot have betrayed his people, his ancestors. His father. I refuse to believe it. I *refuse*. Or if he was tempted to stray even a little from the righteous path of his heritage, then the temptress was you, Dyona, the sin was yours. My son's errors – if errors he made – were born of weakness, not deliberate choice. You deceived him. You seduced him. Darion's death is your fault and you must be held to account. For your crimes against the heir of Ayrion and against the Scytharene race you must be punished.' Gyrion's expression grew sly. 'But not publicly, Dyona. No one must know of your treachery. The Thousand Families must

231

always be seen to be above reproach. You must never be brought to trial, my dear, and yet you must die. You *will* die, and your lies with you, and with your death, my son's memory will be cleansed and will burn brightly forever in the annals of our ancestors.'

Dyona stepped backwards. Gyrion was going to fire. She raised her hands instinctively, helplessly. He couldn't miss. Her eyes widened with the certainty of that one terrible fact.

In a single second she would be dead.

The reunions came first, as joyous as any though soggier than most, then the showers for Travis's sopping party, then a change of clothes facilitated by Enclave Zero's capacious and varied wardrobe, *then* the explanations in Conference Room Two.

Around the table, those Travis had expected to see – the rest of his group, Jessica almost surgically grafted to Antony – and one guy he hadn't, largely because he'd never met Cooper before in his life. The burly teenager who resembled a rather unsuccessful boxer sat on Richie's right and Travis gathered had something to do with the motley assortment of bruisers who comprised the remaining unanticipated inhabitants of the Enclave.

Travis had a lot of questions.

'This Enclave's designed just like the others, Trav,' Mel told him. 'The same three levels, military, scientific, accommodation in descending order, only it's all on a smaller, more concentrated scale. The armoury's been virtually cleaned out, but to give you an idea, you'd have struggled to squeeze a Joshua in there in the first place.'

'The power levels are high, however, Naughton,' intervened Crispin Allerton. After all the traumas it had taken to reach Enclave Zero, he was keen not to denigrate the installation even by implication. That annoying Patrick girl was more trouble than she was worth. 'All systems are fully functional, including those in the monitoring and communications centre as you know. Had they not been, you might still be swimming for your lives in that hideous tube tunnel.'

'Lucky there was an entrance to the Enclave down there,' said Linden.

'Not luck, Darroway,' refuted Crispin. 'Foresight on the part of those who built this complex. There are nineteen different entry points, all of them controlled from the moncom centre as well as individually using the appropriate access codes. Enclave Zero was designed to be a lair, not a trap.'

'What about the labs?' The most vital issue of all. 'Are they equipped with what you need, Crispin? Can you bioengineer the virus here?'

'The facilities, Naughton,' Crispin declared, 'are all that we could wish.'

'They're even better than at Wells,' Geoffrey chipped in, like a child delighted by the contents of a toy-box.

'Thank God.' Relief crashed into Travis like a wave. He closed his eyes. He could sleep now. If he allowed himself to, he could simply fall asleep here and now. But he *couldn't* allow it. It was not yet time to relax or let down his guard. 'Well, you already know how we got here. What about the rest of you?' His eyes opened and fixed on Cooper. 'Do I have you to thank for guiding my friends here before us – Cooper, is it?'

'Yeah, Cooper, and Coop's pleased the Kings of the Ring could help you out.'

'The who of the what?' Antony puzzled.

'The Kings of the Ring.' Cooper provided what he obviously considered to be further elaboration with a quick display of bobbing and weaving from his chair. 'But if it wasn't for our newly crowned champion, we'd prob'ly still be at the gym.'

'Newly . . . so who's that?' said Antony, still at a loss.

'Hi, Tony.' Richie gave a modest little wave.

'Antony, you're not going to believe what happened to us,' said Jessica.

And *still* at a loss: 'Jessie, you could well be right.'

But in the end it was clear enough. The capture. The challenge. The fight. Richie's victory. His first act as King of the Ring, the recruitment of his new-found followers as bodyguards for the remainder of their journey to Enclave Zero. The discovery of the entrance to the installation exactly where Crispin had led them, in the cellars of a deserted Palace of Westminster. The Houses of Parliament directly above them.

'So you were right about Enclave Zero providing refuge for the government in times of crisis, Crispin,' said Travis. 'Pity they didn't see fit to hang around and help the people of London.'

'Oh, but they did, Travis,' said Geoffrey gleefully. 'At least, some of them did.'

'What do you mean, Geoffrey?'

The shaggy-haired boy chuckled. 'Why do you think we're in Conference Room *Two*?'

Conference Room One was occupied. A meeting was

taking place there that must have commenced weeks ago but that would never now be brought to a conclusion. It wasn't the entire cabinet participating – perhaps some had fled to be with their families at the end, or simply died elsewhere – just the bodies of five men in suits and a single power-dressed woman. Clothes and hairstyles helped establish gender. Given the ravages of the Sickness, however, and the extent of decay, individual identities were more difficult to determine, that and the fact that the stench of decomposing human beings was conducive neither to closer inspection nor extended loitering in the room. Even so, Travis thought he could recognise the corpse that had once been the Prime Minister, in life a man famed for a toothy smile of breathtaking insincerity. He wasn't smiling now, and he wasn't taking breaths either. And there too, alongside the Prime Minister, weren't those the remains of the Chancellor of the Exchequer, his fabled dourness and humourlessness in office somehow more understandable now; the dead had plenty to be gloomy about.

'I don't think we can expect much assistance from our wonderful government, do you?' Mel said with grim amusement. 'Not that we could when they were alive. That smell – you reckon it's the whiff of corruption?'

'Are there any other bodies in the Enclave?' Travis wanted to know.

'There were,' said Jessica. 'Mostly soldiers. Richie had them taken away and thrown in the river.'

'We couldn't dispose of them down here,' Richie justified himself. 'And I thought if we started a bonfire or something the Scytharene'd know someone was around.'

Travis regarded Richie curiously, but he didn't disagree.

'Fair point, sadly. We should get rid of the politicians too.'

'I'll get the Kings on it.' Richie nodded. 'Coop, can you take care of this?'

Cooper evidently could.

'Dumped in the Thames,' Mel mused. 'The most powerful men in the country. How the mighty have fallen.'

'Nobody's mighty, Mel,' Travis said darkly. 'Not in the great scheme of things. Not even the Scytharene, as I hope they'll soon discover.'

Soon indeed, Crispin Allerton verified, but there were one or two matters he still wished to discuss back in Conference Room Two before the Paragons could begin work on the gene transfer virus.

'It appears we have you to thank then, Richie,' Antony said as the group re-entered the conference room. 'For saving the girls.'

'Richie the hero,' mocked Mel good-humouredly. '*I* could have taken Cooper if I'd needed to.' But for *girls*, Antony really meant Jessica.

'Thank you.' The blond boy shook Richie's hand warmly.

'Don't worry about it. Bill's in the post.'

'No, you did well, Richie.' Travis nodded his approval. 'Looks like you're becoming an asset to the group after all.'

'Don't get carried away, Trav,' snorted Linden, but found no support for her scepticism from either Jessica or Mel.

Richie didn't look at Linden. He looked at Travis and grinned. 'Reckon I could do your job then, Naughton? Reckon I could be a leader?' A *leader*. His old mum would have been proud of that.

'The way Cooper reacts to you, Richie, I'd say you already are.' Travis laughed. 'Maybe I'd better watch my back.'

'On the subject of the leadership – if we could take our seats?' Crispin called the group to order. Again his fellow Paragons flanked him while Travis's original six automatically congregated together. But from the ambitious glitter in Crispin's eyes, he wasn't expecting such unity to last for long.

'On the subject of leadership, Crispin?' Travis said innocently. 'What, you've got something to say on the matter?'

'Mm. As it happens, I do. Our circumstances have changed now that we're safely ensconced in Enclave Zero. I feel, therefore, that this might be a legitimate moment for a change of leader as well. I propose we hold a new election for that position, and I intend to put myself forward as a candidate.'

'There's a surprise,' grunted Mel. 'A power-grab. The politicians may be dead, but their spirit lives on.'

'You've got a bloody nerve, Crispie,' said Richie.

'No, no.' Travis quietened him. 'Crispin's right. Maybe we should clarify the leadership issue – kind of once and for all.'

'You're more intelligent than you look, Naughton.' Crispin smiled thinly.

'So why don't you tell us why you should be elected, Crispin?'

'Mr Coker is not the only member of our party to have excelled himself, and while an aptitude for physical violence might on occasion be valuable, it is brain power that will finally defeat the Scytharene. In that regard Coker is, lamentably, rather less skilled. I, however, am a genius. It was I who found our way here and opened the door to Enclave Zero. It was I who saved you and your group from drowning, Naughton. And it will be me whose brilliance with genetics

237

will bring about the fall of the Scytharene. Given those incontrovertible facts – I don't believe in false modesty – it seems eminently clear that it is I who should be leader from now on.' Effusive pledges of support from Ruth and Geoffrey. 'But perhaps we have other candidates as well?' Vote-splitting candidates. Crispin Allerton played his best card. 'Clive, perhaps?'

Antony smiled. 'Actually, Crispin, a couple of days ago I'd have said yes. You know, back when you were flattering me into believing I should already have been leader, letting me know how you'd overheard Travis criticising my contribution to the group.'

'Trav?' Jessica was shocked. '*Did* you?'

'Let Antony finish, Jess,' said Travis calmly.

'Yes. Back when, at the same time, funnily enough, you were also letting *Travis* know how you'd overheard me bad-mouthing him behind his back.'

'You didn't, Antony?' Linden demanded disbelievingly.

'He didn't, Lin,' said Travis.

'Which suggests, Crispin,' Antony continued, 'that your hearing is pretty much as advanced as your intellect, and even more creative, because what you claimed to have overheard was actually a pack of lies, wasn't it? Designed to create a rift between myself and Travis.'

Crispin Allerton rose to his feet haughtily, his pale face crimsoning. 'I don't have to listen to this nonsense.'

'We think you do,' said Travis and Antony simultaneously.

'So sit down.' Antony.

'And listen up.' Travis.

'Your pathetic little divide-and-conquer efforts haven't worked, Crispin.' Antony.

'Antony and I had a bit of a talk, cleared the air. Realised the truth.' Travis. 'We're more united than ever.'

Crispin wilted into his seat.

'I'm not standing against Travis, and neither I imagine is anyone else.' A glance at the others confirmed the fact. 'So I don't think another election is a suitable expenditure of time, do you? Travis is leader here, end of story, and certainly end of your scheming.'

'I only said what I genuinely thought I'd heard,' mumbled Crispin in excuse. Only Ruth and Geoffrey appeared to believe him.

'You could have jeopardised the safety of all of us, Crispin,' said Travis. 'Setting us against each other's no good. We need to stand together.'

'Bloody Crispie won't be able to stand at all when I've finished with him.' Richie lunged out of his chair menacingly.

'Keep that Neanderthal away from me,' Crispin warned.

'It's all right, Richie.' Travis's words were restraint enough. Richie settled back into his seat grumbling. 'Bear in mind, though, Crispin, that if we held a vote over what to do with you, right now the result might be to throw you out of here and on to the mercy of the Scytharene.'

'I vote we toss him into the Thames,' Mel said. 'He'll be okay. Shit floats.'

Crispin glared contemptuously at Mel. How he hated her. How, he realised now, he hated all of them, so satisfied with their own wretched mediocrity, hated them for their idiotic plebeian solidarity, for their stubborn refusal to accept his superiority over them or to grant him the respect he merited, hated them for the humiliation they had heaped upon him. *Him*, Crispin Allerton, the pride of the Paragons.

But he had to suppress his feelings for now. His machinations having failed so dismally, he was in a dangerous position. But it was not an irretrievable one. His genius would save him.

'Mm. You can't throw me out, as you so vulgarly put it, Naughton,' he said. 'You wouldn't dare. Who would then create your precious gene transfer virus?'

'That's true,' Travis conceded. 'We need you, Crispin. We need all three of you, Ruth and Geoffrey as well. But we don't need lies and deception and hidden agendas. So just remember. You've claimed you can bioengineer a gene transfer virus that'll infect the Scytharene, and we've believed you – so far. But you've also shown yourself to be capable of the occasional untruth when it's suited you. You'd better start proving to us that the virus is for real, and soon, or we might have to reconsider Mel's Thames idea.'

'You've damaged our faith in you, Crispin,' said Antony. 'You're going to have to work hard to restore it.'

'I think you know where the labs are,' Travis finished.

'Oh yes. But before we go, there's something *you* should know.' Crispin Allerton's trademark supercilious smile was making a comeback. 'We have access to the necessary technology to develop the virus, but bioengineering is about biology as well as engineering. We need living cells to work with, so we need tissue.'

'Human tissue?' Travis shrugged. 'You mean like a blood sample? We can manage that between us.'

'Mm. Not only human. The key to our success will be the splicing together of human and Scytharene genetic material. We therefore also require access to Scytharene DNA. Didn't

240

you realise that?' The six stunned faces before him raised Crispin's spirits again. He would put these inferiors in their place yet. 'In short, Naughton, before we can create the virus, we need a Scytharene prisoner.'

TEN

'Let's go back inside, Trav,' said Mel uncomfortably.

'In a minute. Give me a minute.'

At least one point of access to Enclave Zero was indeed located in the bowels of the Houses of Parliament – the wine cellar, to be precise – and at Travis's request Mel, who'd entered that way in the first place, had led him through it, through the empty, echoing corridors of power, and out on to the street where they stood now, Travis troubled and at times it seemed on the brink of tears. He'd visited Westminster on a school trip to London some years ago. The scene was not as he remembered it.

There hadn't been the barbed wire or the barricades, for a start, or the tanks squatting on the mud of Parliament Square opposite the Houses of Parliament themselves, or the panoply of small armoured vehicles, some of them overturned as though drunk and incapable. Last-ditch defences surrounded the Palace of Westminster which, as Travis's teacher had pointed out, was the correct name for the soaring, ornate, cathedralesque edifice that contained the nation's Parliament. A final attempt to protect the building for the order and stability it symbolised, perhaps, as much as for its value in stone and glass, an endeavour to preserve an idea of England.

If so, it had failed.

The barricades had been breached and the barbed wire pierced. The defenders had fled, abandoning their posts. The iron railings like thin black sentries around the perimeter of Parliament had been beaten down in many places, but the culprits too had long since vanished. Dozens of the Palace's lead-lined windows had been smashed and there were ragged holes like wounds in its imposing Gothic façade. Its regal splendour was violated beyond reclamation. The statue of Cromwell nearby was reduced to a statue of Cromwell's leg – the rest of his body, like the body politic itself, had been shattered. The immortalisation of Richard the Lionheart mounted on a horse and with his sword lifted high had also suffered, the sword hand cruelly amputated. Across the road, fires seemed to have been lit around the base of Westminster Abbey, extinguished now but having blackened its exterior, as if someone in their despair had sought to burn the very notion of religion.

Only sculpted Churchill, solid, resolute and beyond defilement, was unchanged from Travis's previous visit. When flesh and blood, the great man had once saved the country, in easier, more unified times. Now, motionless in marble, there was nothing he could do.

Travis peered into Churchill's sightless eyes. The same was not true for Travis, or for anyone who still lived and who genuinely cared for their nation and their race. The world was under siege, but sieges could be broken.

'Travis,' Mel urged again. 'It's getting late.'

'Mum and Dad'll be getting worried where we are, huh?' Travis smiled bleakly. 'Okay. I've seen all I wanted to see.'

But he changed his mind once they were again inside Parliament.

'What do you want to go there for?' Mel wrinkled her nose as though Travis's request had brought with it a bad smell.

'It was an important place. It meant something.' Like the Palace of Westminster itself, Travis thought. Like the Oxford colleges levelled by the Scytharene. Heritage. History. Hope.

Though Parliament was deserted now, others had been here before Travis's group and the Kings of the Ring. The vandals and the graffiti artists had left their mark in the Members' Lobby, daubing the statues of one-time Prime Ministers unflatteringly with paint and scrawling slogans on the walls.

Hooligans had been busy in the House of Commons itself, too. If any of the country's elected representatives were still alive to take their seats in that august chamber, they'd probably decline the privilege just at the moment pending renovation work. Some of the benches where the MPs sat had been cursorily torched; the green leather padding of others had been slashed and torn. The green carpet was soiled, the hanging lights burst like balloons. The black Speaker's Chair at the north end of the House, however, was surprisingly intact.

Travis and Mel stood in the centre of the darkened, abused chamber. Her expression was cynical and dismissive, his mournful and melancholy.

'It's smaller than you'd think from the telly, isn't it?' Mel sniffed. 'Where did the Prime Minister do his bit?' Travis pointed out the place. 'Yeah, well, politics always was a dirty business full of hollow promises – guess the new-look House of Commons is just a reflection of that.'

'No. You're wrong, Mel,' Travis said quietly. 'Can't you feel it?'

'What? Damp?'

'The dream.'

'Uh, what dream's that, Trav?'

'The dream of doing right. It's still here. The aspiration for justice. The desire to make a difference.'

'You think you might want to sit down, Trav? I wouldn't – not *there*.'

'Mel, can you really not sense it? There's still a power here. The reason for a Parliament, the reason for the existence of a place like this, that hasn't lost its relevance. It still matters. The dream of people coming together to build a better society.'

'Don't you mean the dream of telling the rest of us what to do while feathering your own nest on the side?'

'No, Mel. If politics was in disrepute before the Sickness it was the fault of individual politicians for failing to inspire or be inspired. But they're dead and gone now. The old political parties, the old system, obsolete. I'm talking about the ideals that the older generation might have forgotten but that we can still put into practice. Once we've defeated the Scytharene.'

'That's a hell of a *once*, Trav,' said Mel.

'We can do it. With the gene transfer virus, I know we can do it.' Travis gazed up to the shadowed ceiling of the silent chamber. 'And when we have, we'll need to start again. A new society. A better one. That's what we'll be building. A new future for us all.'

Richie Coker was not interested in politics, unless, maybe, you were talking protest marches that got out of hand and gave you an excuse to kick the shit out of someone on the grounds of principle. He was glad Naughton was politically minded, though. It meant that while Travis and Morticia were doing the grand tour of Parliament, he could sneak a private word with Linden.

Another Enclave. Another corridor. But things would go differently this time.

'Richie, what do you want?' Linden, however, seemed to be expecting the same. 'Another sordid blackmail attempt, is it, while Trav's out of the picture? You seem to have fooled Mel and Jessie into thinking you've changed, but *me* . . .'

'I haven't fooled anyone, Linden,' Richie said. 'I have changed. I reckon.'

'You *reckon*?' Linden snorted.

Richie's brow furrowed. 'It isn't easy. This isn't easy for me, Lin, but you don't need to worry. That's what I want you to know. No more blackmail. No more threats to tell Naughton what we did. I won't tell him. I promise.'

'Really?' Linden said dubiously. 'Like before? And this time I really *really* can trust you, yeah?'

'That's right. This time you can. Like you should always have been able to.'

Linden regarded Richie with increasing confusion. Was he bowing his head, kind of hanging it in shame? And the way his new-found followers looked up to him – she'd noticed it in Cooper and the others – as if he was deserving of admiration. The way Richie looked up to Travis. Linden's mother had taught her that life was a journey and sometimes you took a wrong turn, but even if you did you could always get yourself back on the right road. 'You *have* changed,' she marvelled.

'Not entirely. Not in everything.' Richie lifted his eyes to her and there was pain in them. 'I still feel the same about you, Linden. I still want you like crazy.'

'Oh, Richie.' Backing away, palms raised. 'Just when I was starting to believe. . .'

'No, no. Lin. You don't need to – I know it's not gonna happen. Not between us. Not again. I know that. I do.' He gave a rueful smile. 'The new Richie Coker's gonna have to get used to it. And he will.'

'Talking about yourself in the third person, Richie,' Linden said. 'You're beginning to sound like Cooper.'

'I'm better-looking than Cooper,' Richie grinned.

'You're certainly more attractive than the *old* Richie Coker.'

'So we're sweet?' With hope in his voice. 'We can – what did they use to say to me at school after one of my suspensions? – wipe the slate clean? New start?'

'I don't know, Richie. I'd like to think so. I'm sure you deserve it, but . . . Maybe we should still keep our distance, as far as we can, anyway. I mean, not avoid each other but not go out of our way to be in each other's company either.'

'Why, Lin, if—?'

'I like the new Richie,' Linden said, 'but I'm going to be honest with you. I can't be sure the old one isn't still lurking inside you somewhere.'

'I'll prove to you he isn't,' Richie asserted. 'I'll prove it, Lin.'

'I hope you do, but for now . . .' Linden sighed. 'It's for my good, too, Richie. I shouldn't have slept with you and I hate myself for it. It was all about the physical, the need of the moment, reaching out for whoever was closest to take the fear away, everything that since I've been with Travis I've tried to

247

see beyond. It's not your fault, Richie, but you bring out the worst in me. Travis brings out the best. We should stay apart. I'm sorry.'

'Whatever you say, Lin,' said Richie Coker stonily.

Antony's room. Very late. He and Jessica were lying on the bed tangle-limbed like twin Houdinis in a trap from which neither wished to escape.

'If it's not too much of a cliché, Jess,' said Antony, 'I never want to let you go.'

'I kind of got that impression.' Jessica giggled. 'What if I need to use the bathroom?'

'I can look the other way.'

'Hm. That's sweet.' She kissed him.

'So's that.' He kissed her. 'You know, I was worried – well, at the worst moment, when we were wandering aimlessly in the streets, I *wondered* if I'd ever see you again.'

'I knew we'd be all right. You and Travis together – you were bound to find us. Sooner or later.'

'It might have been later if we hadn't realised Crispin had been playing us off against each other,' Antony reflected.

'That was a nasty thing to do,' said Jessica. She snuggled even closer to her boyfriend. 'I don't understand the Paragons, Antony. The life they've led, kind of shut up in labs doing experiments all day, I want to feel sorry for them, but I can't. Geoffrey's too creepy, for a start. I just don't think I like them very much. And after how he's tried to divide you and Trav, I certainly don't think I can trust Crispin.' She pondered whether this was the moment to broach the subject that was really on her mind. 'I've got my suspicions about Ruth as well.'

'Suspicions?'

'I think she fancies you, Antony.' The slight shifting away of his body told her not only that she was right and that Antony knew, but that something had happened between him and Ruth. 'What?'

'I'm afraid . . . you're not wrong, Jessie.'

A thump of dread in her heart, Jessica extricated herself from Antony and sat up. She might be paranoid, but could that be guilt marring his otherwise perfect features? '*What?*' Was she losing him to Ruth Bell? She couldn't lose him. She was beginning to love him.

'Well, I didn't want to tell you, to be honest . . .'

'No secrets, Antony. Tell me what?'

'Last night.' Reluctantly. 'When we were with the Phantoms – well, I think you can safely say that Ruth tried to seduce me.'

'What,' demanded Jessica, 'happened?'

Like a witness under oath, Antony told her. 'I wasn't interested, of course. I went and slept in the stairwell rather than stay within sight of her. And she should have known. I'd already told her I wasn't interested when she came on to me the other night at the farm.'

'Ruth came on to you the other night at the farm?'

'In the kitchen. You saw us together, remember?'

'Sounds like I arrived in the nick of time. But you didn't tell me *then* she'd made advances, Antony.'

'I didn't want to upset you, and I didn't want to create bad feeling in the group. Besides, Ruth means nothing to me. I didn't think she'd find it quite so hard to take no for an answer.'

'Actually, Antony,' Jessica frowned, 'I'm finding it hard to believe you could *give* no for an answer when a girl with no clothes on who's clearly undressed for a reason somehow finds her way into bed with you.'

'Jessie,' Antony protested, hurt. 'How can you say that?'

Because Mum had always warned her to be careful of boys. They were always after One Thing – except that nice Travis Naughton, of course, Jessica could trust him, and wasn't it terrible about the poor lad's father? But the others, they had one-track minds and it was a dirt track.

But Antony was nice, too. Antony was like Travis. Surely her mother would have been able to see that. Surely she, Jessica, could trust him. She really wanted to.

She didn't want to lose him.

'I'm telling you, Jessie,' he was persevering, 'nothing happened.'

'Really?' Weakening.

'Absolutely really.' With a sudden grin: 'Of course, it might have done.'

'*Might* have done?'

'If the girl last night had been you. I can resist any girl except you, Jessie. You're the one. You have to believe me.'

'I don't *have* to believe you.' With a smile of her own. 'But I do.'

She lowered herself to him and lay alongside him again and let him kiss her, let him hold her. And what else would she let him do? If it had been her with him naked last night, they'd have gone beyond the kissing and cuddling. Tonight, it *was* her with him but she still had her clothes on. But that could change. If he wanted it to. If *she* wanted it to. *Boys, Jessica, are always after One Thing.* But what if that one thing was necessary to keep the boy she loved? If she *didn't* sleep with him, with Ruth ready and willing to slip between the sheets, how long could Antony realistically remain immune to the Paragon's charms?

'Antony, do you want to . . .?'

And he did. Of course he did. Being alone with Jessica was thrilling, exciting, the taste of her lips intoxicating, the tickle of her tongue, the smoothness of her skin. He could get carried away by it all. He could be consumed by the moment. 'Jessie,' he was whispering. 'Jessie.' His hands beneath her sweatshirt, his fingers stroking her back, her belly, easing the garment up.

His friends at Harrington had said, his More Experienced friends, that they all wanted it, girls, even the posh ones, even the ones who looked like butter wouldn't melt, and if you weren't up to the job, if you weren't a Real Man, then the girls'd be off to find someone who was. Real Men did the business. Real Men went all the way.

Antony had always felt the pressure to be a Real Man. He pulled Jessica's sweatshirt off over her head.

Bare arms. Bare shoulders. White bra.

Antony was seeing her in her bra. His fingers were going to fumble with the strap and take it off. She had to let him because she didn't want to lose him, and yet . . .

He wasn't quite sure how bra straps worked but he had to remove the article somehow because otherwise he'd lose her, and yet . . .

One Thing.

Real Men.

'No.' Crimsoning furiously, tears stinging her eyes, Jessica pulled back, snatched up her sweatshirt. 'No. I can't.'

'Jessie?'

She was off the bed, at the door, hauling her top on again, covering herself up. 'I can't do this, Antony. I'm sorry.'

'Jessie, don't . . .' Jumping up, too late. 'I thought this' – the door slamming behind her – 'was what you wanted.'

Jessica rushing down the corridor. *Too far, too soon.* She wasn't ready. She loved Antony but she wasn't ready to *make* love to him or any boy. Too new, too frightening, too big a step.

Time was moving forwards too quickly and she longed for it to stop. She wanted it reversed. If only she could go back, to the old world, to the safe world, to her life at home with her parents and her posters and her modest, manageable fantasies.

She needed somebody to talk to, somebody she could explain to. Someone who'd been there and known her in the past. Refuge in the comfort of the familiar. Trav? Linden would be with him, and he was a boy in any case. Jessica felt she'd prefer the company of another girl tonight. Only one choice, then.

Mel.

Perhaps she should look on the bright side, Dyona pondered.

To begin with, she was gaining far more of a first-hand experience of London than she'd ever managed with Oxford. Being hurried through the desolate streets at night by a small band of armed Blackhearts, their helmet-lights probing the dark, scarcely qualified as an authentic alienological expedition, but it still immersed her in local conditions. She wore no helmet herself though her gold armour gleamed a little light. Perhaps she could request a brief diversion to the British Museum, though she doubted it would be granted. She was neither cuffed nor bound only because there was no chance of her escaping her grim escort. The purpose of this nocturnal excursion was not study but execution.

Her execution.

'It will be so very sad,' Gyrion had assured her in her quarters earlier, 'a proud, patriotic member of the Thousand Families, Dyona of the bloodline of Lyrion, tragically killed during the course of her duties.'

'Is that so?' Dyona had said. 'Excuse me while I wipe away a tear.'

'As well you might, my dear. You see, you should never have gone against the advice of your caring Fleet Commander. He warned you that the streets in that part of London had not yet been made safe by Scytharene military action, he forbade you to undertake an alienological operation in such potentially dangerous territory, but fired by an overwhelming passion to demonstrate yet again your people's cultural and racial supremacy, you disobeyed the one who loved you like a daughter, who might indeed under happier circumstances have become your father-in-law, and unilaterally you chose to venture forth.' Gyrion had sighed in mock grief. 'And you never came back.'

Dyona had smiled bitterly. 'How will our people hear I died?'

'Your expedition was ambushed by murderous Earthers, I'm afraid. You were savagely slaughtered. A plucky lone survivor, one of my loyal Blackhearts, of course, reported the details to me after a painful, plucky . . .'

'That's two pluckies in one sentence, Gyrion.'

'. . . after a painful, tortuous trek back to the *Ayrion III* where he also related to me your final words: "Long live my

253

people! Long live the Scytharene race!"' Gyrion seemed almost genuinely moved by his propaganda. 'Your body will never be found, of course. This plan is the perfect solution to the problem of your existence. While you live, Dyona, you are nothing but a miserable traitor, but in death you will become a heroine and a martyr to the very cause you despise. I hope the knowledge of this gives you pain.'

'And how – in reality – *will* I die?'

'Quickly, Dyona. More quickly than you deserve for your role in my son's death. I only wish I could be there to see you perish, but we cannot have everything we desire and I have a summit to prepare. Farewell, Dyona of the bloodline of Lyrion. May the scaraths gnaw your bones.'

She'd tried to keep a brave face in Gyrion's presence and had probably succeeded. She wasn't doing badly in that respect now, either, but she couldn't banish fear from her body completely. Her breathing was ragged; her legs were weak. Each step could be her last.

'All right,' snapped a Blackheart behind her. 'That'll do. Stand where you are, traitor.'

Where she was. In a street of gutted shopfronts, strewn with debris and burned-out vehicles. Dyona had never envisaged dying somewhere like this.

'On your knees. But carefully. You don't want to bruise them.' Cackles of cold laughter at that.

Dyona knelt.

'Time to die,' gloated the Blackheart.

The machine-gun bullets tore through both his armour and his body. He gurgled blood as he fell, his lifeless form thudding to the road alongside Dyona, who stretched herself

254

out full length and hugged the tarmac. A move made in panic, but sensible nevertheless.

The other Blackhearts managed to fire off a few subjugator bolts, may have inflicted some casualties, but the attackers were invisible in the night and seemed to surround them, and they were armed with weapons they knew how to handle. Their killing was efficient. The Blackhearts were cut down where they stood.

The gunfire ceased as suddenly as it had started. Dyona saw dark figures stepping from the shadows. Her saviours, she thought. Rescued from execution at the hands of her own kind by aliens who ought to be her enemies. Or was she making assumptions? Ironically, Gyrion had got his Earther ambush; perhaps he'd still have his heroine and martyr as well. The Scytharene had a saying: from the warrior's sights into the scarath's jaws.

Their weapons trained on Dyona, the Earthers moved in.

Mel was dreaming.

She was back in the playground in the park where her mother had used to take her as a little girl, and she knew she was dreaming for several reasons. Firstly, the playground no longer existed: both it and the park had been bulldozed years ago to make way for the more commercial priority of a new supermarket. Secondly, her mother – who appeared happy and well in the dream – had looked neither the last time Mel had seen her for real, because by then she was already dead. Finally, there was the little matter of the visits to the playground having ceased when Mel was eight or nine years old, yet as she held her mother's hand and walked alongside her to the roundabout, seesaw and swings, she could see that she

255

was her present age. So she was dreaming but she didn't care. It was a good dream.

To begin with.

Being with her mother again, that was special. That was to be cherished. Mel wanted to speak to her, to hear her mother's voice in return, but the dream was playing like a silent movie and permitted no sound. All she could hear was her own breathing as she slept.

Her mother was sitting her on the roundabout and smiling at her and laughing, and her mouth opened very wide when she laughed like a pit into which a careless child might fall. And Mel was holding on to the bar, holding on tightly as her mother pushed and the roundabout turned, and she felt like a hand on a clock-face and time whirling with bewildering speed. And her mother must have been working out since she'd been dead or something because she was sending the roundabout spinning, spinning so fast Mel could only gasp, and the wind caught her long black hair and yanked at it like a naughty schoolboy. She hoped that horrible Richie Coker wasn't around because he liked to push the roundabout fast too, and when Cheryl Stone fell off that time and cut her knee and blubbed, Richie had laughed.

And he wasn't around but other people were. Other people were sitting on the roundabout with her. She was surprised she hadn't noticed them before. Simon Satchwell. He was there, grinning at her through his glasses. And Rev, in leather as always, though Rev's presence was odd because as far as Mel could remember she hadn't known the biker at Wayvale. And the adults incongruously riding with her, Dr Shiels, Mr Greening, Captain Taber, Dr Mowatt, Darion, they were all kind of perched on the roundabout's rim and they were all smiling at her and their hands were resting calmly on their knees. Which was bad. Which was wrong. Which was dangerous. They should be holding on. They had to hold on because they were swirling so swiftly that if they didn't they'd slip off, if they didn't they'd fall.

Did they want to fall?

Mel didn't. Mel held on. She wanted to tell her mother to slow down, to stop, but when she looked her mother had gone and somebody else was pushing the roundabout. Mel understood now.

She wasn't pleased to see her father again.

Gerry Patrick was whisking the roundabout in blurring circles and Mel could see what he was doing. He was trying to shake everyone off. That was what he wanted. But she *wouldn't* fall. She didn't want to. She'd cling on and she was sobbing.

And her father was cheering because the roundabout had unscrewed from the ground and was spiralling into the sky, up, up, higher, and the world was far below her and Mel couldn't see her father any more nor the playground nor the park. There was a city below her now, a city in flames, a world in ruins. Above the devastation the roundabout revolved.

Dr Shiels slid off. Without a word. No cry or scream or utterance of complaint. The headteacher simply fell, and Mr Greening with her, a faithful deputy to the end. Distance diminished them and everything they'd been, made them small, made them specks. Captain Taber dropped off the roundabout to join them, and Dr Mowatt, Rev. Everyone was slipping away. Darion, tumbling. Mel called out silently to Simon and reached out to him, and he saw her hand extended but he didn't take it. He looked at her in resignation, in acceptance, almost in pity. He fell.

And Mel felt herself slipping too, slipping away. But she couldn't. She wouldn't. She wanted to stay on the roundabout, even though it was hard, even though it taxed all her strength. Her fellow riders had submitted to gravity but she would not surrender. Not yet. There were still things for her to do. There was still Jessie. She had to ensure that Jessica was safe. She had to hold on. But her grip was weakening. She felt herself sliding . . .

It was a moot point whether Mel had forced herself awake to escape her dream or whether the frantic rapping on the door of her room had roused her. She was relieved to be free of the former and obliged to respond to the latter. She checked her watch: almost one o'clock.

'Who is it? You know what time—?'

'Mel. It's me.'

Mel opened the door immediately. When Jessie wanted her, the time was irrelevant.

The issue was, did *she* still want Jessica? Because if she did, now *was* the time. That much was obvious from her friend's distraught emotional condition as she rushed into the room.

'What's happened?'

'Mel, I just – I'm such a coward.' Pacing the room agitatedly. 'I could have – I *wanted* to – but at the same time I was so *scared*. And now I've lost Antony for good I know I have and I can't blame him and what am I going to do it's all my fault what's the *matter* with me?'

'Whoa. Whoa. First thing you're gonna do is sit down,' Mel counselled. 'Then you're gonna take several deep breaths and relax. Then you're gonna tell me what the problem is, with all the punctuation put back in, with all the details nice and clear and in order. Anyone'd need subtitles to understand what you've just said.' Though Mel could probably guess at the gist of what had transpired between Jessica and Antony.

Jessica's hesitant and distressed account confirmed all her assumptions, though the news of Ruth Bell's seduction attempt came as a bit of an eye-opener.

'I had to talk to someone,' the blonde girl said, 'someone I could trust. You, Mel. But . . .' She seemed to register for the first time that Mel was in her underwear – Enclave Zero was not amply stocked with nightclothes appropriate for teenage girls. 'Maybe I should have left it till morning. I – I'm sorry. I've woken you up. This was selfish. I'll go.' Rising.

Pressed back down again by Mel's hands squeezing her shoulders reassuringly. 'No you won't. You'll stay where you are, Jessie. I was only sleeping. I can do that any night. You want to talk, we'll talk.'

'What do I do, Mel?' Jessica asked miserably.

'Do you think Antony's lying when he says he gave Ruth the brush-off?'

'No. I believe him. He's not interested in her.'

Mel sat on the bed opposite the other girl, held her hands. 'Then I guess what you do depends on how interested you are in *him*. It's own up to your emotions time. Forget the recent unpleasantness. If just now had never taken place, what would you say you feel for Antony?' Harbouring a last, slim hope that Jessica wouldn't say what deep down Mel knew she would.

'I love him.'

Told ya. Mel prayed Jessie didn't notice her wince. At least you couldn't physically see another person's heart breaking, finally, beyond repair. 'You love him.'

'Yes, but tonight he wanted me to be with him, sleep with him, and I – I couldn't. So maybe' – venturing a glance at Mel – 'maybe I've got a problem with boys and sex. It's so difficult knowing what to do or what not to do. So much pressure. So many, I don't know, expectations. Maybe it'd be better, easier if' – her green eyes flirting nervously with Mel's blue – 'if I liked girls, after all.'

So here it *was*, after all. After everything. After all those times in the old world that Mel had gazed at her now-lost photograph of herself and Jessica together, wondering what it would be like if they ever *were* together, wishing it could happen. Before, at the first Enclave, she'd attempted to engineer a situation which would break Jessie and Antony up and lure Jessica into her consoling arms, had tried and failed. Here and now, however, at Enclave Zero, Jessie of her own accord, with no prompting from Mel in the slightest, was pretty much doing as the black-haired girl had always longed for her to do – inviting Mel to make a move. All it would take was a caressing hand, a brush of the lips. Neither would be rejected. For the first and, Mel sensed, the last time, Jessica was available.

Ironic, really.

'No,' she heard herself comforting. 'That's not what you really want, is it?'

'I don't know. Maybe. I'm no good at relationships. I don't understand boys.' Flushing. 'I thought it was what *you* wanted . . .'

'That's it, isn't it?' Mel smiled ruefully. 'We all try to guess what other people want when we ought just to ask them.'

'What are you saying, Mel?'

How young Jessica suddenly seemed. How distant from her, like Mel was viewing her friend from the roundabout in the sky. And how could she even have considered what would basically have been exploiting Jessica's vulnerability for her own needs? Jessie belonged with Antony. Mel knew it, painful though that knowledge was. She still loved Jessie herself, of course, but only some kinds of love involved sex. Others focused more on sacrifice.

'Antony didn't try to force you into anything, did he?' she said.

'No, of course not. He just thought I was readier than I was to – well, *be* with him. But I'm not ready. Not yet. It's still too soon.'

'But you didn't speak up, so things went too far and you ended up running out on him in a state.'

'Pretty much,' said Jessica forlornly.

'Well, I told you before I wouldn't give you advice on matters of the heart, but we're girls. We're expected to change our minds. So here comes Dr Patrick's recommended treatment, Jess. In a word, honesty. It can heal misunderstandings and it can cure all kinds of confusion. It can bring people together again. Case in point, you and a certain good-looking former Head Boy of the Harrington School. Be honest with Antony. Tell him what you've told me. You never know, he might have been feeling under pressure himself too, thinking you'd expect him to behave in certain ways, not wanting to let you down. He could be just as happy to wait until the time's right as you are.'

'You think?' Jessica said with cautious optimism.

'I know. Antony's one of the good guys. He proved that to

me when the two of us and Travis went searching for Darion that time. You can trust him, Jess, and if you can trust him, you can afford to be honest with him.' Mel paused, grinned. 'But maybe not right now. Barging in on one person in the middle of the night's probably enough. Best to wait until morning.'

Jessica nodded, then said tentatively: 'Can I stay here tonight?'

'What – here? Tonight? Jessie, I'm not . . .'

'I don't mean and *do* anything, Mel. I mean like a sleepover, like the sleepovers we used to have at my house when Mum and Dad were alive and we were young. I used to love them so much, look forward to them for days.'

'Jessie, I think we've outgrown sleepovers,' Mel said wryly.

'I know. Really, I know.' Jessica sighed. 'But can't we pretend we haven't? One last time? Just you and me, Mel. For the sake of the world we've lost and the little girls we can never be again. Before we move on. Before I go back to Antony. Let's just have one last night together. Please?'

'Okay, Jessie. You want a sleepover? We'll have a sleepover.' Mel could deny Jessica nothing.

Later, she watched her as the blonde girl slept, the two of them stretched out together on the bed, watched her breathing, a stray strand of Jessica's hair quivering over her parted lips. Sweet, lovely Jessica Lane – she deserved better than Mel, anyway. Antony had better take bloody good care of her after . . .

After what?

Mel felt her skin frost. The dream. Herself and the dead high above the earth, the others falling unresistingly, unprotestingly into the void while she clung on. Yet how tiny the world had seemed from up there, how trivial its troubles. The latter could be left behind simply by letting go of the roundabout. All rides came to an end eventually. Maybe her erstwhile companions had had the right idea. Maybe you just had to accept your fate.

Mel leaned over and pressed her lips to Jessica's forehead. The blonde girl stirred but didn't wake. 'Night, Jessie,' Mel breathed. 'Sleep well.'

When her own sleep came, this time it was dreamless.

Antony restrained himself for as long as he could, but he was still standing outside Jessica's door and pounding well before seven. 'Jess? Jessica, are you in there? Please, Jess, if you're in there, I only want to talk. I want to apologise for last night.'

'I've heard of talking to a brick wall,' Mel said as she strode down the corridor towards him, 'but talking to a wooden door's a new one, Antony. Though I'm afraid you'll get just as little response. The other side of that door's an empty room. Jessie slept in mine last night.'

'In yours? Is she still there?' Urgently. 'I need to see her.'

Mel wagged a deterring finger. 'Yes, she is, but no, you don't.'

'But Mel, you don't understand . . .'

'I do understand. Jessie told me everything.' She patted Antony's shoulder. 'She'll speak to you when she's good and ready. Trust me.' With a wink. 'That won't be long.'

'It's what she might say that worries me,' Antony confided.

'Trust me again. *Don't* worry. Come on, let's go and grab a mug of that speciality Enclave coffee – I don't reckon there's any actual coffee in it at all, do you?'

They weren't first in the canteen. None of its current

occupants, however, seemed interested in breakfast, not Travis or Linden, not Richie, not even the several members of the Kings of the Ring. Something more important seemed about to take place.

'I've just sent someone for you,' Travis said. 'Where's Jessie?'

'She'll be along,' said Mel. 'What's going on?'

'Cooper's back,' Richie declared in a gust of pride. '*With* prisoner. He's on his way down now.'

'Fantastic news. Well done, Cooper,' Antony extolled.

'Has somebody told the Paragons?' Mel asked.

'They should be on their way,' Linden said. 'I think Crispin takes a while to get himself dressed in the morning.'

'Forget them,' Richie snorted. 'What about Coop, eh? What about my Kings of the Ring?'

As if on cue, an armed Cooper himself entered the canteen, a group of teenagers with him. And one other significant individual.

'All right, then,' Richie said gleefully. 'Let's have a good damn look at the Scytharene scum.'

The alien prisoner was shoved forward roughly.

Travis gaped. Antony gaped. Mel gaped.

'Never seen a Scytharene like this before,' Cooper said. 'Gold armour. And looks like it's a *she*.' The prisoner gaped. 'And from what we saw, the other aliens ain't gonna give a shit what we do with her.'

'Travis?' said the Scytharene.

'*Dyona*,' said Travis.

ELEVEN

Ruth Bell expected the caller at her door to be another of those grunting and uncouth brawlers Richie Coker had accumulated on his travels. It wasn't.

'I *told* you I'm coming,' she snapped exasperatedly, flinging wide the door.

'You didn't tell me anything, Ruth,' said Jessica, arms crossed and feet planted squarely in front of the brunette.

'Jessica . . .'

'You particularly didn't tell me how you threw yourself at my boyfriend and offered yourself as my replacement. It must have been a bit of a disappointment to you when I turned up alive and well.'

'I don't know what you mean,' Ruth coloured incriminatingly, 'and I don't care, either. Let me by, please.'

'Soon enough. I've got something I want to tell *you* first.'

'I don't want to hear it.' Backing away – literally – from her original intention to push Jessica aside bodily, Ruth made to slam the door on her unwelcome visitor instead.

Jessica grabbed the door first, held it open. 'You're going to hear it, Ruth. Now I'm not used to threatening people. For one thing, before the Sickness I was the kind of girl who wouldn't say boo to a goose. For another, I was taught that making threats was impolite and good girls should always be polite. But attempting to seduce another girl's boyfriend isn't exactly civilised behaviour either, so in your case, Ruth, I'm going to make an exception. You see, my parents used to stand up for me, look after me, but they're gone now so I'm going to have to get used to standing on my own two feet.'

'Can you spare me the biographical tedium and get on to the threat, Jessica,' said Ruth. 'I have a Scytharene prisoner to study and a killer virus to create.'

'You missed out "and a decent personality to develop", Ruth, but that's okay. We can't expect miracles. I'll come to the point. And the point is, Ruth Bell, you don't ring *Antony's* bell. The point is, if you ever come on to my boyfriend again, make eyes at him across the room, lie in wait to catch him alone, even smile at him; if you do anything, basically, that I don't like, then I'm gonna string you up by those ridiculous plaits of yours and take great pleasure in wiping that smile off your face – permanently.'

Ruth tried to sound unintimidated but didn't quite manage it. 'You've been spending too much time with your coarse friend Mel. You're beginning to sound just like her, Jessica.'

'I take that as a compliment. Now, are we clear?'

'Oh yes. We're clear.'

'Excellent.' Jessica seemed to be enjoying herself. 'So you be careful from now on, Ruth. I'm going to be watching you.' She took her hand away and let the door swing shut on her.

'You're going to be watching me, are you, Jessica?' Ruth Bell's teeth gritted. 'Not closely enough, I promise.'

There were embraces and warm greetings, delight from Dyona that Travis, Antony and Mel were still alive, commiseration from the teenagers that Darion was not. Then, while

266

Dyona was given food and drink, Travis explained their prior connection more methodically. Richie, Linden and Jessica – who appeared in the canteen shortly after the Scytharene and shortly before the three Paragons – had not met Dyona personally before. They'd heard about her from the others, however, knew what was owed to her, how she and Darion had saved their friends from a second encounter with slave processing and a sojourn of indeterminate length in a cryotube. They trusted Dyona.

The Paragons did not.

'Would it not be sensible for the prisoner to be bound?' Crispin said in the conference room to which they'd relocated. The prodigies and Travis's group were joined by Cooper, as Richie's loyal second in the Kings of the Ring, and by Dyona herself, as the subject of their discussion. 'Or shouldn't Cooper at least be aiming a gun at the alien's head – just to be on the safe side?'

'The alien has a name, Crispin,' frowned Mel. 'Why don't you try using it?'

'You don't need to be afraid of me,' Dyona assured him. 'I'm not your enemy.'

'As the spider said to the fly,' remarked Geoffrey, scrutinising Dyona's form as if it was indeed that of an insect and he would prefer to see it dead and pinned to a piece of card.

'We don't need to tie Dyona up. We don't need to point a gun at her.' Travis strove to remain calm. He had a damn sight more confidence in the Scytharene than he did in Crispin Allerton. 'She's already proved she's on our side – like I *told* you.'

'That was then,' Ruth Bell put in sceptically. 'This, as the saying goes, is now. She could be a plant, a spy – like that

Simon Satchwell you told us about, Travis. You believed him to be a friend when he was not.'

Ruth's observations hit home and Travis winced. He didn't like to be reminded of Simon. But Dyona was stronger than the boy with glasses. It had been his own weakness that had destroyed Simon and turned him traitor. 'It's not the same thing,' he said.

'It just seems to me a coincidence that the single alien Cooper captures should be the only surviving Scytharene with whom you, Travis, are on amicable terms. Statistically, let me tell you—'

'Don't bother,' Jessica snapped with uncustomary vehemence, causing both Mel and Antony to raise their eyebrows. 'Numbers mean nothing when you're talking about life.'

'I can explain, in any case,' said Dyona, 'if you'll allow me? It was not by accident that I came to be in the London streets at night but by design. Fleet Commander Gyrion's design. His intention was for me to be executed there, in secret, outside the scope of the Scytharene justice system.'

'He found out you're a dissident?' Antony guessed. 'And Darion too?'

'When I was discovered, I took great pleasure in telling Gyrion everything.' Dyona smiled weakly.

'Good on you,' approved Mel. 'I hope the evil bastard suffers.'

'He may well,' the Scytharene continued, 'but not as much as I would have liked. I was apprehended while plotting to assassinate him, and not *only* Gyrion . . .' Dyona briefly related the details of her scheme and the importance of its timing. 'Two days from now, the Fleet Commanders of the Scytharene enslavement force will be gathered aboard the

Ayrion III to celebrate the subjugation of your world. Which also means that you have only two days before my people's warriors storm this final free sector of London and condemn you all to captivity. My own paltry attempt at opposition has failed. I'm sorry.' She gazed round mournfully at the teenagers. 'My friends, as much as it pains me to admit it, nothing now can stop the enslavement of Earth.'

'Dyona,' said Travis, 'I wouldn't be too sure about that.'

'Naughton,' cautioned Crispin, 'the prisoner does not need to be briefed on our plans.'

'Well I think she does.' Travis was emphatic. 'You fancy a vote on it, Crispin? I think Dyona's got a right to know exactly what we're planning, seeing as how she's such an integral part of it.'

'Part of what?' Dyona said.

And Travis told her.

He wasn't sure what kind of reaction he'd expected from the Scytharene. Disbelief, perhaps, or horror or sorrow or even outrage at the fate that lay in wait for her own race if the Paragons proved themselves worthy of their title. He hadn't anticipated eagerness to the point of covetousness.

'A gene transfer virus. And can it really do as Travis claims?'

'Of course.' Crispin shrugged, addressing Travis as if he had asked the question. 'I am prone neither to exaggeration nor disinformation. This virus will work. That is why we required a prisoner.'

'You don't have a prisoner,' corrected Dyona. 'You have at your service a willing volunteer.' She held out her arms, wrists up. 'If my blood can put an end to this madness, I offer it freely.'

269

'Thank you, Dyona,' said Travis.

Crispin didn't even look at her. 'Mm. I am afraid the Scytharene will still need to be incarcerated after a fashion. As soon as we have taken appropriate samples of her genetic material she must remain in an isolation booth on the laboratory level.' Intercepting Mel and Travis's objections. 'For her own protection, naturally. We wouldn't want our noble ally to become accidentally infected, would we? Which could happen while the virus is being perfected unless we take precautions. Bioengineering a contagion to kill aliens will only be a challenge due to the limited time we now seem to have. Developing one capable of discriminating between good aliens and bad aliens, however, that is asking too much even for a genius.'

'But surely, if your lab's properly sealed and secured . . .'

'It doesn't matter, Travis,' said Dyona. 'I'm sure I'll find the isolation booth perfectly comfortable. I'd have been prepared to sacrifice much more than a few days of liberty to strike such a blow against my people.'

'Mm. The prisoner's co-operation is appreciated,' said Crispin dismissively.

Mel still wasn't happy. 'But it won't be a few days, will it? Once the virus escapes into the atmosphere it'll always be there. We're handing Dyona a life sentence.'

'Oh, I'm sure we'll find some way of immunising her,' said Ruth. 'Eventually. But we can only devote ourselves to one project at a time, and time, it seems, is short.'

'Trav?' Mel appealed.

Fortunately, he didn't have to rule on how Dyona's future should be weighed against everyone else's. The Scytharene did it for him. 'Melanie,' she said, 'my life is only one life, and one life is nothing compared to the freedom of a world.' And in her smile, Mel saw the resignation, the acceptance of the riders on the roundabout. Dyona turned to Crispin Allerton. 'Shall we go?'

'Mm.' Crispin rose; his fellow Paragons followed. 'And perhaps Cooper ought to accompany us too, just in case your faith in our Scytharene guest is misplaced after all, Naughton.'

'It isn't. You just start work, Crispin.' Travis's brow furrowed. 'I need Cooper here. Antony and Richie as well. Bearing in mind what Dyona's told us, it's time we held ourselves a little council of war.'

'As it happens,' Travis began when the four boys were alone in the conference room, 'I've already spoken with Crispin about how we can best deploy the virus.'

'Can't we just set it off like some kind of bomb or something?'

'Close, Richie, but the Scytharene will need to be, too. Crispin says he'll be able to provide the virus in a liquid form that'll evaporate on contact with the air, which is good. It'll be supplied to us in capsules, like grenades, which is also good. Because that's what we're going to do – throw the capsules as if they *were* grenades. They'll break open, release the virus, infect the Scytharene. Crispin reckons that the effect should be just about instantaneous, like a dose of cyanide. That's what he hopes, anyway, and we have to hope so too.'

'We're in the shit if it isn't,' muttered Richie.

'The Kings of the Ring'll fight hard for their champion, you can bet your balls on that,' declared Cooper proudly.

'Movingly put,' commented Antony, shifting self-consciously

271

on his chair, 'though I'd prefer not to gamble any of my body parts, thank you very much. So that's the how, Travis. What about the when and the where?'

'The organiser speaks,' grinned Travis. '*When*: when the Scytharene stage their final assault in the city, on *us* – we just have to proceed on the basis that the virus will be ready by then.'

'We're in the—'

'I know, Richie. The brown stuff. Up to our eyeballs. And *where*, Antony: wherever we establish our defensive line to stop the Scytharene in their tracks. The trouble is, and this is *not* good, right now, even with the Kings on our side . . .'

'In your corner,' preferred Cooper.

'. . . there still aren't likely to be enough of us to even slow the aliens down. Yet we're gonna need to hold out for absolutely as long as possible to give the virus the maximum chance to take effect. Bottom line, we need more fighters.'

'Where the hell from?' said Richie. 'You know the number for Dial-A-Resistance, Naughton?'

'The other gangs,' Travis said simply.

Which kind of startled Cooper. His piggy eyes widened. 'No way. That won't happen. The gangs all hate each other.'

'Well, they're gonna have to learn to hate the Scytharene more. They're gonna have to view each other as allies, not enemies, or we'll all end up as slaves. While you two were in the ring, Antony and I were with the Phantoms . . .'

'Mean-arse dudes, man,' said Cooper. 'You need to keep your guard up around them Randolph brothers. And they is definitely fighting out of the black corner, know what I mean? They ain't gonna listen to no white boy.'

'They will.' Travis spoke with unshakeable certainty. 'I

nearly got through to them before, might have done if the Scytharene hadn't attacked. If the Randolphs are still free, and I hope to God they are, they can be convinced. Danny at least was already seeing the sense in co-operation, and now, when we tell them about the virus, that we've got a *chance* . . .'

'How we gonna tell 'em, Naughton?' said Richie. 'And all the other gangs . . .'

'The Cutters. The Hardcore. The Victoria Boys.' Cooper began listing them.

'That's why you're both here, you and Cooper, Richie,' said Travis. 'That's your job. I want the Kings of the Ring to act as our envoys – messengers, Coop. I want someone to go out to each of the remaining gangs – you know where they'll be – and invite representatives from every single one of them to a meeting we'll be holding later today here – or rather, *there*.' He pointed up at the ceiling. 'In the House of Commons. If Gyrion can host a special summit, I don't see why we can't, and we'll get ours in first.'

'But what do you want me to do, Travis?' asked Antony. Liaising with gangs of thugs wasn't his style, though he hoped Travis had in mind some part for him to play, or why was he here at all? The answer gratified him immensely.

'You're going to plan our defence, Antony, just like you did at Harrington against Rev, so that when the gangs get here I'll be able to tell them how we're going to fight as well as what we're going to fight with. When they hear that, they'll want to stand with us. They *must*.' Travis gazed around the table. His blue eyes blazed with adamantine determination. 'Fleet Commander Gyrion's little celebration is going to turn out to be a *lot* premature. He's finished and he doesn't know it – but he will. This is a council of war now like I said, but when the

273

gangs are assembled in the House and I address them, it'll be a call to arms.' Travis's voice grew increasingly fervent. 'And they'll hear it. I know they will. They'll join together and they'll respond. Because we're all human beings and for the first time we won't just be able to fight the Scytharene. We'll be able to *win*.'

'It's not fair we have to keep the alien alive,' sulked Geoffrey Thomas in the lab. 'It'd be much more fun if we could dissect her.'

'There, there, Geoffrey,' soothed Ruth. 'Don't upset yourself. There'll be plenty of dead aliens for you to play about with later. Focus on the Scytharene's DNA for now.'

'Yes, Ruth,' Geoffrey said with a sigh, and shaking his shaggy head returned his attention to the microscope in front of him.

'Mm. Plenty of dead aliens, yes,' Crispin agreed. 'A great victory for the human race; no doubt a great outburst of jubilation to accompany it. But how much credit will be accorded to those most responsible for the defeat of the Scytharene?'

'You mean the three of us, Crispin?' said Ruth. 'What else do you mean?'

'I mean gratitude, honour, respect – or the lack thereof.' Crispin regarded his fellow Paragon speculatively. 'Tell me that you feel yourself as valued by the primitive intellects who are our present companions as you *ought* to be, Ruth, as you *deserve* to be. Or tell me otherwise. Come. We are alone.' He indicated the lab, empty of everyone but the three prodigies. 'We can speak freely and truly among ourselves.'

'I don't like that Richie Coker lout,' Geoffrey contributed

unsolicitedly from the microscope. 'He called me freak-features. *He's* the freak. Some kind of missing link between apes and humans. I imagine we'd be able to revolutionise evolutionary theory rooting around in his skull.'

'Do not speak, Geoffrey,' instructed Crispin tartly, 'unless you are spoken to. Ruth?'

She was thinking of Antony, daring to reject her. '*I'm warning you . . . I don't want you . . . I don't even like you.*' She was thinking of Jessica, daring to threaten her. '*If you ever come on to my boyfriend again . . . I'm going to string you up by those ridiculous plaits.*' She thought of the both of them defying her, denying her what she wanted, frustrating her desires. And yet they also had the gall to depend on her, the temerity to expect her to use her genius to save them. Without her, they would be doomed.

And inside Ruth Bell, those new emotions festered and seethed, unruly children. Resentment. Embitterment. Hatred. She'd named them all and nurtured them. She was about to send them out to play.

'I understand you, Crispin,' she said coldly. 'I agree with you. We are not respected as we should be, and they need to see that. They need to be shown. We three should be lauded and obeyed, not put to work like lackeys. We should lead.'

'I should, shouldn't I?' Crispin amended. 'And I will.'

And somewhere behind that pale, almost bloodless, almost Scytharene exterior, Ruth sensed that the anger boiling in her was also raging in Crispin. The realisation was kind of exciting, almost . . . arousing.

'Do you have something in mind, Crispin?'

'Come now, Ruth. We have a virus to perfect. Mm, but in answer to your question . . .'

A sly smile wriggled across Crispin Allerton's face. Ruth felt her heart beat rapidly. She was surprised she hadn't noticed it before: Crispin was *hot*.

Jessica was waiting outside the conference room when the four boys emerged from their council of war. She was interested in only one of them.

'Antony, can I talk to you for a minute?'

For an hour, Antony thought. All day. For the rest of his life. 'Sure,' he said. But he couldn't ignore reality. 'Better make it quick, though.' He had a battle to prepare for.

'That's okay. It won't take long.' She glanced at Antony's slow-to-disappear companions. Richie in particular was standing there grinning like he was about to thumb through one of those magazines they kept confined to the top shelf of the newsagent's. 'Haven't you got something you should be doing, Richie?'

'Yes, he does.' Travis grabbed Richie's elbow and pulled. 'We're out of here, Jessie, don't worry.'

'Aw, Naughton, I was gonna lend Tony some moral support.'

'*Im*moral support maybe . . .'

The two of them and Cooper moved off down the corridor.

'Back inside,' directed Jessica, ushering Antony into the conference room once more.

'I don't know about you wanting to talk to me,' he blurted. 'After last night I wasn't sure you'd ever want to *see* me again. Jessie, I am *so* sorry. I didn't mean to upset you. I thought—'

Jessica placed one finger on his lips. 'Antony. Ssh. It's all right. I have something to say about last night too.'

276

She took her finger away to accommodate the meeting of lips, to enable her arms to twine around Antony's strong, warm body and squeeze.

'There,' she said triumphantly when she finally broke away. 'I hope you were listening.'

Antony blinked several times, opened and closed his mouth as often. 'Wow. I don't know, though, Jess. My ears – do you think you could say that again?'

She was laughing. She was in his arms and laughing. And she was glad she'd stayed with Mel last night. It seemed that some of Mel's forthrightness and confidence had rubbed off on her. She felt strong and she felt alive.

'Last night was my fault, Antony, not yours.'

'What about we settle for fifty-fifty?'

'I'm sorry I ran off like I did. One night I won't. One night I'll stay.'

The thrill of the prospect surged through Antony. 'I'll go get my diary.'

'It's not yet.'

'I was joking. I didn't mean to rush you and I won't. Whenever you're ready, I'll be ready.'

Jessica sighed. 'Part of me still wants to belong to the old world, Antony. I haven't come to terms yet with the new.'

'Who has?' Antony said glumly.

'But I will. And when I have, that's when we can be together.'

'So, I suppose it's in my vested interest to help you along the way, Jessica Lane.'

'I suppose it is – Antony Clive. If you're willing to do that.'

'Try stopping me.' He kissed her. She responded. 'The old

world, the world we knew,' he breathed, 'it'll never be lost entirely, Jess. It'll live on in us.'

Travis strode briskly through the corridors of Enclave Zero. Like someone who knew where he was going, knew what he was doing. Like a leader.

On many occasions since the Sickness he'd wondered if he would ever feel happiness again. The same terrible possibility had occurred to him during those grief-stricken days following the murder of his father, days numbed with sorrow, time paralysed as if its passage towards the future was a bad thing, taking him further away from the period when his father was alive, parting them more absolutely than death itself. But back then, at least, his mum had been there to help him cope, and relatives, and friends, and the slow-acting comfort of the familiar, the gradual restorative of the continuity of life. The same programmes on the TV. The same shops open at the same times. Dogs being walked. Cars being driven. School. Back then, though one man was dead, the man who'd meant the world to Travis, the world itself lived on.

Not so after the Sickness. The disease had made the planet a cemetery, its countries graves. It had seemed to Travis that there could be no recovery from catastrophe on such a scale, not emotionally. He'd seen ahead only toil and hardship and struggle. He'd braced himself for an existence of anguish and pain. He'd had experience of that. He could survive.

But now, miraculously, *now* there seemed to be more to look forward to than misery. Laughter. Delight. Fulfilment. The future was beginning to seem like a blessing again rather than a curse. Despite the Sickness. Despite the Scytharene. It had begun with Linden, what he felt for her. His love for

Linden had helped him go on. And now, with the hope of vanquishing the invaders . . . Life was making sense again. Optimism coursed through his veins like blood.

The others must be sensing the same. The way they were acting, the way they were changing. Jessica falling for Antony, taking the *lead* back there at the conference room, it had looked like. Travis grinned. That was new. Wouldn't have happened in the old days. Jessie had been too afraid of boys for intimacy then, had shut herself up in her house like Rapunzel in her tower. And Richie's sudden maturity as leader of the Kings of the Ring – who'd have thought that the bully of Wayvale Comp would ever be transformed into someone you could trust. Mel was still on the sidelines, mind, and he couldn't quite shake the feeling that there was something she hadn't told him, but he could sort Mel out in due course. He was confident about that. After he'd dealt with the Scytharene.

Because success there too lay within his grasp. Victory was coming. It was fate. Finding the Paragons in the first place. The fortuitous reappearance of Dyona. The gene transfer virus. The gangs. Everything falling into place. He could unite the gangs. He felt the power in him to do that, the words, the inspiration. He'd unite the gangs and together they'd smash the Scytharene. And Linden would love him and his father would be proud of him and Travis would have made his life matter as he'd vowed to do, all those years ago at his father's funeral. '*I want to be like you, Dad. I'll do what's right. I'll make my stand. I promise.*'

Now where was Linden? He wanted . . . he needed to see her. To share with her what he was feeling. He'd tried her room and the canteen but no. Where *was* she? Travis hurried on, like someone who knew where he was going, what he was doing. Like a leader.

He felt a moment of destiny upon him.

'Richie, you can't do that.'

'Lin, I don't see I've got any choice.'

Richie and Linden, in the monitoring and communications centre. All around them, screens keeping watch on the many entrances to Enclave Zero. Nobody keeping an eye on the two teenagers. Which of course was the point.

'All right, you *mustn't* do that.' Hugging her elbows like they were in need of consoling. Closer to Richie than she'd ever intended to be again.

'It's no good.' His baseball cap jammed down as far as it would go, hiding his face. 'Look, Lin, you've got to see this from where I'm standing. I could reach out right now and touch you . . .'

'Richie, don't.' Linden stepped back warily as if he might be tempted to illustrate words with actions.

'I won't. I told you I won't. But I want to – and every time I'd see you I'd want to. And I couldn't bloody put up with that, it'd drive me bloody mad, and the only way of getting round it is to leave. So that's what I'm gonna do.'

'Richie . . .'

'Me and the Kings. They're out persuading the gangs to come to Naughton's little shindig now, and I won't leave you in the lurch by skipping out before the virus is ready and we take on the bloody Scytharene, but after that, if we're still breathing, after that me and the Kings are out of here.' Richie smiled ruefully. 'Maybe I belong with guys like Cooper more than I ever belonged with the likes of you and Naughton anyway.'

'That's not true, Richie. Listen, I don't want you to go.'

He gave an ironic laugh. 'But you don't want me anywhere near you either. Do you chicks ever bloody make up your minds?'

'This is not about me, Richie,' Linden protested with increasing desperation. 'It's about the group, your value to the group. Defeating the Scytharene's only the start. We'll need to found a new community, one that can prosper and thrive and provide a good life for us all, and we'll need everybody to manage that. You. The Kings. You have to stay, Richie. You have to be here to help Travis.'

'It won't work, Lin.'

'Richie, we can make it work. We mustn't let what happened between us drive you out and damage our chances of—'

'Excuse me.' Travis. At the door. 'Sorry to interrupt.' Travis. Eyes piercing like blue blades. 'What *did* happen between you?'

TWELVE

'Naughton. Shit.'

'Travis . . .' Linden began to move towards him.

He held up his hand to stop her. 'It might be a good idea if you stayed where you are for now, Lin. I can hear you all right from here. I'm just not sure I understand you. So, simple question. I'll ask it again. Between you. What happened?'

'Nothing, Trav.' Linden laughed weakly. 'We were just – we were . . .' Finding it hard to lie directly.

'Fighting, Naughton. Giving each other some verbal,' pitched in Richie, finding it easier. 'You know me and Hippy Chick don't get on, so we were slagging each other off as usual, then – uh – Linden suddenly says maybe we ought to kind of call a truce, put our diffs behind us, you know? Not let what's gone down between us affect the group and – uh – damage our chances of giving the bloody Scytharene a damned good kicking . . . uh . . .' Like a car with very little petrol in the tank, Richie ran out of inspiration and ground to a halt.

'Is that right, Richie?' Travis looked far from convinced. 'Is that right, Lin?' Turning his eyes on her.

She couldn't meet them. 'Please, Trav.' They were like an interrogator's lamp, boring into her, seeing through her. 'Don't look at me like that.' Exposing the truth. She couldn't resist Travis's gaze.

'What happened between you and Richie, Lin?'

'I'm sorry, Trav. I've never been so . . . It was a mistake. It was once. I was stupid and weak and I've regretted it every single second since.'

'You've been with Richie.' Travis said the words in a voice dulled by disillusion. 'You've slept with Richie.'

'It was once, Trav, and—'

'Once is all it has to be.'

'I wanted to tell you, but I was ashamed.'

'Since we've been together. Since you said you loved me. Did you tell Richie you loved him before you let him put his hands on you?'

Linden felt the sting of tears. 'Travis, please . . .'

'It wasn't her fault, Naughton.' Richie stepped forward. There was defiance in his expression, the pride of taking responsibility. 'It was mine. It was all down to me. You can't blame Linden.'

'What,' Travis persisted robotically, 'happened?'

'I made a move on her. I seduced her, if you like. When you, Tony and Morticia were out trying to get yourselves caught so you could find Darion again – when you were out of the way. When Linden was unhappy and upset and kind of bloody lonely. Fair game, I thought. I fancied her. I took advantage of her. Me, Naughton. I'm the one you should be pissed off at, and if you want to take a pop, now's your chance.' Richie stretched his arms out on either side of him and raised his chin in preparation for a punch. 'You want to kick the shit out of me, Naughton, you go ahead. I won't stop you. I deserve it. I'm dirt. But Linden isn't. She's . . . don't blame her.'

'I don't blame her,' said Travis.

'You don't?' The hope of forgiveness surged through Linden's body like a rush of clear water.

'I blame myself.'

'But Travis, you can't . . .'

'For believing you, Linden. For believing *in* you.' And there wasn't anger or sorrow in his tone, but disappointment and defeat and a great weariness. 'I should never have trusted you. You lied to me, Lin. You let me down. You're not the girl I thought you were.'

'I am, Travis. I want to be.' Distraught, she darted forward to embrace him. 'I'm *trying* to be.' If she could hold him, she could convince him. The warmth and the nearness, the life of her body could persuade him. She wasn't so good with words, but *actions* . . . She could prove she loved him if he'd just let her.

Travis stepped away. 'I'd sooner you didn't touch me, Linden.'

'Trav,' the girl wailed. '*Please* . . .'

'Don't be a twat, Naughton. *Listen* to her. It was just once we did it. One time. And she's been telling me where to go ever since because she only wants you, Naughton. Only you.'

'Unless I'm out of the room,' Travis said with quiet bitterness. 'Then she seems quite happy to have someone else.'

'Travis, that's not true. Don't condemn me out of hand.'

'Betrayal condemns itself, Linden. There's nothing I can do.'

Linden shrank back from him then, and it seemed to her that the blue flames in his eyes were flickering and going out. And she realised with a shock of absolute horror that what she'd done had killed something in Travis's soul, something vital, something that had made him who he was. Linden groaned: 'Oh God.'

'What the hell are you on about, Naughton?' She could hear Richie's voice, angry, pleading. 'Climb off your bloody high horse for once and join the rest of us arseholes who make mistakes. Listen, you can believe this or you can tell me to get stuffed, but up till now I've admired you, looked up to you. Yeah, me. Richie Coker. But let me tell you, Naughton, you're losing the plot now. You want to lose Linden too?' Richie was defending her, Linden could hear, but she wished he'd just shut up. *Shut up*. She hated him. 'You're not even gonna give her a second chance? We all deserve a second chance, don't we? Who do you bloody think you are, Naughton, judging Linden like you think you've got a right? God?'

'Richie!' she yelled at him, appalled.

'What? Naughton's got to know he's not perfect.'

'I do know that, Richie. So there's no point in me staying.' Travis turned on his heel and left the room.

His departure was so sudden that it took moments for Linden to react. She snapped at Richie. 'What have you *done*?'

'I was trying to help . . .'

Linden winced. 'What have *we* done? We've broken him. I've got to . . .' Setting off in pursuit of Travis.

Richie following. 'I'll come too.'

'*No*.' Wheeling and punching Richie on the chest. There was still an intensity in *Linden's* eyes. 'I want you to *go*, Richie, and I don't care where. Just get lost. Away. Take your gang with you if you like, but you were right before. I should have listened to you. Clear out. You're scum, Richie, and I never *ever* want to see you again. Do you hear me? *Never*.'

'Lin . . .' But she wasn't prepared to argue. She was gone. Richie stood in the moncom centre alone. He closed his eyes. Breathing was strangely difficult and he felt momentarily unsteady on his feet. Linden's parting words had hurt him almost physically, each one landed like a blow on his unprotected form. He didn't feel like a champion now; he felt like a loser.

He'd always been a loser. He'd always known it. Bullying, that had been his way of covering it up. Until, since the Sickness, since falling in with Naughton, he'd begun to wonder if there wasn't a better way. Not disguising weakness, but replacing it with strength, changing, learning, becoming a person he could be proud of. Naughton's example had led him to hope for a transformation in his life, and how had he treated Travis in return?

He'd wanted to *be* Travis Naughton. Instead, Richie might just have destroyed him.

Vain. Arrogant. Deluded. The self-assessments drove him out of Enclave Zero like the cracks of a whip. Naïve. Self-important. They hounded him through Parliament like catcalls.

Travis walked so quickly he was almost running. He didn't know where he was going or what he was doing, except that he was leaving Linden behind. And more than Linden.

The Palace of Westminster mocked him. Its tainted grandeur taunted him, seemed to be making a derisory statement concerning his own pretensions for leadership. Here, in the dignified corridors of the Houses of Parliament, the lawmakers had once assembled to chart the course of a nation. Travis had had the audacity to believe that he could follow in their footsteps, a boy of sixteen, undistinguished and anonymous before the Sickness, a rootless orphan now. He'd imagined he could plot the downfall of an entire alien race as if the world was a computer game and to win you only had to press the right button. He'd fantasised that he could shape the future for a generation. Idle dreams. Dangerous dreams, for he'd been mistaken enough to persuade others to share them. No longer. The obsolete, hollow shell that now was Parliament reflected the emptiness of all his grand boasts, the poverty of his vision.

He wasn't fit to be a leader. Why should anyone listen to him? Inspire? Command respect? Even his girlfriend was cheating on him. *Ex*-girlfriend.

Simon's accusations before he died had been true, Travis realised. He'd been on an ego trip the whole time. Not only since the Sickness. Before then. Since his father's death. His pathetic little pledge to do the right thing and make his stand. What a load of self-deceiving shit. What kind of stand could he make? What was the point of even trying in a world where your girl goes and gets laid behind your back at the earliest opportunity? A wrecked and ruined world – like his life.

Travis emerged from the Houses of Parliament into the broader desolation of London. There was no way back from this. The Scytharene would come. Nothing mattered any more.

He'd failed.

Jessica called out urgently to Antony even as she ran down the corridor towards him. The blond boy's heart leapt with hope: 'They're back.'

'No.' Anxiety marred Jessica's features. 'Still no sign of Travis *or* Linden. And now Richie's gone too.'

'Gone?'

'As in, not here any more. Not in the Enclave. At least, not as far as I can tell.'

Antony frowned. 'You know, not so long ago I'd have put that down as typical Richie Coker behaviour, vanishing before a crisis, choosing the coward's way out. But not now. Richie's proved his courage. You think it might have something to do with Travis and Linden disappearing?'

'I don't know. Maybe.'

'What does Cooper say, or the other Kings?'

'I don't know that either. Largely because . . .' Jessica trailed away meaningfully.

'They've left as well?' Antony shook his head in bafflement. 'What is this, some kind of secret mass evacuation?'

'There's more. It's why you need to come.' She took his hand. 'Mel's in the moncom centre.'

Antony allowed himself to be led as if he didn't know the way. He only wished he could locate Travis and Linden – and Richie – as easily.

They'd first noticed their leader's absence late that morning when the Kings began returning from their missions to the other surviving gangs. It had been taken as read that Travis would want to hear each party's report on how they'd been received and the gangs' response to the invitation that had been delivered. But Travis couldn't be found – anywhere. Mel had suggested they switch their search to Linden on the basis that wherever Linden was, Travis would probably be close by. A fair assumption that might still turn out to be true, but so far Linden had also proved to be untraceable. The consensus had developed that they both might – must – have left Enclave Zero for some reason, be above ground

288

and outside somewhere. Even if that was the case, however, their companions had lacked the resources to scour the streets for them without at least some kind of clue as to their whereabouts. Besides, they'd been otherwise occupied.

It seemed that in the end the other gangs had been remarkably amenable to the message the Kings had conveyed. Initial suspicion, in some cases threats of violence, had gradually been replaced by a more positive attitude. Whether out of belief in the value of unity and solidarity for their own sake, as Travis might have liked, or due to fear of the Scytharene and a desire for self-preservation, as Antony surmised might be nearer the truth, every gang approached had agreed to send delegates to Travis's summit meeting that afternoon in the House of Commons. Which had been great news then and was great news now, with one important proviso: as long as Travis was there to address them.

At first Antony had imagined that Travis and Linden would be back soon. Travis knew what time the summit was scheduled for and how vital recruiting the gangs was for their cause. But soon stretched from minutes into hours and still he failed to reappear. Antony's fears began to multiply. Travis had ventured outside. The Scytharene were outside, the Scavvies, who knew what other species of undesirables. What if Travis had fallen victim to unexpected danger?

What if he wasn't coming back?

'Mel,' Antony greeted as he and Jessica hastened into the moncom centre. 'At least you're still here.'

'Can't get rid of me, Antony.' Mel smiled grimly. 'I'm like a really hard-to-shift stain.'

'So what do you want? Don't tell me the Paragons have gone AWOL with everybody else?'

'Nah. They're in the lab,' Mel assured him. 'Dyona's in the isolation booth. Other than that, though, as I'm sure Jessica's told you, *we're it*' – melodramatically – 'the final human bastion against the evil alien slavers, *except* for maybe these guys.'

She pressed a button at one of the computer consoles. Several of the screens exchanged internal for external views, displayed not Enclave corridors but streets in the vicinity of Parliament. Groups of heavily armed youths were converging on the Palace of Westminster. Grim, guarded, watchful, cautious of the other bands where others could be seen, hostility suppressed, not renounced. Some dressed in identical colours to denote membership of their gang; others were bonded by the pigment of their skin, in one case by their gender. 'An all-chicks outfit,' Mel observed. 'Must be the Sisters. Wonder if they've got an opening.' One gang wore the scarves and shirts of the same football team, another carried Christian crosses along with knives and clubs and automatic rifles, while another was garbed in traditional Islamic dress and still another, composed entirely of those who once had been termed hoodies, slunk its way to the summit as if the Sickness had never happened and its members were simply on their way to meet with their social workers.

Mel looked to Antony. 'It's hardly the United Nations,' she said, 'but I think the delegates are arriving.'

'They can't be.' Antony's mouth was dry. 'Travis isn't here.'

'*You'll* have to speak to them, Antony,' said Jessica proudly. 'You'll have to take over until Travis returns from wherever it is he's gone.'

'Me? I don't know, Jess. I'm not sure I can.' Liaising with gangs of thugs wasn't his style.

'Of course you can,' Jessica encouraged him, squeezing his hand.

'You'd better,' put in Mel. 'Once they get into the Commons they're not gonna sit around sharpening their knives and polishing their guns for long. They'll want action. If you don't address them, Antony, they'll either end up killing each other rather than the Scytharene or they'll just disperse, with no chance of us ever bringing them all together again. Day after tomorrow's the end, one way or the other. We need that united front now or it'll be too late.'

'I know. I know. It's just . . .' Antony smiled ironically. He'd longed to be leader while Travis was here; now that Travis was gone and his chance had come, he wasn't so certain he wanted it after all. Lately, he'd learned his limitations. 'It's just that I'm not Travis. I don't have the words, the words that Travis has. They're not in me. And even if they were, if I spoke them it'd be like I'd exhumed them from a dictionary. They'd sound dead. When Travis speaks, he brings the language alive.'

'I thought kids who went to posh public schools were supposed to learn self-confidence as well as Latin and Greek and stuff,' said Mel. 'Come on, Antony, let's have a little bit of belief. Your old man was a diplomat, wasn't he? Show us you're a chip off the old block.'

'You'll be fine, Antony, I know you will.' Jessica hugged him. 'I'll be right beside you. Remember the speeches you gave at Harrington after we defeated Rev, after we sighted the Scytharene ships? You united us then. You can unite the gangs now.'

''Fraid the bottom line is,' said Mel, 'you ain't got no choice.'

291

'No,' acknowledged Antony soberly. He didn't have a choice. But with Jessica in his arms that didn't seem to matter. He felt stronger again, more sure of himself. So he wasn't Travis. So what? He'd simply have to rise above his limitations, because he refused to let the girls down, *or* Travis, or himself. He refused to fail.

The success of their entire last stand against the Scytharene depended on him.

Linden found Travis on Westminster Bridge, in the shadow of a Big Ben that would never chime again and gazing out across the Thames towards the shattered wheel of the London Eye, somehow torn loose from its original foundations and toppled into the river. Cullers hovered in the distant skies and the south end of the bridge was blocked by an impassable barricade of tanks and armoured vehicles, but Travis appeared to have no desire to venture further than the point he'd reached. He seemed listless, lifeless, drained of energy, propped up by the parapet he was leaning against. He looked broken in spirit, and Linden's heart went out to him even as guilt racked her without mercy. She was to blame for her boyfriend's despair.

'Trav?' Approaching him nervously, pausing some yards away.

'What do you want?' He didn't look at her.

'To explain.'

'To make excuses, you mean.'

'No. No excuses.'

'You should have sent Richie. He was doing his best to cover up for you before. Had no idea he could be so *gallant*. People surprise you all the time, don't they?' He cast a hurt and bitter look at Linden. Shouldn't have. Shouldn't have looked at her. If he looked at her for too long, he'd love her all over again, and that couldn't be right, could it? Not after what she'd done.

'Richie lied to you, Travis,' Linden admitted, 'but I won't. Sleeping together was my fault as much as his.'

'Thought so,' said Travis, returning his stare to the Thames.

Linden crept closer. 'I betrayed you by doing it, Trav. I know that. I can't tell you how ashamed that makes me feel.'

'Why try? It's not as if I'm interested.'

'I betrayed myself too. That's what I want you to know. I let myself down, allowed myself to be less than the person I want to be. The person you've *made* me want to be, Trav. Before I met you, I thought that love and sex were the same thing and that to show love for a boy all you needed to do was go to bed with him. But I don't believe that now.'

'Do you not?'

'Sex is *part* of love, and it's a good part, but being with you's taught me that there's more to love than the physical. There's faithfulness and honesty and trust. There's the meeting of spirits, becoming soul-mates. They're the things I want now, Trav. With you and only with you. I just . . . for a moment that night with Richie – I'm not making excuses – I let myself be distracted. I was lonely and upset and I needed comfort, someone to hold and . . . my body took over. I let it happen. I shouldn't have.'

'That's right.' Unsympathetically. 'You shouldn't have.'

She was at his shoulder now, her expression pleading. 'But it was a mistake, Trav, a weakness. I'm not perfect. I warned you once not to think I was. I told you. I'm trying to be a better person but in the end I'm only human, and humans make mistakes. We can fall short of what we want for ourselves and I did and I'm so sorry.'

'I worshipped you, Lin,' Travis said. He turned to her with recrimination in his eyes.

'Don't. I'm not worthy of that. Love me instead.' She dared to reach out and stroke his hair, his face.

'I wouldn't have cheated on you.'

'I know. You're stronger than me, Trav. You're stronger than anyone I've ever met – which is why I love you and why you have to come back to us. To all of us.'

With a rueful smile, he took her hand away from him. 'I don't think I can do that.'

'The gangs'll be here soon, Trav. We need you to be our leader. *I* need you to be my lover. Please come back with me – or nothing's going to matter any more.'

'Nothing *does* matter any more,' Travis said resignedly.

'No. You're wrong.' Fierce and fearful at the same time. 'Don't do this, Travis. Don't give up. Not you. Not because of me.' She seized his sweatshirt with both hands and shook him. 'Love matters. Life matters. Always. *Always.*'

'I don't think so. Not now. Not any more.'

'You *do* think so. Inside your head, Trav, inside your soul, you *know* so.' She glanced down at the oily waters swirling beneath the bridge. 'And I'm going to prove it.'

'Linden, what. . .?' She let go of him. She clambered unsteadily on to the bridge's low protective wall. 'What do you think you're doing?' Was that concern in his voice as she held her arms out for balance, inched to the edge of the parapet? She'd soon know.

'I'm going to jump, Trav.' Swaying like a novice

tightrope-walker, fixing her eyes on her feet. 'I'm gonna plunge into the Thames and then I'm gonna drown. It tried to kill me before in the tube tunnel, remember? It won't pass up on a second chance.'

'You're out of your mind . . .'

'This is about *your* mind, Travis. If you really believe nothing matters, you'll let me fall. If you don't, you'll save me. Your choice.' She glanced back at him. 'I mean it, Trav.'

And slipped. Lost her balance. Tottered, flailed for a second, saw the river, dark and deep and waiting, felt gravity forcing her down, felt terror rising inside her . . .

Felt Travis's hand gripping hers. Strong. Warm. Felt him pulling her back from the brink. Linden did jump from the parapet of Westminster Bridge. Into Travis's arms.

And he was holding her, and he was crushing her to him and scolding her and murmuring endearments. And if the end had come for Linden Darroway that very moment, she wouldn't have died unhappy.

They sat on the pavement, their backs against the parapet and their arms around each other.

'You're a stupid, stupid' – punctuating each criticism with a kiss – 'stupid, *stupid* . . . You could have killed yourself.'

'Unlikely. I knew you wouldn't let me fall, Trav.'

'But after the way I've treated you, not giving you a chance to explain, not even trying to understand . . .'

'Travis, I was in the wrong, not you.'

'No. *I* was.' Travis's frown seemed to be directed inwards. 'Too uptight. Too unbending. Too judgemental. You were right about me wanting to put you on a pedestal, Linden. It's the way I think. It has been ever since my dad died. I had to make him proud of me, so he could look down from heaven

295

and be proud of me, and because Dad died doing the right thing, that was what I had to do. The right thing. Every day. Make a stand. Be strong, not weak. Never surrender to weakness. I guess, over time, it's become an obsession, and I've been unfairly scornful of what might be called weakness and I've believed that to be good you have to be perfect and never make mistakes.'

'Travis,' Linden said gently, 'that's not possible.'

'Would you believe it's taken me until now to realise that? It's taken almost throwing our relationship away to make me understand. Imperfections aren't what we should hate about each other. They're what we should love. Listen, Lin, it doesn't matter what you've done or who with, as long as we're together now. I don't want to drive you away. That's the last thing I want. See, I can't imagine life without you . . .'

'You won't have to, Trav. I'm here and I'm going nowhere.'

'I'm glad.'

'Well, nowhere without you, anyway.' She began to get to her feet. 'Come on, leader-boy. You've got a summit meeting to address.'

Travis did not budge. 'I don't know about that, Linden.'

'Trav?'

'When I left the Enclave, I thought I'd lost you. And when I saw the city, reduced to this wasteland, remembered everything else that's happened, the Sickness, the Scytharene, the family we've lost too and the friends, it all . . . it's too much, Lin. It's weighing me down. I feel like I did the day Dad was killed. Useless. Hopeless. Too small to make a difference. Too unimportant to make a stand. Can I change anything? What can I change?'

'Not the past, that's for sure.' Linden knelt with her knees on his thigh and peered deeply, tenderly into his eyes. 'The past is over, Trav. That's why it's no good dwelling on it or letting it be a burden on you. In the Children of Nature we had a saying: yesterday is a crop that has seen harvest; the work of today is to plant the seed of tomorrow. That's what we have to do, Travis, all of us together, but maybe you most of all because like it or not you've got the authority. You're our leader, Trav. You're the one. And you can't deny it or run away from it or try to hide. You have to face up to it.' She searched in his eyes for their blue fire to rekindle. 'Please, Trav. Be strong again. Be who you're meant to be.'

In the event, Antony stepped into the House of Commons with both Jessica *and* Mel by his side, and he drew courage from the girls' presence. He might have felt safer, though, had he also been accompanied by every last member of the Kings of the Ring, fully armed. The atmosphere was not agreeable.

The gangs had taken up positions along the benches on both sides of the chamber as if they were on military operations and might need to defend themselves at any moment. They could have been unruly students in a lecture theatre, they were the right age, except that even the most disruptive elements within the education system tended not to brandish knives with impunity, or wield automatic weapons.

Antony felt intimidated by the blur of suspicious, scowling faces he could make out in the pallid light. They'd placed every portable source of illumination Enclave Zero possessed about the chamber prior to the meeting, but Antony would sooner have been in darkness. There were jeers as he and the girls entered, derisory comments from all around, insults, expletives, like the rattle of ammunition.

'Who the hell are these guys? . . . Hey, baby, over *here* . . . Waste of bloody time . . . This is shit . . . Could be a sodding alien trap far as we know . . . Is that blond ponce Naughton? Looks like a tosser to me . . . Don't trust those Hardcore bastards . . . Where the hell are those guys from before? . . . What the hell are we doing here?'

'This is it, Antony,' said Jessica.

'Yeah.' And in the centre of the Commons he raised his hands for silence. An observer might have been forgiven for thinking that the motion more closely resembled a surrender. 'Please. Good after— please. If we could have some quiet.' Not exactly silence ensued, a dull rumble of restless discontent like a storm outside a window, but it was definitely an improvement. 'Thank you. My name's Antony Clive.'

Temporarily an improvement. 'Where's Naughton? You're not Naughton? They told us your leader was Travis Naughton.'

'Please. *Please.* If you'll listen to me.' And it wasn't that Antony's resove as such deserted him at the crucial moment, just that he realised with cruel certainty that the gangs would never take heed of someone like him. They saw only his privilege, his past, not how he could help them now. They'd never accept his authority. 'Please, if you'll be patient. We'll begin shortly.'

The volume rose again on the gathering's dissatisfaction.

Mel's too. 'Begin shortly? What's that about? Begin now or you'll lose them.'

'All right, Mel,' chided Jessica. 'Antony knows what he's doing.' Turning to her boyfriend: 'Don't you?'

'We wait for Travis. We give him a chance to turn up. A few more minutes.'

'Hey, Clive, man. Where the hell *is* Naughton?'

A voice Antony recognised. Dwayne Randolph and a handful of Phantoms were seated on the front row of benches. Antony crossed to them a little desperately. Dwayne wasn't exactly friendly, but at least he wasn't exhibiting open animosity. 'Dwayne.' Awkwardly offering his hand, which wasn't taken. 'You got away from the Scytharene advance.'

'Some of us did. Some of us didn't.'

'Where's Danny?'

'He didn't.'

'Oh. I'm sorry.' Especially as Danny had seemed the more rational of the Randolphs.

'It don't matter whether you're sorry or whether you ain't. The aliens still got my brother and they are gonna pay for that. Which is why I thought we were here – to find out how we can *make* those bastards pay.'

'That's right. That's right.' Antony felt he was making progress with one gang at least. 'I'm glad you came.'

'We didn't come for your benefit, man. We came 'cause I got to thinking, maybe, if we'd had more people fighting with us yesterday, if the gangs had combined then, maybe Danny would still be with us now. Maybe Naughton had a point about uniting. Trouble is, I don't see Naughton now. Where the hell *is* he?'

'Ah, Travis has been unavoidably detained, Dwayne, but I'm – I'm going to speak to you all.' Antony couldn't delay any longer. The mood in the chamber was growing uglier. He *would* have to make the speech himself. *Rise above his limitations.* He forced himself back into the middle of the floor.

'*Get on with it* . . . If that Cutter looks at me again I'm gonna ghost the sucker . . .'

299

'Please. Listen.' Antony tried again. 'What I have to tell you is vitally important. It's how we can beat the Scytharene . . .'

'Fat bloody chance with this geezer . . . Tosser . . . Waste of bloody time . . . We've left the others open to attack for *this* . . . Let's get the hell out of here . . .'

The gangs began to rise.

'Antony,' cried Jessica. 'Do something. Say something. They're leaving.'

Panic probably wasn't the most potent response, but it was all Antony could muster. He yelled out: 'No. Don't go. Please. You have to hear this. It's for your own good. Don't . . . Dwayne. Stay where you are.'

'You stay where *you* are if you like, Clive,' Dwayne Randolph retorted. 'But if you try to stop the Phantoms from getting the hell out of this shit-hole, we are gonna have *words*.'

A tumult of angry, frustrated voices. Howls and mockery. A general surge towards the doors.

From where the subjugator bolt was fired. It flashed across the chamber like a white lance. Instantly, every gang member's gun was trained on the figure that stood in the doorway. For the first time, total silence.

'Sorry to interrupt, but I think you've been waiting for me. I'm Travis Naughton.'

'Thank God,' exhaled Antony.

Travis strode into the body of the chamber, handed the subjugator to Linden behind him, showing open palms to the gangs.

'Trav,' Mel hissed, 'where the hell have you been?'

'We were worried about you, Trav. And you, Lin,' added Jessica.

'It's okay,' Linden assured her.

'I've been – where I shouldn't have gone,' Travis said cryptically. 'But I'm back now.' And his blue eyes blazed. No Richie around, he observed. No Cooper or Kings, either. He sensed a problem, but he could catch up on current events in Enclave Zero later. His immediate priority was the gangs. They were still on their feet, still on the verge of departure. He'd have to do something about that.

'You all leaving?' He raised his voice, addressed both sides of the House and every gang equally. 'That's fine. You want to leave, you know where the door is. I won't stop you.'

'You *couldn't* bloody stop us,' someone bellowed.

'I can tell you what'll happen, though.' Travis jabbed a finger at the heckler. 'Leave now, and the day after tomorrow you'll either be dead or packed away in a Scytharene cryotube, because the day after tomorrow is when the Scytharene are launching their final assault on *your* territories, on *your* streets. Leave now and you're condemning yourselves to be slaves for the rest of your lives. But that's all right. Maybe that's what some of you want. Maybe that's what *all* of you want. It's what all of you'll get if you leave now. But if you want to be free, if you want to fight the aliens with a chance of victory, then stay. Sit. Listen. I'll tell you how.' Travis noticed the small Phantom contingent. 'Dwayne,' he said. 'Trust me.'

'You found what you came to London for?' Dwayne asked. It appeared so. 'Okay, Travis Naughton, you got your chance.'

The Phantoms resumed their seats. Sceptically, grudgingly, so did everyone else.

'I see you've all come armed to Parliament,' said Travis.

'Did you know they used to have a rule here, no sword-belts in the chamber? Times change. Who wouldn't want to have a weapon handy with the Scytharene out there hunting us down? Trouble is, you're not only armed against the aliens, are you? You're armed against each other. Now I don't claim to possess any psychic powers, but I reckon I've got a pretty accurate idea what's in your minds right this minute when you look across the floor and see the delegations from the other gangs. Suspicion. Distrust. Maybe fear. And that's at best, am I right? At worst, hatred, enmity, hostility. And I know why, too. Because when you look at the other gangs you see what makes them different from *your* gang, and you let difference create division. You see whites or blacks or Asians or Chinese or Muslims or Christians or kids from one area or kids from another, and that's how you want to be seen as well. You define yourselves by the characteristics that set you apart from one another. I can understand it, I suppose. In the old days, the pre-Sickness world, we were told that those kinds of distinctions were what were important, that they gave us our identity – and we all need to be sure of our identity, especially now when we're under siege.

'Because let me get inside the heads of the Scytharene – not that I'd want to stay there for long. If the Scytharene could witness all of us gathered here together, they wouldn't see what *you* see. They wouldn't see differences. Peculiarities like religion or nationality or the colour of our skin, these are things that wouldn't even register with the aliens – too minor, too superficial. To them, we're all the same. They'd see only what *makes* us all the same, the single quality that unites us all in the Scytharene's eyes and that should unite us all in ours – our shared humanity. We're human beings, every one of us

302

here, we're equal members of the human race, and we need to hold on to that fact and celebrate it and stand together and fight together because of it.

'The Scytharene have drawn certain other conclusions about us too. They think we're inferior. We're not. They think we're slaves. We're not. They think we're divided. I think so too. And if we are, when they also think they can defeat us, they *will*.' Shouts of defiance from the benches. 'You can see where I'm going with this, can't you? We can all fight for our lives and our freedom and what belongs to us. The Phantoms can fight, the Cutters can, the Hardcore, the Victoria Boys, you can all fight' – appealing to the chamber as one – 'but if you battle the Scytharene separately, you'll all lose.' Protests from the assembly but ritual, lacklustre, knowing the truth. 'And when the last gang has fallen, the Scytharene will have won and that'll be game over for the human race – *unless* we stand together. *Unless* we combine our resources, unite for the common cause, the greater good. Put aside our differences, put the past behind us. Mend our divisions. Forget that we're Muslim or Christian or British or Bengali. Be *human*. Make our stand as human beings. In defence of our planet. In defence of our race. In defence of our way of life.'

'What then?' Dwayne Randolph was on his feet again, like an accuser. 'What if we did that, did what you want, Naughton?' Anguished, quivering, torn between the cynicism of experience and the desire to believe. 'What good would it do? We might be hundreds then but the Scytharene are still thousands, an army. And those ships and those pods. How the hell can even all of us together kick their arses?'

'I was coming to that, Dwayne,' grinned Travis.

He detected the Phantom's dilemma in the eyes of so

many of the massed teenagers. Despair on the one hand, hope on the other. A wild, crazy, unbelievable hope.

Travis told them about the gene transfer virus.

And he sensed the mood changing in the chamber, by the sentence, by the word, the balance shifting. The gang members' eyes grew brighter, more eager, their body language alert and attentive. They craned forward to hear him. Maybe they didn't follow the details of how the virus would work – Travis only really understood the basics – but that didn't seem to bother them. They knew what the capsules of liquid would mean. The virus was an elixir of death, a magic potion to make the monsters go away. And they believed in it. By the time of Travis's final rallying cry they believed in the gene transfer virus and they believed in him.

'Two days from now,' Travis declared, 'two days from now we'll be ready. When the Scytharene march against us with all their forces we'll be waiting for them, and with the virus in our hands we can beat them. We can send them scattering off into space broken and defeated and wishing they'd never heard of Earth. We can show them once and for all that the human race will never be slaves. Two days from now we'll make our stand. *Who'll stand with us?*'

Everyone. Dwayne Randolph. The Cutters. The Victoria Boys. With roars and whoops of approval. With bursts of gunfire in the air. The Sisters. The Phantoms. The Hardcore. Everyone.

'My God, Trav,' Linden breathed. 'You've got them.'

In the dimly lit chamber of the House of Commons, the gangs rose to Travis Naughton.

As one.

*

The summons came in the middle of the night, brusque and peremptory. Crispin Allerton didn't stand on ceremony.

'Do you know what time it is?' Travis asked as he and Linden entered the lab.

'Actually, no,' Crispin said, 'though judging by Darroway's somnambulistic torpor, I gather it's late. I'm afraid genius does not keep conventional hours.' Ruth and Geoffrey were busying themselves with monitors and test tubes respectively, so absorbed by their work that they didn't seem to register the two teenagers' arrival. 'Besides, even if you were asleep, I assumed you'd want to be woken for this.'

Crispin held up for Travis's inspection a stoppered glass phial the size and shape of a large egg. It was filled almost to the brim with a colourless solution.

Linden gave a little gasp, almost of pain. 'Is that what I think it is?'

Travis took the object in his hand. It was cool and light. He wondered if, in the pre-Sickness world, the generals and the presidents with their fingers on the button had felt the strange, unsettling mixture of fear and excitement that he felt now. He said in an awed whisper: 'You've done it.'

'Did you imagine we would not?' Crispin regarded Travis scornfully. 'The Paragons would like to report that we have successfully combined human and Scytharene DNA. The capsule is only the first of many batches that we will now be able to produce. In short, the gene transfer virus has been perfected.'

THIRTEEN

Travis returned to the lab first thing in the morning with the nervous eagerness of a father in a maternity ward checking on the health of his newborn child. This time, all three girls accompanied him.

The two days from now of which he'd spoken to the gangs were down to one. 'Everything still all right?' he needed to know.

'Mm. It will be,' Crispin said haughtily, 'as long as our work is not constantly interrupted by certain people asking whether everything is all right.'

'And I'd be careful how you handle that,' Ruth pointed out to Mel, who was weighing the virus capsule in the palm of her right hand.

'Just trying to figure out my action for when I throw it at those bastards. Do I just kind of lob it and hope for the best, or do I bowl it like a cricket ball, fast, so they won't even see it coming?' She practised her posture for both options, much to Ruth's consternation.

'*Drop* it,' the Paragon warned, 'and you risk jeopardising the health of your Scytharene friend, even if she *is* in an isolation booth.'

'Ruth's right, Mel,' Travis said. 'Now's no time for fooling about.'

'Can we be sure the virus will really work, though?' Jessica said anxiously.

Crispin did not deign to dignify such an imbecilic question with a response.

Geoffrey's eyes, however, lit up. 'We could *show* you,' he said, crossing to a table heavy with equipment. 'With this.' He lifted from its stand on the table a glass and metal hybrid of syringe and pistol, the former functioning as the barrel, its contents administered through the needle by depressing not a plunger but a trigger on the handle. The weapon was loaded. 'We have a dosage of the virus solution primed and ready in the syringe-gun as well. We could trial it by injecting it directly into the veins of our alien captive. We'd learn exactly how long the infection takes to kill. That would be useful for tomorrow, wouldn't it? And if this Dyona really wants to help—'

'You're sick, Geoffrey,' said Linden with revulsion.

'Out of the question,' ruled Travis. 'Dyona's not a captive, she's an ally. It's not normally done to harm an ally. We get through tomorrow safely, you can start work on a vaccine or whatever to immunise her and any other dissident Scytharene against the gene transfer virus. As for testing – thank you, Mel' – plucking the capsule from her hand and giving it to Crispin – 'we'll find out how effective the virus is soon enough. Just produce as much of it as you can, Crispin.'

'Mm,' said the Paragon. 'We will.'

From the lab, Travis and Linden went to the isolation booth to update Dyona on the situation. Travis thought she deserved at least that much. He was aware that while he'd denied to the Paragons that the Scytharene was a prisoner, it did look suspiciously as if she was languishing in a cell. The room might have been more comfortable than those traditionally found in jails, but the sheer Plexiglas walls were just as incarcerating as bars – and Dyona's sentence could yet turn out to be as long as any criminal's.

The Scytharene seemed unconcerned by any of that. 'Good. Good,' she approved as Travis outlined each development. She stood close to him, the two of them separated only by the Plexiglas. 'You have the warriors. You have the weapon. I only wish I could be there tomorrow to fight by your side.'

'I wish you could too,' said Travis. 'I wish you didn't have to stay in this damned bubble.'

'But I do,' Dyona accepted without rancour. 'And I would rather be here alone than back aboard the *Ayrion III* surrounded by those I despise. I have lived a lie for so long, Travis, Linden. You have given me the chance to live true at last, and whatever happens in the future, I thank you for that.'

'I notice that you didn't tell Dyona about Richie and the Kings disappearing,' Linden said after she and Travis had left Dyona to her own reflections. 'Why not?'

'I'm hoping they'll be back, that's why not,' said Travis, a little edgily. The subject of Richie Coker was still kind of raw.

'It's my fault that they've gone. Richie was going to stay until after tomorrow but I told him to get lost, screamed at him, called him scum. I'm sorry.'

'It doesn't matter now. With the other gangs coming in we're not reliant on the Kings for manpower. That's not the issue. But Richie's been with us practically since the beginning, and though I can hardly believe it, I was actually starting to like him, to respect him, even to think of Hard

Man Richie Coker as a friend.' Travis touched Linden lovingly. 'I've worked my way through what happened with *you*, Lin. I can make my peace with Richie as well. We can't afford to lose him.'

'Maybe we could send a search party out – see if they're at that gym where the Kings had their base . . .'

'I'd like to, Lin,' Travis said, 'but it's time and it's resources. The gangs should already be on their way to Parliament from their own territories. They need to be directed, organised, fed. They need to learn tomorrow's plan, build our defence perimeter, scavenge as big an arsenal and as much armour as possible. I want Richie back with us and I'm hoping he'll come, but we can't go looking for him. He knows where we are.'

'Speaking of where people are,' Linden said, happy enough to change the subject, 'I haven't seen Antony this morning.'

'No. Antony's busy.'

'Doing what?'

'I'm hoping,' Travis said, 'he'll show us.'

That afternoon he did. It was a kind of guided tour London had never seen before.

From the Houses of Parliament, Antony led Travis and the three girls away from the Thames and Westminster Bridge, along Great George Street towards the junction of Horse Guards Road and Birdcage Walk.

'The river will form our rear line of defence,' he explained. 'As far as the bridge is concerned, we've probably got sufficient explosives to blow a hole right through it, but we lack the expertise to set the charges in the first place. So we've got volunteers to hold the bridge and defend against any Scytharene attack from south of the river.'

'Can see you're taking precautions against trouble from the west as well, Antony,' said Mel.

Birdcage Walk, the tree-lined thoroughfare that bordered the west side of St James's Park, was thronging with urgent activity. The road itself was being converted into something more like a fortification, an uninterrupted pile of vehicles intended to slow the advance of any Scytharene warriors on foot. Sandbags were being transferred from defence emplacements elsewhere that no longer required them and being put to similar use here, providing a series of makeshift walls behind which the gangs could fire at any oncoming enemy; cars and trucks tore across the open spaces of the park, wove between its trees, transporting weapons and ammunition as well as non-military materials to the site. Everyone was working with an almost manic intensity to construct the defences. Everyone was working together.

Pity it had taken pretty much the end of the world for it to happen, Travis thought grimly.

'This is the front line. We're going to run our defence perimeter along three sides of the park,' Antony said, continuing north. 'Here, obviously. The opposite side at the Mall, and ahead of us in front of Buckingham Palace. It's not too large an area for our people to cover during Stage One of the engagement, and the parkland will make it easier for us when we move to Stage Two.'

'Aren't we going to try to protect Buckingham Palace, Antony?' Jessica asked, a little crestfallen.

'No point, I'm afraid, Jess. We wouldn't be able to even if we wanted to.'

The palace appeared before them now, remarkably untouched by the tumultuous events that had unfolded around it, as if nobody, not even the aliens, had dared to trespass on royal territory. Yet at the same time the once-proud edifice seemed lonely, forlorn, smaller than its size, like a prop in a movie, a front. No flag flew from its roof.

'My parents brought me here once,' Jessica remembered. 'About a hundred years ago. The big house where the Queen lived. I thought I was going to see her too, and that maybe she'd invite me in to tea – and Mum and Dad, of course. I thought all I'd have to do was let the soldier in the sentry box know that I was a princess like my parents told me I was, and he'd bow and salute or something and escort me inside to the queen, who'd be playing with her corgis and *very* pleased to see me – and probably give me a crown to wear.'

'Instead, don't tell me. Soldier-Boy marched you off to Paddington Green police station where you were charged with terrorist offences, right, Jess?' Mel gave a strangely sad smile.

'Of course not. I didn't see anybody. The Queen didn't even come out on to the balcony.' Jessica sighed. 'Mum wouldn't let me speak to the soldier, either.'

'So Stage One' – Travis got back to business – 'we defend the park. For as long as we can.'

'Perhaps not as long as we can,' Antony moderated, 'but long enough to convince the Scytharene that we desperately want to. So that when we switch to Stage Two, they fall for it, hook, line and sinker.'

'Stage Two being?' prompted Linden.

'Run like hell,' Antony confided. 'Total retreat. Abject, headlong, all-screaming, all-panicking flight.'

'Only the retreat's not really either total or abject, right, Antony?' Mel hoped.

'Exactly. It's a tactic, a manoeuvre. The setting of a trap. Similar to the way we drew Rev's bikers in at Harrington, making your enemy overconfident and therefore – hopefully – careless, or at least incautious. So everybody falls back simultaneously—'

'How are you going to manage the simultaneously?' Linden said.

'Two-way radios,' Antony replied. 'What my friends and I used to call walkie-talkies. The Enclave has practically a roomful. We use them to synchronise our movements and we all converge on Horse Guards Parade' – he turned to position his back to Buckingham Palace – 'the far side of the park *ahead* of us.' Setting off in that direction through the park itself. 'It's vital our people reach Horse Guards before the Scytharene do.'

'Why?' said Mel.

'Because there on the parade ground is where we really *do* make our stand,' Antony revealed, 'where the Trooping of the Colour ceremony used to take place. We're already rein-forcing a position there and we'll be holding a fair proportion of our forces in reserve expressly for that moment, armed with the virus capsules. As the Scytharene pursue the park's defenders, duped into believing they've got the inferior Earthers on the run again, then and only then do we deploy the virus.'

'Sounds good, Antony,' said Mel, 'but why not lead with the virus when the Scytharene first show their ugly faces?'

'I thought it might be better to lure them into a smaller area, concentrate their numbers. The virus might spread among them more quickly.' Antony glanced to his leader as if for approval. 'Travis?'

'You know what I said before about communities needing organisers,' Travis said thoughtfully, then broke into a smile. 'I was right. You've come up with a heck of a plan, Antony. Well done. Now it's up to us to make it work.'

'Oh, Antony,' squealed Jessica, flinging her arms around him and kissing him exuberantly, 'I'm so *proud* of you.'

Linden congratulated him too, though rather less physically. Mel made the approbation unanimous with a 'Yeah. Great plan, Antony.' But she could see in the lake of St James's Park the rusting, half-submerged wrecks of vehicles and the bloated bodies of drowned Londoners that the spider-robots must have missed, and she couldn't help but recall what, according to the saying, so often happened to even the best-laid plans . . .

The others seemed happy enough, though. That evening, Travis's core group, the Paragons and the gang leaders crammed into Conference Room One for a meeting to ensure that everything was prepared for the conflict to come. Crispin Allerton reported that sufficient liquid virus had been produced so far to fill fifty capsules, an amount that could be doubled by dawn, the hour that Dyona had warned was traditionally favoured by her people for the commencement of hostilities. Antony reiterated the details of their defence one last time, confirming that each gang knew where its members should take up their positions and what their roles entailed once the aliens' assault began.

'We don't want any misunderstandings,' he reminded his audience anxiously. 'We don't want anything to go wrong.'

'Chill, man,' said Dwayne Randolph. 'Give me an AK-47 in one hand and one of those virus capsules in the other and it ain't gonna be *us* shitting ourselves.'

Travis's voice cut through the laughter. 'One last thing. If something *does* go wrong, or even if it doesn't, I don't want to leave Enclave Zero undefended. As far as we know the Scytharene aren't even aware of its existence, but if they find it . . . We can't afford to lose these facilities. Crispin, Ruth and Geoffrey will have to remain here out of the firing line in case we need more virus later, but I want a small armed force to stay behind as well.' Addressing the gang leaders: 'To make it fair, one guy from each gang? I'll leave it to you to decide who.' While they did, Travis spoke more quietly to Mel: 'I want you here with them too, Mel, to protect Dyona. Any set-back in the battle and some of our less discriminating friends might start looking for a scapegoat. Antony and I obviously have to be with our main force, and other than the two of us, Dyona only really knows you. Sorry. I know you'd sooner be out there fighting.'

But if Travis had expected protests from Mel, unusually they never came.

Which might have explained why he turned up at her room later, and the expression of concern on his face.

'Shouldn't you be with Linden, Trav?' Mel said, a little defensively.

'Linden's fine. I'm not sure you are.'

'There's nothing wrong with me.'

'Subtext: nothing I want to talk about.' Travis shook his head. 'Come on, Mel, we've known each other too long to play games. I hope you know you can trust me.'

'That's one of the few things I *am* sure of these days,' Mel said with a faint smile.

'So what's wrong?' Plumping himself down on the chair and folding his arms in a gesture of stubbornness. 'I'm not shifting until you tell me, not even if I have to wait here all night. Not even if I'm still here tomorrow and we've got Scytharene knocking on the door.'

In the security of Travis's company, Mel opened up a little. 'It's tomorrow I'm worried about.'

'I'm not exactly ecstatic about facing a Scytharene army myself, Mel, but we've got the virus. We've got a chance. We can't ask for more than that.'

'Why not? I want to ask for more. I've got a very bad feeling, Travis.' Then, with a stifled sob, she opened up a lot. 'Not all of us are gonna make it.'

'Hey. Mel, hey. Don't . . .' He rose, embraced her. She pressed her face to his chest and he stroked the black spill of her hair. 'This isn't like you. Where's all this coming from? Listen, I for one have every intention of making it, as you put it, and I'm going to be doing everything in my power to ensure that the others do too.'

'It won't do any good, Trav.' She gazed up at him, her eyes wet with fearful tears. 'I've been having these dreams. Nightmares. All so ominous. I've been seeing dead people in them.'

'What, like that kid in that Bruce Willis movie?' Travis wasn't sure how seriously to take her.

'My dad's been in them.'

'Oh.'

'Yeah. Oh.'

Travis knew only too well how Mel had felt about her

315

abusive father. He'd despised and hated Gerry Patrick himself. In a few cases, the Sickness had done the world a favour. 'Your dad can't hurt you any more, Mel. He's dead.'

'I know he's dead, Trav.' She wiped her eyes on her sleeve so that they were dry when she added: 'What you don't know is that I killed him.'

'What?' Subsiding to the bed this time, holding Mel's hand so that she was forced to sit alongside him. 'You're . . . don't be ridiculous. The Sickness killed your father, Mel.'

'It would have done, sure, if I hadn't got in there first.' And because Travis was too shocked to speak, Mel filled the silence with explanation. 'It was that day you called to say you were going to the hospital to look for help. After you'd gone . . . Dad had heard someone at the door. Thought I'd sent a paramedic with a cure away to spite him. I stalked off in disgust, up the stairs. He followed me, lunged for me.' Mel pulled her hand away from Travis's. She was in the past, re-enacting events. 'He grabbed me. He was hurting me. I didn't want that. No more. I didn't want him even touching me. I couldn't bear it. So I turned, I whirled, I tried to shake his hand loose and . . . he lost his balance and . . . he was flailing and I can't remember whether he screamed or not. He broke his neck at the bottom of the stairs.'

'I don't believe it. Mel, why didn't you tell me? You told me he died of the . . . So that's why when I came back for you, you wouldn't let me in the house.'

'I couldn't move him, Travis. I couldn't even touch him.' Mel's features contorted in horror and disgust. 'I left him there, lying on the floor. He must still be there.'

Travis clasped her hand again. He had no real sympathy

316

for Gerry Patrick: all of it was devoted to Mel. 'But did you push him, though? You didn't say you pushed him.'

'Does it matter? I turned. He fell. I killed him.'

'No, Mel, of course it matters. If you didn't push him then you're not responsible. It was an accident.'

'I *feel* responsible, Trav. I didn't actually push him, I know I didn't, but part of me *wanted* to, wanted to shove his ugly fat carcass away from me. Part of me was glad when he . . . and it's still my fault anyway, Travis. If I hadn't been on the stairs in the first place . . .'

'If he hadn't been chasing after you,' Travis countered. 'If he hadn't been abusing you for years. You mustn't feel guilty about this, Mel. You've no reason to.'

'I don't think guilt listens much to reason, Trav.'

'And you've been carrying this burden around with you the whole time? Punishing yourself for nothing? Mel, why?' He hugged her. 'You should have told me.'

'I know. Maybe I'm a masochist.'

'Or Jessie. You could have told Jessie – someone.'

'Linden knows. She kind of guessed. Back at Harrington. Seems I talk in my sleep. And before you get mad with her' – anticipating the furrows in Travis's brow – 'I made her promise not to breathe a word, not even to you.'

Travis nodded. The possibility of him getting mad with Linden now was as remote as the Scytharene homeworld, and as unappealing. He was simply proud that his *girl*friend could so readily be trusted by his *oldest* friend. 'What did Linden say?'

'Same as you. Wasn't my fault. It was an accident. I shouldn't feel bad.' Mel smiled briefly. 'She's the perfect match for you, Travis. Don't mess it up.'

'I won't,' said Travis.

'But Dad appearing in my dreams, it's like he's coming for me, looking for revenge. It's like the dreams signify that something terrible is going to happen.'

'Dreams aren't real, Mel. They don't mean anything and they can't predict anything. I dreamt about my dad after he was killed.' Travis's expression darkened at the memory. 'I think – I think what they *can* do, all they can do, is to kind of dramatise your – the dreamer's – emotional state, remind you while you're sleeping of how you're feeling *in* the real world. But dreams can't affect reality. Only people can do that.'

'What if dreams affect people, though,' Mel responded, 'like mine are getting to me?'

'Everything in our lives can be an influence on us, Mel,' Travis said. 'The people we've met, the books we've read or films we've seen, the happiness or sorrow we've experienced, tragedy, joy, all the things we've done or haven't done, promises broken, promises kept – maybe even our dreams too, I suppose. And time. Time's always trying to change us, shape us and reshape us. All we can do is try to stay true to ourselves, try to be the people we most want to be, and resist the pressures from whatever sources to be less than that like – I don't know – like a rock rising from the ocean. Mel, you didn't let your father break you while he was alive. Don't let him do it now he's dead.'

Tears again in Mel's eyes, and a longing for the impossible. Dreams. 'I wish I'd been your sister, Travis. I wish your parents had been mine. If your dad had been my dad, I could have been so different. Better . . .'

'Nobody's better than you, Mel,' Travis said sincerely, 'and I'd have been proud to have you for a sister.' He kissed her. 'I think, though, I'm gonna sound more like your mother now. We should try to get some sleep. Big day coming.' He squeezed her hand and stood. 'Hey, and try not to dream, huh?'

'Even if I do,' Mel said, 'after telling you about my dad, I don't think they'll bother me any more. Oh, but Travis . . .'

'Yeah?' He paused at the door, looked back at Melanie Patrick.

'Be safe tomorrow.'

A few short hours later and there was no more time for private words with Mel. The screens in the moncom centre showed night's darkness gradually ceding ground to the dawn, like an amorphous army in slow retreat.

The moment of truth was upon them.

Barked orders and bursts of frenetic activity in both Parliament and Enclave Zero as the gangs mobilised, moved out to their stations in St James's Park, on Westminster Bridge, at Horse Guards Parade, the latter groups bearing with them, as jealously guarded as treasure chests, the briefcase-sized receptacles that contained the virus capsules.

'Mel's staying with you,' Travis told Dyona. 'You'll be all right.'

'I pray you will too, Travis Naughton,' said the Scytharene, pressing her palm against his through the Plexiglas. 'Think of Darion when you strike today. Do this for him as well as for your own people.' Travis nodded. 'In my culture we have a saying: may your ancestors be strong beside you. Let it be so.'

Travis thought of his father. Today was the day he'd prove himself his father's son.

'One hundred capsules of virus exactly,' said Crispin

Allerton as Travis made a final visit to the lab. 'We have done our part in the human race's great struggle. Now it is your turn to do yours.'

'We will,' Travis assured him. 'You don't need to worry about that, Crispin.'

'Mm, I won't,' the Paragon said. He twitched his trademark smile. 'I'm sure everything will go precisely according to plan.'

Dawn. A warm summer's day in prospect, the weather forecasters would have said, had any of them still been alive to comment. Early sunlight dancing on the Thames, on the bodies, on the wrecks of boats. On Westminster Bridge, hooded teenagers with wild, feral eyes, crouching behind a wall of ownerless cars, unwashed fingers nervous at the triggers of automatic weapons. *Earth has not anything to show more fair.* The poet's words ghosts of a lost, forgotten age. *This City now doth like a garment wear the beauty of the morning.*

Dawn. Above the lonely London canyons, the gutted, looted stores, the workless offices and derelict monuments, cinemas without movies, restaurants without diners, churches lacking congregations. *Silent, bare, ships, towers, domes, theatres, and temples lie open unto the fields, and to the sky.* The grope of crematorium smoke as black above the disposal pits as ever, though seeming darker by daylight. The charred parks become burial grounds. The cruel architecture of slave camps gleaming like torturers' teeth. Alien ships in alien shapes. The Cullers rising with the sun like counterweights, cold, lightless sickle moons.

Ne'er saw I, never felt, a calm so deep. And prayers and pleadings mouthed by irreligious lips as young defenders counted down to combat. Silence heard, and swearing, and sobs. *Dear*

God! the very houses seem asleep. The barricades of vehicles around the park, the sandbagged gun emplacements, the armoured cars idling on the grass, a stillness born of dread, frozen before the frenzy.

At Horse Guards Parade, an obstacle of wood and wire built hastily across the open side of the parade ground's square, in sight of the Cenotaph. The mass of young people behind it unlike their comrades armed with more than guns. One hundred glass grenades. Lethal eggs in trembling hands. Travis at Horse Guards, ready to hold the line. Linden beside him. And Jessica. Wondering how long they had until the Scytharene came. How long they had, perhaps, to live. *And all that mighty heart is lying still!* Scarcely able to breathe.

Dawn. On a morning like no other. '*Two days from now we'll make our stand,*' Travis had pledged to the gangs.

Time up.

Antony saw them first. As chief organiser he'd felt it incumbent upon him to be in the front line when the Scytharene launched their attack. He couldn't have placed himself any closer to the likely action than at the defence perimeter immediately opposite Buckingham Palace. This was where the remnants of the Phantoms had elected to fight, and Dwayne Randolph accompanied Antony as he inspected their position. But when the battlepods flashed across the sky, Dwayne was reassuring one of his followers that yeah, they really *were* going to kick arse. Only Antony was looking up.

Battlepods above Buckingham Palace.

'This is it!' In a mixture of awe, fear and a quickening of anticipation. 'They're coming.' Antony was on the radio to Travis at once, even though those at Horse Guards would see the pods themselves in seconds.

The Phantoms already had. Curses and yells exploded from their mouths like dynamite. Gunfire crackled from St James's Park, ineffectual as the dozen glittering spheres swooped and soared. 'Reconnaissance,' Antony guessed. 'They're establishing how strong we are.' *Or how weak*. A rocket wheezed into the sky. Like an old man trying to chase children it missed everything but the ground as it faltered and fell somewhere in the park. The earth shuddered with its explosion. The battlepods circled swiftly, unmolested.

'They ain't firing. Why ain't they firing?' demanded Dwayne.

'They don't want to kill us,' Antony suddenly realised. 'They want to keep casualties to a minimum. Dead slaves have no value. They'll be pulling their punches, Dwayne.' Excitedly. 'That gives us an edge.'

'We'll need one.'

Warning cries from the Phantoms had alerted Dwayne to the area off to their right, where the Mall bisected St James's Park and Green Park. Not too much green visible at the moment, not with the ranks of black-armoured Scytharene warriors advancing steadily towards them, silent and steely-eyed behind their menagerie of helmets, no doubt, rifles resembling elongated subjugators clutched across their chests.

Radio messages coming in from Westminster Bridge, from Birdcage Walk, from every point in the line. Different voices, raised, unnerved. The same intelligence. The aliens were on the move.

'They just gonna come on at us like that?' Dwayne said.

'March directly at the enemy. Show no fear. Rely on your own firepower to break their lines and shatter their will to resist. It's the way the British Army used to fight.' Antony's

322

expression hardened. 'No doubt the Scytharene employ the same tactics to make some kind of statement about their racial superiority. They're demonstrating contempt for us, showing us we're not their equals.'

'Yeah, well, listen, man, while we've got a chance – talking of guys who reckon they're better than the rest of us,' Dwayne said, 'I reckoned you might be one of 'em. At first. The whole upper-class thing you've got going on, you know what I mean? But I was wrong.'

'I'm pleased to hear it,' said Antony curiously.

'Your main man Travis is right. We're all in this shit together. But you are the man with the plan, Tony, and – what I'm saying is, I wish Danny was here fighting with me, but as he ain't, I'm glad you are.'

Antony nodded. 'Feeling's mutual.' Maybe he could do this inspiration thing, after all.

'Me and you, man,' Dwayne said. 'Let's give these bastards hell.'

The Phantoms opened fire in earnest. Machine guns, pistols, automatic rifles, shells from bazookas and hand-held rocket launchers. Bullets raking through the front ranks of the alien advance, their perfect lines disrupted by explosions and fire and erupting soil. Warriors falling as silently as they'd marched. But the Scytharene kept on coming.

And it seemed to Antony, armed with his subjugator, that now the battle had begun the tension had lifted from him; he felt stronger, surer. The waiting was the worst. Waiting forced you to think, and into your thoughts could creep doubt and dread and fear of failure. In action, there wasn't time to think. Fighting was better.

But now the warriors in unison thrust their firearms forward and retaliated. A dazzling burst of energy bolts, searing white. Almost perversely, Antony's heart leapt with hope. He'd been right. White blasts meant temporary paralysis and unconsciousness, not death. The Scytharene were seeking first only to incapacitate their foe. Where the energy bolts pierced the uneven barricades of vehicles and boards and sandbags, defenders were hit, cried out, crumpled. But the white beams didn't have the power to penetrate solid obstacles. The casualty rate was still higher among the aliens than the humans. But the Scytharene kept on coming.

Almost at the road now, trampling over their fallen comrades without pity or pause, the fire of their subjugator rifles incessant, the air sparking like electricity. And their numbers seemed endless.

A few anxious faces began to glance at Antony. Dwayne translated. 'Stage Two yet?'

'No. We stay put. We can hold them a little longer.'

Dwayne grinned. 'Tony Clive, you the *man*.'

But the Scytharene kept on coming.

And maybe the deployment of the battlepod had always been integral to the attack or maybe it had been necessitated as a result of the defenders' staunch resistance. Either way, the 'pod swooped low, its gunport open, and yellow lightning scorched to earth. Its target barricades combusted, the force of the explosions scattering the Phantoms, swatting them to the ground. Devastation and confusion in the lines. Deaths. Burning bodies and screams. Massive holes in the teenagers' defences, like mortal wounds. The relentless onslaught of energy bolts now had little to stop it from claiming victims. The aliens were across the Mall. Antony dropped one, two with his subjugator, only for them to be replaced by ten, twenty more. The warriors seemed to multiply as they reached the blazing barricades. The human forces seemed only to be shrinking. People had no option but to retreat and regroup, their cover gone.

And still the Scytharene kept on coming.

'Antony?' Dwayne.

'I know.' The radio. His heart thudding as he yelled into it: 'This is Clive. Fall back to Horse Guards. Now. We're moving to Stage Two.'

They'd gathered in the moncom centre, Mel, the Paragons, the dozen or so gang members assigned to protect Enclave Zero, everyone in the complex except Dyona, and they hung on every word of every radio transmission. Mel would have liked to see what was happening too, both to Antony and at Horse Guards, but the Enclave's hidden camera network above ground didn't extend that far. The screens did show Westminster Bridge, however, and the Scytharene warriors striding imperiously across it, smashing their way through the resistance. So maybe it was preferable *not* to have a visual fix.

A mêlée of voices from the radio receivers: 'Stage Two. Did he say Stage Two? . . . Move. *Move* . . . Stage Two. Go! . . . They got Nicky. Nicky's down . . .'

One she recognised, one that gave her hope. Travis was still in control. 'Back to Horse Guards. Quick as you can. Everyone. We've got the virus capsules ready. Keep to the plan. Keep to the plan . . .'

The virus capsules were ready. Mel felt sick with anxiety. What if they didn't work after all? What if, after everything they'd been through, the gene transfer virus was ineffective, useless? What then?

But no, she couldn't think like that. She didn't dare. Giving up on the virus was like giving up on those she loved, Travis, Jessica. She would never do that. The virus *would* prove as deadly to the Scytharene as the Paragons boasted. It would. They'd win. They'd beat those bloody aliens.

Mel glanced behind her, to where Crispin, Ruth and Geoffrey were loitering by the door. The Paragons had faith in their fatal creation. Clearly. Otherwise, why would they be smirking?

At Horse Guards Parade, the survivors of the initial Scytharene assault streamed behind the final barricade. They arrived in small, random groups, no longer differentiated by the gangs to which they'd belonged. Some were bleeding, wounded, and some disorientated by the reality of combat, staggering and speechless; these were led to the middle of the parade ground by youngsters who'd claimed earlier to have a working knowledge of first aid. Other new arrivals, however, jaws set and eyes fixed like bayonets, were determined to fight on. Those joined their comrades at the wall.

Comrades with their potential salvation in their hands. The virus capsules had been distributed.

'There he is!' Jessica, whose eyes were hurting from straining in search of Antony. She screamed his name as at last she spied him racing from among the trees.

And Dwayne, Travis registered. Jessica darted to the narrow opening they were keeping available between rolls of barbed wire to admit their retreating forces. 'Go with her, Lin,' Travis said. 'Make sure he's all right.'

'Don't go anywhere without me.' Linden smiled weakly.

No chance of that, for several reasons. Travis scanned the

park. A handful of teenagers still sprinting for sanctuary but no more. Anyone he couldn't see now wasn't coming. A quick estimate. They'd already lost over half their strength. Travis swore under his breath by way of consolation. The virus had better take effect damn quickly, because if it didn't, they'd be discussing where they'd gone wrong from a cell aboard the *Ayrion III*.

Glimpsed through the foliage, a second wall advancing upon their own, a living wall of flesh and blood and armour. The Scytharene warriors in a single uninterrupted line, marching, purposefully but hardly rapidly. They obviously felt they didn't need to rush. For the moment they'd even ceased firing.

'Trav.' Antony. Gasping, dishevelled, his face streaked with smoke, but uninjured. The girls and Dwayne Randolph were with him.

'Am I glad to see you.' Travis embraced Antony relievedly. 'You too, Dwayne.' Shaking the Phantom's hand.

'One hell of a party, man.'

'It's not over yet,' Travis said, holding up a virus capsule. 'This is one party where it's the gatecrashers who get the present.'

'Travis,' Linden alerted. 'Look!'

At a distance of some fifty metres from the barricade the Scytharene halted. A deathly quiet descended on the scene. Even the battlepods, Travis noticed, had vanished.

'What have they stopped for?' Jessica wanted to know. And why was she whispering?

'Maybe they think we're gonna piss ourselves and surrender,' Dwayne scoffed. 'No way, man.'

'The 'pods scouted the whole area,' Antony said. 'They know this is all we've got.'

'All we've got.' Travis's fingers curled tightly around the glass phial. For the first time, it truly did seem like a grenade to him. 'They know shit.'

A command barked in what must have been their guttural native language issued from the heart of the Scytharene formation. The warriors responded with a unanimous yell of aggressive intent, their subjugator rifles primed, in one fluid movement trained on the humans' defences.

The next cry, Travis knew, would signal the final attack. Time to get in some orders of his own. 'First wave ready,' he called. 'Second, third and fourth behind them.' A lot of jostling behind the wall as three lines of twenty-five and one of twenty-four kids took up their positions. Travis himself would complete the last rank. Jessica and Linden stood with the first. One hundred capsules in one hundred hands. 'When I give the word, deliver your packages.'

The Scytharene commander, apparently not wanting to be outdone, bellowed even louder. But his words were subsumed by the pyrotechnic blaze of his warriors' weapons. A barrage of energy bolts broke against the barricade.

'Now!' Travis shouted, his voice cracking. 'Now! Now!'

With a collective holler of defiance, the first wave hurled their capsules. It was the last act many of them performed. They were cut down by the white blades of the energy blasts.

But the virus capsules struck the road and shattered. The virus solution splashed and spilled. From the violently released liquid, Jessica thought she saw vapour rising. *Hoped* she did.

'Second wave!' Travis urged. 'Now!'

He had no idea what the aliens must be thinking as two

dozen more glass spheres flew through the air to smash with apparent harmlessness on the ground. What must seem like a preposterous new tactic was certainly not deterring them. The advance was on again, the blinding, blistering onslaught of energy bolts. The final big push.

'Third wave. Now!'

The Scytharene would be at the wall in fewer seconds than there were metres between it and them. Scytharene boots were crushing the fragile shells of the splintered capsules.

Scytharene lungs were breathing air polluted by the virus.

'Fourth wave.'

Travis joined them. Several fell before they could throw their capsules, lit up briefly like pale fireworks. Others stepped in to make their contribution for them. Antony. Dwayne. Travis's own capsule hit a Scytharene breastplate, splattered it with liquid. The breastplate's wearer threw back his head as if in great hilarity.

Travis hadn't known quite what to expect once the virus had been released. Maybe the aliens slowing, stumbling, tottering, sinking to their knees. Or maybe clutching at their throats, writhing, screaming, tearing off their helmets to expose white faces carved red with the scarlet circles of the Sickness. Or frothing at the mouth. Or gargling blood. Like cyanide, Crispin had said. Or whatever. Something. He'd expected something to happen. Not nothing.

Nothing.

On either side of Travis, teenagers dropped. Others, seeing the Scytharene advance proceeding unchecked, fled their posts with wails of panic.

It wasn't working.

'Trav. Get back. Get the hell *back*.' Antony and Dwayne, grabbing for him amidst a hail of energy bolts.

The virus wasn't working.

'Did you hear him?' Mel whirled to confront the Paragons. They had. Everyone in the moncom centre had heard Travis's chilling words over the radio receivers. 'It's not working. Why not? What can we do? How can we help them?'

'Maybe it's just taking a while to kick in,' someone suggested.

'No. You said the effect would be immediate,' Mel accused Crispin Allerton.

'Mm. I did, didn't I?'

'So what's gone wrong? What's . . .?' And why wasn't Crispin expressing horror and dismay and alarm like everybody else? Everybody but Ruth and Geoffrey. Why were the Paragons' superior smirks still in place? Why were they widening into schemers' smiles? With the sudden, sickening impact of a blow to the stomach, Mel realised. 'You knew this would happen, didn't you? You let Travis and Jessie and the others go out there to fight and you knew the virus would fail.'

Crispin Allerton shook his head primly.

'Poor Melanie,' said Ruth pityingly.

'The virus didn't fail, Patrick,' Crispin assured her. 'We simply didn't supply it.'

'You . . . what?' Mel's skin prickled with fear.

Geoffrey tittered. 'Those capsules – they've only got water in them.'

'*Bastards!*' Fear converted into instant fury. Mel lunged at the Paragons.

330

Didn't reach them. A flourish of the guns they magically produced stopped her in her tracks. Between them, Crispin, Ruth and Geoffrey had the whole room covered.

'Mm. I would advise any of you so considering *not* to indulge in reckless displays of heroism,' said Crispin. 'Or this will happen to you.'

He shot Mel in the stomach.

FOURTEEN

It was over.

Rationally, even Travis would have had to concede, his ragtag coalition of street gangs had never stood a chance against the massed might of disciplined Scytharene warriors, but the gene transfer virus had lured them into believing otherwise. The virus had been a magic potion, a warrior's spell, their last hope. They'd placed all their faith in it but, it seemed, the age of faith was past. The virus had failed, the aliens were upon them in a coruscation of energy blasts, and it was over.

Travis gazed into the sky. Rising above Buckingham Palace, where the tinier battlepods had flitted like flies, the more prodigious crescent of a Scytharene mother ship appeared ominously, like a wrathful god observing with cold pleasure the carnage its servants had wrought. The *Ayrion III*, Travis assumed. Gyrion and the Fleet Commanders come to gloat and witness the final fall of London. The slavecraft was flanked by twin Cullers, their tractor beams setting to work.

'Travis, we've got to move.' Antony still, trying to haul him away from their feeble barricade. 'We can't stay here.'

He was right about that. White bolts switched briefly to yellow, pulverising the barrier into splinters and shards.

Any last pretence of concerted resistance crumbled with the wall. All around Travis, people were retreating, routed, crying out. Only a hardy few stood their ground, with a fatalistic fanaticism preserved on their faces as the subjugator rifles mowed them down.

But Travis felt an affinity with them nevertheless. 'We have to *fight*, Antony.' Insistently.

'Not here. It's suicide. What good is that?'

'You're crazy, man.' Though Dwayne sounded kind of impressed.

'If we run we can regroup.' Travis heard Antony making an organiser's sense. 'Linden, tell him.' But what would his dad have done under these circumstances? Travis allowed himself to be backpedalled towards the centre of the parade ground. What was the right thing to do? A diminishing circle of survivors clustered together. Very few options remaining. Scant seconds available to flee.

'Trav, please.' Linden, imploring. 'Antony's right.'

So Linden wanted to get out of there too. His dad would have refused to go. Maybe that was one reason why he was dead and Linden was alive. Maybe, sometimes, ideals had to give way to practicalities. So he had to choose. Flight or fight. Freedom or captivity. The past or the future. Dad or Linden.

'*Travis.*' With the Scytharene scenting victory, picking off their human adversaries almost at leisure.

He couldn't choose. But he *had* to.

The shells whistled shrilly to announce their arrival. Their impact tore up the parade ground, threw gravel and concrete and Scytharene warriors into the air indiscriminately. Blood spouted from severed alien limbs.

'What the hell . . .?' gaped Dwayne Randolph.

The Scytharene barely had time to register that they were under attack from a second quarter before bullets ripped through their formation as well as bombs, before armoured cars screeched into view along Horse Guards from the direction of the Mall, a small force of eight or nine vehicles, like swifter tanks, some with manually operated rocket launchers mounted on the roof, others with machine guns to create havoc. The Scytharene's attention divided, the remaining defenders fired their own weapons with renewed vigour and determination. For the first time, the enemy was confused.

Of course, so was Travis. The newcomers were welcome, that was for sure, and they were teenagers, he could see that, but as to their exact identity . . .

Several armoured cars ploughed straight into the Scytharene, bulldozed the warriors, broke their ranks and their bones simultaneously, crushing the bodies of those unfortunate enough to slip beneath their wheels.

Several other vehicles sped directly to their fellow humans, formed a shield between besieged and besieger. While the machine-gunners on the roof maintained a frantic covering fire, driving back the startled Scytharene, in one armoured car a side door opened vertically and someone leapt out.

He was wearing a baseball cap.

'Yo, Naughton. Fancy a lift?' grinned Richie Coker.

Mel was on her knees. She couldn't recall collapsing but she must have done, self-evidently. The pain perhaps was impairing her memory as it filled her mind, the pain that burned in her belly as if her innards were aflame, and yet the sticky wetness she could feel on her fingers as she clutched her middle in no way seemed able to douse that fire, the red liquid oozing over her fingers and soaking through her clothes, the blood. Mel was on her knees and bending forwards, her forehead resting against the cool steel of the moncom centre's floor, her vision screened by the black curtain of her hair.

She thought she could hear Ruth Bell ordering Geoffrey to turn that annoying radio receiver off and everyone else to place their weapons on the table – carefully – then to back away with their hands on their heads. That was what it all sounded like but Mel couldn't be sure. Getting shot played hell with your perceptions as well as your memory.

Crispin was crouching beside her. She *sensed* him. When she turned her head to the side, and when helpfully he smoothed her hair out of her eyes, she saw him. He looked pleased with himself, like Judas after the kiss in Gethsemane.

'May I?' he said, removing her subjugator from her belt. 'I don't think you'll be needing this again.'

Mel hoped her features expressed hatred rather than pain. 'You bastard,' she whispered with a venom that didn't require volume. 'Why?'

'Why did I shoot you, Patrick?' said Crispin conversationally. 'Mm. It's something I've wanted to do since we first met, I'm afraid. Why have we made such fools of your friends? Because they deserved it. Because we Paragons have been shown no respect. At every turn our rights and our desires have been flouted or obstructed by Naughton, by Clive, by Lane. Dear Ruth should have been indulging in' – wincing abstemiously – 'unsavoury physical intimacies with Clive by now, but Clive spurned her and Lane threatened her. They shouldn't have done that. I expect, just about now, they rather wish they had not.'

335

'I wish,' gritted Mel, 'you were dead.'

'Mm. Of course you do. And Naughton, attempting to deprive me of my destiny as leader of humanity? The effrontery of one with such a low-grade intellect, an ignorant rabble-rouser. But he is paying for his temerity, as are those who inanely elected to follow him. All of them, most probably enslaved by now. Best thing for them, I say. Might help them to realise that authority should belong only to superior beings.'

'You?' Mel might have spat at Crispin Allerton had her mouth not been so dry. 'Superior my *arse.*'

'Mm. The relevance of your nether regions to the issue under discussion rather eludes me, Patrick, though it does provide further evidence of your own unspeakable vulgarity.'

'If you're so clever,' Mel struggled, red-hot pincers goring her insides, 'if you're so . . . how come you couldn't develop the virus?'

'Oh, you poor simpleton,' Crispin chuckled pityingly. 'Don't you understand? We *have* formulated the virus. A Paragon never shirks a challenge, and never fails one, either. We merely neglected to provide it to those degenerate brutes gibbering after Naughton. A viable gene transfer virus exists, let me assure you. Who knows? In the future we may have need of a bargaining chip, should the Scytharene prove as unappreciative of true genius as you and Naughton have been. But as your future is very brief, I wouldn't worry about it.'

'Crispin, are you ready?' Ruth Bell.

'Yes, yes. *Distractions.*' Crispin stood, sniffed dismissively at the gang members lined up against the far wall with their hands on their heads. 'Mm. Well, I suppose we'd better march these morons out and lock them up.'

'What,' Mel croaked from the floor, 'are you going to do with me?'

'With you, Patrick?' Crispin lowered himself to her level once again. 'Mm, nothing. We're going to leave you here to die.'

'You . . . can't.'

'Tut, tut, Patrick, haven't you realised even now?' Crispin gave her a parting smile, dagger-thin. 'We can do whatever we like.'

Mel couldn't stop the Paragons, that was true enough. She could only gasp in agony while the others departed, Geoffrey giggling. She slumped over on to her side. Pain squeezed her eyes shut and she could see only scarlet. They'd left her to die, and as the burning inside her somehow turned to ice, a paralysing cold spreading through her limbs, and as the crimson before her eyes became black, as she descended into darkness, Mel feared she couldn't do much about that, either.

'I know,' said Richie. 'Questions. Where've we been? What've we been doing? No time now. 'Specially as' – glancing into the skies above St James's Park – 'the bastards have sent for reinforcements.'

The battlepods were back, zeroing in on the combat raging. Beyond those, Cullers and the *Ayrion III*.

'In the back,' Richie yelled to the entire group, indicating the armoured cars. 'Get your arses in there.'

The survivors needed little encouragement. Double doors in the back of each vehicle opened up to reveal ample space inside for the transportation of troops – or teenagers. Metal forms protruding from the walls provided some seating; the floor was already littered with spare weapons.

'No questions, Richie, but one thing,' said Travis. 'It's good to see you.'

Richie nodded, the chaos of conflict all around them. 'I bet it bloody well is.' He turned to the driver of his own vehicle, another familiar figure. 'Coop, get us out of here.'

'No worries, boss.' Giving a cheery thumbs-up. 'Cooper drives like Lewis Hamilton on *speed*.'

And hardly had Travis's closest companions, Dwayne Randolph and as many others as possible crammed into the armoured car's interior, Richie bringing up the rear, than Cooper set about proving his claim to be no idle boast.

'Bloody hell,' Linden cried, 'if the Scytharene don't kill us, Cooper will.' The sudden acceleration propelled her rather awkwardly into Richie's arms.

'You glad to see me too, Lin?' he said, a sadness in his eyes. He'd noted her with Travis. He knew what that meant.

'You should never have left in the first place,' Linden answered. Richie didn't resist as she pulled herself free of him and lurched back to her boyfriend.

'Where *have* you been, Richie?' said Jessica. 'And why?'

'More to the point,' Antony added, 'where are we going now?'

He was peering through the narrow strip of window that was their only visual access to the outside. Every armoured car was racing towards the Mall now except two – they were in flames, their personnel immolated, and would never race anywhere again. The Scytharene warriors had recovered. The battlepods were in pursuit.

'Me and the Kings were gonna set up for ourselves,' said Richie. 'Naughton can tell you why later. And Tony, with

338

alien bastards up our arses you're not getting picky about final destinations, are you? Anywhere but here.'

Two 'pods in concert blasted a nearby armoured car. It might as well have been made of paper. *Yellow* energy bolts. The insolence of the attack was clearly going to be severely punished. Those whose lives ended as the vehicle exploded, overturning in a whoosh of fire, may indeed in their last moments have regretted incurring Scytharene anger and its consequences; on the other hand, they might have been grateful to die free.

'Why did you come back?' said Travis.

'Thought you might like to see all the shit we found,' Richie replied. 'Thought it might help you out, case the virus didn't work according to plan, *which* . . .'

'It didn't,' said Jessica, who was glancing from the tense expression on Travis's face to its mirror image on Richie's, 'and is there something going on between you two we should know about?'

'No,' declared Travis. 'Nothing. Or if there was, there isn't any more.'

Richie appeared visibly relieved. 'Naughton, you don't know . . .' *What that means to me*, he would have said, if it hadn't been likely to sound so bloody poncy, so un-Richie Coker. 'I came back 'cause of *you*, Naughton. I couldn't let the aliens take you. Not you. You're—'

He never got to finish his sentence. The vehicle was suddenly swerving crazily from side to side, throwing its passengers about with maniacal glee.

'What does Cooper think he's doing?' Linden cried.

'Bobbing and weaving,' Antony said from the window where he'd heroically kept his balance, 'trying to keep away from his opponent's sucker punch. A boxer to the end.'

339

They were spurting beneath the grand curve of Admiralty Arch, but even though the battlepods were forced to divert above it, they swiftly swept back down again, mercilessly closing in for the kill. Left and right, armoured cars erupted. Fewer targets meant greater focus on those remaining.

'Hold on!' Antony advised.

But whatever they might have held on to would have made no difference. When the yellow bolt struck the road to their left, mangling the vehicle's wheels, blackening and denting its side, flinging its machine-gunner to his death, sending the twenty tons of moving metal rearing up and over, nobody could possibly have kept their grip on anything. They didn't. There were screams as the armoured car, still striving valiantly to escape, skidded on its side for half a street, its steel flank scraping, sparking on the tarmac like tinder and flint.

Then silence.

Another gap in her memory.

Mel had no idea how she came to be here, in the ruined streets of a deserted city – London? It was dark but somehow it still didn't seem like night. She was lonely and in need of company. She called Jessie's name, and Travis's, but she couldn't hear her own voice. She couldn't see where she was going.

If only there was a sign, a clear way forward.

A light.

Not so much at the end of the tunnel as the end of the road. The glow of a pure white light, like a beacon, like a brand. Alluring amidst the darkness like spring in winter.

Mel made towards it.

She felt a sudden need to reach it, to attain the light, to

bathe in it as if it was water, to be cleansed by it and made new, her pain washed away, her loneliness, her regrets. The wound in her stomach would be healed, she felt, if she could only . . .

The wound. Her stomach.

Mel halted with the light still some distance off. She'd been shot, she remembered that now. Crispin Allerton had shot her and left her to die. Was she dead now? Was this death, this urban wasteland? She sensed not. She sensed she was alive but unconscious, sleeping, dreaming, slipping away.

But she couldn't do that. Not while Crispin Allerton still wore that smug, superior smile. Not while Jessie, Trav and the others might still need her help, could still be saved. She couldn't just let herself die, and she wouldn't. She had things to do. The light would have to wait.

She'd learned about not giving up from Travis. *Wake up, Melanie*, she forced herself. *Wake up*.

On the floor. In the moncom centre. Bleeding. Her hands dripping with blood. The pain seemed less than before, maybe dulling with familiarity. Nobody watching her. The Paragons no longer considered her to be a danger to them, not with a hole in her belly.

Big mistake.

About the pain easing, too. As Mel heaved herself to her feet it felt like she was splitting herself open. She badly wanted to vomit but preferred to direct what physical energy she could muster more beneficially. Jessie. Trav. She fixed their images in her mind. She needed to concentrate on *them*, not on the pain, on her reason for *enduring* the pain. And on the one person she could still rely on as an ally.

Dyona.

Mel didn't have time to find out where the Paragons might have imprisoned the gang members, but she knew where to find Dyona. The isolation booth wasn't far – luckily. As she dragged herself along the corridor, the wall she leaned against like a crutch to keep her upright, she was leaving a trickling scarlet trail behind her, like bright, spilled paint.

A lot of blood. She was losing a lot of blood, and she had such a limited supply.

Had to make it to the isolation booth. Had to make it to the isolation . . . place quickly. While she could. While her strength . . . slipping away. *Jessie. Trav.* Up ahead. Just up ahead. Like the light. Could settle for . . . the light. Slip off the roundabout. Fall.

No. Don't fall. Mel steadied herself against the wall. Her legs were like liquid. Should have worked out more. Should have built herself up. When she'd had the chance.

Jessie. Trav. One foot before the other. Don't worry about standing tall. If you can get to the iso . . . *whatever* only by bending double like some old bag lady, then do it. *Dyona.* Open the door for her. Remember how to open the door. The glass room. She was there. The door had a fancy kind of – mechanism thing. She only had to activate it. If she could only remember how to . . .

Door was open. Two people inside. Dyona seeing her but not showing it. The other not seeing her, back to her, pointing a gun at Dyona. Plaits.

Speaking: '. . . little experiment on you, alien, if you'll come with me . . . make personal acquaintance with our gene transfer . . .'

'*Ruth!*' The way Mel howled it, definitely a four-letter word.

Ruth Bell turning, startled for a second.

And in that second Dyona smashing her in the jaw with one clenched white fist.

'Way to go, Dyona,' Mel smiled wanly as the floor once more rose up to meet her.

Coughing. Groaning. An anonymous whimper of pain.

'Someone,' gasped Antony, 'get the number . . . of that driver.'

'Found that sense of humour, Tony, huh? Just in time.' Inside the crippled armoured car, bodies piled unceremoniously on top of each other, the world seemed to have turned upside down – the kids were used to that. Richie squirmed from beneath a girl with a broken neck, kicked the rear doors open. 'If you're alive, *move*.'

Grabbing the first weapon that came to hand, he scrambled out on to the scarred road. Battlepods were circling above like vultures waiting for their prey to die. Waiting for further orders, Richie thought. Do they kill or capture any human survivors? Not that there was much loss or gain in either option. With dismal horror he saw that the other armoured cars were blazing wrecks. Only a handful of teenagers were still alive to limp and stagger and stumble a desperate path towards Trafalgar Square.

He wouldn't let the Scytharene take Naughton.

Who was helping Linden out of the armoured car, both standing, both cut and bruised but otherwise uninjured. That was good. Tony and Jessica following, in one piece too. A few of the others. Also good.

'Can I – you think I can get a hand here?' Cooper, bleeding from a head wound, lacking the strength to haul himself out of the front compartment through the hole where a door had been.

'Naughton, get Coop,' Richie said. 'Then take Lin and everyone else and get the hell away.'

'Antony.' Travis delegated the rescue of Cooper. He was more concerned for Richie. 'What about you?'

Scytharene warriors appearing through Admiralty Arch.

'I'll hold the bastards back.'

'Hold them back?' Linden blurted. 'Richie, that's insane.'

'Buy you some time. Whatever. Make a stand.' He appealed to Travis for understanding. 'Like I should have done a long time ago.'

'Travis, don't *let* him.' Linden in anguish, realising only now how much she was going to miss Richie Coker, despite everything. 'Force him to come with us.'

'Trav! Lin! Richie!' The others calling frantically.

'What happened between you and Linden, it doesn't matter now,' said Travis.

'I know. Makes no bloody difference.' Under the baseball cap, Richie's eyes shone. 'I wanted to be you, Naughton. Let me. Just once.'

'Travis, you *can't*.' But Linden saw the acceptance in Travis's expression, the admiration. They were losing Richie.

'We'll remember you,' Travis said.

'You'd bloody better. Look after her.' His final gaze was reserved for Linden. In it there was something like love.

But he was turning away and opening fire at the advancing Scytharene. The machine-gun rattle meant Linden doubted he could even hear her hopeless pleas for him to come with them. Then Travis was grabbing her hand and yanking her after him and she was running with Travis and Antony and

Jessica and Cooper, and if she looked back now she might see Richie taken, might see him die.

Linden didn't look back.

Neither did Richie glance behind him. One, he didn't need to: if anyone could lead Lin and the others to safety, that'd be Naughton. Two, he had enough to deal with in front of him. A couple of Scytharene went down but he wouldn't delay them for long. Not that that was the point. Standing his ground was the point. Being someone he could be proud of, whatever the cost.

'Come on, you bastards. *Come on* . . .' Richie Coker, fighting like a soldier. His old mum would have been proud at last. She'd always wanted him to join the army. If she could see him now. . .

But the warriors weren't returning his fire. Why weren't . . .?

Bastards. Cheating bloody bastards.

The whoosh of air. The crackle of electricity.

Richie looked up. *Naughton, I hope I helped.* The bolt from the battlepod was yellow.

'Oh, shit.'

Richie Coker was incinerated where he stood.

And in Trafalgar Square, further Scytharene forces lurked. Nelson on his column and the lions on their plinths had observed their arrival but had seen fit not to warn Travis's people of their presence. Soon it was too late, in any case. The white spears of subjugator blasts were a bit of a give-away.

'Travis!' Terror in Linden's eyes. They were surrounded. They were helpless. The few weapons in their possession could offer only token resistance.

'Stay with me. Lin, stay *with* me.'

She would have liked to have done, but the subjugator bolt that struck her robbed Linden of choice as well as movement.

Cooper falling. The others with names Travis didn't know.

Antony shielding Jessica with his body so that he was hit first, crumpling, sprawling on English flagstones.

Jessica crying out, crouching down at Antony's side, keeling slowly over him as she blazed briefly white.

Travis alone. No time to mourn their losses. No time to despair at their defeat. No time to think at all. Beneath Nelson's Column and the London sky, time only to breathe, a deep, final gulp of native air, sweet and pure.

Who knew *what* the hell the air would be like where he was going?

In the lab at Enclave Zero, Crispin and Geoffrey were expecting Dyona to join them, marched in at the point of Ruth Bell's gun.

They weren't expecting the Scytharene prisoner to burst in on them brandishing a firearm of her own and, more startling than that, accompanied not by their fellow Paragon but by the roaring rabble from the streets they *thought* they'd locked up. Yet this was how Dyona appeared. Which, had either of them been capable of the slightest amount of humility, might have suggested to them that even the most exceptional prodigies on the planet didn't know everything.

'Crispin! Crispin!' squealed Geoffrey, kind of like a pig about to be slaughtered. His habitual bobbing up and down became exaggerated into a jump. Until a flurry of eagerly vengeful fists pounded him to the floor.

Crispin snatched for what had been Mel's subjugator. He'd

placed it on a table. If he'd thrust it under his belt, he might have been able to loose a few blasts. Instead, the butt of an automatic rifle slamming down almost shattered his hand. Crispin Allerton wasn't a fan of physical pain.

'Don't kill me!' he blubbed, the barrel of several guns keen to do just that jabbing into him like accusing fingers. 'Do what you like with *him*' – pointing to Geoffrey – 'but let me live.' Seemed Crispin wasn't big on loyalty, either.

Geoffrey was tugged into standing by his hair. 'Freak's like a bloody sheep,' someone jeered, a generous tuft of the boy's shaggy fleece in his fist. 'Maybe we should shear him.'

The rifle butt that had all but broken Crispin's hand now sought diversion by ramming repeatedly into his stomach. 'Nah. Let's just shoot 'em. It's what they deserve.'

'That's true,' said Dyona, 'but not yet. We might need their expertise. Put them with the girl.'

The Paragons were dragged towards the lab door.

'Alien scum,' Crispin spat as he passed Dyona. 'I hope the virus is in the air down here. I hope you're contaminated and die slowly, screaming.'

'I'll take my chances.'

'At least your wretched little friend is dead,' Crispin gloated.

'Melanie?' Dyona tilted her head in amusement. 'Really, Crispin, I thought you were supposed to be intelligent. Who do you think helped release me from the isolation booth?' She leaned forward. 'Somebody wants a word with you.'

The bridge of the *Ayrion III* was more crowded than usual. As well as the typical complement of red-armoured techs at computers, black-armoured warriors at attention and

Gyrion presiding over all in the golden robes and armour of the Thousand Families, the latter's twenty-three fellow Fleet Commanders were also present. As only those who belonged to the Scytharene elite could even hope for elevation to the exalted rank of Fleet Commander, Gyrion's guests too gleamed goldenly. Ranged along the crescent shape of the bridge, they gazed down at London through the panoramic floor-to-ceiling windows, and if applause had been an acceptable element of Scytharene military etiquette, the assembled dignitaries would have applauded their host there and then for what he had achieved.

The Cullers were at work. Their expansive white tractor beams lifted the bodies of unconscious Earthers into the bellies of the ships – from that park, from that parade ground, from that square with the statue of a totally insignificant, long-dead Earther hero. London had fallen. England had fallen. Earth had fallen.

Fortunes would soon be made in the slave markets of Homeworld.

'A most satisfying sight, my lord Gyrion,' acknowledged Atrion of the bloodline of Syrion.

'It is indeed, my lord Atrion.' Basking in the approbation of his peers.

'A tragedy that your son Lord Darion is not here to witness this final enslavement, my lord.' An observation from Fleet Commander Urion of the bloodline of Davion.

'He is here,' Gyrion asserted coldly. 'Darion watches us now with the eyes of his ancestors.' The likes of Urion might match his own social rank, Gyrion reflected, but they were not his equals where it mattered, in their hearts, in their spirit, in their commitment to the Scytharene cause.

348

'A tragedy too about the loss of Lady Dyona,' pursued Urion.

'Indeed, my lord Urion.' Through gritted teeth. Why didn't the infuriating nonentity *shut up*? 'But she died as she would have wished, in the service of her race. Like my son.'

'You are certain, then, Gyrion, that the Lady Dyona is dead.' Atrion again. His bloodline had close ties with Dyona's.

'I am afraid so,' lied Gyrion. 'The search party I dispatched as soon as Dyona's expedition failed to return at the designated hour found no trace of either her or any of her companions.' Another lie. He'd sent nobody after Dyona's missing group, though he *almost* had. The non-appearance of his Blackheart executioners meant that something had gone wrong with his original plan. 'We must assume that Dyona and all her party fell victim to a savage and cowardly Earther attack.' An assumption with which he was secretly comforting himself. It had to be true. Dyona must be dead. *If only he knew it for a fact.*

'These Earthers deserve punishment for their crimes,' declared Atrion.

'Agreed, Lord Atrion,' said Urion, 'but in our zeal for retribution, let us not risk damaging our merchandise.'

Relieved to steer the subject away from Darion and Dyona, Gyrion said: 'Oh, I think we can strike a powerful blow against these primitives without jeopardising our profits.' He snapped an order to the helmsman and the *Ayrion III* repositioned itself slightly. 'You see the building below us, my lords?' Overlooking the river, by indigenous standards palatial, a clock tower at one end. 'This hovel was once the seat of this paltry nation's government. It stands while its people have fallen. An incongruity there, I think.'

'Indeed, Lord Gyrion,' nodded Atrion.

'Are we to see explosions?' hoped Urion.

'Oh, I think we can promise you explosions, Lord Urion,' said Gyrion. He turned to the techs. 'Engage energy beams.'

Dyona had advised her to rest. They'd patched her up as best they could, as the bandages wrapped round her midriff testified – 'What?' she'd said. 'You want to turn me into a mummy?' – but she had lost a lot of blood already and her overall condition was still deteriorating. Any further exertion, Dyona had warned gravely, could prove counterproductive. By which Mel knew she meant fatal. But she couldn't just languish on a bed groaning while Jessie and Travis were still out there, maybe still at liberty, maybe enslaved. Maybe worse. She had to do something to find out and to help her friends if at all possible.

And that process started with the Paragons.

'Patrick,' greeted Crispin Allerton from the isolation booth which, it seemed, was rather cramped for three. He sneered. 'I'm delighted to say you look terrible.'

'As long as I never look like you, arsehole,' Mel gritted. She was leaning on Dyona. Her legs seemed to be in the middle of a strike. A pair of armed male gang members completed the visiting party.

'Such a wonderful conversationalist,' Ruth Bell observed.

'What's it like, Mel?' Geoffrey Thomas pressed his nose to the Plexiglas like a child to a sweetshop window. 'Being shot, I mean?'

'With any luck, you weird little boy,' Mel said, 'one day you might find out.'

'Is that what you intend to do with us, Patrick?' Crispin

350

more cautious now. 'You ally yourself with alien scum like her, yet threaten your own kind with violence. No wonder society was in such a parlous state even before the Sickness.'

'The only scum I see here, Crispin,' glared Mel, 'are sealed up in an isolation booth, and what *happens* to you is *up* to you.'

'They still want the virus, Crispin,' deduced Ruth.

'Oh yes,' said Mel.

Which made Crispin smug again. 'But Patrick, to what end? To save your pitiful friends? Naughton, Clive and the others . . .'

'Jessica Lane,' gloated Ruth vindictively.

'. . . they must have been overrun and captured or killed by now. Are you able to make radio contact with them, may I ask?'

Mel cast her eyes down momentarily. They'd tried to, but the moncom centre had remained disturbingly silent: nobody from Travis's force was broadcasting.

'I thought not.' Crispin smirked. 'You should face the inevitable, Patrick. It's all over for you.'

'Not yet it isn't. Not *yet*.' Not until she'd seen the bodies.

'Let the three of us out of here,' Crispin coaxed. 'We can take care of everything, Melanie. We can look after everything.'

Mel laughed sardonically, winced at the pain the action caused her. 'You shot me in the stomach, Crispin, not the brain. You're staying where you are. Now back to the point. The *virus*. You said you had some, so where is it? Where's a sample of the real thing?' Even if the others were in the cells aboard Gyrion's ship, if the virus could be deployed before they were squeezed into cryo-tubes and transported into space . . . 'Tell us – help us – and you might yet see tomorrow.'

'Will it be a tomorrow with the right people in charge, though?' Crispin said.

Mel shook her head in exasperation. 'I don't believe you. Even now all you're interested in is your own selfish agen . . . duh.' She uttered a sudden cry.

'Melanie? What is it?' Dyona was thinking relapse. 'Help her,' she called to their companions.

'No. It's okay. I'm okay.' Mel waved them away. 'I've just – why didn't I think of it immediately? Change of plan, guys.' Addressing the Paragons, her words like razor blades. 'What happens to you is now up to *us*. *We* can take care of everything. We don't need you after all.'

'What,' said Crispin, smugness diminishing by the second, 'do you mean?'

'The real virus is in that syringe-gun, isn't it? The one Geoffrey wanted to inject Dyona with.'

'Crispin?' Geoffrey eyed his elder woefully.

'It *is*.' Mel was triumphant. For a moment she even forgot the pain in her stomach – almost. 'Dyona, the lab.'

They'd have got there, too, if it hadn't been for the sudden, deafening boom about their heads, above *ground*, and the subterranean rumbling like a rockslide in a mine, and the juddering of Enclave Zero's corridors.

'What the hell . . .?' The floor shook beneath Mel's already unsteady feet. She held on more tightly to Dyona.

'Are we under attack?' the Scytharene said fearfully. 'Do my people know we're here?'

A Chinese boy was pelting along the corridor. Mel knew his name. Ling. She'd posted him in the moncom centre. Whatever he might have seen or heard there – news of Jessie? – had terrified him. 'The aliens,' he reported between gasps. And was it her imagination, or could Mel really, faintly, hear the distant grinding of metal on metal? 'They're destroying the Houses of Parliament. They're blowing them up.' Which didn't trouble Mel unduly, except for one rather significant consideration. 'They're bringing the whole thing down on top of us!'

FIFTEEN

'What do we do?' Mel's companions looked to her for direction.

'I don't . . .' It was so hard to think, clearly and coherently. Why was it so hard to *think*?

The Enclave's vibrations seemed to have ceased. A moment of stillness and silence ensued. But the atmosphere below ground remained tense, anxiously expectant, the calm before the storm.

Which began again with clanging, clashing percussion, sounds like the slamming of an endless succession of heavy steel doors, a giant blacksmith hammering perpetually on his titanic anvil, metallic peals that reverberated through Enclave Zero. Floors and walls renewed their trembling. Ceilings quaked like a desert on a fault line.

Crispin Allerton had a good idea of what he wanted done. 'Let us out of here.' Joining Geoffrey at the Plexiglas. 'Patrick, let us out. This tin can of a complex is about to be crushed.'

Was it? Mel glanced up. Was she seeing what she appeared to be seeing, the solid steel ceiling rippling like water? 'Dyona?' Second-opinion time.

'The outer shell of this installation has been damaged, weakened by my people's destruction of your Parliament building,' the Scytharene said. 'And now, with the added weight of those thousands of tons of rubble bearing down on top of it . . .'

'Crispin's right? The roof's just gonna cave in?'

'It might. Unless it can withstand the pressure.'

'I know I can't,' muttered Mel. And she doubted the Enclave could either. She thought of steel buckling, rivets popping like buttons on a fat boy's coat, metal torn open like a bag of crisps. 'We can't take the chance, not when Jessie and Trav and the others need us alive. Time to go.'

'My sentiments precisely,' concurred Dyona.

'We'll take the Downing Street exit,' Mel said. 'That'll probably be safest. Ling, get everybody else together and out. Now.'

'Yes, Mel.' Ling departed as swiftly as he'd arrived.

'You others,' Dyona instructed the two male gang members, 'take Melanie with you. She's in your charge.'

But even as the boys moved in to support her in Dyona's place, Mel resisted: 'No. I can't leave yet. Have to get to the lab, find the syringe-gun. Without it—'

'I'll find it,' Dyona intervened. 'I'm more mobile than you are. I'll fetch it and I'll follow you. Now please, Melanie' – as the complex shuddered like a man in a fever – 'we don't have time for arguments.'

'No,' accepted Mel, and put her arms around the necks of the two gang members.

'I'll see you soon.' Dyona ran off as Mel herself was helped down the corridor.

'Wait. Wait!' Ruth Bell made it a full set of three Paragons at the transparent wall of their prison. 'What about us?'

'Yeah, Ruth.' Mel glanced back. 'What *about* you? You were happy enough all by yourselves at Wells. Thought you might like more of the same now.'

'But you can't just leave us locked up in here.' Ruth was aghast. 'If the Enclave collapses . . .'

'This is murder, Patrick,' Crispin accused. 'Cold-blooded murder.'

Geoffrey whined like a dog refused its walk.

'Murder like shooting someone in the stomach, Crispin?' Mel retorted. 'Thanks to that, I don't know how much blood I've got left, cold, hot or otherwise. And what are you complaining about anyway? You're a genius, so you keep telling us. If you are so bloody clever, genius your way out of that.'

Enclave Zero groaned in its suffering. Along the length and breadth of the highest of its levels, its ceilings bulged as if suddenly and unfeasibly pregnant. They quivered. They stretched. To breaking point.

While Mel was being hurried into the tunnel to Downing Street and Ling was forging ahead with the rest of those who'd been designated the Enclave's defenders, Dyona was reaching the lab where the Paragons had worked. She hoped that soulless trio of Earthers – so similar in many respects to her own people – had not taken steps to conceal the object she was searching for. Needless to say, they had not. The syringe-gun was there on the table, placed on its own stand like an exhibit in a museum. Why *would* the Paragons have hidden it? They hadn't anticipated Mel freeing Dyona from the isolation booth and the turnaround in events her liberation had brought about. Like the Scytharene, the Paragons had arrogantly assumed they'd have everything their own way. They'd been given a rude awakening. As Dyona lifted the syringe-gun with both hands, its barrel brimming with viral fluid, she trusted that the same would soon be true of the Scytharene.

356

She knew what she had to do.

As every metal surface in the complex seemed to become ductile, malleable, as steel plates twisted and scrunched into shapes unenvisaged by Enclave Zero's architects.

As the prisoners in the isolation booth spectated in horror.

'Patrick! *Patrick!* Come back here!' Crispin was bawling into empty corridors. 'You can't leave us! Don't you know who we are? We're Paragons!'

Shaggy-haired Geoffrey Thomas was whimpering in Ruth Bell's arms, like a frightened child with its mother. 'Ruth, we'll get out, won't we? We won't die, will we? It's not fair. I don't want to die.'

'Statistically,' said Ruth with a calmness that surprised her, 'our chances of survival at this juncture, Geoffrey, are nil.'

She sat with the younger boy on the bench that doubled as a bed and waited patiently for the end to come. There was no point in doing anything else. Not even Ruth Bell could defy the dictates of numbers. Numbers were everything.

Yet Crispin continued to pound on the Plexiglas in vain protestation. 'I'm better than any of you, do you hear me?' Not above the rending and tearing of reinforced steel from the higher level. Not above the avalanche of soil and stone cascading into the complex. 'I'm Crispin Allerton. You've no right to leave me here. Listen to me. Patrick! *Patrick!*'

Sudden, spidery cracks in the Plexiglas wall, as if Crispin's fists had had more effect than his words. They hadn't. It was pressure from overhead that was splitting their prison open, the unsustainable stress of steel forced to bear impossible weight, steel straining, rupturing, giving way.

And the countless tons of earth and debris that crashed through Enclave Zero, the foundations of the Houses of

Parliament, the fallen towers and the shattered spires, they were as little interested as the departed Mel in what Crispin Allerton had to say.

Which now was nothing at all.

Could be she was getting worse.

Mel felt herself lapsing in and out, if not of consciousness, exactly, then certainly of full awareness of where she was and what she was doing there. Locations blurred by. A tunnel, long and narrow, illuminated by a single strip of electric light in the ceiling. Rooms of leather and mahogany: she'd always wondered what the interior of Number Ten Downing Street looked like. The open air, studded in the distance with Cullers. If the others were alive at all, they had to be inside one of the scythe-shaped ships. The even larger hulk of a Scytharene slavecraft. War-zone streets. Kids around her she scarcely knew, appearing concerned for her, like relations at hospital beds. Lying on a sofa in a large, airy room in some government building or other. Gasping, having to think about breathing to do it.

Blood seeping through her bandages to wet her clothes again.

Worse, yeah. Definitely worse. But she said to the half-dozen kids standing round her, she said she was holding on for a while yet, wouldn't let go for a while yet. She wouldn't let herself fall from the roundabout till she knew that Jessie and Travis and the others were safe.

'The roundabout?' Dyona said, and here Mel was thinking she'd been talking to a group but it was just herself and the Scytharene. 'Melanie, I don't understand.'

'Doesn't . . . doesn't matter.' Willing her eyes to stay open and her senses alert. 'You're here. Dyona, did you bring it? Where is it?' She groped for the Scytharene's hands. They were empty. 'No. . .' Struggling to sit up. 'The syringe-gun, Dyona. The virus. Where is it?'

'It's all right. It's all right,' Dyona soothed. 'Lie back, Melanie. Rest.' Easing her into a recumbent position. 'Conserve your strength.'

And Dyona crouched by Mel's side and the wounded girl saw that the Scytharene looked as if she too had been shot. Or something. She didn't look well. She was sweating profusely, yet her hands where they touched Mel were cold and clammy, amphibian, and the pure white of her skin, particularly of her face and hairless skull, was pinker in tint now, like it was slowly being boiled from within.

'I didn't bring the syringe-gun with me,' Dyona said. 'I didn't need to.'

'Didn't . . .? Do you know what – you've just condemned my friends to slavery.'

'No. I hope I've saved them. Melanie,' Dyona confided with a mixture of pride and horror, 'I injected myself with the virus.'

'Dyona . . .' Mel's voice expressed only horror.

'It was the best way. The only way. We have so few fighters left. We might not be able to get close enough to my people for the infection to work. But if I return to the *Ayrion III* alone . . . By the time Gyrion apprehends me it will be too late. For him. For all of them.'

'And for you, Dyona,' Mel said. 'You've just killed yourself.'

'I can feel it working inside me now, Melanie.' A shudder thrilled through Dyona's whole body. 'The virus. I can feel it changing me, modifying me, manipulating the core of my being. It's like fire. But the pain, I can – I *will* endure it. Crispin Allerton must have exaggerated the speed of the process. I have time yet – to find my way back to the *Ayrion III*.'

'You're dying.' Mel couldn't get further than that single, devastating fact. 'For us.'

'As my beloved Darion died, Melanie.' Dyona smiled wistfully at the thought of him. 'Can I do less? We both pledged our lives to the cause of freedom, the end of slavery and the equality of all races. Those were our beliefs, and what good are beliefs if you are not prepared to die for them?' A serenity settled upon her, a kind of transcendence, as if Dyona of the bloodline of Lyrion was already above and beyond the obsessions of mortal life. 'And in dying like this I have found freedom too. Freedom from my own species. From the tyranny of my own biology. The virus is violating my cells, corrupting the integrity of my bloodline with the genetic material of an un-Scytharene race, a so-called inferior race. So, I have been made impure, and I rejoice in that. When I die, it will not be as a Scytharene. I will die as a human being.' Her final note was one of almost messianic triumph.

Not shared by Mel. 'Couldn't we . . . Dyona, there had to have been another way.'

'I am the carrier of your kind's salvation now, Melanie, and soon I will be more.' Dyona stared distractedly into space. Her voice grew colder, more remote, a true Scytharene voice. 'When I walk among my people again, when I greet the Fleet Commanders at their warped celebration tonight, as I will, I will become as the Reaper and I will leave death in my wake. Everyone who comes into contact with me will be infected and become carriers in turn.

The Sickness that we ourselves seeded here will spread throughout our fleet. Your planet will be saved. Your friends, Melanie, will return to you. I truly believe that.' She focused her gaze on the injured girl and tenderness, humanity were restored to her voice. 'Do not despair. Stay strong for the reunion to come, Melanie. Stay alive.'

'I will,' Mel promised. There were tears in her eyes. Her last sight of Dyona was splintered with tears.

'I must go.' Squeezing Mel's hands in farewell. 'While I can. Your companions will show me the way. Melanie, it has been a privilege knowing you. Remember me to Travis and Antony.'

Mel nodded. She wanted to say something too, something profound, appropriate as final words to be spoken to one who was departing and would never return. 'Dyona,' she said, with sorrow and gratitude and love, and perhaps that was sufficient. Mel thought she saw Dyona smile as she rose, but she might have imagined that. Difficult to be sure. She seemed to have drifted off once more. When she was certain of her consciousness again, something else was certain too.

Dyona was gone.

The Scytharene as a race had little time for music. Music, it was said, encouraged emotional incontinence and physical indolence, neither of which were conditions suitable for a martial life. Composers won no battles. And, as alienologists had pointed out, it clearly wasn't coincidence that so many inferior and subsequently enslaved civilisations wallowed in singing, dancing and the playing of instruments. Instruments of war, it was said, were all that a loyal and decent Scytharene needed to master.

So the celebration of London's enslavement that Fleet Commander Gyrion hosted in the Chamber of the Triumph aboard the *Ayrion III* unfolded to an absence of musical accompaniment. Gyrion was glad. More tuneful to his ear in any case were the compliments and words of praise offered by his twenty-three noble guests. Beverages of an intoxicating nature did not fall under the same puritanical proscription as melody – shared inebriation fostering solidarity and comradeship among warriors – and the pluvium was flowing liberally as Gyrion circulated. Everyone was attired in their full ceremonial regalia. There was so much gold in the chamber that lighting was all but rendered superfluous.

'A great day for the Scytharene race, my lord Gyrion.'

'Thank you, my lord Lorion.'

'I have no doubt your place on the Council of the Thousand Families will be guaranteed after such a glorious enslavement as this, my lord.'

'Do you think so, Lord Petrion? Thank you.'

The Chamber of the Triumph was austerely decorated, in keeping with Scytharene taste. Its only architectural feature of note was the glittering steel sickle that seemed to be slicing its way out of three of the room's four walls, the other being glass and providing panoramic views of whatever lay beyond the ship. The sickle's blade gleamed well above head height, and the effect of its apparent emergence through the walls was supposed to symbolise the advancing power of the Scytharene race and the inevitability of their victory over any foe.

An interpretation of an inanimate hunk of metal that Gyrion normally scorned as pretentious, indulgent and downright fanciful. Tonight, however, as he stood beneath the

362

crescent and quaffed his goblet of pluvium, he was graciously prepared to concede there might be something in it. Particularly the reference to victory over any foe.

The Earthers had certainly been no match for him. Neither had the treacherous Lady Dyona. It appeared that he, Gyrion of the bloodline of Ayrion, like his revered ancestor had been born to crush his enemies.

'My lord?' The black-armoured officer of the watch reporting, something of an inane grin on his face.

'You've left your post, Turion,' Gyrion observed. 'I instructed you to disturb me in the event of an emergency only. And from your expression, I doubt that such a situation currently exists.'

'My apologies, my lord, but I thought you would wish to be informed personally. More good news,' said Turion. 'The Lady Dyona has returned.'

'What?'

'The Lady Dyona, my lord . . .'

'I *heard*, Turion.' As would everyone else if the overeager buffoon didn't keep his voice down. 'Good news indeed.' Disguising fear with favour, steering the officer of the watch to the corner of the chamber. 'Tell me how this happy circumstance has come about.'

'The lady made herself known to one of our perimeter patrols, my lord, and was brought aboard ship immediately. Her party was attacked by Earthers as you'd feared, but Lady Dyona managed to escape and find her way back.'

'Where is she now, Turion?'

'In her quarters, my lord, resting. I have been told she has refused medical attention.'

'Very well.' Gyrion's mind raced. What did Dyona think

she was about, placing herself voluntarily again within his clutches? Surely she knew that he would make no mistake concerning her elimination a second time? Was she perhaps insane enough to believe she could carry out her original scheme after all? 'Turion, tell no one of the Lady Dyona's reappearance. We wouldn't want her unduly disturbed by well-wishers until she has fully recovered from her ordeal, would we? Order those who have seen her also to hold their tongues until I allow otherwise.'

'As you wish, my lord,' Turion said, a little curiously.

'Now return to your post.' Gyrion detected the puzzlement on his subordinate's brow. He attempted to clear it with a smile of the most outrageous falseness. 'But you were right to inform me of this development, Turion. My heart is gladdened by it, so much so that I must make excuses to my guests and hasten to the Lady Dyona's quarters myself. I cannot *wait* to see her.'

Many levels below the Chamber of the Triumph were situated the slave quarters. Not so many minutes before the commencement of Gyrion's enslavement celebration, their latest batch of prisoners began to regain consciousness. Some did not find their surroundings unexpected: the school-hall-sized silver room, featureless, windowless. Travis, Linden, Jessica and Antony had sampled the hospitality of Scytharene cells before.

At least they were together, Travis consoled himself. That was something. At least he could hold Linden close as they sat on the floor and find hope in the feelings they had for each other. Antony and Jessica were clasped in a similar embrace. Dwayne Randolph and a Cooper shiny with fresh bruises made up the remainder of their immediate circle, while maybe fifty other former gang members lolled in glum, listless groups around the cell, wondering what was going to happen to them next.

'Processing, I imagine,' said Antony in answer to exactly that question from Dwayne. 'Though I'm surprised they haven't started already.'

'I'm *glad* they haven't,' Jessica shuddered. 'I hope they never do.'

'Assuming we're aboard the *Ayrion III*, if Gyrion's hosting some kind of party like Dyona told us,' Travis mused, 'maybe they'll leave processing until the morning.' As their personal effects had not yet been confiscated, their watches were able to inform them that it was evening. 'Which still gives us time to find a way out of here.'

'Another breakout, Trav?' Antony smiled wistfully. 'I wish. Unfortunately, I think we're out of Scytharene allies.'

'There's still Dyona,' said Linden.

'And Mel.' In whom Jessica had every faith. 'They must know what happened. They might mount some kind of rescue attempt.'

'The Phantoms damn well would,' claimed Dwayne Randolph. 'If we weren't either all locked up in this shit-hole already or dead.'

'The Kings of the Ring wouldn't throw in the towel nei-ther,' said Cooper staunchly, and then, more forlornly, 'not if we still had a champion to lead us, anyway.'

Linden gnawed her lip. 'What do you reckon *did* become of Richie, Travis? You think he's still alive?' *Hoping.* Hoping he was.

'I don't know,' Travis admitted grimly. 'If he was, I kind of think he'd be here with us, wouldn't he? With the other prisoners? Before, aboard the *Furion*, we didn't get divided until processing. I could be wrong, though. Richie *could* be alive, Lin. But I've got a feeling he's gone.'

Linden gave a half-nod. She had that feeling too, and a worse one that accompanied it, if that were possible. Guilt. If it hadn't been for her turning so venomously against him, Richie might never have left Enclave Zero in the first place, certainly not when he actually did. If it hadn't been for her . . .

'If he is dead,' Antony said solemnly, 'he died bravely. He showed us there was more to Richie Coker than we ever gave him credit for. He proved himself, and I don't think you can ask for more than that.'

Linden could. She could ask for Richie to be alive again. But the age of miracles was past.

'So many questions,' sighed Jessica. 'What about Mel and everyone we left at Enclave Zero? And why didn't the virus work? Crispin seemed so sure . . .'

'We might never find out, Jess,' said Antony.

'So was it worth it, then?' the blonde girl pursued. 'All those sacrifices. The pain. The deaths. All that loss. Richie. The others. And for what? To end up pretty much back where we started, in a cell.'

'It was worth it, babe,' Dwayne Randolph said. 'If only 'cause all of us fought as one. My brother Danny would have been proud of the stand we made today and that's damn well good enough for me. You gave us a chance to battle those bastards, Travis, to really take 'em on. We might have got our arses kicked in the end, but so the hell what? We were right to join up with you and I'm guessing everyone in the other gangs would say the same.'

'Well, I'm not ready to concede we've lost yet, Dwayne,' said Travis, 'but I appreciate your sentiment. And even if it is all over, you're right. Simply by resisting them we sent a message. That humans aren't just going to roll over and surrender to the mighty Scytharene.' The last words thick with sarcasm. 'Hopefully we've set an example for somebody else to follow. There might be other kids out there better equipped than we were, or Crispin might find a way to make the virus work after all. Or something. Even if we've failed, what we've done might still inspire others to succeed in our place. That's what we have to believe.' He raised Linden's hand to his lips and kissed it. 'We have to believe it.'

Dyona got changed as quickly as she could. Gyrion could be here in her quarters any minute.

It was probably folly for her to even be thinking about clothes – especially as it was becoming harder for her to think about anything but the pain burning inside her – but she couldn't grace the celebration in the Chamber of the Triumph garbed in the tarnished gold armour she'd been wearing for the past several days. The eminent assembly of Fleet Commanders would expect an outfit more in keeping with the grandeur of the occasion. If she disappointed, they might suspect something and she couldn't risk that.

She was reaching for a gown of spun gold when she doubled up in agony, felt the room reeling around her. *No.* Forcing herself to stay on her feet. She couldn't collapse now or submit to the pain. There were so many people depending on her. Melanie. Travis, Antony and the rest of them, languishing in the slave quarters aboard this very ship, no doubt. She couldn't let them down by faltering now. And what about those she'd loved who were dead – the faithful Etrion, her darling Darion? What she was doing, she was doing for them, because the sickness of the Scytharene empire had to end, and she, Dyona, would end it. And when she stumbled and fell against the wall, when she felt herself sliding helplessly to the floor, it seemed to her that Darion was with her again, his spirit close, his strength steadying her, bearing her up.

Somehow, her golden gown was on. Now, if she could only rest for a moment, gather her wits. If she could just sit down. For a moment.

Gyrion would be here. In that moment, Gyrion would be bursting into her quarters with Blackhearts at his side.

But perhaps that didn't matter. Every pore in her body was on fire. Her innards felt molten, her bones carbonised and brittle. Hadn't she done enough? She must already have infected the warriors in the patrol that brought her back to the *Ayrion III*, the medtech she'd sent away rather than let him examine her, the Scytharene guard who'd escorted her to her quarters. Six she'd breathed her pestilence on, whose vulnerable cells were secretly under attack. Six who would come into close proximity with six more, and the twelve another twelve. The chain reaction of contagion. The multiplication of death. The inevitable had begun. So perhaps there was no need to drag herself to the Chamber of the Triumph to look in on the Fleet Commanders she despised. Perhaps she'd done enough.

It was tempting to stay where she was, and rest, and wait for Gyrion to come to her. So tempting . . .

He overrode the activation mechanism on the door to Dyona's quarters. Gyrion and a quartet of loyal Blackhearts burst in, subjugators drawn.

'My dear, *foolish* Lady Dyona . . .'

Her rooms were empty.

'By the *ancestors*.' Her absence did not make Gyrion happy. 'Find her!' he snapped to his underlings. 'Check the slave quarters first. She loves the savages so much she might have returned to free them. And notify security. Nobody leaves this vessel without my express authorisation. Is that clear? I must return to my guests.' Hoping that by now they'd imbibed too much pluvium to detect that something was wrong. 'I want to know the *second* you have her, do you understand?'

The Blackhearts understood. They raced off immediately to do their commanding officer's bidding. In the event, however, they needn't have bothered. In the event, Gyrion found Dyona himself.

'My lord, why didn't you tell us?' Atrion called cheerily as soon as Gyrion re-entered the Chamber of the Triumph. 'Here is cause for celebration indeed.' Atrion, whose own bloodline had always valued its links to that of Lyrion. 'For one we thought dead is alive again.'

There, resplendent in a golden gown, one hand placed decorously over Lord Urion's while the Fleet Commander politely kissed the other, was Dyona. Smiling. Regal. Poised.

Dyona.

Who observed Gyrion's entrance and was delighted. Already she felt her feeble strength failing. The tremendous effort of will to get here had sapped her last reserves. The pain was returning to claim her and this time she could not deny it. But this time she didn't care.

She welcomed the end.

Gyrion striding towards her, his fury and his hatred barely

369

contained. 'Dyona,' he said, spurning the formality of her title. '*Dyona.*'

She wondered if he'd strike her. He'd be killing himself if he did that.

As she was killing Lord Atrion, whose particularly arrogant bloodline she'd always loathed, killing him with the brush of her fingertips, and Lord Urion as his mouth pressed lightly against the back of her hand. And all the other Fleet Commanders she'd greeted since her arrival.

She couldn't leave her beloved's father out, now could she?

And she could tell that Gyrion was taken aback when rather than flinching from him fearfully she approached him smiling with an innocent's exuberance. 'My lord Gyrion, I never thought I'd see you again. I'm so glad I have.'

And the entire gathering was frankly astonished when she threw herself on him, flung her arms round him, kissed him deeply on the mouth with a lover's energy.

And when, as Gyrion pushed her away with a cry of revulsion, she broke into shrill, hysterical laughter, laughter as at some magnificent yet unspoken jest, laughter that seemed as if it would never cease, the Fleet Commanders actually began to wonder whether all was quite well with the lovely Lady Dyona.

She was closer now to the light, so close that she needed to shield her eyes against the glare. And as she neared the source of brilliance, she saw that the adjacent rubbled streets seemed to melt into it and vanish away, as if all the shadows and the darkness and the despair that they'd contained had been washed clean. The light throbbed like a thing alive. It pulsed like a heartbeat. And it extended – oh, as Mel gazed up into the dazzling sky – it extended far beyond the range of her narrow vision, a beam shone from above like a signal or a beacon. For a moment she thought of the tractor beam in the Scytharene's Cullers, but she sensed that if she stepped into this pillar of brightness, she would not be conveyed into slavery.

But where?

For it seemed to her that the pole of light was like a bridge between the ruined city, the dismal earth, and the heavens, a bridge that someone with a mind to might cross.

Others evidently felt the same.

Mel became aware of them only now, though they were crowding round her, the people, emerging from buildings and from streets, converging on the light. Adults and children alike, at first they seemed troubled, but as they approached the light their expressions uniformly gladdened and they appeared at peace. So many people. Mel had not seen such a multitude of adults together since before the Sickness – and that was notable too.

Not a mark of the Sickness on any of the faces. Not a scar on the skin. The legacy of their death had been wiped away.

Dr Shiels was healed. Mel saw the Headteacher as she passed by. And Mr Greening. And Jessica's parents, hand in hand. And Travis's mum.

And hers.

As if they'd never died. As if they never *could* die or be taken from those who loved them. *Restored*.

And some of the youngsters were familiar too, faces and names Mel had known from school. Simon Satchwell, of course, no blood where the Scytharene had shot him. And Richie, still in his baseball cap. *Richie*. She'd never dreamed of him before. Why now? What did that mean?

Mel knew what that meant. Poor Richie Coker.

She was thankful not to see Travis or Jessica among the throng who were now beginning to enter the light, dissolving into it, becoming light themselves. Crossing over.

Those she knew were waiting for her to join them. Smiling. Expectant. Hands extended. How could she not want to take their hands and join them?

Mel glanced down at herself. Blood still oozed from her wounded tummy. And there was Trav to think about. And Jessie. Antony and Linden. She couldn't leave them yet. Not without knowing.

So she turned her back to the light and averted her eyes. She gazed upon the dull grey streets of London again.

And woke on the sofa in the office of the government building, a blanket around her, the dullness and greyness transferred to the dawn, woke to the pain of her wound, and to fear for her friends.

Elsewhere, but at the precise same time, prisoners stirred.

'Lin! Antony! Jess!' Travis coming to quickly, leaping to his feet instantly. Or maybe neither. He could still be asleep and dreaming. Surely he had to be. 'Up! Get up! Look!' Because though the artificial lighting aboard the *Ayrion III* was functioning as efficiently as ever, he kind of felt he needed visual confirmation from others before he could truly believe what his own eyes were claiming.

The cell door was open.

'Trav!' Linden clutched him, a wild excitement in her eyes.

'No guards. No instructions,' Jessica said perplexedly. 'What does it mean, Trav?'

'It means let's get the hell out of here.' Dwayne Randolph was on his way.

Until Antony grabbed his shoulder. 'Not without thinking, Dwayne. This could be some sort of trick.'

'Get real, Tony. What sense would that make?' Dwayne retorted.

'What sense would leaving a cell door open make *unless* it's a trick or a trap?' Travis countered.

Which was sufficient to give the Phantom pause. The rest of the company too, all woken by the commotion, all standing, murmuring nervously, uncertain whether to move towards the door or away from it.

'Well somebody had better see what's outside,' Linden suggested. 'Maybe this is some kind of initiative test.'

'Whassat?' said Cooper.

'You just stay where you are for now, Coop,' advised Travis. 'Shall we?' To Antony.

'Why not? If you don't look for answers, you don't find them.'

While their companions hushed instinctively into silence, the two boys edged to the doorway, leaned their heads through. Travis glanced left: empty corridor, though every door open. Antony glanced right: 'Trav.' He saw the Scytharene first. The black-armoured warrior sprawled on his front on the floor.

'Wait here,' Travis ordered the others, before loping with Antony to the prostrate alien's side. And 'My God,' he breathed when they got there.

It wasn't a trick. It wasn't a trap or a test. They could tell at once that the Scytharene was dead. They knew as immediately *how* he'd died. The killer had signed his work.

The hairless skull was encrusted with the livid rings of the Sickness. The boys turned the alien over. And so was the face.

373

If anything, the scarring was even more revolting than on human beings. The raised scarlet ridges of skin had split open, had wept blood and a kind of pus that had dried but still streaked the features. The warrior's eyes were open but the red fire in them had been extinguished. In death, a Scytharene's eyes turned black.

'The Sickness.' Antony's heart raced.

'The virus.' So did Travis's mind. 'It must have worked after all. Just – took its bloody time.' He half laughed, half sobbed.

'All things come to those who wait,' said Antony, quoting received Harringtonian wisdom.

'Too damn right. Hah!' Dwayne Randolph had disobeyed his leader and ventured out into the corridor himself. 'Bastard's dead. Alien bastard's *dead*.' Linden, Jessica and Cooper were following behind him.

'Keep it down, Dwayne,' Travis urged. 'There might be others.'

'Other stiffs,' Dwayne grinned. 'Man, let's bloody hope so.'

'He's right.' Antony's eyes shone. 'He's got to be right, Trav. If the virus has worked, if the Sickness is inside the ship, all the Scytharene could be infected. Every single one.'

'All of them – dead?' Linden said without relish.

'Don't bet on it until we've seen it,' Travis cautioned. He relieved the corpse of its subjugator. 'But they could be. This could be the turning point. The human race's comeback. Victory.'

Linden hung her head.

'So are we getting out of here or what?' Dwayne Randolph demanded.

'Let's check the rest of the cells first,' Travis said. 'Dwayne,

Coop, get the others. And keep your eyes open for Scytharene, dead or *especially* alive.' In a softer voice, noticing her anguish: 'You okay, Lin?'

'Not really. Victory, you said, Travis, and I hope you're right. I'd sooner win than lose. But think about it another way. Victory in war is always built on death. The winning sides are those who turn out to be the better killers. If that's us, Trav, the better killers, are we supposed to celebrate?'

'We're alive, Lin,' Travis said. 'And life is good. Let's make do with that for now.'

They searched the slave quarters. It didn't take long, a pattern of emptiness swiftly established on the other side of invitingly open doors. Travis had harboured the slimmest of hopes that Richie might be in one of the cells, unconscious or tied up or something, to explain why he hadn't made it to the corridor of his own accord. He'd have been overjoyed to find Richie in one of the cells.

He was shocked, instead, to find Dyona. Then horrified. Then stricken with grief.

Poor Dyona was difficult to identify at first, disfigured by the Sickness. For some reason, she was robed in a gown of gold.

Travis and Linden gently laid her on her back, straightened her legs, crossed her hands over her chest. Jessica sobbed in Antony's arms.

'What happened to her?' the blond boy said in bafflement.

'I would have thought that was obvious, Antony,' snapped Linden.

'I meant, why is she here? If the Scytharene managed to find and overrun Enclave Zero, where are Mel and the others?'

'You don't think Mel's . . .' Jessica couldn't say it.

'Mel's fine.' Travis's turn to be testy, instantly regretted. 'Sorry, Jess. But wherever she is, Mel's fine. I know it. I don't think Dyona *was* brought here from the Enclave, not as a prisoner. If she was, why dress her up like she's guest of honour at some awards ceremony or something? I don't know.' He shook his head in frustration at his own confusion. 'I don't understand.'

'At least,' Jessica said, 'at least she's with Darion now.'

'Yeah. I hope so.' Travis squeezed the Scytharene's hand. 'Goodbye, Dyona of the bloodline of Lyrion. We won't forget you.'

'Don't forget us either, man,' Dwayne Randolph called from the door. 'You can do the whole funeral bit later, let's get our arses off this tub first.'

'Soon,' Travis said, in a tone that brooked no disagreement. 'There's one more place I want to see first, and one more person.'

Up through the ship. From the slave quarters to the higher levels. Scytharene bodies littered everywhere. Black armour. Red armour. Spreadeagled on corridor floors. Propped up against walls. Some expressing the final agonies of the Sickness. Others calmer, more peaceful, but no less deceased. Up through the innards of the *Ayrion III*. To the bridge.

No orders to be given from this quarter any longer. Though communication channels were open, they emitted only static; the comscreens flickered as though dying. Techs slumped over consoles. Blackhearts crumpled at their posts. In his command chair, frozen in lifelessness, sitting erect and staring blindly forward, the gold-armoured Scytharene Travis knew must be Fleet Commander Gyrion.

The boy stared at Darion's father with an expression like stone. His blue eyes burned fiercely. Had it been Gyrion who'd taken the decision to enslave the Earth, or a Scytharene just like him? Did it matter now? Gyrion and his ilk between them had devastated the world and pushed the human race to the brink perhaps of extinction. But the teenagers had fought back, the young, those very humans the Scytharene had bioengineered the Sickness to spare because of their weakness, their helplessness.

'Not so weak now, are we, Fleet Commander Gyrion?' Travis said. 'Not so helpless after all. How the mighty have fallen, hmm? It's just a pity Darion isn't here to see this day. But you brought it all upon yourself, Gyrion, you know that? The deaths of all your people are down to you. You sowed the wind, Gyrion. Now you've reaped the whirlwind.'

Travis turned to gaze across Regent's Park, and there were dark heaps of bodies there too, and in the early morning light not a living thing was moving.

It was the same as they made their way back to Enclave Zero. Silence and desolation the only residents in London but for the several scores of young people, all armed again now, thanks to the late crew of the *Ayrion III*, who hurried in a combination of anticipation and dread towards Westminster.

Mel, Travis was thinking. Jessica too, and Linden, and Antony. Mel had to be alive.

Fire and smoke from the riverside did not bode well.

The heat hit them like a wall, the smoke so black and choking it seemed as if the sky itself was alight. It was difficult to discern details in the billowing miasma, but one thing could be seen. Or not. The Palace of Westminster no longer existed. Where Big Ben and the Houses of Parliament had stood just yesterday, a deep and blazing pit now gaped, as if in some respects the political stretch of the north bank of the Thames had simply, calamitously subsided into the river.

The teenagers stared in horror.

'Again,' Antony murmured despairingly. 'They've done it again. Everywhere important to us, every meaningful place, the Scytharene destroy. They steal them from us. Harrington. The Enclave. Parliament. Every single damned place.'

Right now, though, while she comforted her boyfriend, Jessica wasn't so concerned for bricks and mortar, however symbolically significant. 'What about Mel? Enclave Zero's . . . down there.'

The pit.

God, she couldn't have survived, Travis knew. Anyone still in the Enclave when Parliament came crashing down would have been crushed. Their only hope. . .

'*Travis.*' Dwayne Randolph alerting him. A solitary teenager was approaching the larger group. Immediately, subjugators stabbed at him.

'It's all right,' somebody said. 'It's Ling. He's one of us.'

'They got out.' Linden clutched Travis's hand eagerly. She recognised the Chinese boy herself now. 'They must have got out.'

'Ling.' Travis ran towards him. 'What happened? Where are the others?'

'Safe,' Ling said. 'Whitehall. Most of us are safe.'

'Most?'

'Travis, I've got some bad news.'

*

378

Mel tried to sit up but she was too weak. Travis told her just to rest there, she needed to conserve her energy while she recovered. Jessica told her she was going to be fine. Linden and Antony provided well-meaning, sincere but hollow echoes. They all knew they were lying.

They were alone with Mel in the government office as the day ebbed towards dusk.

'Did they tell you?' said the girl with the black hair. 'What the Paragons did? What Crispin did?'

'They told us,' Travis said. He was *glad* the Paragons were dead. It saved him the trouble of killing them himself.

'And what about Dyona?'

'Yes. Don't worry about that now, Mel. Don't worry about anything.'

'Don't need to, not any more.' Mel attempted a smile, managed that. 'You're all back. You're all well. Want to tell me how?'

'Dyona did it.' Jessica started strongly. 'She got to the ship. She . . .' Couldn't finish. Grief for her friend thickened her throat.

Antony's arm was around her shoulder. He took over. 'She spread the virus before it killed her, Mel. Her sacrifice worked. It's because of Dyona we're here.'

'We were in the cells,' Linden added. 'We would have been cryo-tubed. But not now. The Scytharene are dead. Gyrion. All of them. The *Ayrion III*'s a ghost ship. And if the Sickness infects the rest of the fleet . . .'

'Looks like you did it, Trav,' Mel said, kind of drowsily. 'You did the right thing, made your stand. I knew you would.'

'It's only the beginning, Mel,' Travis said. 'Soon as you're well enough, we're gonna get out of London and find somewhere better, found a proper community, build for the future, all of us . . .'

'All of us, Trav?' Another smile, fainter than before. 'All of us is a dream. Richie didn't make it, did he?'

'How do you . . .?'

'I saw him, Trav. I saw lots of people. It's really not so bad.'

'What's she talking about?' Linden mouthed to Travis.

He shook his head to suggest it didn't matter. 'We lost Richie, yes,' he admitted to Mel, 'but he went down fighting. And the rest of us, we have to be strong. We have to go on.'

'You do, Travis. So many people . . . are relying on you.' Mel lifted her hand. Travis knelt by her side and took it, kissed it. 'I'm proud . . . you've been my friend.'

'Don't talk like that. Mel, you mustn't talk like that.' Jessica on her knees, too, torn between scolding and sobs. 'Like you're . . . You mustn't give up. We'll get medicine. We'll get stuff to treat you with.'

'I waited for you, Jessie.' Mel's voice wearier with every word, her speech slurring. 'I wouldn't go before I saw you again.'

'You're not going anywhere except with us.' Jessica adamant. 'Mel, I love you.' And tearful.

'I love you. And I'm not the only one.' A sly and sleepy smile. 'Jessie, you've got Antony. Trav, Lin. You don't need me.'

'We do. *I* do.' Jessica's eyes burned with anguish. 'Hold on, Mel. Stay with us.'

The slightest nod of the dark girl's head. 'All right, Jess. I just . . . I'm kind of tired, I think. Just . . . Trav, can we talk

380

again later?' Eyes closing in a shadowed room. 'I think I'd like to sleep now . . .'

Now here was a strange thing. No more blood. No more pain. Mel felt her stomach, pressed in with both hands. Her wound had healed. It was as if she'd never been shot in the first place, as if she'd never . . .

The light was intensely strong now, mesmeric and fascinating. Serenely benevolent. And close indeed this time, so close she only had to reach out her hand to touch it. And she felt she'd quite like to do that, did Mel, to reach out her hand and touch the light.

The dead people wanted her to. The dead people clustered all around her almost as if she belonged with them now, as if she herself . . . Simon, Richie, Mr and Mrs Lane. Her mother.

Her father.

Gerry Patrick, his neck intact. Gerry Patrick, beaming at her as he'd never done in life, the light playing over his body, sparkling. If her father had believed she'd been responsible for his death, he seemed to have forgiven her now.

And with the light so near, Mel thought she could forgive him too. Former differences and disagreements, past pains and animosities, they seemed so trivial now, irrelevant, clothes they'd grown out of. The old days, the old life, they were behind them like the ruined streets they'd walked.

Mel glanced over her shoulder. London was shadow now, was mist, intangible. She imagined, in the distance, that she could see Travis and Jessica, and they seemed sad, but they didn't need to be. Not for her.

She turned her face again to the light. She didn't want to

delay any longer. But if Mel did still harbour the faintest of fears of what was to come, these vanished as she took her mother's hand, as she took her father's, as together they stepped forward into untainted brightness.

The light embraced Mel Patrick.

EPILOGUE

Light again. Shining from a brilliant summer sky as a long column of vehicles wound its way through the countryside north of London. It was a motley and in many cases ramshackle convoy, veteran family estates bumper to bumper with sportier open-top models, white vans with company names on the side right behind top-line 4×4s. Smashed lights here, a missing windscreen there, buckled wings and battered doors. But every vehicle in the formation had at least one thing in common, direction, and every passenger in every vehicle shared other traits too, like purpose, and belief, and trust in those who led them.

Travis's car was at the head of the convoy. Antony, Linden and Jessica were crammed into the back while Travis rode in the front, but he wasn't driving. Since their departure from London, Cooper had taken it upon himself to be chauffeur. He seemed to have transferred his allegiance – and presumably that of his fellow Kings of the Ring – from Richie to Travis without the latter having to prove his champion's credentials by donning a pair of boxing gloves and smashing someone's face in. It was as if Coop was leaving the familiar rituals behind him with the city, consigning the Kings to the past.

This was a development that Travis had detected evolving

throughout the now hundred-plus-strong group – they'd picked up a few recruits on the outskirts of town. The old gang enmities were being forsworn, forgotten, the old gang loyalties subsumed into a wider sense of belonging, a broader, deeper unity.

The journey was proceeding today as it had done since its commencement, at a leisurely pace. No need to hurtle along with frantic, fearful haste. No need to be continually and anxiously craning the neck upwards for Cullers or battlepods. Not any more. The skies were safe again. The Scytharene were dead – or gone. And nobody really cared which.

They'd passed several alien craft on their way out of London, all of them reduced to silver sepulchres. The gene transfer virus had done its job well. Travis's people tended not to linger at these sites of death.

But not all the Scytharene had been killed. Once they saw a mother-ship, a slavecraft like the *Furion* and the *Ayrion III*, scything its way into the heavens, soaring higher and ever higher, rising towards the limits of the Earth's atmosphere, until it was beyond the sight of their straining eyes. Retreating, Travis prayed. Fleeing the planet for ever. Never coming back. Because if Dyona had infected the Fleet Commanders as she'd planned, and if those Fleet Commanders, carrying the virus, had returned to their own ships, then the carnage they'd seen wrought among the aliens here in London would be replicated all over the world. The Scytharene would have no defence. The masters would have been overthrown by the slaves. Revolution. What goes around comes around. Any ships able to isolate themselves from infection would have no choice but to seek refuge in deep space, on the Scytharene homeworld, and the invisible yet implacable deterrent of the Sickness virus in the air would keep them there.

Of course, it was possible that the aliens' scientists might in time find a means to immunise their kind against the virus. It was possible that at some point in the future the slavers might again seek to target the Earth. It was possible, perhaps, that one day the Scytharene might return.

But not today.

Travis told Cooper to pull over. Here was a good place for a break, fields on either side of the road for the younger kids to run about in, expend some energy. They'd accumulated a number of under-tens lately.

'The future,' Linden said, watching the little ones while she and Travis stretched their legs.

Jessica and Antony joined them.

'You know,' said the blonde girl, 'if you took a photograph of that – just that – the kids playing, it could be a shot of the old world, like nothing's happened, nothing's changed.'

'Except that everything's changed,' said Travis.

'But do you think they'll remember what it was like, the time before the Sickness?' Jessica pursued. 'The very young ones, I mean. We're old enough not to forget what we've lost, but are they?'

'We'll tell them,' Antony answered. 'We won't let them forget. When we start up our school, we'll teach them everything they should know about the old world, all the good things.'

'Still big on the school idea, Antony?' Travis grinned. 'What with the day-to-day running of the community, that's a whole lot for you to organise.'

'That's why I'm the organis*er*, Trav,' the other boy grinned back. 'And as I'm sure I must have said when we first met, we need two qualities if we're going to survive: courage and knowledge. We all benefit from a little bit of learning.'

'Can't disagree with that,' said Travis.

'They ought to be told about Mel as well,' Jessica said in a voice charged with emotion. 'And Richie and Dyona. What they did, how they died, *why* they died. We mustn't ever forget them.'

'We won't, Jess. I promise.' The loss of Mel in particular still ached in Travis's heart, alongside the older wounds he'd received there, wounds that never quite healed and which, in a way, he never quite wanted to. So many deaths in his life now; so much death in all their lives. Yet they hadn't been crushed by the horrors they'd witnessed, the tragedies they'd suffered. They'd survived. They'd endured. They'd stayed strong. That was what truly counted. And they'd been rewarded with victory over the invader and a chance now to move on, to do *more* than survive. The opportunity to build a new world.

'And we'll look after them, won't we? The children.' Linden's brow was furrowed with the memory of five young charges of her own, lost to the cryo-tubes weeks ago.

'Sure we will.' Travis snapped out of his reverie to reassure her. 'Like you said, Lin, they are the future. And while we're right always to remember the past, it's the future that has to concern us most. Because it's us who are going to be responsible for it. No adults. No aliens. Nobody to guide us or tell us what to do. Nobody but us to blame if things go wrong. Do you realise? For the first time in history, kids of our age are on their own. What we do will shape the world. The future lies in our own hands.'

Jessica smiled. 'If Mel was here she'd say something like: Yeah? I *knew* I should have cut my fingernails.'

'It is a responsibility, Travis. An awesome one,' said Antony in the tone of someone more than willing to rise to it.

'Something Lin said to me,' Travis recalled. 'Yesterday is a crop . . . how does it go, Lin?'

'Yesterday is a crop that has seen harvest,' Linden supplied. 'The work of today is to plant the seed of tomorrow.'

'Sounds about right, doesn't it?' said Travis.

'Hey, Naughton.' Dwayne Randolph yelling from his car. 'We staying here for the rest of our lives or what?'

Travis gave a laugh, hugged Linden. 'I think we can improve on that.'

After all, they'd be at Willowstock soon, a promising place to found a community. They could even venture a few miles further and build anew on the site of Harrington. Antony was keen.

The convoy moved off again, Travis's lead car setting a faster pace than before. Leisurely was all very well, but not when there was work to be done. The future they wanted wasn't going to grow of its own accord.

They'd better get planting.

About the Author

Andrew Butcher was once an English teacher but now devotes his time to a ragtag group of orphaned teenagers fighting a desperate resistance against alien invaders. He lives in Dorset with an unfeasibly large comic collection.

Find out more about Andrew and other Atom authors at www.atombooks.co.uk

A PREVIEW OF ANOTHER FANTASTIC ATOM BOOK . . .

SCOTT WESTERFELD
parasite
positive

Okay, let's clear up some myths about vampires.

First of all, you won't see me using the V-word much. In the Night Watch, we prefer the term *parasite-positives*, or *peeps*, for short.

The main thing to remember is that there's no magic involved. No flying. Humans don't have hollow bones or wings – the disease doesn't change that. No transforming into bats or rats either. It's impossible to turn into something much smaller than yourself – where would the extra mass go?

On the other hand, I can see how people in centuries past got confused. Hordes of rats, and sometimes bats, accompany peeps. They get infected from feasting on peep leftovers. Rodents make good 'reservoirs,' which means they're like storage containers for the disease. Rats give the parasite a place to hide in case the peep gets hunted down.

Infected rats are devoted to their peeps, tracking them by smell. The rat brood also serves as a handy food source for the peep when there aren't humans around to hunt. (Icky, I know. But that's nature for you.)

Back to the myths:

Parasite-positives *do* appear in mirrors. I mean, get real: How would the mirror know what was *behind* the peep?

But this legend also has a basis in fact. As the parasite takes control, peeps begin to despise the sight of their own reflections. They smash all their mirrors. But if they're so beautiful, why do they hate their own faces?

Well, it's all about the anathema.

The most famous example of disease mind control is rabies. When a dog becomes rabid, it has an uncontrollable urge to bite anything that moves: squirrels, other dogs, you. This is how rabies reproduces; biting spreads the virus from host to host.

A long time ago, the parasite was probably like rabies. When people got infected, they had an overpowering urge to bite other humans. So they bit them. Success!

But eventually human beings got organized in ways that dogs and squirrels can't. We invented posses and lynch mobs, made up laws, and appointed law enforcers. As a result, the biting maniacs among us tend to have fairly short careers. The only peeps who survived were the ones who ran away and hid, sneaking back at night to feed their mania.

The parasite followed this survival strategy to the extreme. It evolved over the generations to transform the minds of its victims, finding a chemical switch among the pathways of the human brain. When that switch is thrown, we despise everything we once loved. Peeps cower when confronted with their old obsessions, despise their loved ones, and flee from any signifier of home.

Love is easy to switch to hatred, it turns out. The term for this is the *anathema effect*.

The anathema effect forced peeps from their medieval villages and out into the wild, where they were safe from lynch mobs. And it spread the disease geographically. Peeps moved to the next valley over, then the next country, pushed farther and farther by their hatred of everything familiar.

As cities grew, with more police and bigger lynch mobs, peeps had to adopt new strategies to stay hidden. They learned to love the night and see in the dark, until the sun itself became anathema to them.

But come on: They don't burst into flame in daylight. They just really, really hate it.

The anathema also created some familiar vampire legends. If you grew up in Europe in the Middle Ages, chances were you were a Christian. You went to church at least twice a week, prayed three times a day, and had a crucifix hanging in every room. You made the sign of the cross every time you ate food or wished for good luck. So it's not surprising that most peeps back then had major cruciphobia – they could actually be repelled by the sight of a cross, just like in the movies.

In the Middle Ages, the crucifix was the big anathema: Elvis and Manhattan and your boyfriend all rolled into one.

Things were so much simpler back then.

These days, we hunters have to do our homework before we go after a peep. What were their favorite foods? What music did they like? What movie stars did they have crushes on? Sure, we still find a few cases of cruciphobia, especially down in the Bible Belt, but you're much more likely to stop peeps with an iPod full of their favorite tunes. (With certain geeky peeps, I've heard, the Apple logo alone does the trick.)

That's why new peep hunters like me start with people they used to know, so we don't have to guess what their anathemas are. Hunting the people who once loved us is as easy as it gets. Our own faces work as a reminder of their former lives. *We* are the anathema.

So what am *I*? you may be asking.

I am parasite-positive, technically a peep, but I can still listen to Kill Fee and Deathmatch, watch a sunset, or put Tabasco on scrambled eggs without howling. Through some trick of evolution, I'm partly immune, the lucky winner of the peep genetic lottery. Peeps like me are rarer than hens' teeth: Only one in every hundred victims becomes stronger and faster, with incredible hearing and a great sense of smell, without being driven crazy by the anathema.

We're called *carriers*, because we have the disease without all the symptoms. Although there is this one extra symptom that we do have: The disease makes us horny. All the time.

The parasite doesn't want us carriers to go to waste, after all. We can still spread the disease to other humans. Like that of the maniacs, our saliva carries the parasite's spores. But we don't bite; we kiss, the longer and harder the better.

The parasite makes sure that I'm like the always-hungry snail, except hungry for sex. I'm constantly aroused, aware of every female in the room, every cell screaming for me to *go out and shag someone!*

None of which makes me wildly different from most other nineteen-year-old guys, I suppose. Except for one small fact: If I act on my urges, my unlucky lovers become monsters, like Sarah did. And this is not much fun to watch.